A Box of Crosses

A Box of Crosses

C. Coolidge Wilson

RESOURCE *Publications* · Eugene, Oregon

A BOX OF CROSSES

Resource Publications
An Imprint of Wipf and Stock Publishers
199 W. 8th Ave., Suite 3
Eugene, OR 97401

www.wipfandstock.com

PAPERBACK ISBN: 978-1-5326-4092-6
HARDCOVER ISBN: 978-1-5326-4093-3
EBOOK ISBN: 978-1-5326-4094-0

Manufactured in the U.S.A.

All quotations from the Holy Bible come from the Revised Standard Version.

Illustrations photographed by Michael Good
Photographic Trends, Bethel Park, Pennsylvania

This book is dedicated to

Elizabeth Slayton Wilson
Keeper of my heart,
preserved like a dried flower
between the pages of an inimitable symbiosis

and

Essie Belle and Albert Edward Wilson
Infinite sources of profound faith and pure delight

Every cross possesses its own mystery, its unique story to reveal,

the story of the one on whose back that cross is carried.

—STIRLING McCUTCHEON

Many might doubt there were a God above

Who sees and permits evil, and so die:

That faith no agony shall obscure in me.

—PERCY BYSSHE SHELLEY, *The Cenci,* III,1,100-103

Contents

Illustrations

Author's Notes

A Box of Crosses features numerous characters with various nationalities—not only American, but also Scottish, British, French, Danish, and German. For the ease of reading dialogue smoothly, I have composed conversations among characters in American English without the respective European dialects.

This book is a work of fiction. Names, characters, churches, judicatories, organizations, places, events, and incidents are either the product of the author's imagination or are used fictitiously. Any resemblance to actual persons, living or dead, or to events or locales, is entirely coincidental.

Good Friday

IN HIS TWENTY-SIXTH YEAR as Senior Pastor of Madison Avenue Presbyterian Church, the Reverend Dr. Sinclair Chamberlain hanged himself in front of his congregation. The lights came on after the blackout, and he was exactly where he was not supposed to be: in the noose at the end of the rope, dangling from a substantial branch of the cut tree lashed to the stone lectern in the sanctuary. He was still clothed in Judas's robe while swinging. The stool for his feet lay on its side at a slight distance.

This was not the first time he had performed *The Death of Judas* on Good Friday. Nearly every year on this annual dark night in winter, the Reverend Dr. Chamberlain presented this particular dramatic monologue to a mesmerized audience either in his church or in some other. On numerous occasions he had travelled a considerable distance to honor requests to do so. Anyone who had witnessed his performance as Judas—or, for that matter, anyone who had listened to him preach on Sunday mornings—fully understood the demands for his dramatic appearances. His understanding of theater was immense, his delivery of lines enthralling, his sense of timing flawless. He was deftly skilled at swaying the collective emotions of an attentive congregation; and to the amateur theatergoer, he was the best of Olivier and Gielgud blended into one. If this indeed was not the first time he had performed *The Death of Judas* on Good Friday, it surely constituted the last.

For nearly a full minute, the congregation sat stunned, attempting to discern if this spectacle before their eyes was part of the play script—a revised ending, perhaps. When finally he didn't extricate himself from the noose, however, many parishioners leapt to their feet and rushed forward. One called for an ambulance. Three men lifted him while another removed the rope. Gently they laid him on the chancel floor as a physician attending the play checked his pulse. There was none. His neck was broken. He was dead.

Freda Chamberlain hung back against the sanctuary wall, standing beneath a tiffany window portraying the crucifixion of Christ. Other women stood beside her, supporting her. When the physician delivered the news, she dropped into the nearest pew and wept.

"I have always hated this presentation," she moaned. "Every time he did it . . . every time I saw it, I desperately feared the image would someday become the reality. He had to make everything so real, so authentic! 'What if there would be a mistake?' I'd ask, 'a slip of the foot in the dark,' I'd say. Oh, no! That could never happen! But now it . . . has . . . happened!"

Freda rose and went to her husband's lifeless form, sat on the floor beside him, and laid her head on his chest. "You would not listen, dear, dear Sinclair. Only to yourself. Now I shall be so alone . . . alone completely. If only you could take me with you!"

The ambulance arrived, then departed with the golden-tongued orator amidst a wave of boundless bewilderment and unfathomable despair.

For two years the bewilderment and despair lingered, mitigating only slightly with time. At last, however, the Reverend Dr. Chamberlain's successor was selected, and the Reverend Stirling McCutcheon appeared from Scotland to assume his duties as the new Senior Pastor of Madison Avenue Presbyterian Church in Albany, New York.

Now Freda Chamberlain faced involuntarily a cataclysmic adjustment. For twenty-six years she had stood beside her husband center-stage in the church. For twenty-six years she had wielded a benign influence on the congregation's culture, its spirit and tone. For twenty-six years she had reigned supreme as matron of the manse, keeper of the house, guardian of her husband's availability. In the past two years, however, she had felt upstaged, subtly maneuvered from center-stage to the invisible wings; she had perceived her former influence tacitly diminished and her personal significance obscured; her reign as matron-of-the-manse had come to an unsolicited end. Beneath her deep, frightful disappointment, though, she detected a remnant satisfaction in learning that mention of her momentous reputation had passed from the lips of church members to the ear of the Senior Pastor elect.

With that momentous reputation lodged in the recesses of her mind and her fervent agenda secured in her hand, Freda Chamberlain, assertive widow of the prominent former Senior Pastor, was among the first of those most keen on meeting with the Reverend Stirling McCutcheon the first week of his arrival.

1

Matron of the Manse Deposed

ANTICIPATION GAVE WAY TO apprehension. A knock on McCutcheon's study door announced his appointment with Freda Chamberlain and their meeting for the first time. Caryn Corrigan presented her. Stirling rose to greet her and offered her the prominent place in the wingback chair in the sitting area of the study. Obviously she was no stranger to this milieu, nor to this wingback chair, which she had undoubtedly occupied so often in those previous twenty-six years, nor to the large mahogany desk, which her husband had leaned upon for an equal tenure.

"May I offer you your usual tea, Mrs. Chamberlain?" Caryn asked with apparent affection.

"Yes, please, Caryn, with just a touch of milk, thank you," she replied with a cultured air of propriety. Turning to McCutcheon, she intimated with a slight smile, "Sinclair and I always drank tea at this time of day."

"Pastor McCutcheon?" Caryn inquired, reaching for his coffee cup.

He hesitated, wondering if he should follow suit with a request for tea but chose coffee as an initial statement of differentiation. "Another coffee, please, Caryn," he said innocuously. She left and closed the door.

Waving her hand with a raised index finger at the closed door, Mrs. Chamberlain stated emphatically, "Now that, my dear sir, is the most efficient, devoted administrative assistant a pastor could ever find anywhere in the northern hemisphere or, to be sure, anywhere in the United Kingdom. I am aware that many new pastors adhere to the notion that a new broom sweeps cleanly, but I want to tell you, Mr. McCutcheon, that I sincerely hope you will not sweep her out the door as you could be so inclined by your adopted duties at staffing the church. To do so would most certainly do yourself and this church a grave disservice. The same is true for our Danish sexton, Trudel Swenssen, who is by all standards the most assiduous of custodians."

McCutcheon smiled politely and responded with an element of surprise at her opening remark, "I can assure you, Mrs. Chamberlain, I have no such inclination."

Settling into the other wingback chair opposite Mrs. Chamberlain, McCutcheon found that her entire image filled his vision, so prominent a figure she presented.

Upon her entrance, he recognized how large a woman she was and what an imposing manner her aura commanded. A sitting posture diminished nothing of the image. She was just as erect and engrossing seated as she was standing. Her complexion was unusually white and smooth for a woman in her early sixties, and her ample white hair was full, thick with no signs of gradual thinning as is common with women of her age. Her eyes were hazel, a most engaging shade, intense and burning with inquisitiveness, making her pupils remarkably large. Her eyelashes were noticeably long, her cheekbones high, and her smiles were characterized by downward, rather than upward, turns, but always ever so slightly. As she placed her forearms on the arms of the wingback chair, her hands drooped downward and appeared curiously large and coarse with raised veins, as if she were accustomed to hard physical labor or kneading bread perpetually or merely to everyday housework. Freda Chamberlain's overall appearance summoned up the descriptive phrase *matron of the manse,* arrayed in a plain blue dress, subdued rather than garish, yet which understated tone could not successfully disguise the enormity of her bust or her plentiful hips. Despite the accentuated traits of her muliebrity, she presented an attractive figure that was not void of lovely contours created by a small waist.

"I see that the study has gone through an extensive transformation," Freda began with the skillful glance of a surveyor at work. "Just as it should be! This is your study now, Stirling . . . ah, may I call you *Stirling?"*

"Of course," McCutcheon nodded warmly. "Please do!"

"Call me *Freda.* I have been *Mrs. Chamberlain* to so many here for so long that it seems my identity is still tied up with Sinclair," she said as she surveyed the credenza with McCutcheon's photos of Heather and the children. "We had no children, Stirling. I desperately wanted to give Sinclair children, but he was too absorbed with his work, and he believed that children would be a distraction."

Caryn knocked and entered again, tea tray in hand, which she set on the coffee table between Freda and McCutcheon. "And here are your favorites, Mrs. Chamberlain, scones with clotted cream. Is there anything else, Pastor McCutcheon?"

"No, thank you. I believe we're all set," he answered with an extra note of gratitude, which Caryn heard as a hint of apprehension related to this impending conference between representatives of the past and of the future.

When a new pastor is issued a call to serve a Presbyterian congregation as its Minister of Word and Sacrament, the former pastor should stay out of the way. According to the definitive guidelines of the presbytery—the judicatory that oversees all Presbyterian churches located in a specific region—a former pastor should remain apart from the corporate worship and sacramental life of the people he or she had served previously—or better yet, move to another city or to another part of the country. In all circumstances, that pastor should not be seeking to marry couples, baptize children, or conduct funerals for members of a former congregation and should, in deference to the new pastor, refuse any request to do so. This simple guideline makes up an integral part of Presbyterian polity and applies to all churches and pastors in the Albany Presbytery. Of interest to Stirling McCutcheon is the fact that the same principle applies to pastors in the Church of Scotland. So it wasn't a matter of his having to adapt to a new policy in the United States in contrast to that which prevailed in Scotland. Quite to the contrary! Presbyterians, for centuries now, have looked much the same on one side of the Atlantic as on the other.

When McCutcheon accepted the call to ministry at Madison Avenue Presbyterian Church, none of this was an issue. There was no living former pastor to interfere with the transition at Madison Avenue Church. Only his widow remained. They had had no children. By the same token, Freda Chamberlain was a strong woman, imperious in her deportment, tenacious in her opinions, and resolute in her endurance; consequently, her widowhood allowed her no leeway for weakness or self-pity. While black adorned the average widow throughout her first year of mourning, Freda refused to let mourning assume a lengthy residence in her stalwart disposition; she discarded her black apparel the very evening of her return from the Sinclair's burial in England. Though an Englishwoman herself, her avowed intent was to remain in America, in Albany in particular, and most certainly as a member of the congregation of Madison Avenue Church. If McCutcheon had had an illusion about any of this before he accepted the position, such an illusion would have been categorically dispelled the first week he arrived at the church to assume his duties as pastor. While the presbytery policy applies to a retiring pastor, there is no definitive guideline regarding a former pastor's widow's remaining in the congregation of her choice and none that mandates her having to leave—either here or in Great Britain.

When the door closed behind Caryn, Freda went directly to the point, without a hesitating exordium, without preliminary groundwork, without so much as a by-your-leave.

"Stirling, I trust that it will be no problem for you if I remain a member of Madison Avenue Presbyterian Church while you are pastor here," she said matter-of-factly. She paused, waiting for an answer in the affirmative.

"I shouldn't think so, Freda," McCutcheon rejoined slowly, giving emphasis to each word, "since I presume you would be adverse to causing any problem at Madison Avenue Presbyterian Church while I am pastor here."

There ensued an uncomfortable silence. Their eyes remained locked.

Freda looked away, first to the photos of his family again, and then to the Celtic cross mounted on the wall behind his desk. "I hesitate, Stirling," she answered slowly, "not because I have any intention contrary to absolute and undying support of your ministry here but, rather, because I readily acknowledge that any and every transition is difficult . . . not only for me, of course, but for everyone who gives up something precious to take on something new. I am ready to do precisely that, but I admit to you straight out that, apart from Sinclair's death, accepting new leadership here at the church will be the most difficult transition I have ever had to make, even more than moving to Albany from London. I have come here to tell you unequivocally, however, that I am intent on making that transition and that you can count on my unswerving support, even during times I might disagree with your methods of leadership. I believe what I am proposing is . . . allegiance . . . yes, an active allegiance."

Taken aback by her forthrightness, McCutcheon rejoined, "Freda, there is no way I could ask you to leave people who are your friends here, those who have become family to you."

"But do you want to?" she asked without varnish.

"Do I want to what?"

"In your heart, do you really want to ask me to leave?"

McCutcheon leaned back in his chair, placed his elbows on its arms, his chin upon his folded hands, looking at her inquisitively, attempting to assess her integrity.

"No," he attested at last. "Of course not!" McCutcheon gestured toward the family photos and ventured, "I'd like you to think of it this way, Freda: we are the newest members of your family."

The corners of Freda's mouth turned down into a characteristic smile, slight but definitive. "Thank you, Stirling. I'll be a worthy sister-in-Christ to you."

"And I . . . and I a worthy brother-in-Christ to you, Freda," McCutcheon said, cognizant of the appropriate parallel.

"For over twenty-six years, I have been the matron of the manse here at Madison Avenue Presbyterian Church. I am grateful to the elders of the congregation—and I have told them so in an official communication—for allowing me, after Sinclair's death, to continue living in the manse until just two months ago. Then I moved to an elegant apartment on St. James Street. But I am keenly aware that I am no longer the matron of the manse . . . that, indeed, that role belongs now to Mrs. McCutcheon, and I can only hope that—in that special role—she will serve you and the congregation as faithfully and as ardently as I served Sinclair and this church in all those stellar years."

In his mind's eye, attempting to picture Heather McCutcheon as a contented player in that designated role, McCutcheon rejoined, "Well, we shall see, Freda, won't we? We shall see."

They helped themselves to Caryn's scones and clotted cream, sharing a British custom common to both their English and Scottish heritages.

"So, Freda, you chose not to return to London, where you could have daily English Tea with lovely treats like these?" McCutcheon asked good-naturedly.

"I returned to London for Sinclair's funeral and burial," responded Freda with her stately English gravity. "I'll return to London for my own as well when the time comes, but London is no longer home for me. It wasn't for Sinclair either, but he was buried in London according to his own wishes . . . simply because, after all, he is an Englishman: he lived as an Englishman."

"I presume he died an Englishman," McCutcheon offered innocently, "possessing to the end that noble element of English pride."

"What do you mean, Stirling?" Freda asked suddenly distressed, failing to appreciate another parallel of speech: lived as an Englishman, died as an Englishman.

"As a Scotsman who has bowed to the invincibility of the English," he explained, "I know that Englishmen live vigorously and die proudly."

Freda looked down at her hands folded in her lap. "Sinclair didn't die proudly, Stirling. His death was an accident . . . a tragic accident that snuffed out his life prematurely. He had many more years of ministry ahead of him, and in one misbegotten moment, all his sweet twenty-six years here came instantaneously to a sour end. Hadn't you heard?" she asked incredulously.

"Yes, Freda, I had heard. The Call Committee informed me that he had died accidentally while presenting a phenomenal dramatic monologue on Good Friday. But emphatically they made the point that your husband was a man of pride—not *hubris*—authentic pride, who conducted ministry with pride of the office, who attended to everyone's most desperate needs with the privilege of compassion—a *nobles oblige*, if you will—who preached charismatically with the pride of intellect, and who, at the very end, met his death with the pride of faith, utterly confident that life goes on eternally. I believe that is exactly what they conveyed to me. Did I misunderstand, Freda?"

"No . . . no, not at all," Freda said sadly, "but I think in these short two years since his death there is a bit of embellishment that has occurred in the retelling of the incident . . . not a rewriting of history exactly but an investing of each person's own perception of how it happened, what Sinclair was thinking and feeling when it happened, and what great pronouncement of faith Sinclair was actually making by this last act. You understand, I'm sure, Stirling, the gospel according to so and so, according to whoever is retelling the accident and according to whoever is interpreting its ultimate meaning. I hope I don't sound cynical, but there was no ultimate meaning to Sinclair's death. It was categorically a meaningless cessation of life, and for someone to say that he died proudly is nothing more than a hermeneutical embellishment."

This entire comment was soft and measured. It occurred to McCutcheon that anyone else he knew would have become animated, more intense in delivering these lines, as theater people would say; but Freda did not raise her voice; she refrained from gesturing; she held his attention with her riveting gaze; she demonstrated the power of the quiet word.

"I understand, Freda," McCutcheon began cautiously, "or, more accurately, I understand this congregation's need to attach meaning to a tragic event that snatched the pastor they loved for so many years out of their reach. I understand that. What I don't understand, of course, is who Sinclair Chamberlain truly was in essence. I suspect that you alone possess that intimate, privileged knowledge."

Freda had finished her scone and tea, used the finger bowl to wet her hands, and then wiped them on her napkin, placing it with a gesture of finality on the tea tray. "Well, Stirling, that could be another discussion for another time since I'm sure you are extremely busy settling in this week," she said with a gracious air of dismissal.

"Freda," said McCutcheon as he leaned intently forward in his chair, "I have time now if you are inclined to share your understanding of your husband. As you know, everything has a context, and the content within any specific context cannot be fully understood without understanding that context. The context of this church and its congregation was principally composed by you and my predecessor. It would be a gift to me, and indeed of great assistance, if you would talk to me about your husband."

Whatever else can be said of Freda Chamberlain, it was quite apparent to McCutcheon that she was not afraid of silences. She sat motionless, staring off to the left of his head as if she were scanning eternity for a suitable response. It must have been minutes before she turned to McCutcheon again and, in clear tones, commenced an astounding narrative.

"It is far beyond my limited comprehension, Stirling," Freda said puzzlingly, her right hand upon her chin, "as to why this congregation, apart from any other in the area, seeks pastors from Great Britain; but for certain there seems to be a dominating will that persists among the people here to call pastors from England and Scotland—Sinclair twenty-eight years ago, directly from London, and now you, straight from Edinburgh. During the two-year interregnum—between Sinclair's death and your arrival—I have given this question considerable thought, and I think it has something to do with grief at the perceived disappearance of civility in this country, as represented by the adulteration of language, the growing disregard for intellect, and what others have dubbed the dumbing down of America. This condition of decaying civility and diminishing regard for intellect feature the preeminence of vulgarity, a state in which the stupid fellow—what the French call *bête noir* or the dark beast—inexplicably ascends to superiority.

"Knowing the people of this congregation as I do, Stirling, it is my conviction that most of them are misoneists in a strict sense of the term: they are not afraid of new ideas *per se,* but they fear, even detest, the innovation of moral, linguistic, and intellectual decline. Unless I am mistaken, these people have looked to Great Britain as its source for pastoral selection as a concerted attempt to maintain the principles of scholarly preaching and to testify to the moral imperative of unmitigated civility. Whether that confidence in England and Scotland is well-placed could be debated, but what cannot be debated, I believe, is their motive for confidence in a traditional system of tried and true antiquity. This congregation had all of this in Sinclair for twenty-six years."

As McCutcheon listened to Freda, he remained visibly still, but his viscera were churning. There could be no doubt that her expectations were finely articulated in her analysis of the congregation's purpose in seeking British pastors. She would definitely anticipate sound intellect, impeccable civility, and imaginative language to characterize his preaching and pastoral work.

"As you may know, Stirling," Freda continued concertedly, "Sinclair was an Oxford Fellow with a focus on philosophy. Though he seldom, if ever, alluded to his concentration, he was a Nietzschean scholar in particular, who believed that Friedrich Nietzsche was more Christian than atheist. I admit up front, Stirling, that all I know about Nietzsche could be inserted into this compact reticule—with nothing overflowing—while leaving room for other items," she asserted, raising the small handbag that had accompanied her. "He insisted that Nietzsche's *Superman* was actually a description of the Christ, since only a Superman could intentionally endure the excruciating cross of Golgotha. How he ever came to that conclusion is far beyond me, but he was adamant about it. Further, he maintained that Nietzsche's sister, Elisabeth Förster-Nietzsche, in later works, distorted his ideas and made him appear to be both a racist and an atheist. I mention all of this, Stirling, because I believe Nietzsche made a major impact not only on his preaching—characterized by keen intellect, rich philosophical tones, and theological discernment—but also on his dark demeanor."

"What do you mean, Freda . . . dark demeanor?" McCutcheon inquired delicately. She looked down at her hands, raised her eyes again and searched the room, as if looking for an answer from the spirit of her husband in its walls. McCutcheon continued, "I ask simply because no one of the congregation has intimated anything of the sort."

"Of course not, Stirling. No one ever saw that side of him, I'm sure. It was manifested only at home. Night after night—whenever there was no meeting to oversee or other people's needs to attend to—he would sit in his study at the manse, usually in the dark, and drink a glass or two of Courvoisier . . . and think. Invariably they were what could be described as melancholy states, in which—as he once explained to me—he felt a propinquity with the psalmist, who ruminated, 'my only friend is darkness.' Perhaps he would fall into this state three or four times a week; and then, on Sunday mornings, without having made a note on paper, he would stand in the pulpit and preach an utterly riveting sermon, absolutely brilliant and impeccably profound. Stirling, I tell you this without bias. It is a matter of record. His skills at oratory surpassed those of most other preachers that congregations listened to on either side of the Atlantic. It was his greatest strength; it was his greatest weakness."

"His greatest weakness?" McCutcheon repeated with a measure of incredulity.

"Yes, his greatest weakness."

"How could that be, Freda?"

"His unparalleled oratory," explained Freda, looking intently into McCutcheon's eyes, "the dramatic force with which he presented the truths of the gospel, his clarity of language, his vivid imagery, his poignant illustrations, all of that which held the congregation spellbound Sunday after Sunday convinced his people that he actually believed what he was preaching . . . but he didn't . . . he couldn't."

"Why?" McCutcheon asked compassionately.

"Nietzsche's darkness had claimed residency in his soul. Even in the brilliant light of his preaching there resided the darkness of Nietzsche, like a deadly nightshade infecting and dominating a glorious garden of faith. So if you were to paint his portrait to hang on a prominent wall of the church—and believe me, Stirling, I am adamantly opposed to such an idea—but if one were to paint his portrait, the artist would have to be especially adept at chiaroscuro and integrate both light and dark . . . with perhaps an excessive emphasis on shadow. While Sinclair believed that Nietzsche intended his Superman to be the Christ, Sinclair also concurred with Nietzsche that Christianity makes the mistake of focusing on the next world and making it impossible for us to deal with the present world. But he would never say this from the pulpit. He simply justified preaching what he couldn't embrace theologically by contending that these are the truths to which holy scripture subscribes, and his job was to serve as a mouth-piece for a power that was way beyond his comprehension. In his tacit preoccupation with this world rather than the next, however, by the time of his accidental death, he was spending more nights in the dark, drinking more glasses of Courvoisier, and falling deeper and deeper into a world-weariness, which he himself called the specter of *mal de siècle*."

"Freda, would you say more about his notion that Nietzsche likened his Super-man to the Christ?" McCutcheon asked quietly after a long pause in Freda's narrative.

"I believe it was a conclusion that grew out of Sinclair's own experience. As I mentioned earlier, Stirling, he believed that only a Superman could go through with the intention of enduring execution on the cross, and he knew for certain that he could never have endured it himself. He occasionally referred to Martin Luther's sermon in which Luther claimed that Jesus's resurrection could hardly be astounding, since God as God could raise anybody from the dead. But for a man to choose to go to the cross was indeed a mystery. That mystery not only baffled Sinclair but also terrorized him. Every time he preached on the mystery of the cross, he would break out in an involuntary sweat, and his hands would tremble so visibly that he would have to stop gesturing and keep them at his side, out of view. These were the only times that his voice would quiver, his throat would constrict, and his countenance would become as ashen as Marley's Ghost. Lent was the cruelest season for Sinclair, and all its cruelty fell upon him with full force every Good Friday, when he had to preach on the mystery of the cross and endure the images of his own form on that torture stake, knowing full-well that he himself could not have actually endured the agony of it all . . . and in that pulpit, and in that exercise of preaching that mystery, and in that vicarious agony, all the guilt about his underlying and overarching fears—all-consuming in the moment—took him to his knees and convinced him that he was growing into death . . . took him back into his dark study, where he was leveled until Easter."

"Fears, Freda? These were fears that surfaced during Lent?" McCutcheon asked delicately.

"Yes, especially during the days of Lent . . . but actually . . . every single day of the year."

Silence took over. McCutcheon could feel his heart beating faster and his silent breathing more rapid and shorter.

"There are hundreds of people who would swear to a belief that the very foundation of Sinclair's life was that of faith and courage. His preaching alone would be a testimony to that belief, they would say. But the truth of the matter, Stirling, is that the foundation of his life was fear. It was fear that drove him into his darkness. It was fear he saw manifested in the bottom of his every glass of Courvoisier. It was the fear of death that was lurking as a specter in the shadows of his Nietzschean preoccupations. But because of his theatrical dexterity, no one but I ever detected the slightest trace of fear in his nature." Her eyes took on a vacant aspect as she looked to the Celtic cross behind McCutcheon.

"Was knowing him so intimately too heavy for you?" he asked carefully.

"Ah, of course, but I'd have it no other way. It was too wonderful for me as well. I had the unparalleled privilege of knowing the whole man; but, as you undoubtedly suspect, it was too heavy for me when there was nothing I could do to allay those penetrating fears that on occasion morphed into veritable paroxysms." Freda paused for an unduly long time, until a look of grave remorse clouded her eyes and, actually, her entire countenance.

"There was one occasion," she continued slowly, "which I regret to this very day . . . every day to this very day," she repeated. "Only months before Sinclair died, he officiated at the funeral of a forty-seven-year-old woman who predeceased her mother of seventy-four. At dinner the following evening, Sinclair told me about it with a noticeable tone of empathy, remarking, 'it is a horrible thing for a woman to lose a child, no matter how old the child has become. There is a wrenching of the heart,' he said, 'that wrings the essence of life out of a parent who is subjected by fate to such a loss. Though we have never had children, Freda,' he conceded to me, 'my imagination is too insufficient to grasp how I could ever deal with the death of our child.' I listened to him with a grim, perhaps bitter aspect. For some reason, whether it came from a resentment that he had never concurred with my desire for children or whether I simply wanted to strike an eloquent man's Achilles's heel, I said to him, 'Most everyone I know would say, *God, take me before you take my child,* but not so with you, Sinclair. I believe you would pray, *God, take my child before you take me . . . take anyone before you take me.*' He placed his fork on his plate, sat motionless in thought. Then, as if he were evaluating the truth of my statement, he stared at the centerpiece of flowers on the table, lifted his face to mine and ponderously said, 'No, I don't think so, Freda.' He stood up, waited a moment by his place, and exited the room, leaving the rest of his food untouched.

"Stirling, it is the heaviest thing on my conscience in all the years we were married. For one god-forsaken moment, I played upon his most poignant foible, his life-confining fear, to touch him to the quick, to level a crippling blow at his self-questioning manhood . . . an arrow to his throat. And I—only I—had the power to engage in such a heartless act of emasculation. If I only had it to do again . . . differently!"

No word of consolation occurred to McCutcheon. There could have been none. No such word existed that once expressed—however compassionately—could alleviate the deep remorse and the indelible regret Freda harbored inexorably since that unfortunate, god-forsaken moment. There was no balm in Gilead for her self-recriminating perseveration. Freda took a tissue from her purse, dabbed her eyes gently, and returned the tissue to its place.

McCutcheon broke the silence, changing the subject. "How did you and your husband meet, Freda?"

"We met at the University of Oxford. As I mentioned, Sinclair attended the University of Oxford, Trinity College specifically. In order to pay for his education, he served as a Teaching Fellow in the philosophy department. As a student, he was particularly studious and immoderately conscientious, his face always in a book, always in the same chair, always at the same table at Bodleian Library when not in class. Bodleian Library was where I first met him. At the time I was a student at the university's Harris Manchester College. Three years older than Sinclair, I had matriculated at Harris Manchester College after I had worked two years in the marketplace, in the world of business, in order to cultivate a much-needed exchequer for my education. One evening I sat beside Sinclair at his study table in Bodleian Library, and we both broke for late tea in the refectory. It was then that we spoke to each other, shared our initial stories, and began a relationship that continued nearly every evening we studied in Bodleian . . . always at the same places, always at the same table. We graduated from university the same year, were married the following summer, and then made our way to the States, to Union Theological Seminary where Sinclair earned his doctorate in theology. After serving two pastorates back in London, we returned to the States to accept this position at Madison Avenue Church. You know the rest of the timeline, Stirling."

"Yes, Freda, but before university? Did you come from similar backgrounds in England?" McCutcheon asked with considerable interest, but then added, "if I'm not being too personal."

"That's all right, Stirling," she said reassuringly. "Then sometime we must talk about you."

He nodded benignly and smiled.

"Neither of us ever had a taste for or possessed the trait of aristocracy, either in our blood or in our associations. Even at university, though there was an abundance of aristocracy among the student body, its manifestations appeared at a distance. We seldom rubbed shoulders with it, never socialized with it. I had come from an agrarian background, ironically the daughter of highly cultured parents, at nineteen had gone to London to make the most of a business opportunity, and then on to Harris Manchester College. Sinclair, on the other hand, had experienced a traumatic childhood. Born in Coventry, he was only five years old when the Coventry Blitz occurred in November of 1940. His parents, who were highly respected, wealthy haberdashers, were killed in the bombing; but, by the grace of God, Sinclair was spared by a quirk of destiny, when his nineteen-year-old French nurse had taken him to the basement of their house to shelter him as much as possible. When the bombing ceased, they discovered the bodies of his parents, arm-in-arm, on the living room floor. Bridget, the French nurse, took complete charge of Sinclair for the next four years, making their way to her original home in Marseilles, France. At twenty-three, Bridget fell in love with a French pilot. They were married within the year, and there was no room in the pilot's plans for Sinclair, who was then taken to his uncle's back in Yorkshire. His uncle and aunt then sent Sinclair to boarding school in London, where he excelled academically. From there, he made his way to Trinity College. Other than his nurse, who filled the intimate role of a mother as best she could, Sinclair has no recollection of a loving, stable family. His dominant memory regarding familial relationships was characterized by loss." Freda broke off her narrative abruptly, shook her head sadly, and then took on an involuntary tone of contrition. "Stirling, forgive me. I have rambled on unmercifully here."

McCutcheon hastened to reassure her. "Not at all, Freda! I asked you."

"No, indeed!" she insisted, apparently concerned about having revealed too much at their initial meeting. "I apologize for taking so much of your time this first week of your arrival, but I thought it important to meet with you before your first Sunday in the pulpit . . . actually to pass this on to you from a long line of your predecessors." While making this comment, Freda drew from a wooden case, which she had been holding with her reticule, a large bronze cross on a substantial link chain. Handing it to McCutcheon, she explained, "it has been the custom here at Madison Avenue Presbyterian Church for the Senior Pastor to wear this cross every time he is in the pulpit—as a seal of the office of Senior Pastor—which imbues you with the authority to preach the good news of Christ to our people. I suppose you could think of it as a comparable manifestation of Elijah's mantel passed on to Elisha. Sinclair's predecessor passed it on to him when we arrived from London to take on the pastoral responsibilities twenty-eight years ago."

As McCutcheon held the cross in both hands on his lap, a sense of awe overwhelmed him, perhaps emanating from an awareness of the profound tradition it represented. "I shall wear it dutifully, Freda," he said, "and with a humility that is suitable to the office it signifies. Ordinarily I wear a stole as a sign of the office of servant ministry . . . "

"Oh, no, Stirling," Freda interrupted emphatically, "stoles are not a part of the Madison Avenue Church tradition. All clergy here wear academic hoods. Whatever changes you implement in the future, I hope you will find it agreeable to comply with this tradition in particular."

"Yes . . . of course," McCutcheon responded thoughtfully, deliberating upon the essential differences implied in academic hoods as opposed to clerical stoles. Once again he studied the bronze cross in his lap. It was a Greek cross, and on the two crosspieces was inscribed in raised German letters: *ICH BIN BEI EUCH ALLE TAGE.* "I am with you always," McCutcheon read as he translated the statement.

"Sinclair didn't believe it," Freda said wryly.

"He didn't believe what, Freda?" McCutcheon inquired, pursuing her meaning.

"He didn't believe that God is always with us. 'In point of fact,' he contended, 'if God could abandon his son on the cross, why would I expect God to fulfill an hyperbole that he is with us every day?' And because he couldn't embrace the statement as true, he hated wearing that cross every Sunday when he preached. It became an albatross around his neck, a heavy confinement that weighed him down. He detested this tradition; he detested this cross; he detested his own duplicity."

"But did he always wear it in the pulpit here?" McCutcheon asked, looking first to the cross and then back at Freda.

"Yes, but it was a curse to him, not a blessing."

"And you knew, of course, of his inordinate discontent?" he asked, knowing that he was restating the obvious.

"Yes, I did." She paused, looked down, and then handed him the wooden case, which had served as a casket for the Greek cross. "If you haven't met Sinclair's closest friend, Marcel DuBois, I'm sure you will very soon. Marcel is a professor of philosophy at Vassar College. He possesses a penchant for what he considers the compatible discipline of anthropology. On one of his recent trips to Ethiopia, he learned of the practice of the Hummer Tribe there, that when a woman is married, a metal ring is welded around her neck, and that ring has a metal handle that the husband holds firmly while he beats her, so she cannot get away. When Marcel related this new knowledge to my husband, Sinclair took it as a simile for this link chain he wore around his neck every Sunday, and the cross was the handle God held to beat him . . . and he could not get away. That's how seriously he applied Isaiah's description of the Suffering Servant: *smitten by God and afflicted.*"

They sat quietly, locked by an iron gaze between them. She then said in a whisper, "Sinclair was wearing that cross as he dangled in the noose. If you choose to wear it, Stirling—as, of course, you must—please be careful. This is a friendly admonition, dear brother-in-Christ, not from the matron of the manse but, rather, from a devoted member of your congregation."

Freda stood to her full height. McCutcheon rose as well. Surprisingly, she bent forward, embraced him, and touched his cheek with her lips. McCutcheon's eyes followed her imperious figure as she left.

For a number of minutes McCutcheon remained standing, examining the bronze cross: *ICH BIN BEI EUCH ALLE TAGE.* "I certainly hope so," he mused.

Recollecting his moving into the study with his retinue of books, McCutcheon recalled the strange sight of starkly empty bookshelves . . . no books whatsoever, with one exception: on the lowest shelf at the far left lay one book facedown. Picking it up, he had noticed it was a book titled, *Contes Français / French Stories.* On the left pages was the French text of each story and on the right, the English translations. The sixth story was Paul Claudel's *Mort de Judas / The Death of Judas,* the pages dog-eared. McCutcheon had kept it. Now he lifted it again off the shelf and leafed through its pages.

On the last page, at the end of the story, there in pen was written: *I am Judas!*

2

A Nietzschean Manifesto

It happened every day at five o'clock in the afternoon. Invariably. McCutcheon returned to the church, walked into the main office while Caryn, the last remaining staff member, was packing up to leave. She would stay longer if he wanted her to, if he needed her to make notes or take dictation. She had intimated as much numerous times since his installation as Pastor/Head of Staff three weeks ago. Anything that isn't done by five o'clock, however, can usually wait until morning.

Today—a damp, cold day—was an exception. It had been raining incessantly and the chill bit like a rapacious pit bull. Earlier in the afternoon McCutcheon had officiated at the funeral of a seven-year-old girl who had been struck down by meningitis . . . the fatal kind. Despite tireless, round-the-clock efforts of the medical profession, in two days she was gone, a flower whose petals had been deftly, brutally plucked off the stem of an earth-connection all at once by some invisible ghoulish hand. She was the child of a wealthy, prominent family in the Madison Avenue neighborhood. They were not members of McCutcheon's congregation or, for that matter, of any congregation. McCloyd's Funeral Home simply called McCutcheon to officiate at the funeral, even as the funeral director had done in the past with Dr. Chamberlain.

McCutcheon had remained with the family after the service, the burial, and the late afternoon formal tea. Helpless. Nothing he said made a whit of sense. He was hardly a novice at this business. He had officiated at numerous funerals in his years of ministry, but for the first time, he actually witnessed a family's self-flagellation, beating of the breast, wringing of the hands, primal screams. Rachael's weeping for her children, refusing to be consoled because they were no more took on a full-rounded meaning. Any attempt at consolation was pointless, sternly rebuffed. He had failed to offer an effective word of hope, peace, or tranquil assurance.

When he returned to the church at 5:00 o'clock, Caryn was packing up to leave. Her eyes met McCutcheon's inquiringly.

"I can stay longer if you have something for me to do."

McCutcheon looked away, silently. His eyes were burning. Rain on his face disguised the stinging tears.

"What do you need?" she asked.

Revealing his first fleeting thought of a mother's arms would be unacceptable.

"Nothing," he said.

"Are you sure?"

He looked out the office window behind her. Rain was drumming on the pane with a ferocious, rapid cadence. He suspected the glass would break any instant, like fine china. Motionless, he stared at the pelting rain on crystal.

"No, I'm not sure. Everything I see is so fragile."

Caryn came from behind the desk, approached him and lifted her hand to his face, brushing away droplets of rain beneath his eyes.

"Including you," she said softly.

He nodded slightly.

"What do you need?" she repeated.

Though aching to weep, to shout, to issue primal screams of his own—all of which he had previously witnessed but not expressed—McCutcheon stood stock-still. He could feel an internal storm raging beneath his skin, pushing to erupt like a tsunami with a pounding, pulsating rhythm, one enormous squall in quick succession after another.

"I'll be all right, Caryn, soon. I'm sure of it. Thanks!"

McCutcheon moved to the study. Caryn gathered her belongings and left. She closed the door and locked it behind her. As he sat back in his desk chair, his head in his hands, feeling like a stifled scream, Caryn's compassion pleased him.

She was not his hire. She had been at the church office as administrative assistant long before McCutcheon arrived. She worked quietly and efficiently, cultivated genuine loyalties easily, seldom made references to the previous pastor, listened intently to anyone speaking to her, kept confidences better than anyone he had ever known, greeted everyone with a cheery salutation, was inclined to ready embraces and appropriate touches, and—by her actions—intimated that, for there to be success in the workplace, one's competence must be laced with a healthy attitude. Why would he ever consider replacing Caryn with a hire of his own? On that rainy afternoon—within this first month of his call to Madison Avenue Presbyterian Church—it occurred to him that there had always been a healthy reserve between the two of them—an assumed professionalism—and, at the same time, a respectable warmth of relationship; that afternoon confirmed it.

The door she had locked behind her was soon to be unbolted on that same chilly, rainy autumn day and opened to a labyrinthine past of helplessness and despair, of dark faith and resolute apostasy.

McCutcheon sat motionless, musing. Seven years old. *Where was God in all of this? How could God allow this to happen? This is not the God I know, the God I worship! This is no God of love!* For eighteen years McCutcheon, on occasions such as this, had felt the earth heaving beneath him in an unappeasable agony, expostulating these laments incessantly, vomiting the black bile of biting bewilderment, finding no original expressions of furor at a perceived divine, cosmic indifference. What is original in the hackneyed laments is the uniqueness of the existential catastrophe that devastated the victim and his or her family personally. *This time it's me,* the devastated mourner laments, looking to heaven with an angry, jeremiad visage. Until this moment, catastrophe had happened to someone else, and while that victim's tears elicited empathy, they courted no despair in the observer. Until today, McCutcheon had never had to be original in expressions of emotive grief. He had not been practiced in the art of sorrow, but now he genuinely felt like straining every creative nerve to express his lamentation with a unique protestation against a God who is deemed all-powerful and all-loving, yet is apparently neither.

This was the language of despair and disillusionment he had heard that frigid afternoon. Who could blame them? What could be said to them by way of scriptural assurance that would change their minds, settle their stomachs, cool the flames licking their skin and scorching their minds, a word that would shed a brilliant light upon them, or imbue them with a lasting note of hope while the earth was heaving and regurgitating another death of innocence being tamped down its raw throat? Who could reveal the ultimate consolation in a word or a phrase? *Not I,* he thought. And that's the hell of it—literally, the *hell* of it. That's the all-consuming never-consumed hell of this profession. There are no answers. Worse than quantum physics that researches the most outlandish suppositions but with enough discoveries to encourage the physicist to persist, even perseverate. On the other hand, the pastor and theologian stand holding a reticule of suppositions and revelations that crumble when held out as authentic at a seven-year-old girl's funeral. A little girl. A very little girl. Once she jumped, skipped, played hopscotch, shared the sandbox, cuddled up to her mother's side, laughed at her father's antics, played dolls with her older sister, and pretended to be a mother to her four-year-old brother. She has her very own sandbox now: a child's coffin beneath fresh sod at the north end of an Albany cemetery. *God is love,* McCutcheon had said. *You're a fool,* they whispered through clenched teeth.

He opened his desk file drawer to place the funeral service bulletin, homily notes, and prayer of thanksgiving in the funerals file. There must have been residual torque of anger in his right arm. He had yanked too hard on the file drawer; it extended the full way and beyond, landing upon the floor beside his chair. It was when he lifted the drawer by the front handle and the back partition that he felt something rough on the back end. A note attached by tacks onto the hidden side of the back. Chances are that no one in a matter of decades would ever discover this attachment so long as this elegant, large mahogany desk drawer remained in place. Only by a quirk of circumstances had it come to light.

With the larger blade of his penknife, McCutcheon pried out the four tacks and retrieved the three-by-five index card. *Archives fourth floorboard.* Three words, that was all. They must bear the weight of some particular meaning, but he had no idea what that meaning could be. Was the note referring to the archives of this church or to some other archives? Although he had been in this church little more than a month, he had visited its archives on the initial tour, when the Call Committee had shown him every nook and cranny of the building. That was a particularly memorable room due specifically to the uneasiness he felt in the eerie, high-vaulted space in close proximity to the gigantic belfry. Dust lay on everything. No one took care of anything. In contrast to active archives in a museum or historical society, the archives of Madison Avenue Presbyterian Church apparently lay dormant for incalculable years, like a weed-infested garden, abandoned, apparently without a gardener.

McCutcheon made his way up the dark, narrow staircase toward the belfry, the uppermost extension of a church completely Gothic and stone—Gothic and stone in its architectural majesty of the symmetrical walls on the outside; Gothic and stone in its winding mystery on the staircase inside; Gothic and stone in its aspiring reach in the sanctuary; Gothic and stone in its towering splendor in the belfry; Gothic and stone in its spacious offices, classrooms and hallways; Gothic and stone in its dark foreboding in the archives. Its massive door was unlocked. McCutcheon pushed. It resisted. He pushed hard. It gave a little, then opened reluctantly, creaking continuously as if responding to some inaudible ghostly command. What he saw for the second time was hardly a cave of hidden treasure but, rather, a compilation of artifacts and relics of previous decades, apparently of little interest to the present congregation.

A flash of lightning lit up the dim room, and a deafening crack of thunder accompanied it, the natural pyrotechnics featuring the huge stained glass window ensconced in the stone wall to his right. The percussive, impetuous rain still beat its cadence, this time on patterned glass. McCutcheon switched on the light and glanced again at the note in his hand: *Archives fourth floorboard. Fourth from the left or the right?* he wondered. That ghostly portal of entry to this eerie chamber was closer to the fourth floorboard on the right, and that floorboard lay beneath a long rectangular oak table stacked with papers and photographs, which, if one could estimate by the thickness of accumulated dust, obviously belonged to an era of antiquity. Each plank floorboard must have been eight inches wide. McCutcheon examined the portion of the fourth floorboard visible beneath the table and could detect no particular disruption in its running seams. This suggested to him that nothing had been ensconced beneath this area of the floor, so he moved across the cavernous room to the plank floorboards on the left. There in front of the left wall stood a gigantic oak chest of drawers with brass handles on each, the breadth of which extended from the front of the room to the back, and the depth of which reached into the room by eight floorboards. Needless to say, the fourth floorboard was completely covered. McCutcheon glanced skeptically at the card in his hand. A successful conclusion to this cryptic clue seemed dismal at best.

Since his quest had been thwarted, McCutcheon casually pulled open the huge left middle drawer of the chest and lifted out documents that dated back to the Civil

War era and earlier to the founding of the church in the late seventeen hundreds. Dust. Covered with dust. We all come to dust. Archives remind us of coming to dust . . . *for dust thou art, and to dust thou shalt return.* Why would anyone want to work in archives where there is a perpetual reminder that we all come to dust? He couldn't think of anyone in this congregation who would want to look into the drawers of this chest and see mirrored there a foreshadowing of his or her inevitability. He closed the drawer.

When McCutcheon closed the mammoth drawer, its weight rocked the chest. It had been attached to the wall, he thought. But not so. It rocked. He knelt down, looked at the feet of the mammoth and discovered they were mounted on inconspicuous casters . . . efficient casters, apparently casters with ball bearings that allowed this gargantuan chest to effortlessly roll away from the wall and out into the room, exposing six plank floorboards. A four-foot segment of the fourth floorboard was loose. McCutcheon raised it and shone a light into the hole. There between two ten-inch joists was wedged a rectangular cedar wooden box—covered by a black felt cloth—perhaps twelve by fifteen inches in size. Gingerly he lifted it from the cubicle, raising first the left end and then the box in its entirety.

A sudden moment of reverence came over him—a sudden sensation quite inexplicable. What contents could be so private, so sacred, that it should be hidden from sight like a casket buried for eternity and shrouded in complete, complex obscurity? He held it cautiously. Surprisingly the wood still emitted its cedar aroma. He waited. He waited longer. His hands trembled. What is this phenomenon? What was he waiting for? Afraid. He thought he was afraid, but of what he had no idea. He had often confused awe and fear, could seldom distinguish one from the other. Right now it was one of them. He had no idea which one. What puzzled him was the absence of dust, either on the cloth or on the box.

McCutcheon closed his eyes, breathed a prayer for calm, and then simultaneously opened his eyes and the dust-free coffer. A gleam reflected from off the contents. There, within a black velvet-lined rectangular space, lay a book—a thick book with a black leather cover. An appellation and subtitle were inscribed on the first page— *A Nietzschean Manifesto: the Confessions of an Ecclesiastical Atheist.* The signature scrawled on the same page was that of Sinclair Chamberlain. A hand-written journal, or, if not a journal, a document. McCutcheon looked around, surveyed the cavernous room with high-vaulted, cathedral-like ceilings in search of a chair. Having succeeded, he sat for hours, reading, devouring Chamberlain's secrets, absorbed in the darkness that gathered around him inside these archives while the night grew thick outside in the stormy streets of Albany.

A Nietzschean Manifesto:

The Confessions of an Ecclesiastical Atheist

While not a meticulous scribe of sequential events, I vividly recall the stroke of midnight that sounded upon this dark soul of mine, drawing a dramatic conclusion to the pretentious day of faith. And here, I record it for none to ever read, but for me to finally acknowledge.

That stroke of midnight that descended like a vast, shivering, resonating shroud upon a long-held pretense occurred in late spring of the fourteenth year of my serving as Senior Pastor of Madison Avenue Presbyterian Church here in Albany. Precisely one year before, I had been elected Moderator of the Synod of the Northeast, a one-year position of non-stipendiary leadership held concomitantly with my pastoral position at Madison Avenue Church. Duties included the task of interpreting the work of the synod to the twenty-one presbyteries that compose that northeast middle judicatory. Another rather public duty was to moderate the annual meeting of the synod at which I was elected. The following year, at the annual meeting at which I was to step down, after having visited all twenty-one presbyteries during the previous twelve months, I chaired the opening session of the annual meeting, sought approval for all the reports of synod staff, Synod Mission Council, standing committees, and task forces, and presided at the election of the next Moderator. It was during the review of—and assembly action on—my report as Moderator that my great awakening occurred. A commissioner—officially seated as an elder representing a particular presbytery—rose to be recognized. Having gained the floor, he moved that the term raison d'être *be deleted from my report. I called for a second to the motion, which was immediately offered by a fellow commissioner from the same presbytery. Speaking to the motion, the mover objected to my use of the term* raison d'être *on the grounds that the Moderator's concepts, reasoning, rationales, presentations, and vocabulary should be within the reach of the common people, that any hint of pretentious intellect excludes the common person of the pew, and that such intellectual pretense flies in the face of our Lord Jesus Christ, who was a down-to-earth teacher of simple truths, who spoke in parables without unintelligible French phrases.*

As a reminder to myself—which I deem essential while recording this incident, this turning point—during those years among Presbyterians nationally, the synods that comprised the denomination were fighting to justify their existence to the General Assembly, the highest judicatory, and, subsequently, were continually redefining their identity, both function and form. Within my moderator's report, I had written a comprehensive, well-documented justification for the existence of synods, and the term raison d'être, *in my view, was particularly apropos. The kicker to the motion occurred immediately after the second to the motion and the justifying words of the mover, when I called for discussion of the motion: silence. No discussion. No one rose in opposition, predicating a rebuttal with the fact that Presbyterians are supposedly known as the learned branch of the Christian church, that scholarship—even mass education—is central to John Calvin's*

foundational thoughts about the church's essence. There before me sat a sea of silent ac-
quiescence, the most profound manifestation of the dumbing down of America, an entire
ecclesiastical body's embracing the lowest common denominator of intellect, concurring
with two voices representing the daft and the dregs. Motion passed unanimously.

All my personal raison d'être *for being in ministry—namely, a fierce love of philo-*
sophical, theological, and ecclesiastical scholarship—was curtly and mindlessly coun-
tered by one simpleton's motion, another simpleton's second, and a voting body's torpor,
indifference, and stupefaction. Raison d'être. *Strike it from the record. Some said it was*
a small thing, too trivial to think about at any great length. No, it was a large thing, a
looming foreshadow of the dismal decline of the Presbyterian Church sinking fast into
the vortex of an emotive faith devoid of intellectual inquiry, with blue-jeaned preachers
strumming guitars and carrying on ad nauseam *about their own personal experiences of*
sickly faith, as if those examples epitomize the ideal of Christian devotion, the summum
bonum *of life in Christ.*

There ensued a fifteen-minute recess to allow for one hand to lay down the gavel
with tacit disillusionment and another to take it up with naive anticipation. As I stepped
down from the dais, finality of office gripped firmly in hand, I walked past a synod staff
person—one known for his clever, biting cynicism—who quipped, "How does it feel to
be a has-been?" It felt extraordinarily liberating to be released from a blood-sucking
swarm that demanded much and gave little. Aware of classified information that this
staff member would soon lose his job due to the reorganization of the synod, I thought
with a wry, silent smile: "if you only knew!" It was a silent response that echoed the
deafening taciturnity of those hundreds of expressionless accommodators who, in my
perception, proffered no personal raison d'être *of their own. Theirs also had been struck*
from the record . . . or, more accurately, had never been recorded! The midnight shroud
fell in that instant and suffocated faith, sounding its death knell—intellect and reason
alone surviving.

The days—and particularly the nights—following the five-day annual assembly of
the synod, I moved immediately into my mental inner sanctum with a centripetal force
that virtually attacked and swiftly surrounded the center of being; and there the comfort
of Nietzsche's philosophical constructs—on which I had dwelt so studiously throughout
my years at university—brought me an immeasurable comfort, unlike any I had ever
experienced in the church of Christ. If the man on the street knows little of Nietzsche,
the chances are that what he does know—and the only thing he can remember hear-
ing—is the philosopher's contention that the thought of suicide is a great consolation;
by means of it, one gets successfully through many a bad night. Such was the case for
me since that dreadful epiphany on the dais. I became submerged in a bottomless well
of melancholy, the nature of which was both delicious and distasteful, exhilarating and
terrifying. Often the thought of suicide sustained me as a great consolation. In that state
of self-contradictory melancholy, the sour image of that silent assembly continually as-
saulted me. Then, without faith, transported often back to that feckless scene, the fierce

irony every time tapped not Nietzsche's most commonly-known words on suicide but, rather, another sentiment contending that the masters have been done away with and the morality of the vulgar man has triumphed. Within days—after so many sleepless, melancholic nights—I came to admit what I had known for over a decade, like a song without words, that I shared Nietzsche's utter and complete distain for all mankind, pathetic whimperers, sick inhabitants of a still sicker world. Up until these recent nights, such thoughts—though unarticulated—consistently seemed judgmental and, therefore, vile. But now, another extraordinary liberation—not unlike that I felt at the words of the synod cynic, chortling at my newly acquired has-been emeritus state—I joined Nietzsche on his seat of judgment from which he surveyed humanity with disparagement, freely voicing his scorn. No apologies! I, as well, make none from this time forward. Judgmental? Perhaps! I choose to think, perceptive . . . an accurate observation of human life, of so many, "the much-too-many," endowed with exceptional character traits, who miss their way and deteriorate, who vomit up their human potential mixed with the black bile of their misbegotten desires and hasten shrieking to their graves unfulfilled.

Every evening—when there wasn't one of those notorious, superficial, banal committee meetings at the church—I entered my study in the manse, closed the study doors, and poured my intellectual inquiries into Nietzsche's brilliance, reveling in the revised realization—after so many years of neglect—that opus opificem probat (the work proves the craftsman). At the same time, during the course of the evening, I poured myself two or three glasses of Courvoisier, and from there—propelled by Nietzsche's ingenuity and Courvoisier's opiate—I made a swift descent into the darkest depth of melancholia, into what Nietzsche called "the melancholia of everything completed!" There in that vast, consoling darkness I came face-to-face again and again with Nietzsche's madman lifting his lantern in daylight, searching for the God who is dead, indicting the stupefied crowd who had killed him with their indifference, and entering diverse churches where he requiemed God and queried rhetorically, "What are these churches now if they are not the tombs and sepulchers of God?" And there, in good company with his madman, I came at last to embrace Nietzsche's full, incontrovertible conviction that God is dead, and that he has been killed by simpletons, the much-too-many, the mob of men who have no raison d'être either in their scant vocabulary or in their essential being.

While every evening I was thus sequestered, Freda invariably thought I was crafting sermons, when in actuality I was sculpting my destiny in a milieu that required faith, a resolute, unquestioning faith sounding forth with clarion call from an immutable pulpit. The scintillating challenge at hand was to exude faith when there was no faith. I had willingly and willfully abandoned illusions. Others looked to me to shield them from the debilitating pains of coarse life—characterized by vicissitudes and catastrophes—with romanticized images of a better life in faith or an infinitely better life to come in eternity. As for me, however—as one who at the stroke of his soul's midnight had relinquished faith, had discarded illusion, and had chosen to live by his own ingenuity—the delectable challenge was to simultaneously hold on to my newly acknowledged hostility to the

Christian faith and preach passionate, brilliant sermons based on the so-called biblical truths. The people of my church—like so many Pontius Pilates—want to know truth. What is truth? they ask. Little do they know—and far be it from me to enlighten them— there is only one truth: God is dead, and this church on Madison Avenue is his sepulcher. But only a self-destructive fool would disclose that truth. Being neither self-destructive nor a fool, I shall continue to weave bright illusions of a better world, detailed descriptions of the City of God, for a people who stand on the precipice of despair—on the brink of defeat—vanquished by the cruel blows of life, who cannot transcend beyond a tragic vision. By fashioning bright illusions—woven with brilliant imagery and delivered with passionate theater—I held my place in this sanctuary and guaranteed the uninterrupted flow of my lucrative emolument. What else would I do? What else could I do?

Two definitive acts—one of hand and the other of mind—seemed imperative as I moved forward with this new massive mindset. The first pertained to the very pulpit itself. On the beautifully hand-carved wooden pulpit desk were engraved two sayings, one from John 12:21—"Sir, we would see Jesus"—the request of Greeks to Philip; and the other from Richard Baxter, seventeenth century English theologian, poet, and hymn-writer: "Preach as never sure to preach again; preach as dying man to dying men," a preaching directive to the Madison Avenue preacher based on Baxter's own declaration, "I preached as never sure to preach again / And as a dying man to dying men." I covered these sayings with rubber matting, fitted neatly within the raised edges of the pulpit desk.

The second act was related to a sacred tradition known universally by all Madison Avenue congregants and held sacrosanct by every member for past decades. Every Sunday, on a chain around his neck, every Senior Pastor in the church's history wore a heavy Greek cross with a German inscription: ICH BIN BIE EUCH ALLE TAGE. When one pastor died or moved on to another parish, the cross was passed on to his successor with the irrefutable expectation that the new minister would wear that cross every time he preached from the Madison Avenue Church pulpit. Not even in my most radical estimation could I conceive of laying that cross aside as I continued to preach. That alone would bring the walls of God's sepulcher down upon my head. The second act, therefore, was one accomplished by a cognitive denial. Every Sunday, though that cross was a dangling, weighty stone about my neck, I put it on and consciously repudiated its assertion: I am with you always. No, no! I have known only God's absence.

Having admitted this, it is not without some sadness—even chagrin—that I acknowledge my own pain at the shattered vision of a God who guides history and intervenes in people's lives. But I see no such guidance of God's hand in the rise and fall of nations or God's intervention in the birth and death of humanity or any specific saving acts of the Son of God who represents a God of providence and protection. I'm inclined towards Albert Schweitzer, who recognized that the Jews of Jesus's day thought Jesus was not the Messiah but the forerunner; but, contrary to the Jews' thinking, Jesus thought he was the Messiah. Schweitzer thought that Jesus was correct in this self-perception but that he was wrong in his thinking that the kingdom of God would soon appear. In *his disappointment, Jesus read Isaiah and decided that he must die: conclusion—the disillusioned Jesus, lashed to the wheel of history, goes on being mangled by the stupefied crowd who have strapped him to the wheel with their myopic apathy, even as King Lear's two evil daughters bound him upon a wheel of fire by their calculated indifference.*

I, too, am confined to that mutilating wheel of history and to that scorching wheel of fire, not by indifference, however, but by abject fear. I could never conceive of willingly throwing myself on that wheel of history or willingly trudging up some barren, dreary pathway to a windswept, scorching hill to lay myself willingly upon a cross, waiting for some Father's will to be done through the ghastly instruments of hammer upon nails. If I recall my Luther readings accurately, Martin Luther intimated, "God—as God—can raise anyone from the dead; but for a man to choose to go to the cross is a mystery." Some mysteries are nearly comprehensible, but this mystery is far beyond anyone's comprehension. One of the finest preachers I have ever heard contended that the true joy of Easter is inextricably bound to the sacrifice of the cross; Easter joy comes only at a costly price, graciously paid on our behalf by a Lord who goes willingly to death. Willingly, no doubt, was the operative term in that assertion: it couldn't have meant gleefully but rather it described an act of will, of choice . . . choice of the Christ; and that is the mystery no one can possibly understand. Though I find myself bound upon a wheel of fire, choosing to throw myself on that wheel is an act of will I could never intend. The torment. The contortions of suffering would be so ugly, impossible to behold, say nothing of to endure. He would have to be a superman, which leads me to believe that this Jesus of Nazareth—whom centrists as well as conservative Christians declare to be both fully human and fully divine (an astounding paradox that assaults all human reason)—qualifies as Nietzsche's Superman, his Übermensche, his Beyond-Man, his Overman, the one who is capable of transcendence, excessiveness, intensity. Nietzsche's Übermensche had no intention of bringing in a kingdom of God but, rather, creating a new-world value. Undoubtedly, only an Übermensche could willfully slog up a rocky hill with a shivery cross as his medium for ultimate transcendence, all the while spat upon by dolts and dullards, an earlier blood-sucking swarm calling for his blood to be upon them and their children.

Given any similar day, given any similar night, given any similar demand, neither could I nor would I willingly make myself vulnerable to people's folly or nature's calamities. Fear is my castellan—my turnkey. If Glynnis Vandeusen knew the truth about that day on the State Street hill, she would realize that I am not the Good Shepherd who lays down his life for the sheep. Most categorically, no. *I am the hireling who runs away in fear at sight of the wolf. Only those who are too dull, too dim-witted to taste the acidity of fear in their mouths—when the gift of fear would warn them of imminent danger— rush in for vainglory, such as that fool-hearty Honeysuckle!* Manu fortis—personally *brave, she said. That grotesque miscreant, that misbegotten mishap of nature! Contrary to whatever grace her words bestowed upon him, he is in truth the rival of Quasimodo or Richard III for trophies in ugliness. Ignorant offspring of a no-known father, that honey-sucking Honeysuckle! Now must I be saddled with the unbecoming appellation of* hireling, *though I alone know the truth of the matter. How soon will it become too much to bear on my own, before I must regurgitate the bits of undigested, indicting facts in some fabricated confessional to relieve my simpering spleen?*

Lay down your self-incriminating pen, Chamberlain. Pick up your script on Morte de Judas, *and play the part yet again, for you have played it well on stages, in chancels . . . wrapped belligerently in your cloak of fear.*

McCutcheon closed the book. He recalled his recent conversation with Freda Chamberlain. All of those incredible elements in her description of her husband were verified here in this document. How clearly she had seen into his soul . . . even more than Sinclair Chamberlain had realized. She had not been fooled—only bewildered, saddened, helpless, committed to secrecy.

The storm that continued to rage outside could not measure up to the storm newly raging in McCutcheon's head. The sudden moment of reverence that had come over him upon discovery of the box dissolved into utter dismay. What McCutcheon had discovered to be hidden, private—and therefore deemed sacred—he found to be an enormous contradiction. God dead? Preach as if God is alive when God is dead? No. God is not dead. This church is no lie! McCutcheon's adopted creed—tasted, savored, and ingested from one of the great literary giants—attested to the essence of Jesus the Christ as the One who, with or without truth, brings in the kingdom of God.

He laid Chamberlain's clandestine journal back in the box, closed the lid, and placed it in the very spot he had found it. He replaced the floorboard and rolled back the gigantic oak chest against the wall. Dark was descending upon the stormy streets of the city and upon those making their way against the saturated winds howling in that darkness, lighted only by dim streetlamps.

And who are these in the streets of Albany who have been wounded by that darkness within and without? Who are these in Albany related to the rest of humanity by their common despair, their passionate love, their fervent aspirations, their mutual dreams, their flawed affections, their broken loyalties . . . their resonating disbelief? In his twenty-six years among them, Chamberlain obviously knew them, for he resided with them in the bleak shadows of an ever-threatening and overarching death, diminished only by the natural barbiturates of flagrant denial, wanton hedonism, calculating treachery, and self-induced ignorance. In his view, they all drank from a common, bottomless well of abundant despair found in the central square of center city marketplace. Their melancholy fed his melancholy; their despondence matched his despondence; and according to Chamberlain's *die Weltanschaaung,* his worldview, they all—every one of them, without exception—lived Thoreauvian lives of quiet desperation.

While McCutcheon disputed Chamberlain's conclusions and could not embrace his predecessor's internal inconsistencies, he leveled no judgment at Chamberlain's state of mind or his faith's demise. What McCutcheon comprehended all too well was the undeniable reality: pastors are made of the same stuff as the people they are called to serve, comprised by the same hope, faith, fears, doubts, and speculations. They laugh with the same gusto, weep with the same profusion, speak with the same bravado, fail to speak out due to the same fear, are bowed down with the same fractured self-esteem, are lifted up by the same restoring inspiration, wounded by the same concupiscence, planted like a new tree beside streams of living water by the same grace.

The only difference between pastors and the people of Albany is that pastors are called to muddle through the messiness of ministry, called to touch the blood of bleeding humanity and—with the blood of humanity's crosses on their pastoral hands—say, *God is love.* When the wounded say, *you're a fool,* pastors nod their heads and say, *yes, a fool for Christ . . . and God is love.* Do pastors believe it? McCutcheon would like to think so. *But we are so flawed,* he mused, *at times it is hard to tell. Apparently, not all of us do.*

3

Devotee of Fractured Beauty

ENTERING THE SCHUMANNS' DRAWING room, the dinner guests felt a magnetic pull into a captivating time warp. It was as if they had left a spot where the Albany twenty-first century sidewalk ended and had free-fallen into a Victorian manor of a previous century, perhaps some 150 years past. Certainly a couple of couples—the McCutcheons and DuBoises—were well acquainted with Victorian monoliths in England and France, but such a magnificent structure of this architectural style and vintage in Albany was undoubtedly rare, if not unique.

"Come in, come in, come in," boomed the host with a sonorous cordiality as he rose from his high wingback chair of opulent brocade. Though they had come separately, all three couples had arrived simultaneously and entered the drawing room *en masse*. Marcel and Chantal DuBois, long acquainted with the Schumanns, were the first to greet their host, followed by Heather and Stirling McCutcheon, newly arrived in Albany and Madison Avenue Church the previous month. Then Francesca Harlansworth advanced while her husband Keith held back until acknowledged. Barbara Schumann made her entrance through the arch that delineated the drawing room from the library and descended upon the group with characteristic flourish, embracing each guest with exuding warmth that radiated throughout the chamber.

As yet unknown to Stirling McCutcheon at this early period in his tenure as Senior Pastor, William and Barbara Schumann were the highest financial contributors to Madison Avenue Presbyterian Church, where Babbs had been baptized as an infant and Bill had taken on membership and responsibilities as an elder soon after they were married in the church's stately sanctuary thirty-two years ago last month. In those thirty-two years, they had been blessed by a son and a daughter as well as six lively grandchildren—three from each, the two families residing in the Midwest and on the west coast respectively.

Along with a small percentage of the tri-city populace, the Schumanns inhabited an elite sphere of the *nouveau riche*. Most of the wealth and influence in the Albany industrial tree grew from its deep roots—from old money. In the last two decades, however—with burgeoning technology start-ups—the most colorful and the fullest blossoms on that money tree were nurtured by business innovations resulting in a bona fide class of new rich. Bill Schumann had positioned himself on the crest of the initial wave of that escalating phenomenon with an inventive microchip that—patented and rushed to market—sent the stock of his start-up company off the charts. Since then, through sharp ingenuity and generous employment practices, he maintained his competitive edge with a large cadre of loyal, brilliant employees.

"Well, Mrs. McCutcheon, my dear lady, welcome!" exclaimed Schumann. "What a delight to have you and your fine husband here this evening as honored guests!"

"Thank you! It's our pleasure, I assure you," rejoined Mrs. McCutcheon. "Please call me *Heather.*"

"Surely, as you wish," hastened Schumann to concur. "So long as you understand that we and the rest of your congregation hold you both in very high esteem."

"Granted. How pleasant esteem is when it possesses an identifiable mutuality! I'm sure my husband and I shall experience that mutuality with all of you and the rest of our congregation as well."

"I dare say, you all must have come together in the church van," ventured Babbs with marked joviality, "or you cleverly synchronized your watches. I don't recall ever seeing such collective punctuality."

"A providential phenomenon, Babbs, nothing more than that," quipped Marcel DuBois.

"Come, come, come!" insisted Schumann. "Sit wherever you please. Plenty of room! Plenty of room!"

Rather than sitting, Marcel moved toward the fireplace and gazed at the wall-hanging above it. "Bill! This troubadour is new since we were here last." It wasn't a portrait, nor was it a tapestry but, rather, a rendering of a medieval minstrel cast in iron, raised upon a black metal background. The large portrayal measured easily four feet wide and six feet high. Seated on a decorative gold stool, dressed in a forest green poet's shirt with high collar, puffy shoulders, tight sleeves, and flourishing cuffs, the minstrel held a long-neck lute which he strummed with slender fingers. He had a strikingly handsome face with pointed features that shone vividly beneath his bright orange, two-cornered minstrel hat with tassels hanging from each corner. His close-fitting tights matched the brilliant orange of his hat, and his forest green minstrel shoes—also tasseled—completed his haberdashery.

"Yes, yes, yes!" attested Bill with abundant conviviality. "We couldn't leave the museum without it. Had to have it, you know! Truthfully, I'm convinced Babbs was taken with those orange tights and muscular calves."

"William Blythe Schumann! You incorrigible tease!" retorted Babbs. "There's not a whit of truth in that speculation. It's simply a matter of wanting someone to keep me company when you're off on your insufferable business trips." Then referring to the colorful wall-hanging with a graceful hand gesture and an amiable countenance, she turned to the group and said demurely, "he sings to me."

Two waiters entered the drawing room with trays of champagne and hors d'oeuvres. When everyone had received a glass, Schumann—as host—raised his chalice and proposed a toast: "To the McCutcheons, Heather and Stirling, may they prosper in our midst and flourish in their ministry at Madison Avenue Presbyterian Church for many, many, many years to come! Here! Here!" Champagne flowed freely before the congenial gathering adjourned to the dining room for a sumptuous repast in an elegant setting.

By nearly anyone's standard, this was an unusual coterie of people, all seated at the same table, all brought together in this given instance, all connected by chance or by destiny to the same underlying search for meaning. Was it chance? Or was it providence? Could there be some overarching divine hand shaping this moment, this instance, this time and place, this specific configuration of collective individuals? Who can divine the intentions of the Divine? What an objective observer could divine, at the very least, was that the makeup of the guest list was imbued with carefully calculated intentionality. Unabashedly Bill Schumann had an agenda, one that would come to light during the main course of the elegant dinner. He and Babbs had selected six of the most obvious intellectuals in their church to engage in a unique encounter around their dinner table: Francesca Harlansworth, a PhD Professor of Romance Languages in the Arts and Humanities Department at the College of St. Rose, and her husband Keith, a chemist at Bayer Pharmaceutical Corporation; Chantal Laurent DuBois, French translator at the United Nations, and her husband Marcel Pierre DuBois, Philosophy Professor at Vassar College; and, of course, the guests of honor, Heather Chisholm McCutcheon, author of two published books—*The Pauper's Soul* and *Medea's Bitter Anguish*—theologically trained, daughter of Scottish landed gentry, mother of three children, and her husband Stirling, Scottish pastor, newly-installed Senior Pastor of Madison Avenue Presbyterian Church. Not to neglect mention of the hosts of this calculated occasion, Barbara Schumann, graduate of Vassar College with a doctorate from SUNY Albany, Dean of Students at Skidmore College, and William Schumann, graduate of MIT, inventor, developer, founder of an abundantly successful start-up company, and current member of Tufts University Think Tank.

"Heather," said Schumann, directing his comment to his right—the place of honor at the table—when he recognized a lull in the numerous conversations among the group, "Keith informed me that you have written and published two books."

"Really!" remarked Heather, casting a glance at Harlansworth and smiling, "How could he know a thing like that?"

"Because he read them," answered Schumann "perhaps the only one here who did. Anybody else?"

"I did," smiled McCutcheon, "I'm proud to say."

"Of course you would, Stirling," chortled Schumann.

"How did you know Heather published these books, Keith," asked Chantal inquisitively.

Harlansworth looked self-conscious, as if he had been accused of something devious. "When I served on the Search Committee and we met with Heather and Stirling in Edinburgh for interviews, Stirling mentioned that Heather is a published author, so I bought the books and read them."

"What do you think of them?" pressed Chantal with a winsome challenge. "What I really want to know, Keith, is what they're about. Putting you on the spot!"

"Heather should tell you," suggested Keith without picking up the gauntlet.

"No, no! You can't get off that easily," shot back Chantal. "You said you served on the committee. You said that you bought the books in Edinburgh and you read them. Now you have to tell us what they are all about."

Keith thought for a moment, assumed a story-telling tone, and said, "The title of the first one is *The Pauper's Soul* and is an extensive treatment of Jesus's torment in the Garden of Gethsemane, which is all related to the predicament of his identity. He has nothing except his identity as Son of God with which to bargain for his survival and for the transmuting of his divine death sentence. As pauper, he has no other collateral to buy off this moment of garden anguish. In point of fact, his identity as Son of God, as Messiah, as Savior of the world—who takes away the sins of the world by the only means possible, namely, his death—works against a stay of execution and thrusts him forward into the ghastly resolution of his mission. The one thing he possesses and the one thing he cannot turn his back on is his identity, which determines both his fate and his destiny: his fate in that he has no choice consistent with his identity other than to carry the cross, and his destiny in that his identity is his pathway to ultimate glory.

"Heather's second book is titled *Medea's Bitter Anguish*. Medea, who used her powers to help her husband Jason overcome three enormous obstacles and secure the Golden Fleece, represents the contemporary woman who has put her own personal ambitions on hold for a lover or husband, works while he acquires degrees, and then feels the serpent's sting of ingratitude when he casts her off for a mistress or new wife, leaving her and her children to fend for themselves. Medea's bitter anguish foams up in the moment of choice: to take revenge and destroy something he loves—their children—or to embrace what he left behind and draw them all the closer to her bosom. Heather included pictures of Medea, which show her naked as she reaches for her children to kill them, indicating that her anguish completely exposes her to the tyranny of a callous husband. Heather uses the story of Medea as the defining metaphor for the predicament of abused and abandoned women in our global society. And, Chantal, as to your question—*What do I think of them?*—I think they are profound, brilliant, relevant, compelling, and should be required reading for all adult members of Christian churches, Protestant and Catholic alike."

Chantal turned to Heather with playful cunning. "And how did he do, Author McCutcheon?"

"Impeccably!" she said, smiling at Keith. "Spot on!"

Schumann set his fork on his plate and admitted, "I have a confession to make, although I must tell you that I have no remorse whatsoever. The central theme of *The Pauper's Soul* provides the perfect transition into my confession. Babbs and I invited you this evening because we want to hear your best thinking about the cascading scientific developments around genome editing, which has a transformative impact on the nature of identity. Six months ago I was invited to join other scientists, ethicists, clerics, and academics in a Think Tank on Genome Editing that meets every two weeks at Tufts University. The basic question that underlies all the discussion is whether altering the DNA in a mosquito, or a fruit fly, or a rat, or a gorilla, or a horse, or a human embryo will alter the identity of the entity and/or its offspring? While much of the genome editing can be for purposes of good and ultimately for curing diseases, there are enormous risks that raise ethical questions about the potential destructiveness of unleashing altered organisms into an unequipped society. It could be that the formation of the Think Tank on Genome Editing is behind the curve. There are scientists who maintain that the genie is out of the bottle and can't be put back in. Undoubtedly you read about all of this, about CRISPR and how it edits DNA. What I want to know is what you think about it. An altered organism is presumably not the same organism it was before it was altered. The identity it had before presumably is not the same identity it possesses afterwards."

"Of course, Bill, you're right," DuBois remarked, "undoubtedly we've all read about this immense concern, but it's very complex. I've noticed that students and we as faculty find it difficult to describe our basic initial identities to say nothing of the complexity of the challenge to describe our identities if we were to become an altered organism. Indeed, Heather has written an entire book on Jesus's identity as tested in the Garden of Gethsemane. We have to assume that his identity was consistently the same. But did he discover it as it always was, or did he forge it in his adult years, or was he told it at his baptism?

"When Chantal and I were in France recently, we drove from Paris to Bordeaux, where we would spend some time with her parents on the Bay of Biscay. I related to her the discussion the students and I had in my course on the Philosophy of Values. On the one hand, I asked, is our personal identity established at birth, or, on the other hand, is it formed as we grow? On the one hand, is identity set and discovered, or, on the other, is identity fluid and forged? On the one hand, is identity something that is unveiled or unfolded, or, on the other, is identity an entity that is conceived and created by each individual? Is identity static and never changing, or is identity continually being recreated, going through transformation?"

"Ah, here we go," interjected Chantal, "just wait to the end and see who wins this one!"

"You may be surprised to know," smiled DuBois drolly, "that Chantal and I don't always see eye-to-eye on these kinds of questions, or that we failed to come to consensus on the nature of identity. My point of view was simply that identity is given, static, and one simply discovers it. Chantal's point of view, on the other hand, was that identity is developed and is ever-changing as we recreate our essence. Of course we knew that this has been a classic debate historically, but we waded right into it regardless. I reminded her that in the *Dialogues of Plato*, Socrates encounters his fellow citizen Meno, who asks Socrates how he will inquire into that which he does not know. Socrates insists that knowledge does not consist in the accumulations of external facts but, rather, in the unfolding of truth, already latent in the soul, under the stress of persistent inquiry. A Greek slave—who belongs to Meno, lives in Meno's house, and, according to Meno was never educated—comes on the scene and is introduced to Socrates. Through an intricate process of inquiry, Socrates elicits from Meno's slave certain mathematical conclusions that he had never previously learned in Meno's house or anywhere else. Socrates concludes that either the slave acquired this knowledge in a former state of existence, or he always knew it. This knowledge is innate! Truth, the idea of God, virtue, understanding of morality, and identity are innate, already established! It's simply a matter of inquiry and discovery, unfolding what is already there. 'Chantal,' I said, 'I rest my case.'

"Then from somewhere on the passenger-side of the car came a challenging and persistent voice.

"'But, Marcel! What about John Locke?'

"'What about John Locke, Chantal?'

"And she said, 'in his essay *Concerning Human Understanding*, Locke insists that nothing is innate. There are no innate speculative principles, no innate moral principles, no innate understanding of virtue. An understanding of truth, or worship, and of God is learned, not innate; and, as a matter of fact, Locke specifically states that identity and the idea of identity are not innate. We are a *tabula rasa*, Monsieur Professor. We are given the opportunity to start from the beginning—a clean slate. To begin with, our minds are unformed and featureless before they receive impressions gained from experience. Identity is formed and dynamic, not preset and static. Our identity is subject to various contexts and altered by unique experiences.'

"I sat silently. I don't think I was sulking, just silent. Chantal turned to me, smiled what appeared to be a gotcha Mona Lisa smile, and victoriously said, 'Checkmate!'"

Marcel's story ignited a spark of conviviality that lasted as the dinner plates were removed, coffee and tea were poured, and dessert was served.

Francesca Harlansworth picked up the theme at the conclusion of dessert. "I can't be sure about CRISPR or the expansive ramifications of genome editing, but I think it's worth noting that there is a metamorphosis that occurs naturally, and the best example of that, of course, is the emergence of the butterfly from the chrysalis. In the chrysalis shell the insect has one identity but then emerges into the butterfly, a completely different identity with different characteristics, different functions, and different form. If the scientist can alter the DNA of an organism in such a way that it develops into something beautiful from something gross, or into something whole and transcendent from something broken and limited, then I'm in favor of it, even in face of the known risks. In that regard, I agree with Chantal, in that we—all of nature—are a *tabula rasa.* I for one could not describe my identity, and I don't know whether it is principally determined by form or by function; but I know I am ready to forge it from something prosaic to something poetic."

"If I understand Babbs's point of view," said Schumann, "she would be standing in the same breadline with Marcel."

"True," rejoined Babbs, "and my viewpoint can be simply stated and simply understood. I believe God has dealt each of us the cards we have to play with, and how we play those cards determines the heights to which we climb or the depths to which we fall. But there is no way to change the hand we've been dealt, an ace for a six or a king for a three. The DNA we have is the DNA we should live and die with, without any attempt to alter the God-given identity we receive at birth. As Marcel posited, it's a matter of discovering it. As God declared to Jeremiah, *before I formed you in the womb, I knew you.* Obviously God knew Jeremiah's identity before he formed him in the womb, and it was up to Jeremiah to discover that particular identity, which, I believe, was related to function rather than form: his function as God's prophet. In my opinion CRISPR is carrying us dangerously close to a bottomless abyss into which we will not want to slip."

The room fell silent momentarily, until the waiters appeared to refill cups of coffee and tea. Schumann looked to the other end of the table, to Stirling sitting at Babbs's right.

"Stirling, your dear, creative wife got us into this robust discussion on identity," cajoled Schumann, "and we haven't heard a word from you . . . ah, except we know you read *The Pauper's Soul* and *Medea's Bitter Anguish.* What say you to CRISPR and genome editing? Or, better yet, what about your identity? How would you describe it?"

"Like the rest of you, I've read about genome editing but understand less about it than I've read about it. I think it's a truism to say that if the DNA is altered, the identity of the altered organism is definitely altered. That has to be obvious. Whether that new identity is something that is given and must then be discovered by the altered organism, or whether that new identity must be forged on a *tabula rasa,* I can't say because, as far along as the scientists are in this experimental phase, I don't believe there are any rational altered beings at this time who can speak about their experience. If the genie is out of the bottle, as some scientists have said, we can only hope that the course that this ship is charting shows us the direction to positive and rehabilitative destinations rather than to negative and destructive outcomes. Actually, we must insist on it. The medical ethicists that are dealing with these questions, Bill, must be objective."

Bill nodded affirmatively.

"As to my own identity," McCutcheon continued, "I can't say for sure whether it was set at birth—like Jeremiah, known before God formed me in my mother's womb—or whether I forged it in later years. I don't mean to equivocate here, but it seems as if I have always been this way and, then to the contrary, it seems that the awakening came to me in college and seminary.

"When I was at Bowdoin College, in my junior year, I became enamored of Fyodor Dostoyevsky, and I discovered a letter he had written to a friend, a letter that contained his creed. I memorized it quite some time ago, and essentially he said: 'I believe that there is nothing lovelier, deeper, more sympathetic, more rational, more manly, and more perfect than the Saviour; I say to myself with jealous love that not only is there no one else like Him, but that there could be no one. I would even say more: If anyone could prove to me that Christ is outside the truth, and if truth really did exclude Christ, I should prefer to stay with Christ and not with truth.'

"It stuck with me. I rehearsed his words every day. I envisioned the essence of Christ as inimitable beauty. Then when I returned to Scotland to attend seminary—where Heather and I met—one of the very first objects that captivated me was a rendition of Grünewald's Isenheim altarpiece portrayal of Christ's crucifixion, depicting his horrific agony, his emaciated body with nails driven through his twisted hands and contorted feet, his body covered with gaping sores, and his head pierced with thorns. This beautiful Christ was broken. It was an elegantly framed print that I passed in the hallway every day to class. It drew me in and spoke to me of fractured beauty. Having placed Dostoyevsky's affirmation of the beauty of Christ in juxtaposition with Grünewald's broken Christ, I concluded that I was a devotee of fractured beauty. It's my identity. As Heather claimed in *The Pauper's Soul,* one cannot turn one's back on his or her identity."

From that night on, there was an invisible thread that bound the souls of these eight people, each to the others. Perhaps none of them could describe the tether, but each of them knew intuitively that that invisible thread yoked them to *The Pauper's Soul*. It must have been providential.

4

Agony of the Hireling

MARCEL CHOSE A WINDOW table. The conversation over the meal was light, somewhat meaningless, not at all indicative of an agenda or even a purpose for meeting. DuBois had requested the luncheon, and by the time the check came, McCutcheon was convinced that the reason for their time together was simply that: time together. Time together to affirm that they are two beings whose common destiny threw them together in a common location with uncommon backgrounds. For McCutcheon, it was enough. Time together. There have been too many occasions when he had sat alone with the beating of his heart. This time together—with its meaningless, even banal conversation—caused him to rejoice in the simple company of a learned friend. Just as he was about to thank Marcel for lunch and rise to leave, DuBois reached across the table and laid his hand on McCutcheon's arm to detain him. Then he withdrew his hand.

"Stirling," he ventured, "you have asked about Sinclair Chamberlain. Numerous times, I believe. I have held back each time you broached the subject, but now I'm ready to talk about him."

McCutcheon settled back in his chair. "All right," he said, looking into his eyes with an unarticulated question as to why now.

"When I accepted the appointment to the Austin Chair of Philosophy at Vassar College eight years ago, Chantal and I preferred to live in a larger metropolitan area with more cultural advantages than Poughkeepsie had to offer, so we bought a house in Albany. I've been commuting by train every term since then, and Chantal takes the train to New York when the United Nations is in session.

As I mentioned to you soon after we first met, my heritage belongs to the French Huguenots, so the first summer I spent some time visiting Protestant churches in the area, particularly Presbyterian churches in deference to my French kinsman John Calvin. The first Sunday Chantal and I attended Madison Avenue Presbyterian Church, Sinclair Chamberlain was holding forth in the pulpit. He literally astounded me with his preaching. As we subsequently found out, he was a consistently brilliant preacher. Some would say that he shared the depth of insight of a Karl Barth, displayed the theological agility of a Martin Luther or a John Calvin, and had cultivated a speaking style that rivaled Laurence Olivier's Hamlet. We needed to look no further. We joined the church the following autumn.

"Sinclair and I were of a similar age, and at the time I first met him we were in our mid-forties. Initially, we convened occasionally for coffee, but then I believe we both recognized—though neither articulated the sentiment—a peculiar propinquity that readily led to a close friendship. Fridays were ordinarily light days for me at the college, so every other month or so, when I had no Friday classes, I'd have lunch with him at the University Club. As the months and years passed, I realized that Sinclair's life had taken shape on a foundation of apprehension, even fear. He was given over to periods of melancholy, at which time he would sit in the dark, drink Courvoisier, and brood. Is that an Englishman's proclivity? I don't know, but being French, I'm biased enough to think so.

"I respected his brilliance, the raw gem that his stellar education at the University of Oxford had polished. I honored his doctorate earned at Union Theological Seminary but, for the life of me, could never understand why he had remained in the United States when he could have had an extraordinary ecclesiastical appointment in London. At the time, however, I never questioned his decision to remain on this side of the Atlantic. After all, I had done the same. Besides, I was pleased to be spiritually nourished by such an astounding mind every Sunday.

"On one of those occasions when we lunched at the University Club, Sinclair said, 'Pierre'—he preferred to use my middle name—'Pierre' he said, 'I need to tell you something I have never told anyone until now.' I nodded and listened.

"'A few months before you and Chantal joined Madison Avenue Church, one of my parishioners named Glynnis Vandeusen, a middle-management executive at Key Bank on State Street, on her lunch hour, was walking along Broadway. Inexplicably an empty school bus careened down State Street hill and struck her with such an impact that multiple bones in her body were fractured. It was a freakish accident, freakish in that the bus then flipped over and remained teetering just a foot or two above her. She couldn't move, but miraculously she was conscious. As the crowd gathered around the scene of the accident, she cried out for someone to reach under the bus and hold her hand until help arrived. No one would. She then asked if someone would call me, her pastor, to come and hold her hand and pray.

"'The telephone rang in my study. The situation was described, and the request was made, to which I reacted with an immeasurable surge of terror. *What if the bus falls on both of us*, I mused. I told the person on the phone that I was in the midst of another crisis at the church and would get there as soon as possible. But I hung up the phone, walked to my credenza, poured a glass of Courvoisier, closed my study door, sat down and waited until Glynnis's emergency had passed.

"After a restless, introspective night, I visited Glynnis in the hospital the following morning. She lay on her bed in a full-body cast, in which she would subsist for the next six months. I greeted her, sat down, and took her hand—ironically, too little too late—and then apologized for not being able to get to her due to another crisis at the church. Pierre, this was Glynnis's response: *That's all right, Dr. Chamberlain, Honeysuckle came.*'"

"Honeysuckle! I exclaimed to Sinclair. The village idiot?"

"'Yes, Honeysuckle,' rejoined Chamberlain, 'the village idiot, that endomorph with an enormous, grotesque face and a protruding nose that never stops running, who carries that large, dirty, white handkerchief to wipe his face and to shoo away children who taunt him. Glynnis said to me: *You know, Dr. Chamberlain, I have always been terrified of Honeysuckle, and when he looked under the bus and showed his face, I nearly screamed in horror. But he put his hand under the bus, took my hand in his. Then he crawled under the bus and cradled me in his arms. In that moment, Dr. Chamberlain, his grotesque face took on the countenance of Christ; and I was at perfect peace.*'"

"Chamberlain stopped, looked down at his coffee, and then looked up at me again. 'Pierre,' he said, 'just like Prince Myshkin, the Christ figure in Dostoyevsky's *The Idiot,* Honeysuckle became the Good Shepherd who will lay down his life for the sheep—and I? . . . and I? I was the hireling.'

"On numerous occasions after that I would stop by the manse and find him sitting in the dark, sometimes shaking his head and exclaiming in a hoarse whisper, 'Myshkin! Myshkin! Myshkin!'

"A few months later I lunched with Chamberlain again, and he started the conversation by saying that he had done something he had never done before. He said, 'at our presbytery meeting last Saturday, a young theological candidate was being examined for ordination. He read his statement of faith . . . nothing extraordinary or remarkably creative; but it covered all the doctrinal bases: you know, the complex trinity, the divinity of Christ, the pervading Holy Spirit, doctrine of the church, a right understanding of the sacraments. When he had finished, the usual questions from the floor followed, and when those seemed to wind down, I went to the microphone and addressed the young candidate: I said, *I see you have a pending call to a church in this presbytery. Yes, sir,* he answered. *Presumably you will serve as pastor in that congregation?* I inquired. *Yes, sir,* he answered. *Well then,* I ventured, *this is my question: Will you lay down your life for the sheep?* A palpable quiet fell upon the assembly. The young candidate remained motionless, absolutely silent, staring straight ahead. Then the assembly became restless, shifting their feet, implying the absurdity of the inquiry. After a moment, I repeated: *Will you lay down your life for the sheep?* Then the young candidate said softly, *I don't know . . .* And I said, *My young friend, that is the only authentic answer to the question.*'

"'Pierre,' said Chamberlain to me, 'we know that the Good Shepherd lays down his life for the sheep. But until the moment the wolf appears in front of us and bares its lethal teeth, we will never know whether we shall imitate the Good Shepherd or run away like the hireling.'"

Marcel sat quietly for a long time as he stared out of the window at the noonday traffic. Then he said slowly, deliberately, "You know, Stirling, I am convinced that, as a scholar, Sinclair Chamberlain knew of Bonhoeffer's contention that Christ's call summons one to come and die; but, as he conveyed in his confession, when Sinclair heard Christ's call, he could not answer it. What I don't know and what I cannot resolve in my own fits of self-recrimination is whether an actual pronouncement of absolution by me—as one of the priesthood of all believers—that day, following his confession, might have liberated him from an oppressive guilt and unbearable despair. Consequently, he lived the rest of his days as a haunted man until the occasion of his untimely death."

McCutcheon and DuBois's eyes met, locked in a mutual stare of bewilderment.

"Do you actually think so, Marcel?" McCutcheon inquired incredulously. "Do you even speculate that a pronouncement of absolution, either from you of the priesthood of all believers or from a pastor or priest of apostolic succession, could have alleviated Chamberlain's despair?"

"Why not?" persisted DuBois.

"You said it yourself. He was a haunted man," McCutcheon rejoined with a quiet, fervent emphasis.

"But what if my reticence to offer absolution contributed to his death?" Marcel fired back with an equal accent.

"How could it?" McCutcheon continued. Giving himself over to the party line as it had been recited to him numerous times, he pointed out, "Freda told me it was an accident. The entire congregation knows it was an accident."

Marcel gazed at the traffic again, endured a pregnant pause, and, looking back at McCutcheon, said with certainty, "It was no accident."

Puzzled, McCutcheon sat startled into silence. Then leaning forward, placing his elbows on the table, and fixing his eyes on DuBois with a controlled intensity, he eventually asked, "What do you mean, Marcel?" If what he had just uttered in his presence was true, all the myth surrounding a commonly held explanation of Chamberlain's death was about to be dispelled.

"What I mean, Stirling, is that Chamberlain's death was intentional—a suicide." He maintained his stare, assessing McCutcheon's response to his disclosure. McCutcheon leaned back in his chair as if he had been dealt a blow to the chest, leaving him nearly breathless, even dazed. DuBois remained motionless.

"How do you know, Marcel?" McCutcheon inquired softly after he had regained an inner composure.

"I don't know how much Freda has told you about the actual death that night," DuBois began hesitantly. "I suspect she has described it in detail, so what I tell you may carry with it an element of redundancy, but the new information is what is essential, so bear with me, Stirling."

McCutcheon nodded assent, assuring him of his patience.

"It is common knowledge," Marcel continued with a penchant for meticulous narrative, "that Sinclair Chamberlain frequently presented religious monologues—costumed and staged with a full complement of lighting—in churches throughout the city and in surrounding suburbs. His was chancel drama at its best: vibrant, intense, forceful, masterful in its execution, captivating in its delivery . . . all with a charming, riveting, native British accent. At any of those productions, I could close my eyes and imagine Laurence Olivier was holding forth in this dimmed sanctuary. What is not commonly known, however, is that Sinclair harbored a bitter resentment that destiny had neglected him in favor of Olivier. He evidenced this to those of us who knew him intimately—a paltry few of us. He admitted to a perpetual discontent that he had not been born a Laurence Olivier. While he sublimated that frustration into two dramatic mediums—unparalleled preaching and compelling chancel drama—it was never enough to be the popular and debonair Sinclair Chamberlain; rather, the self-incriminating, fateful reality was that he wasn't Laurence Olivier.

"His dramatic repertoire was extensive: biblical characters and scenarios such as Peter in his act of denial, Saul on the road to Damascus, Simon of Cyrene carrying Christ's cross, Barabbas set free by the crowds; but the most popular of all was his portrayal of Judas. Sinclair actually wrote most of the presentations, but the one featuring Judas was adapted from Frenchman Paul Claudel's short story titled, *Mort de Judas / The Death of Judas*. I can't recall a single Good Friday evening in the years I knew Chamberlain that he did not present, in one church or another, *The Death of Judas*.

"I do recall, however—and quite vividly at that—the simple but profound staging for the monologue. He would actually cut down a small tree and lash it to the stationary stone or wooden lectern beside the chancel steps. The tree was positioned so that a small stool could not be seen behind it. As the sanctuary went dark, Chamberlain would slip into the noose of the rope tied to a limb of the tree, and when the spotlight came up on him, he was hanging. Then after a moment, Judas would come to life, extricate himself from the noose, climb down from the tree, dress himself in his tunic and robe, and then—for a full hour—relate his past experiences with Jesus of Nazareth and the other disciples. At first Judas comes off as calm and rational, simply relating facts, dynamics, and intricacies of the disciples' relationship with Jesus. Then his narrative takes on a vitriolic tone as he manifests a pecuniary self-defense for dipping into the funds of the disciples and rationalizes his betrayal of the Christ. From the penultimate scene of throwing down the thirty pieces of silver in the temple, the monologue builds in intensity until Judas—throwing off his robe and tunic—mounts the tree, slips into the noose, and then shouts out into the night, 'Behold . . . Judas . . . hanging!'

"Chamberlain elongated each of these last three words, letting the final utterance reverberate throughout the sanctuary. Then he would drop to a hanging position and hold that pose until the sanctuary went completely dark. When the lights came on a minute later, the noose was empty, and Chamberlain had disappeared from the chancel."

Marcel DuBois interrupted his account to signal the waitress for more coffee. She filled their cups and left. After a few sips, he continued with a measured solemnity.

"During the season of Lent before he died, Chamberlain had turned down numerous invitations from other churches to perform *Mort de Judas* on Good Friday. He had already decided to present the dramatic monologue again at his own church. You may know, Stirling, that for six weeks prior to that fateful evening, I had been conducting a mission trip in Ethiopia, leading twenty-two Vassar students through an intensive study of religious observances and tribal practices as contrasted by our cultural, classical philosophies. My colleague Vivian Sager, Professor of Cultural Anthropology at Vassar, played an equally prominent role in the six-week program.

"The mission trip was scheduled to conclude on the Wednesday of Holy Week, and our travel plans called for us to land at the Albany Airport at 4:15 p.m. on Friday. By the time I arrived at my house, it was after five o'clock. I remembered that Sinclair was slated to present *Mort de Judas* that evening at eight, so I rested an hour or so, freshened up, and left for the church at seven forty-five, arriving a few minutes before the sanctuary lights dimmed. Chamberlain's performance topped all of his others. Of all the ones I had attended—which was virtually all of them—there had never been one that riveted an audience spellbound to a transported state than this one had. At his final speech from the rope, members of the audience issued little heart-wrenching sighs, barely audible, but distinguishable all the same. Finally, Judas slumped in the noose, and the blackout occurred on cue. The audience waited breathlessly, moved beyond any suitable utterance, expecting the lights to come on at the appointed moment. At that point they would rise and leave silently as had been the custom in the past. But when the lights rose, Sinclair was still in the noose, swinging, even as he had predicted in that final speech. We all sat aghast, paralyzed. Realizing that this was certainly not a part of the script, I leapt to my feet and dashed to the chancel. Others followed. The stool on which he had many times before clandestinely supported himself was at a distance from his dangling feet. He had obviously kicked it away. Yet, as people initially viewed the scene, all the visible elements that made up the incident could be collectively construed as a tragic accident, neither willed nor planned. A number of us men lifted Chamberlain down from the noose and laid him on the chancel floor. He was not breathing; his neck was broken, his limbs completely limp. Dr. Tillman, a member of the congregation who had attended the performance, examined him and found no pulse. Upon their arrival, ambulance attendants concurred with Dr. Tillman's assessment and declared him dead before transporting him to the hospital for an official medical verdict by a pathologist. Close friends took Freda to the hospital, and the rest of us remained in stunned bafflement, disoriented and dismayed, convinced that the universe had just come unhinged."

"What led you to believe that the tragedy wasn't an accident, Marcel?" McCutcheon asked, mentally struggling to discern a basis for his deduction from the description he had portrayed of the incident.

"For the remaining hours of that night—and, as a matter of fact, for the two days following—I believed much the same as everyone else who had witnessed the sickening event and had concluded that the stool slipped from beneath his feet. But then on Monday morning, I went to the post office to pick up all the mail that had been held for me during the six weeks I had been in Ethiopia. Careful sorting of the pile turned up an envelope from Sinclair Chamberlain. Inside was a simple note in his handwriting, these three words in capital letters: *I AM JUDAS!* I knew then for a fact that Sinclair Chamberlain—who could never forgive himself for deserting Glynnis Vandeusen, who detested himself for being a cowardly hireling and Honeysuckle for being the representation of the Christ, who was tormented by thoughts of dying on a cross, who maintained with Nietzsche that it was only thoughts of suicide that could get him through the night—had ended his life by his own will and by the exercise of his own thrusting foot. In retrospect, Stirling, the stool was far too far from his feet to merely have turned over. It had to have been kicked . . . in one last gesture of self-determination to be free, to finally belong to himself, and at long last to have gained autonomy and independence from his castellan: fear."

Both men remained inert and silent for a sober interval. While believing, McCutcheon sat in a state of disbelief. What he had heard others describe as a hot flash seemed to wash over him, a tingling of needles attacking every pore of his body, his face flush with a burning sensation. Images of Chamberlain swinging from a tree beside the lectern at Madison Avenue Church flooded his mind, sending him into a temporary trance.

"Marcel . . ." McCutcheon started after refocusing, "Marcel, who else knows this?"

"No one," said DuBois.

"Not even Freda?"

"Especially not Freda . . . no one," he reiterated with conviction. "What good would it do anyone to bear this knowledge?"

"No good," McCutcheon rejoined. "I was not suggesting by the question advocacy for general disclosure. You are a devoted friend, Marcel, to have carried this secret all this time to protect the golden reputation of a silver-tongued orator. I commend you."

"Thank you, but I had no choice. Freda would have been devastated by the truth, and the congregation would have been marked by an ineffaceable curse. So, needless to say—though, as you see, I'll say it—I value your confidence, Stirling. Your carrying this with me will help, and your confidentiality will vouchsafe Sinclair Chamberlain's memory the untarnished quality it actually deserves, despite his foibles and failures, despite his final self-destructive act."

McCutcheon nodded assent. "All right, Marcel. You have my word."

"Before we leave, I have something for you, which I hope will remind you of our conversation today." DuBois pulled a small box from the right side pocket of his suit coat: an *étui,* he called it. "Stirling, do you recall after the dinner party at the Schumanns'—when we walked with our spouses together in the night on the way home to our respective houses—that I told you about my French Huguenot background and related to you how the Huguenots' history had influenced my philosophy and shaped, in particular, my Protestant theology? Then before we went our separate ways that night, I removed my Huguenot cross from around my neck and gave it to you as a sign of my loyalty to you as the new Senior Pastor of Madison Avenue Presbyterian Church. My intention at the time was to signal to you my singular transference of allegiance from Sinclair Chamberlain to you as our new, our rightful, our duly-called and installed pastor. I trust that in the coming years I will give you every reason to believe in my loyalty to the Christ and to you as his duly-appointed servant."

"Without a doubt, Marcel," McCutcheon sincerely attested. Then with a smile, he added, "As you Frenchmen would say, *sans doute!*" This French acknowledgement did not go unappreciated. "To be sure, I often look at your Huguenot cross in my box of crosses on my desk and think of your vow that night."

"While on the mission trip in Ethiopia two years ago, I purchased a Lalibela cross, which I have here in this *étui.*" He opened the small case and lifted out a cross, an elaborate, intricately formed cross. "The Lalibela cross has its genesis in the 12th century, and every year there is a lavish festival known as Meskel observed in Lalibela, the counterpart to Christians' and Jews' Jerusalem. Meskel is the Festival of Finding the True Cross, and Ethiopian Christians believe that the Lalibela Cross is precisely that." He held it up across the table for McCutcheon to examine closely and said, "Here, Stirling, it's for you."

Stirling took it in his hand and studied it from various angles. "It's magnificent, Marcel. Thank you!" He paused, looked up, and asked, "Why now?"

"To be honest, Stirling, I need to tell you that I originally brought it back for Sinclair. But, obviously, that fateful event on that dreadful night precluded my giving it to him." Dolefully DuBois added, "it precluded any gift to him with the exception of keeping his secret. It has required considerable introspection for me to relinquish this cross. Despite my full trust in you at this time, it has taken me excessive deliberation to confidently lay this matter into your care. Stirling, this gift of the Lalibela cross is a sign of my ultimate trust in you. Though it was originally intended for another, I hope you can receive it as it is given, in the spirit of companionable reliance . . . and confidentiality."

Again McCutcheon nodded consent. He stared down at the cross in his hand and reflected upon so many of his parishioners who, soon after his arrival at the church, had repeated the tragic account of Chamberlain's death, invariably attributing it to fortune's most regrettable accident. It was a story that had never worn out. Now, as of today, he knew that every one of those woeful recitations unwittingly contained a naive fabrication; and McCutcheon had a cross in his hand to remind him. Looking up, McCutcheon expressed his gratitude once again to DuBois and placed the cross around his own neck. DuBois signed the chit and stood to leave. McCutcheon rose at the same time and offered his hand.

"*Au revoir . . .* Pierre."

"*Au revoir,* Stirling."

DuBois smiled in recognition of the devolution, turned toward the main door of the dining room, and subsequently disappeared. McCutcheon sat down again at the table by the window and thought about the profound secret hidden in this Lalibela cross resting upon his necktie. With that thought, the cross suddenly felt heavy.

5

In the Stranger's Guise

IN CONCERTED ATTEMPTS TO become familiar with the names of all the members of the congregation, Heather and Stirling stood together to greet the people following each Sunday morning worship service. By the end of the fourth month at Madison Avenue Presbyterian Church, both of them had a firm grasp on the church roster and could call virtually every member by his or her name, including the names of children. Stirling was quick to admit that the children's names came more readily and nimbly off Heather's tongue than off his.

By the fourth month as well, there were clear indicators that the McCutcheons with their three children had become endeared to the church congregation, and the transfer of the people's affection from Sinclair Chamberlain to Stirling as their pastor was occurring smoothly, an affection they were extending freely to his family as well. Freda Chamberlain had been honest to her word, supporting the McCutcheons in every ostensible way, exhibiting no detectable resentment at the transfer of position from her husband to Stirling.

On the fourth Sunday of this aforementioned fourth month, Glynnis Vandeusen—the first time since the McCutcheons had arrived in Albany—passed through the greeting line and introduced herself to Heather first and then to Stirling. Hers, of course, was a familiar name to Stirling, who—since his conversation with Marcel Du-Bois at the University Club—had called Glynnis numerous times but without results.

"My apologies for not returning your calls, Mr. McCutcheon!" said Glynnis without self-effacement. "Work has been intense, and there have been personal matters that required my close attention."

"Not a problem," rejoined McCutcheon. "As you might suspect, I'm simply getting around to members to become acquainted."

"But of course," said Glynnis with a diffident smile and an odd nod of the head. "I occasionally take a two-hour lunch break when there's important business. Could you meet me any day this week for lunch?"

"Yes, Wednesday would work especially well for me," suggested Stirling. "And you?"

"Wednesday's good. How about noon at Hampton Plaza? I'll need the two hours if you can spare the time."

"Yes, of course. See you then," said McCutcheon warmly, shaking her hand again before she turned to leave.

The rest of Sunday could be described as an incongruity. Invariably, during every Sunday afternoon and evening in the previous four months, Stirling had booked back-to-back commitments—whether meetings, or hospital visits, or pre-marital counseling, or home visitation—but on this day, he settled in with his family. Following a long, unhurried dinner, they changed into riding clothes and headed north to Stony Creek Ranch Resort north of Saratoga Springs. While it had been a common family activity in Edinburgh—at Farquharson Heights, Heather's parents' estate—this marked the first time since they had been in the States that the family had ridden the trails together. Having grown up on the Farquharson Estate with its vast acreage, open spaces, as well as wooded lands, Heather was an expert equestrian. As a youth, she had taken principal responsibility for overseeing the care of their harras of riding horses. After she and Stirling were married and the three children arrived, horseback riding became a Sunday afternoon family occupation. It was one of the phenomena that melded the five family members into an indissoluble union. While Stony Creek Ranch Resort could not compare to the expansive beauty of Farquharson Heights, on this day the five were alone together at last, and each was riding the trails as one seasoned in the sport and well acquainted with the experience. For the moment, nothing could be better.

Angus, age sixteen, and Annabella, age fourteen, and Fiona, age twelve: each had been endowed with a cosmopolitan spirit, but it was no secret among the family of five that the move from Edinburgh to Albany had been especially difficult for the three siblings. Being torn away from their Scottish friends left in each a vacuum too deep to fill with new, tentative school relationships. The heaviest remorse for them, however, was their father's preoccupation with work. But today, it was all different, and the immeasurable joy of chasing the breezes while mounted in a saddle could not be assimilated . . . only exuded.

On their return to Albany, they stopped in Saratoga for supper at Longfellows's Restaurant. The atmosphere was electric with laughter, teasing, Scottish jokes, and the restoration of a pleasing familial union. In all the jocularity, for a fleeting moment, Heather thought she caught a hopeful glimpse of a future that looked manageable . . . if not edifying or fulfilling, at least manageable. Reflected in her bemused smile was a comfort taken in the end of a perfect day.

As the crescent moon rose in full view from the sill to the top of their bedroom window, Heather and Stirling lay silently watching its trajectory until at last it disappeared from sight. Stirling drew Heather closer, unbuttoned her nightgown, and removed all other encumbrances between them until they achieved the pure state of mutual intimacy. What they achieved after that was, without question, the perfect end of a perfect day.

† † †

"I like things understood right upfront, Mr. McCutcheon," said Glynnis with a warm smile and a definitive tone as she and Stirling were seated at a secluded table near the back of the restaurant. "This lunch is on me, so eat heartily."

"Please call me *Stirling*. And you must know that I have an expense account, so I could certainly pick up the tab."

"As do I, Stirling, and it was my suggestion," she indicated with a slight laugh. "So it's settled."

"Where do you work, Glynnis?" asked McCutcheon. He deemed this a legitimate question as a starter, even though DuBois had told him in one of their previous conversations.

"Just up the street. I'm the manager of Key Bank, the State Street branch. It's an easy walk from here."

They set aside the menus and ordered lunch when the waiter came with waters and lemons.

"How have the first few months been for you and your family here in Albany . . . at Madison Avenue Church?" asked Glynnis as she placed her napkin on her lap and set her flatware in the etiquette-prescribed arrangement in front of her.

McCutcheon looked down at the table and considered the acceptable party line, but then he answered without varnish. "It has been a major adjustment, but we're working at it, and there's hope for full assimilation. One should think that two cultures wouldn't be inordinately different since we all speak English, but there seem to be cultural and linguistic nuances that trip us up. More so for Heather and the children. As you may know, I had four years undergraduate at Bowdoin College, which gave me a leap ahead of the others. But thank you! We're managing."

"I trust it will be a good experience for all of you . . . ultimately," rejoined Glynnis compassionately.

"Thank you. I feel sure it will be," smiled McCutcheon. "You indicated, Glynnis, that we shall need the full two hours. Is there something particular on your mind?"

"Yes!" Glynnis said with a sad, wry smile. "Yes, Stirling, there is." She paused, pushing her knife around slowly, twirling it gently in a circle. "This week marks the fifth anniversary of a severe accident that landed me in Albany Medical Center in a full body cast for six months. While I'm grateful to be alive, it makes me wonder what it's like to be dead . . . since I came within a handbreadth of my own demise."

"Are the anniversaries of the accident particularly difficult . . . more than other days?" asked McCutcheon softly.

"Yes, usually, but there can be recurring flashbacks any given day without warning, flashbacks that are virtually debilitating."

"What happened, Glynnis . . . if you don't mind telling me?"

"It was a runaway school bus that had been parked at the top of State Street hill, without driver or children occupying the vehicle. Inexplicably—I mean inexplicably! In these five years no one has ever figured out why or how the bus let loose and careened down the hill, going straight to the bottom of the hill, crossing over Broadway. I was on my lunch hour and looking the other way, my back to the hill. I had no warning of the impending impact. I was knocked to the ground, the bus flipped and landed on a low stone wall, teetering dangerously over me, perhaps two feet above my body. It felt as if every bone in my body was broken. I couldn't move a finger, but I was conscious. Immediately I fell into a chasm of panic . . . of an uncontrollable fear. Within minutes, from beneath the bus, I could see people's feet gathering around the scene. I wanted a little comfort. So I pleaded for someone to reach under the bus and hold my hand, just until the medics came. No one would. No one did. So I asked if someone would call my pastor, Sinclair Chamberlain, to come to be with me . . . to hold my hand and pray. I thought that someone ran off to call him, but he never showed up. After a few minutes I made a second plea for someone in the crowd to reach under the bus and hold my hand. Much to my surprise—actually, much to my terror—my gaze fell on Honeysuckle, the village idiot, who was actually climbing in under the bus. He reached for my hand, took my hand in his, and held it tightly, making reassuring, though unintelligible, sounds. I closed my eyes to dispel the image of his grotesque face. Before I knew it, he had crawled all the way under the bus and had taken me in his arms. I opened my eyes, Stirling, and his face had taken on the countenance of Christ, and in his arms I was perfectly at peace . . . no fear, no panic. He remained there until the bus was lifted up and the medics placed me in the ambulance."

"Honeysuckle, you say, Glynnis," McCutcheon said with an element of awe.

"Yes, Honeysuckle. I can't adequately describe my aversion to Honeysuckle before that day . . . his repulsiveness, his grotesque form and repugnant appearance, his ridiculous mannerisms and animal-like sounds, his runny nose, his filthy white handkerchief. I have known Honeysuckle for more than twenty years, back when I was a child with other children in my neighborhood. When I was nine or ten years old, my friends and I would go to the afternoon matinee nearly every Saturday. Invariably we caught up with Honeysuckle, a much younger man at that time of course but much the same in demeanor and mannerisms . . . just as gross as ever he was. He waddled along, his nose running, and the huge white handkerchief in his right hand. We children tormented him, teasing ruthlessly, calling him names, jeering and making fun of him, imitating the way he walked, coming up close to him—but not too close—and making faces at him. In his frustration he would shoo us away with his handkerchief, as if it were a protective weapon. The sounds he made were inhuman, but anyone could tell they were sounds of agony, pain, even torment. I participated in the taunting every time with the other children, but it always spoiled the Saturday afternoon matinee for me. When I arrived at the Strand Theater, I was awash in shame. I hated what I was doing, but I was one of a tribe of monkeys that mindlessly mimicked what the first one did. Because others were doing it, and because I was afraid of losing friends if I didn't participate, I played along with the rest, regardless of how terrifying it was for Honeysuckle.

"After this had gone on for months, I began to have a recurring dream, if not every night, most every night, the same dream, the same in every detail, without variation in the slightest. The dream always began with my being asleep on the long sofa in our parlor, one of our three huge living rooms in our mammoth house. In the dream I would be awakened by the ringing of the bell at the front door. When I'd make my way to the door and open it, there was Honeysuckle with a sinister look; he came into the foyer and asked for my mother. When I called, no one answered since no one was home. When Honeysuckle became aware of that, he said he was selling scissors, and he was going to cut me up into little pieces. Over and over again I dreamt this nightmare, realizing that Honeysuckle and I had this macabre bond of mutual tantalizing and torment. The aversion to him on Saturday afternoons became all the more intense, and I detested him with the deepest and most horrific hatred. It became self-evident that the very sight of his face on Saturday afternoon would strike a paroxysm of terror throughout my body. I began to wonder how I could taunt him without looking at him. Then I came to my senses, stopped going to the Saturday afternoon matinees, pulled away from my friends, and seldom saw Honeysuckle after that. Over the last twenty years I would see him walking along the streets of the city at intermittent occasions but would purposely turn down another street to avoid him. Eventually the Honeysuckle nightmare subsided, and only rarely would it recur.

"Given that, Stirling, surely you can imagine the compounded fright I experienced when—while under the bus and pleading for someone to reach under and hold my hand, longing to have my pastor come to the scene—it was Honeysuckle who appeared, not only reaching under the bus but actually crawling under the bus to take my hand and to hold me in his arms, making unearthly sounds of reassurance and comfort. At first his face was the face I saw in that recurring nightmare, identical to that face, except that there was nothing sinister in his countenance. The moments from the time he appeared and the time he took my hand seemed an eternal hell of retribution and demonic justice. But then once he took my hand and settled in beside me, the world became placid, his face took on a divine aspect, there was an inexplicable serenity that cradled my mind and lent me a confidence that all was going to be well. I even fantasized that if the bus suddenly gave way, Honeysuckle would hold it up with his other hand. How unreal was that! But it brought me a great sense of security. I could close my eyes and drift off to sleep, and when I opened my eyes again, Honeysuckle was still there. His had always been a ghastly face, but now when I'd look into his eyes, I could see a countenance that was the sweetest I believe I had ever known."

"Remarkable, Glynnis!" McCutcheon exclaimed quietly. "What happened after that?"

At this point, the waiter brought their lunches. Glynnis continued while they ate.

"As I mentioned, I was in a body cast for six months. Prior to that, when I arrived at the hospital, I was on the operating table for twelve hours. It took twelve hours for the doctors to put me back together again and six months to heal. During that time, I suffered recurring night terrors from flashbacks. They occurred so frequently that the nursing staff would have to sit with me for long periods of time. After suffering the recurring flashbacks for two months without relief and receiving daily visits from a staff psychiatrist who attempted to help me through the psychological recovery, I asked to see Honeysuckle. Arrangements were made by the hospital staff to transport Honeysuckle to my hospital room, much to the dismay of hospital personnel who watched him walk the corridors to my room. When he arrived, Honeysuckle entered the room and gingerly approached my bed. 'Will you take my hand, Honeysuckle?' I asked haltingly. He did. I'm not ashamed to admit, Stirling, that a river of tears flowed down my face as a flood of fears flowed out of my body. Honeysuckle sat down, held my hand, and I slept a peaceful sleep I had not had until that moment. For the remaining four months, Honeysuckle came at night whenever I suffered flashbacks and held my hand while I slept.

"One night, I asked one of the nurses to give Honeysuckle a gift: it was the silver Shepherd's cross I had worn around my neck at the time of the accident. It was originally given to me, as well as to others at the church, as a part of the Shepherds program, in which lay people are trained to serve as shepherds to designated small groups of people in the congregation. He loved the cross and now wears it constantly."

The waiter took away the empty plates and served coffee.

"There were two months of rehabilitation after the six months in the hospital. During that time I would go to Honeysuckle's house and hold his hand, but then when I went back to work, I saw Honeysuckle less. There were times, however, when I would wake in the night with flashbacks. In a wash of panic, I would make my way to Honeysuckle's house, where he would open his door and welcome me in, and agree to hold my hand. It was the only thing that could bring me any comfort.

"During this time, I learned that Honeysuckle still walked to the Strand Theater every Saturday afternoon. One day I went the old route and, from a distance, watched him walk to the matinee. The scene was all too familiar. New children were tormenting him as he walked along. I parked my car, jumped out and ran to Honeysuckle's side. I took his hand and walked with him as the children ran away. From that day to this, Stirling, I go to the Saturday matinee with Honeysuckle, and no one bothers him anymore."

"Mutual shepherds to each other!"

"Stirling, all of this narrative finally brings me to my reason for meeting with you."

"All right, Glynnis," rejoined Stirling warmly.

"Honeysuckle is now in hospital with congestive heart failure. Would you be willing to visit him? Perhaps you could cultivate a rapport with him and serve as his pastor during this extended illness. Would you mind?"

"Of course not. I'd be honored to do that. We could go to hospital right now if you have time."

"I do."

Glynnis picked up the check, set the money on the table, and they left. Stirling drove.

To the casual observer, Honeysuckle was every bit as ugly, grotesque, and repulsive as Glynnis had described—the most accentuated features exacerbated by tubes and needles and oxygen lines and a urinary catheter all protruding from various parts of his body. But to McCutcheon, who had the sacred benefit of Glynnis's story, Honeysuckle was a man of infinite beauty.

Glynnis took his hand in hers and said, "Honeysuckle, this is my pastor, Stirling McCutcheon . . . and now he is your pastor, too. He will visit you here . . . often. You can rely on both of us to love you."

Stirling spotted Glynnis's silver Shepherds cross around Honeysuckle's neck, which filled McCutcheon with a powerful surge of credulity. "Honeysuckle, I'm glad to know you! I'm honored to be your pastor now. At the same time, somehow I believe you will be my shepherd as well. I think your silver cross tells me so."

Stirling took Honeysuckle's other hand, joined hands with Glynnis, and prayed the most ardent, genuine prayer from the heart he can ever remember praying. When Glynnis and Stirling turned to leave, Glynnis indicated she would be out in a minute. Stirling left but then looked back to see Glynnis holding Honeysuckle's hand and kissing him firmly on the cheek. She put a handkerchief to his nose, wiped it, placed it in his hand, and said, "Goodbye, my lovely Honeysuckle."

As they walked toward the elevator, Glynnis said, "There's one more matter, Stirling. Could we make our way to the coffee shop?"

"Sure. We're still within your two-hour parameter," he said jovially.

The hospital café occupied the second floor. Stirling paid this time, and they chose a small table by the window.

"Dr. Chamberlain never showed up at the accident," Glynnis said, her face clouded. "I think he was called, but I can't be certain. I'm told that Honeysuckle and I were under the bus for an hour and a half before the rescue could be completed and I was transported to the hospital. I asked him when he came to visit me in the hospital the next day. He said he was sorry that he couldn't be reached. I asked him what he meant by not being able to be reached. He could never say what he meant. 'I was tied up at the time,' he said. But he never gave a reason why he couldn't come. I had no intention of putting him on the spot or being critical. It was because I missed him desperately in that terrifying circumstance. I had felt extremely close to Dr. Chamberlain ever since

I was a child in his church. Actually, I wanted him to know how much he meant to me and that no one could do what he always did with such authenticity and such ease. He was a phenomenal preacher, addressing issues of life with confidence and vigor. His prayers were masterpieces, so spiritually moving, perpetually stirring the soul. Everyone said so. I wanted one of those prayers under the bus. I wanted him to lend me his strength with the healing warmth of his hand in mine while he prayed. It never happened, and I don't know why it didn't happen, but now that he's dead, I feel guilty that I wanted him beside me and was disappointed that he never came. I have to admit that I even felt abandoned. How childish, Stirling! It has taken me all this time to get over it," she admitted, looking out the window with a sadness that struck McCutcheon as perennial, "but, obviously, I'm not."

"Undoubtedly, it's a mystery why he didn't—or couldn't—appear on the scene of your accident. Unfortunately, like all mysteries characterized as unknown and unknowable, there apparently is no definitive answer—nothing that you can know for certain; but this much I know, Glynnis: you have every good reason to expect someone you love and admire to live up to that admiration; but when the disappointment occurs, for the sake of your love for him as your pastor, it would be well for you to understand that he would have been there if he could have been . . . if the circumstances that constricted him were different. It is such a truism to say, if it were different, it would be different. But it wasn't, and your love for him as your pastor entitles him to some leeway: a gift of blind understanding on your part without understanding a definitive why on his part."

Glynnis stared out the window again. A gentle breeze nuzzled the leaves on the trees in the garden below. Wistfully she said, "Dr. Chamberlain had agreed to officiate at my wedding, which had been scheduled for two months after the accident."

"Ah. You were engaged to be married, Glynnis?"

"Yes. *Was* engaged to be married. Ryan and I rescheduled the date, giving me time to recuperate; but then he called it off three weeks before the big event."

"Because of the accident?"

"No, because of Honeysuckle . . . when I started going to the matinee with him, holding his hand. Ryan was chagrined. 'He's just an idiot! Don't you see that? He's an idiot, and you're holding his hand for the whole world to see? You're making me a laughing stock: *she prefers an idiot to Ryan!*'"

"I'm sorry."

"Don't be, Stirling. He got it right. He was actually right on. I did prefer Honeysuckle to Ryan. Besides, Honeysuckle never made fun of my newly-acquired limp."

"Thank you for today, Glynnis!"

"I had better get back. Will you drive me?"

"Of course. But before we leave, one question. Did you say that, as Honeysuckle held you in his arms beneath the bus, when you looked at him a second time, his face had taken on the countenance of Christ, and you were at perfect peace?"

"Yes, Stirling. It was exactly like that."

"There's an old Celtic Rune of Hospitality . . . a poem or incantation that ends with this verse: *Often, often, often, goes the Christ in the stranger's guise.* I thank God that Sinclair Chamberlain could not attend to you. He made room for the Christ to cradle you in his stead."

6

Confined to the Chair

"THE BULLIES BANGED ON the door, bellowed, *State Police, open up!* . . . and then broke it down. I heard it all: hollering as if they were three counties away in the next state. How could I hear it any other way! I had been in the bottle three days, and I had been sleeping on the living room sofa all that time. They rushed in as if they were dashing into my dreams . . . carnivorous interlopers!"

McCutcheon sat attentively in a chair near her bed in her bedroom, or, rather, her former bedroom in her mother's house. Jocelyn Hudson, sitting on the edge of the bed, was clad in a loose nightgown, the top of which flopped open whenever she leaned forward to make a point emphatically.

"As I said, interlopers," Jocelyn continued, "rushing in and shouting—at least it sounded as if they were shouting, piercing my head with a hunting knife—yeah, they were shouting, 'Where's your husband, Mrs. Hudson? We haven't seen him for three days. He's not suppose to be on vacation, and we haven't seen him at the barracks in all that time.' Then one of them said, 'Hey, Captain, what's that smell?' They looked at the stains on the carpet, and then they started searching the house, following the trail of stains, until they found his body in the first-floor master bedroom. 'Here, Captain, we found `im! You'll want to see this! Blood all over the room, the floor and the bed!' And then they began to question me . . . a horrendous third degree, like vultures pecking at my bones incessantly . . . no letup, no reprieve.

"'What happened here, Mrs. Hudson? Jim hasn't reported to work for three days, and now we know why.'

"He came in and saw I was drunk again, I told them. He loved to beat me whenever I was drunk. He'd go for his handcuffs and nightstick, cuff me to a chair and rough me up real good with that damned nightstick. He was a sadist of the highest order, all the time saying this would teach me a lesson. With every stroke he'd shout that this would teach me a lesson. So, I said to them, three days ago he came home, looked at me drunk on the sofa, and went to the kitchen for his extra handcuffs. I heard the cupboard open, and I knew he was going for the handcuffs and nightstick. But I outsmarted the tyrant! For the first time in all our lousy marriage, I outsmarted the sadistic tyrant! I made my way through the dining room and into the kitchen by the other door. I grabbed the butcher knife out of the butcher block and stumbled back into the living room. He was looking for me. His back was turned, and I drove the blasted knife into his hairy back. When he swung around, screaming, I drove it into his gut and then his chest, until he was dead. I dragged him into the bedroom and somehow lifted him onto the bed. Let him rot in his own gurgling blood, I said. I slammed the door shut and smiled to myself, knowing that was the last time he'd ever touch me with that bloody Billie club."

"And when did this all happen, Jocelyn?" McCutcheon asked quietly.

"Three weeks ago yesterday is when they busted through my front door. They used their own handcuffs to take me to the police station, where they charged me with murder. Last week a grand jury heard the charges, and I'll go on trial in two months. I was released on $100,000 bail, which my mother acquired by mortgaging her house . . . this house. She has hired the best criminal attorney in the tri-city area. He's renowned for never having lost a murder trial, but he comes at $50,000, half of which my mother has already paid him."

"I guess you know I'm here because your mother called me . . . asked me to come," McCutcheon said by way of explanation regarding this first encounter.

"She told me," Jocelyn responded with a matter-of-fact tone. "But I don't understand why."

"Why what?" McCutcheon rejoined.

"Why would she call you? She's not a member of your church," she stated wryly, if not caustically. "So far as I know, she's not a member of any church . . . never has been . . . I always assumed she never would be. What she believes about God could fit into the pocket of one of those million angels that dances on the head of a pin."

Taken aback by Jocelyn's sardonic reaction, McCutcheon retorted, "Didn't you just say she put up bail for you, mortgaged her house to do so . . . and, above and beyond that, paid half of the lawyer's fee upfront?"

"Sure," countered Jocelyn, "but to save face, not because she loves me or ever did. She has to save face with all her bridge clubs and social butterflies and inquisitive neighbors. Undoubtedly that's the same motive for calling a pastor who lives just up the street from her."

McCutcheon sat silently, speculating about the association of this forty-four-year-old woman and her seventy-seven-year-old mother, deducing the obvious, which was that they had at best a stormy relationship and probably had for decades.

"I have no intention of adding to your consternation, Jocelyn," said McCutcheon. "Here's my card. Feel free to contact me if I can be helpful to you." He stood to leave, but she reached up and laid her hand on his arm.

"No, no. Please don't leave. That's just a lot of baggage I've attempted to deal with for years, and I haven't been successful in resolving any of it. Were I absolutely honest, however, I'd have to admit that I am principally to blame and haven't been an attentive or kind daughter for a very long time. This is especially true since my marriage to Jim."

McCutcheon returned to his seat, prepared to listen again. Though the light in the bedroom was dim, he could see that Jocelyn's countenance bore the features of an inveterate alcoholic and one—now that she had told him her initial story—who had been abused consistently. He could imagine that at one time she had been strikingly beautiful, with long brunette hair, smooth skin, a delicate nose, a finely shaped face, narrow in its aspect and comely in its appeal. He judged her to be five-feet-six inches tall and imagined that she had been stately when she stood. Her stature presented a modest bosom, a slender waist, and attractive legs. Now, however, what McCutcheon saw sitting before him was a desperate woman with an ashen face, hollow cheeks, unkempt hair, and a body stooped and weary-worn.

"If you don't mind my asking, Jocelyn, how long have you been subjected to your husband's abuse?" McCutcheon ventured.

"It started soon after he became a state trooper. Before that we had had a good marriage. If not perfect, it was tantamount to ideal, better than I had ever expected it could be. In those days, it was by far better than what I had seen in my parents' marriage; so I felt gratified. We were good lovers, good companions, good friends as well as good husband and wife. Then Jim, who had a great job as a financial planner, got the itch for more thrilling work, something with more excitement than a column of figures. He studied, took the state police entrance exam, passed it, and entered the state police academy. That seemed to change him. He became cocky, proud to wear the uniform, authoritative. He expected everyone to jump when he spoke and resorted to bullyism if he didn't get his way. It wasn't long before his focus changed from columns of figures to multiple feminine figures, which kept him at so-called work longer. When I questioned him about any of this, he became verbally explosive, insisted I should trust him, and told me to pay attention to the house. When I discovered I couldn't trust him, I moved from the social drinker status to alcoholic status."

"How did Jim handle that transition on your part?"

"That's when he became physically abusive. But it was such a paradox. He set up occasions for us to drink heavily, and then he lambasted me when we did."

"I don't quite understand, Jocelyn," said McCutcheon inquisitively, "how did he do that?"

"We lived in an upscale neighborhood in Clifton Springs. It was all perfectly fine when we were first married. We had great neighbors, and I had developed close friendships with many of the women in our development. Jim played golf with the men a couple of times a week. We attended cocktail parties two or three times a month. Then when Jim became a state trooper, he cultivated a magnetic aura about himself. The neighborhood parties took a vicious turn; people developed sordid playfulness, displaying the worst of cocktail party games. Perhaps it was six months after Jim had become a full-fledged trooper, when I had begun drinking more heavily, Jim suggested that he and I play a game for the other guests, a game he called *Confined to the Chair*. Most of the neighbors at the party were already three sheets to the wind, so they encouraged us to play for them. Jim sat me in a straight chair in the center of the room, pulled out his handcuffs from his suit coat pocket—which I didn't know he had with him—and handcuffed me to the chair spindles. Then he mixed a French martini and waved it under my nose, taunting me with singsong invitations to drink heartily. Every time I leaned forward to drink it, he would pull it back, tantalizing me, and then repeat the routine over and over again, much to the raucous delight of our friends who were watching. By the time we left for home, I was thoroughly humiliated and furious. I immediately went to our wet bar and drank myself silly. That's when he handcuffed me to our own chair and beat me."

McCutcheon remained motionless, stunned. "I assume you had had enough when he came into the house three weeks ago, and you expected the same treatment."

"Yes," said Jocelyn grimly, weeping quietly.

After a long pause in the conversation, McCutcheon asked, "What can I do for you, Jocelyn? How can I help?"

"I don't know, Mr. McCutcheon," she answered. "You remember that I wasn't the one who asked you to come to see me." She hastened to add, "I don't mean that unkindly; it's just that I have no concrete expectations of you . . . or even any idea how you might be helpful. If you have the time or the inclination, I could be happy to have a pastor by my side—or at least somewhere near—during the court proceedings. But maybe that's too much for someone who's not a member of your church to ask."

"No, not at all," McCutcheon said, assuring her as well as he could. "I can do that."

"Thank you," rejoined Jocelyn, "and thank you for coming today."

"You're welcome." McCutcheon thought momentarily before he asked, "Are you free to go about while you're on bail? I assume you're not confined to the house, are you?"

"No. No, not at all. As you no doubt realize, I can't leave the state, and I have to check in with my lawyer before I can go outside the county, but otherwise I'm free to go where I wish. As you might suspect, I haven't returned to my house or even talked with the women in my old neighborhood. Much better that way. I do go to AA, however, three times a week. Really, what choice do I have, Mr. McCutcheon? It's a mandate of the court."

"Of course," said McCutcheon as he rose to leave. "You have my card. Call me if you need me. Otherwise I'll stop in to see you next week."

Jocelyn pushed herself up from the bed, her loose nightgown revealing a gold cross—a Latin cross—dangling from a gold chain as she stood. McCutcheon looked away and then back again when she was upright.

"What if they ultimately give me a lethal injection, Mr. McCutcheon?"

"No, I trust they won't, Jocelyn. Your lawyer, I'm sure, will make a strong case for self-defense. Keep in mind—when that thought overwhelms you—that he has never lost a murder trial in his entire career. You have the best! Trust him!"

"But if they do, will you be with me at the end?"

McCutcheon remained silent. Then he said, "Yes. Of course I will."

"Thank you."

"Would you like me to pray before I leave?"

Jocelyn looked down at the floor, and then at her folded hands, by which she had not intended to connote an attitude of prayer. "No, thank you, Mr. McCutcheon. Maybe next time."

McCutcheon nodded with benign acquiescence, left the bedroom and then the house after a brief, cordial conversation with Jocelyn's mother.

† † †

During the next six weeks, McCutcheon kept his word, visiting Jocelyn once each week. Jocelyn adhered to the court mandate by attending AA every Monday, Wednesday, and Friday evenings. What impressed McCutcheon most was how closely she was beginning to resemble the beauty he had imagined her to possess before he met her for the first time. The first two of these subsequent six weeks McCutcheon met with her in her mother's living room. Each time, she was casually dressed and neat, her hair washed and free-flowing. After that they met for coffee in the local café three blocks from the church. On Friday of the sixth week, over coffee, Jocelyn told McCutcheon she had something to share with him in confidence.

"Stirling, can I count on you to keep this confidential?"

Before McCutcheon answered, he inadvertently glanced at her bodice and was struck by the fact that she was wearing the delicate, plain, gold Latin cross on a gold chain around her neck. He repeated her question to himself and then responded, "Sure . . . assuming you aren't planning something that will harm either you or someone else."

"No, I'm not. So can I?"

"All right," said McCutcheon somewhat reserved but good-naturedly. "Go for it."

"I've met someone at AA, a guy whom I like very much."

"Really! What's he like?"

"He's a good guy, gentle, soft-spoken . . . the entire opposite of what I've been used to for so many years."

"Does he know about your past and what you're facing next month?"

"I told him, Stirling, and he said he understood and wanted to be there for me throughout the ordeal."

"Do you trust him?"

"Yes. So far he has given me no reason not to."

"Where do you want this to go, Jocelyn? Where do you think it's leading you?"

"I want to get more serious. I've agreed to spend tonight with him at a motel just outside the city."

McCutcheon, dubious, skeptical, raised his coffee cup to sip what had cooled slightly, vying for time to consider what Jocelyn had just laid on him.

"Jocelyn, do you think this is wise? Isn't it too soon for another relationship?"

"Yes, it is. But I'm lonely, Stirling. Who knows what lies ahead for me? I'm sure it will either be years in prison—if not years on death row—or death by injection on a hard, unforgiving gurney."

"Wouldn't this violate your bail, Jocelyn? You have to consider that, don't you know?"

Yes . . . that's why I'm telling you in confidence. You promised, Stirling!"

"I know," acknowledged McCutcheon regretfully. He stared at her with compassion, wishing he hadn't agreed to confidentiality before he heard her ludicrous—in his assessment—plans. "I promise . . . What motel?"

"The Castaway in Troy."

"Tonight?"

"After the AA meeting. Just one night, Stirling."

"Be careful, Jocelyn," warned McCutcheon intently. "And your mother? What does she know?"

"Nothing. She's under the impression I'm staying with a new girlfriend for an overnight."

As they stood to leave, Jocelyn leaned forward and gave McCutcheon a friendly embrace, which he returned willingly, all the time concerned for her well being in this ill-timed adventure.

† † †

Heather and the children all noticed McCutcheon's preoccupation at dinner and later into the evening. This was no different in kind, however, but only in degree. They all played a few board games, but there were numerous times when someone had to tell him it was his turn to move. By ten thirty the entire family had gone to bed. Stirling endured at best a fitful night's rest.

By nine o'clock the next morning, he was at his desk in the church office, editing his sermon for Sunday worship services. At half-past eleven the church phone rang.

"Stirling McCutcheon here."

"Hello, Rev. McCutcheon, this is Herb Remington on the front desk at the Castaway Motel in Troy."

McCutcheon knit his brows, indicating a sinking suspicion that all was not well at Castaway Motel. "Yes, Mr. Remington. Good morning, sir. What can I do for you?"

"I have your card here, sir, which was giv'n to me by a young lady—oh, well, not so young perhaps . . . I mean not a teenager or such—a lady who gave me this here card and said that if she didn't check out on time, that is, eleven o'clock, I should give you a call and tell you where she is, and that she may need your help, sir; and here it is at 11:30 in the morning, sir, one half hour past official check-out time, and she hasn't checked out. So what I'm doin' here, sir, and why I'm callin' you is that she told me to."

"Thank you, Mr. Remington. I'll be there as quickly as I can." McCutcheon wrote down the address and left immediately for the Castaway.

Herb Remington was ready for McCutcheon's arrival, key in hand. "Room 132, Rev. McCutcheon, sir. Let me know if you need any help."

McCutcheon walked briskly to Room 132, knocked on the door and waited for an answer before he inserted the key, opened the door cautiously, and walked in. The curtains were drawn closed, but there was enough light to see that the room was in unbelievable disarray: clothes strewn around on the floor and over chairs, empty liquor bottles overflowing three baskets, unfinished drinks in dirty glasses on nearly every piece of furniture in the room, and pizza leftovers in the middle of the desk. McCutcheon drew back the curtains on the side window. Jocelyn was lying deathly still on the bed, facedown, naked. Spotting a blanket at the bottom of the bed, he pulled it up over her and tucked it securely around her sides.

McCutcheon checked to be certain that Jocelyn was breathing and then shook her by the shoulders. "Jocelyn, wake up! Wake up, Jocelyn, wake up!"

Her eyes opened, slits only. McCutcheon was convinced her head must be throbbing but, given the looks of the room, he wouldn't have bet that she had escaped brain damage.

"Stirling! . . . Stirling, where am I?" She raised her head, scanned the room, and lay back again. "Oh, yes! Where's Milton?"

"Apparently he's missing. Taking a powder, as we say in the UK. So he was a good guy, Jocelyn? Good enough to get you smashing drunk, good enough to take advantage of you, but not good enough to stay around for the afterglow or, no doubt, to pay the room bill."

Jocelyn rolled to her side and faced the wall. "Ah-h-h," she groaned.

"Jocelyn, listen to me. You need to get up and get dressed. I'm going to the main office to settle accounts with Mr. Remington. I'll be back in fifteen minutes, and you need to be ready to leave. Do you understand?" There was no response. McCutcheon raised his voice. "Do you hear me, Jocelyn?"

"Yeah, Stirling, I hear you. I'll be ready."

"Well, sir," said Remington, "I hope the lady is all right?"

"Yes, Mr. Remington, she is certainly in a fine state, one she has found herself in many times before . . . one that is both familiar and comfortable to her. You'll find the room is in an unusually untidy condition, however, so I'm here to pay you for the night's lodging with an extra generous gratuity for your extra generous understanding . . . sir!"

"Yep, Rev. McCutcheon! I both understand you and thank you, sir."

When McCutcheon returned to Room 132, he was actually surprised that Jocelyn had not only dressed but also had packed her leather valise and picked up the trashed room.

The ride to her mother's house occurred in silence except for Jocelyn's incomprehensible mumbling, her head back on the headrest and her eyes closed. Stirling's knuckles were white on the steering wheel, his head whirling with conflicting thoughts and bewilderment. He castigated himself for getting into such an insoluble conundrum. He had handled this situation poorly. He had no formal training in alcohol or drug addiction and, therefore, no right to be involved in Jocelyn's escapades, whether alcohol sprees or sex capers.

As the car approached her mother's home, Jocelyn became agitated and began shouting, "Stirling, where in hell are you taking me!"

"Home! To your mother's home," said Stirling emphatically.

"I don't want to go there! All I'll hear is a litany of lectures, screaming, and declarations of disappointment—slurs of deprecation. I've heard it all before. I can't stand to hear it again!"

Jocelyn reached for the car door handle, yanked it, and started to jump out. McCutcheon reached for her, grabbed her coat and held on. He slowed the car until they reached the driveway. Jocelyn closed the car door she had been holding open. She laid her head in Stirling's lap and said, "I love you, Stirling." He laid his hand on her shoulder while she rested for a considerable number of minutes before he lifted her to a sitting position.

When he had finally helped her into the house and to her bedroom, he suggested to her mother that she allow Jocelyn to sleep it off, intimating that he was quite certain lecturing wouldn't accomplish anything.

Back in the church study, he thought how rich a life it would be if he could only sit here in this leather desk chair day after day, hour after hour . . . and read . . . and read . . . and read. He walked to his windows, drew the drapes closed, looked back at his desk and mused: I wouldn't mind being confined to that chair.

He picked up the telephone and dialed the number for Alcoholics Anonymous.

7

The Final Gesture

YEARS AGO, IN AN organizational development seminar sponsored by the Albany Presbytery, the presenter drove home a central point so vividly that Stirling McCutcheon had never been able to shake the image. *If your house catches on fire at night, before you rush to retrieve the children from their bedrooms, be sure that you seize your Day-Timer* from the nightstand and tuck it in your pajama pocket.* Of course, hyperbole usually remains with us, but McCutcheon wasn't so sure that the presenter was exaggerating. He had already confessed to an inflexible organizational development manifesto, the first tenet of which purported that it is only the organized person who accomplishes great goals and ultimately moves the world in a constructive direction; the second tenet: that there are twenty-one modules in every week, three for each of seven days, and each of those twenty-one modules must be planned; and thirdly, each of those modules is comprised by fifteen-minutes segments in which an individual objective will contribute systematically to the specific module of morning or afternoon or evening. *Your Day-Timer,* he maintained, *is the indispensible instrument of your planning. Without it, you cannot plan your work or work your plan.* Then he drove home his point with the aforementioned hyperbole.

The indelible image had implanted itself as vividly on McCutcheon's memory as a Midwestern cowpuncher's brand burnt into the hide of his herd. Placing his pocket Day-Timer into the inner right-breast pocket of his suit coat before he placed his wallet in the opposite breast pocket had become an unconscious, conditioned preparation for leaving home or the office. To be sure, it was an instrument of organizational excellence.

At the same time, however, McCutcheon's Day-Timer took on the function of a slave-driving overseer, as relentless as those of the Cyprian copper mines. He had designated no modules for spontaneity, or for recreation, or for doing nothing; and outside of the late-night retrospectives in his manse study, his twenty-one modules were saturated with specified pastoral duties. Heather had said—no, to be accurate—she had raised her voice and exclaimed emphatically: *You are a driven man, Stirling! A driven man!* True! He wasn't chained to another slave in the Cyprian copper mine; he was chained to his inseparable Day-Timer.

While this was invariably the case, it was never more pronounced than during the season of Lent. Freda Chamberlain's comment at their first meeting together three years ago rang in his ears as a quotidian reminder at this time of year: *Lent was the cruelest season for Sinclair.* Unlike other years, the climax of Lent and Easter occurred this year in April, early in spring with a period of unusually heavy rains.

The first Sunday in April was the Fifth Sunday in Lent. Despite the torrential rains that had been unremitting since Friday, a larger-than-usual number of church members had made their way through the flooded streets to attend one of the two worship services. It was a communion Sunday, which customarily swelled the numbers of attendees. As the continuous downpour thundered on the slate roofs over the sanctuary's high-vaulted ceilings, McCutcheon conducted worship and preached the sermon titled, *Words to the Cross: Come Down.*

After the noon-time greeting of his people at the door, McCutcheon returned to the office study, lifted the Greek, German-inscribed cross from around his neck, removed and hung his robes, slipped on his suit coat, placed his Day-Timer and wallet respectively in his breast pockets, and, as he was about to leave, spoke to the sexton— Trudel Svenssen—a gentle man of enormous size. Sinclair Chamberlain had taken him on staff when he learned that Svenssen had no family and had made his way from Denmark to Albany with only cents in his pocket and a lapel pin of Denmark's national red flag with a white cross. Trudel, whom the congregation affectionately called *The Great Dane,* always wore his Denmark lapel pin attached to his left shirt collar.

"Are we dry in all of the rooms, Trudel?" McCutcheon asked with a note of dread in his voice. "No leaky roof anywhere?"

"No, no leaks, Mr. McCutcheon, thank God!" Svenssen replied with a sad smile.

Noting the incongruence between his words and his countenance, McCutcheon asked, "Are you concerned, Trudel?"

"Not about the roof, sir," he explained in his Danish broken English, "there is no disaster regarding our roof, no leaking . . . no collapse. But I have been listening to the radio, and there was a disaster on the New York State Thruway, just west of us at Fort Hunter, near Fultonville."

"What disaster?" McCutcheon asked.

"About eleven o'clock this morning, the Schoharie Creek Bridge collapsed from all the flooding. The commentator said that several vehicles fell into the raging creek. No one knows yet how many people were lost."

McCutcheon stared in disbelief at Trudel. It immediately occurred to him that they have parishioners who live in that area and make the trek to Madison Avenue Church every Sunday, but he couldn't recall seeing them this morning at worship. His legs felt weak. He sat down on the outer-office sofa, stunned, looking at the floor.

"Is there anything more to report, Trudel?" McCutcheon asked hesitantly looking up at Svenssen.

"That's all I know, Mr. McCutcheon."

Regaining his strength, Stirling stood up. "Do you remember seeing the Douglas family this morning?"

"No, sir, I don't."

"Neither do I," McCutcheon said with as much concern as the sexton had initially exhibited. "I'll call them directly. Thanks for the information, Trudel! Will you be leaving soon?"

"No, sir, I intend to stay here for the rest of the day . . . to keep an eye on the roof."

McCutcheon nodded a gesture of acknowledgement and gratitude, picked up an umbrella from the umbrella rack, left by the side door of the church, and sloshed his way through rising puddles to the car.

As soon as he arrived at the manse, he shed his raincoat, removed his shoes, and went directly to the study. Locating their telephone number hastily, he rang up the Douglases. Much to his relief, Myrna answered and informed him that they had simply stayed home due to the heavy rains and the danger of hydroplaning. "And now we're glad we did," she said with a slight quiver in her voice. "We cross that bridge every time we head for Albany. One of those automobiles in the creek could have been ours . . . with us in it, Pastor McCutcheon."

An unseen plethora of unknown factors surround us in any given moment, McCutcheon thought. A twist of fate sends unsuspecting victims over a precipice into a deep, swirling creek while that same twist of fate preserves others . . . safely in their homes, all because of a random choice they make.

"I'm glad you didn't come to church today, Myrna," McCutcheon said with all the sincerity the occasion warranted. "Actually, what I mean is: I'm glad you're safe . . . you and your family."

When he hung up the phone, he sat back in his chair and wondered which pastors would be receiving the news of their parishioners' untimely, horrific deaths and, by virtue of their calling, would be charged with comforting the victims' families and, of necessity, proclaiming the truths of eternal life. While any and every human being is undoubtedly subject to the heinous sin of *Schadenfreude*, McCutcheon could feel no joy at anyone's misfortune in these circumstances, nor did he thank God that he was spared the arduous task of speaking a word of eternal hope to bereaved families. Having acknowledged that, however, he was free to admit his delight that the Douglas family was safe and that he need not bury five members of his congregation in a water-soaked, flooded Fultonville cemetery.

Later that afternoon, as was his custom on communion Sundays, he delivered home communion to four shut-ins. Everywhere he visited, television sets were tuned to news broadcasts of the sunken Schoharie Creek Bridge. In spite of rough, dark waters, the systematic search for bodies was underway in full force. Early that afternoon

Governor Mario Cuomo had arrived by helicopter to survey the scene and to determine what emergency funds would be required to launch a suitable fiscal response to the catastrophe. It would not be until later that night that the first vehicle and the body of the driver were found in the west bank of the creek, a little less than a mile from the fallen bridge.

Serving home communion with strains of the macabre issuing from televisions proved to be a challenge; but, in each case, once they had become acclimated to the background noises of commentators' voices—diminished slightly with a stealthy turn of the knob—it also became an opportunity to include the victims and their families in the Eucharistic Prayer, commending to God all for whom they prayed, trusting in his mercy.

Early evening McCutcheon arrived home to an empty house. Heather and the children were spending spring break in Saratoga Springs, where they had checked into the Gideon Putnam Hotel. McCutcheon knew that Heather was equally repelled by the prosaic in Albany as she was attracted to the poetic in Saratoga.

He prepared a light supper, and then retired to his study. In spite of the need to be further informed, he could not brook the thought of turning on the television. He settled into his easy chair and opened John Calvin's *Institutes of the Christian Religion*, searching for some practical, theological answer to this inexplicable event of the Fifth Sunday in Lent. Like every other time he had raked through these and other Christian works for a definitive answer to suffering—an answer that could be universally accepted as the key to cataclysmic calamity—he failed to find any sensible reason.

Closing the book, McCutcheon rose and poured a glass of Scotch, mused over it for an hour and, completely clueless about the ultimate meaning of the day's misfortune, he ascended the stairway to his bedroom, where he lay alone on the bed—much in need of Heather—and slept to the sounds of screeching owls and the unearthly squeals of their vulnerable prey, suffering at their own twists of fate in a dread-filled night.

When McCutcheon awoke in the morning, groggy and wearied by incessant dreaming, momentarily confused by the interweaving of reality and delusion, one indistinguishable from the other, he discovered he had slept the entire night in his clothes. As he undressed, shaved, and made his way to the shower, events of the previous day came to mind. Images of cars sailing off the truncated highway into the icy waters below had tormented him in the night, and now they returned to dominate his waking thoughts.

This morning's module in his Day-Timer called for sermon planning for the coming Sunday, Palm Sunday. However, after devotions—comprised by daily lectionary readings and prayers—as a deviation from the norm, he decided to walk a few blocks to Michael's Diner for breakfast and listen to what the people on the street, so to speak, had to say about yesterday's devastation. At long last, the rain had subsided, and while the earth was still saturated with pools of water, he could walk the streets without having to carry a change of socks and shoes to his destination.

Michael's Diner was packed with people breakfasting. The conversational hum sounded more intense and higher in pitch than McCutcheon could recall ever hearing there before. The television set mounted high on one of the prominent walls carried on with the latest details of the sad saga. He waited patiently until a table became available. The hostess seated him directly next to two apparent artisans, their work clothes covered in a fine white dust, as if they had come directly from the Star Cement Plant in Hudson.

"Good morning, gentlemen," McCutcheon said as he sat down in close proximity, with only a narrow space of four or five inches separating the two tables.

"Mornin', sir!" responded one of them sonorously while the other kept his head down and attended to his bacon and eggs. McCutcheon could see that, as he turned to him, the man who spoke had a broad, handsome face with a long, strait nose. His lower visage wore a day or two of white whiskers, while the top of his visage was graced by thick, silver hair, curly and uncombed. Perhaps a man of sixty, he sat high in his chair, higher than either his compatriot or McCutcheon sat, which indicated a long torso, all of which gave him a commanding air. His hands were those of a craftsman, somewhat gnarled and knotty with raised veins. His friend across the table was a younger man, probably in his forties, with coal-black hair, long and straight. He sported unusually thick eyebrows, which gave a weighty cast to his ruddy countenance. When he wasn't eating, he frequently thrust his lower lip and jaw forward, well beyond his upper lip, which was a common gesture when he listened intently to his partner, as if he were straining to comprehend the spoken words. Occasionally McCutcheon caught a frontal glance of his visage. His nose was crooked and a bit too short for his long, narrow face. His eyes were deep-set, dark . . . the darkest brown McCutcheon had ever seen, significantly sunken in their sockets. His hands also were those of a craftsman but not as seasoned as the other's and possessing longer fingers.

The waitress appeared; McCutcheon ordered from the menu and cast a glance at the dominating television.

"Horble shame, ain it, sir," exclaimed the man with the sonorous voice, following Stirling's gaze shot furtively at the television. "Nerrie had a chance, did they! Me and Clod here was jes talkin' 'bout it. Wernt we, Clod?"

"Yah," rejoined Clod without lifting his head from his plate. "We was jes' sayin' how aorful a thing it ud be to tumble into them wadders and nerrie ha' a chance to say goobye to nobody, to none of th' people ya care 'bout." Surprisingly, at this point Clod lifted his head for the first time, thrust out his lower jaw, and looked directly at McCutcheon, holding that pose for a long moment of silence. His eyes moistened. "Yah know wha' I mean, sir?"

McCutcheon nodded. "I know what you mean, Clod," he answered slowly.

"Eh! How'd ya knowd my name, sir?" Clod asked with a wide grin.

"Your friend used it . . . sir," McCutcheon said, wondering if he had offended him with too much familiarity too soon in the conversation.

"Oh, yah, tha's righ'!" he said as the explanation dawned on him as true. "My name *is* Clod, sir, an' this here is Muggins." With this formal introduction, the man with the sonorous voice extended his hand at the same time as Clod.

"I'm delighted to meet you, gentlemen," McCutcheon said as he shook hands. "My name is Stirling McCutcheon."

"Likewise," boomed Muggins.

Turning to the younger man, McCutcheon remarked, "Yours is an unusual name, sir. Is *Clod* your Christian name or your surname?"

"Oh, I'm a Chrisian, all righ', sir, bu' tha' ain' my Chrisian name," he said emphatically.

"Your family name, then?"

"No, sir. It's my nickname," Clod explained with a look of pride.

"Ya see, Mr. McCutcheon," Muggins interjected promptly, "we're gravestone carvers. We chisel all those names and pictures into gravestones, and then we set them in the cemeteries at the head of all those people who are buried there." Pointing to his friend, Muggins informed McCutcheon with a filial benignity, "Clod here, sir, has the honor'ble name of Higgins, somethin' like mine but differ'nt. That's his family name. His Chrisian name is Franklin, but you see, sir, his nickname is more honor'ble yet, `cuz there is no one in all of the State of New York who can take a clod of earth out o' the ground more perfectly than Franklin Higgins . . . jes' the exact measurements for the headstone: length, width, and depth. He's done so many of these so perfec'ly, sir, that he earned the honor'ble nickname of *Clod.*"

"That certainly explains it, Mr. Muggins," McCutcheon began warmly.

"*Muggins,* sir . . . jes' *Muggins,* sir," corrected the sonorous voice.

"Well, Muggins, that certainly explains it. Thank you. It must be an honor for the two of you to work together."

"`Tis, sir," acknowledged Muggins, "nothin' else we'd rather do!"

"Where is your business located?" McCutcheon asked as his breakfast arrived.

Without raising his head or his voice, Clod answered, "Pine Street, sir."

Placing his napkin on his lap, McCutcheon lowered his eyes to return thanks, then lifted his fork and commenced to eat.

"I see yer a religious man, Mr. McCutcheon," observed Muggins. "Like Clod said, we ourselves is Chrisian men . . . no' always Chrisian-like in all our thoughts and behaviors, I admit straight out to you, sir, but at heart, sir, we are Chrisian men . . . men of the cross, ya might say. Every time we chisel a cross on a gravestone, we stand back and say, 'Yep, now there's a sign that gets a man into heav'n!' And then we cross ourselfs. 'Cuz that's the thing to do when a soul, by the cross, has made its way to heav'n . . . to its final resin' place: in the arms of the Lord . . . forever. Amen!"

By this time, Clod had finished his breakfast, had wiped his mouth on his sleeve, leaned forward with his elbows on the table, and stared at McCutcheon, who set down his fork, touched his lips with the napkin, and sat posed to listen. "Yes, Clod?" he asked.

"Do you think, sir, that any of those people who went over into the drink had time to cross thaselfs?" he asked emotively, maintaining his stare.

McCutcheon thought a moment. "I'd like to think so, but I doubt it."

Clod thrust out his lower jaw and somberly said, "Me neither, and it's a cryin' shame!"

"Prob'ly couldn't see three feet ahead of thaselfs in that hor'ble rain," added Muggins, "an' down they went. I keep wonderin' how many seconds they had before they hit that wart'ry death, or drownded in the warters that come into th' windoos . . . and they couldn't get out. Yep! Tha's a mighty miser'ble way to meet the Maker, I say! I wouldn't want it myself or for anybody I knows, nope! I wouldn't, sir!" Looking to his partner, he sought confirmation of his expressed opinion, "Would you, Clod?"

"No, sir, Muggins!" attested Clod, who had been looking at his plate again as if it were a crystal ball auguring some fateful future for himself and his colleague. Then returning his gaze to McCutcheon, he took on an expression so serious it could rival a judge's countenance while delivering a sentence of death by hanging.

"Believe it or not, Mr. McCutcheon," said Clod after glancing to the left and then to the right to determine if anyone else was listening to their conversation, "yesterday marnin' I myself came this close to drivin' inta that gas'ly fate." He placed his elbow on the table as he raised his right hand and positioned his index finger and thumb just an inch apart. "Yes, sir, Mr. McCutcheon, this close, and I 'scaped death by the very skin of my teeth, to quote the great Shakespeare! Yessir, I was traveling that part of the thruway yesterday, drivin' through that terr'ble storm, when the taillights of the car jes' ahead of me disappear, you see. Disappear righ' out o' sight. Righ' out o' sight so a man coun't see 'em. So, payin' attention to some kind of instinct . . . or maybe an inner voice . . . or, as Muggins and me here jes' now specalated, prob'ly the voice of God . . . I pulled my car to the right and slamm'd on the brakes. Gettin' out of my car, I walked slowly ahead of myself, and there jes' a few feet in front of me, I saw the end of the highway where the cars had gone down ahead of me. I thought quickly—yessir, Mr. McCutcheon, I was agile of mind!—an' run back to warn other cars, an' sur nuff, a big Cadillac was crusin' towar' me. I waved my arms fran'ically, trying to stop the vee-hicle, but it kept on comin', so I jumped out of the way jes' in the nick of time, an' as the Cadillac whizzed by me, the guy in the passenger seat flipped me the bird! Yep! He stuck up his middle finger to me, to the very man who was tryin' to save his life. Jes' think of it, sir! That was the final gesture of that feller's life before he toppled into the crick . . . an' it sur wan't no sign of the cross."

Throughout Clod's narrative, Muggins had been intermittently nodding his head or shaking it back and forth in dismay. When the narrator had concluded, Muggins offered his own commentary to supplement his partner's. "Me and Clod here ha' been talkin' about this ever since we set down here to eat this here breakfast of ours. As Clod said, jes' think of it, sir, stickin' up yer middle finger jes' before you die and takin' that d'rogatory attitude with you into eternity. Well, sir, Mr. McCutcheon, sir, let me ask you a quesion, sir. Do you know what a raised middle finger means? Do ya, sir?"

Reluctant to admit it—as if such an admission on his part would imply a frequent or occasional use of the gesture—McCutcheon paused before nodding, "Well . . . yes, I do, Muggins."

"Well then, sir," Muggins continued, "since you know what it means, then you know that it was a crude and rude gesture to make to a feller human bein' . . . it is a gesture, sir, that lacks civility, which is to say that there ain' no civility whatsoever in that gesture, an' beyond that, it's unkind, pugnashus, an' flippant. That, sir, is prob'ly why they call it *flippin' ya the bird*, because the act is down-right flippant. Now to look at this more finely, I'm sayin', to examine this act of incivility with more refinement, I would put this to you, Mr. McCutcheon: if you are a married man, say, an' you want to be close to yer woman, an' you want to bed her since you have already wed her, then to think of the hidden meanin' behind this gesture could be a beautiful thing, a intimet thing, an' could even lead to popalatin' the world with little McCutcheons. But, sir, anybody who's flippin' the bird to somebody he don't know, ya gotta believe it ain' intimate, or lovin', or a kind *Howdy-do*. Nope! It's flippant . . . and uncivil . . . and crude. I'd place a bet of twelve baskets of loafs and five fishes on it, sir, that that last gesture was a windoo to that man's soul . . . yep! It revealed a life full of discontent, anger, and animosity. Say what'cha will, but that's what I believe, sir! Other than zooming off a collapsed bridge, we don't know how he died. Maybe he banged his head against the cracked windshiel'. Maybe he sat terr'fied as the warters filled up his Cadillac and he drownded. Maybe he was so scared that he had a heart attack on his way down. But this I can tell you, sir, his ultimate cause of death was that he disintegrated in his own vile acid. Yep! He disintegrated in his own vile acid."

With this pronouncement, Muggins and Clod stood to leave, extended their hands once again—while Clod extended his lower jaw—and departed the diner. McCutcheon sat bemused as the waitress cleared the plates and filled his coffee cup. "Now there's a pair for you," she said with a wry smile. "They come here nearly every day, and I've never met two people with a greater primitive wisdom than they have." McCutcheon smiled and nodded assent.

Leaving Michael's Diner, McCutcheon headed directly to the church office. Caryn had taken a personal day and, by a stroke of good fortune, the phones were quiet, allowing time to work on Palm Sunday's sermon. Three or four times, McCutcheon read slowly and deliberately Matthew's Gospel account of *Jesus's* triumphal entry into Jerusalem, Matthew 21, then worked up the sermon outline. By late morning, he had the outline in hand and had titled the sermon, *God on a Donkey*, which in and of itself carried within it a statement of the Incarnation: *God*, heavenly, *donkey*, earthly; *God*, eternal, *donkey,* finite—the heavenly, eternal God coming into the world in his divine/ human son transported through the streets of Jerusalem upon the earthly and the finite. With that initial accomplishment, McCutcheon headed to the manse, assured by the volunteer receptionist, who had arrived at 11:30, that she would field phone calls and leave messages on his desk.

A steaming bowl of soup filled the bill for lunch, and visits to parishioners at three different hospitals in the tri-city area filled the subsequent hours. Late in the day, he returned to the manse in a doleful state of mind, with a leaden heart. Even as yesterday afternoon's visits had been marked by announcers' voices, so in every hospital room today the dreadful discovery of one body after another, one vehicle after another, was portrayed and discussed on every major television station. He turned on the television in the den and listened for less than four minutes, during which time a local fundamentalist pastor was interviewed and asserted, by way of some bizarre conclusion, that it must have been the will of God for these people to die since nothing happens in our world without the divine imprimatur of almighty God. Sickened, McCutcheon switched off the television. "Right, brother! Tell that to one of the decimated families," he muttered.

It was a blessing that he had no church or community meeting scheduled for the evening. He was in no frame of mind to sit in on a gathering this evening, even if it were urgent business. With a dinner plate of food before him, he dabbled at leftover chicken, cooked spinach, and a boiled potato, but he finally admitted to a loss of appetite and left most of it untouched.

Adjourning to the manse study, he filled his pipe with a bowl-full of Borkum Riff, lit it, and settled into the overstuffed chair. Immediately the words of Dietrich Bonhoeffer, in a letter from prison to his parents, came to mind, when he told them he was out of pipe tobacco and requested them to bring him some; that it was more difficult for him to do theology without his pipe. He was hardly thinking of doing theology this evening, for he was already stymied theologically about the senselessness of the previous day's events. Skirting the related theological quagmire, his mind returned to Michael's Diner, summoning up the countenances of Muggins and Clod, their expressive features conveying all their indignation at the passenger in the Cadillac, his flippant gesture and his unsuspecting demise.

A Retrospect

After numerous, lengthy draws on his meerschaum pipe, he laid his head back on the arch of the overstuffed chair and narrowed his eyes to a squint. Through the haze of pipe smoke, Bowdoin College campus came into view, an image that took him back twenty-five years. It was providential—or at least he had thought so at the time—how he had decided to attend there for undergraduate work. He thought of Mr. Sumner, his American Literature teacher, an American who had taken a position at his high school in Edinburgh during his next-to-last year. Sumner was a Bowdoin College graduate before he had gone to Columbia University for doctoral studies. If there were any obsession he manifested—other than his absorption with Melville's *Moby Dick*—it was Bowdoin College. All McCutcheon's classmates knew it. All McCutcheon's classmates made sport of it behind his back . . . not cruelly, but certainly in jest, imitating his American accents of the English language and his readiness to wax long and eloquently on the inestimable merits of Bowdoin College. While McCutcheon didn't rush to his defense, he refused to join the jesting, not because of any particular virtue but, rather, because, in all of Sumner's discourse about this New England college, McCutcheon had become infected by an insatiable curiosity. Eventually he approached his parents with an inquiry.

McCutcheon's parents were people of modest means, not poor by any stretch of the imagination, but classified as what Americans would term middle-class entrepreneurs, who had worked assiduously for what they had acquired. As Scottish Covenanters, they followed the Calvinist work ethic religiously, to be literal about the adverb. They never looked for favors or handouts but, at the same time, made the most of every business opportunity. They resided with other Covenanters in the Calvinistic camp of those Presbyterians who believed that financial success and pecuniary prosperity indicated the God-favored aspect of predestination. While they would not go so far as to declare that those in poverty were predestined for eternal damnation, they believed—with invincible certitude—that one's prosperity reflected God's election of the prosperous for eternal salvation. Therefore, they worked tirelessly for it.

It was an evening after the haberdashery shop had closed for the day that Stirling approached his parents with the inquiry. Dinner had concluded; his mother—with Stirling's calculated assistance—had washed the dishes and tidied up the kitchen; and they sat reading by a cozy fire in the living room.

"I've been thinking about college a lot the past few weeks," Stirling began with an adopted confidence in his voice.

His parents looked up from their books. "Have you now, laddie!" responded his father, betraying an element of surprise in his tone. "What about it?"

"Well, I want to know what you'd think about my going to the States to college . . . actually to a college in New England." Stirling paused, looking from one to the other, unable to read the expressions in their faces. He had expected more than surprise . . . actually he had anticipated alarm and an immediate rejection of the idea. There was only silence and, apparently, consideration.

"Bowdoin College, Stirling?" his mother inquired quietly. "Has Mr. Sumner been talking to you about Bowdoin College?"

"No, Mum," he answered, recalling the times over tea at the kitchen table with her when he spoke of his teacher's discourses on Bowdoin, "no, not to me personally, Mum. But, of course, he talks about Bowdoin often to groups of students. I'm curious. I think it could be a great educational adventure."

"What's wrong with the University of Edinburgh, laddie?" asked his father seriously. Much to McCutcheon's relief, it was an interrogative that came off as earnest, but not pointed or defensive. "Your sister did well there."

"Oh, nothing's wrong with University of Edinburgh, Father," Stirling quickly reassured him. "Outside of Bonnie's distaste for rivers of beer that flowed through her dormitory, she had a great experience there . . . superb academic preparation. It's just that it's . . . well, it's Edinburgh. Bonnie's still in Edinburgh, doing her thing with students in Edinburgh, and I suspect she'll be teaching little children the rest of her professional life in Edinburgh. I'd like to cultivate a bit more of a cosmopolitan taste, Father . . . if I could."

"We wouldn't see you much, Stirling, during the year, don't you know!" lamented his mother softly. "We couldn't afford to bring you home for holidays and then for summer as well."

"I know, Mum, I'd miss you and Father, I know. But that's a part of growing up, too," Stirling ventured to say to make his case further. "Bonnie's on her own now, and she did it after she graduated from Edinburgh. I think I'd acquire a similar desirable independence—albeit not financial—while at Bowdoin, learning to live on my own."

McCutcheon's parents looked at each other somberly and fixed their steady gaze interminably, it seemed, as an eternity of disquiet settled upon him. His father then turned to him and promised, "Your mother and I shall pray in earnest about it, laddie. We'll let you know as soon as we've received an answer."

"Thank you, Father," Stirling said as he rose from his chair. He walked to his mother, bent down and gave her a kiss on the cheek. "Good night, Mum," he said affectionately and ascended the stairs to his bedroom.

A few days after his aforesaid request in front of the fireplace that brash and brazen evening, his parents gave him their answer over a family dinner at which his sister Bonnie was present. His father was nearly done with his beef and Yorkshire pudding when he lay down his knife and fork, looked at Stirling, and smiled. "Your mother and I have made our decision, laddie. We've prayed about it for a couple of days, and we think God is leading you to a life larger than a confining residency in Edinburgh. Such a life works for Bonnie here, but she'll make her way around the world a bit more, she says, when she has stored up a few more pecuniary advantages in order to use her summers traveling."

"That's so, Stirling!" exclaimed Bonnie. "You needn't think of me being stuck in Edinburgh. This is where I want to be, and who knows? Perhaps I'll just flit across the ocean one of your holidays there and visit you at school. Wouldn't that be a surprise! So you best be on good behavior all the time you're there, lest I appear when you're least expecting it," she warned with a carefree laugh and dancing eyes. "*You never know the day or the hour,* as the Good Book says."

Bonnie was five years older than Stirling, had made her way through the University of Edinburgh with flying colors, graduating with numerous academic awards, all of which put her in a prime position in the queue for a teaching post in prominent private schools. As of this occasion at the dinner table, Bonnie had been teaching already six months in the Lower School of St. George's School for Girls on Garscuba Terrace, Center City Edinburgh. Bonnie and Stirling had experienced little of the typical sibling rivalry reportedly so common. Perhaps its dearth had more to do with the five-year interval between them than with any other reason, such as sanguine or phlegmatic temperaments, or a natural disposition for Covenanter compatibility. Actually, Bonnie manifested an enormous penchant for protectiveness, a maternal proclivity to keep Stirling not only safe but on the straight and narrow as well. He learned at a young age that submitting to this identifiable characteristic in his older sister made life at home as pleasant as a rhapsodic etude. Life at secondary school, on the other hand, where she had made her mark as a young, studious academician, was quite a different tale to tell. The five-year interval between them made little difference there. She was still remembered as one of the most brilliant students their Edinburgh school had ever graduated. Undoubtedly this contributed significantly to Stirling's interest in attending college in the States rather than entering the University of Edinburgh to hear more of the *summa cum laude* praises he had heard throughout his school days. Yet, when making the case for considering Bowdoin, Stirling submitted none of this to his parents as one of the rationales for studying abroad. This personal struggle on his part, out of deference to his sister and his love for her, remained forever unspoken.

As it turned out, Stirling matriculated at Bowdoin College in Brunswick, Maine, the autumn after graduating from secondary school in Edinburgh. McCutcheon's years in New England numbered among those of the best of his younger days. He initially stood out in the student body for no other reason than his Scottish brogue, and he wondered if his classmates were jesting behind his back, making sport of his pronunciation of English words even as classmates in Edinburgh had done in reference to Mr. Sumner. They soon came to know of McCutcheon's Covenanter background and demonstrated—at least at first—an intense interest in those Presbyterian Scots, at times so austere and fixed in an apparent rigid theological posture. They used the terms Calvinists, Covenanters, and Cameronians interchangeably. While Stirling spent numerous hours the first year explaining his religious background—even defending his Calvinist roots—the second and third years required less of him in subsequent bull sessions, a rather odd American phrase, he thought, for a serious discussion. It was during the second and third years that his sister Bonnie visited him twice. She struck a rather dashing figure when she arrived on campus and seemed to captivate a few of his dorm mates with her innate Scottish loquacity. She was as articulate as any of them in the nightly bull sessions that occurred while she was there. Her use of language engaged them; her understanding of international politics surprised Stirling; and her air of distain regarding their drug experiments and binge-drinking rituals made no apologies for her stringent Covenanter morality. Inclined as McCutcheon was to play down her intransigence, to take on the role of mediator, he refrained from contending with her, knowing full-well that his disinclination to do so grew solely out of his people-pleasing propensities . . . his shameful discomfort with conflict, whatever the magnitude or severity. It required little assessment on his part, however, to recognize that his dorm mates didn't need his defense any more than Bonnie would have appreciated his countering her on these occasions. Thus Stirling remained a silent observer. As a result, no one had the slightest inkling where he stood on any issue—either political, economic, sociological, military, or industrial . . . except they knew he was a Calvinist, a Covenanter, and, they thought, that must look a lot like a Bonnie McCutcheon.

McCutcheon's final year at Bowdoin College began with a turn of events that escalated into sheer demagoguery. During his previous three years, he had played snare drum in the Bowdoin Marching Band, a talent he had cultivated in the bagpipe band in Scotland. When he returned from home for his senior year at Bowdoin, the music professor reported that the student who had been selected to be the drum major had transferred to a different college at the end of the summer. The professor needed a drum major post haste. After going through the training, Stirling agreed to do it, rehearsed the marching band twice each week, directed the half-time formations at the football games, and was catapulted to stardom—albeit as transitory and delicate as the gossamer wings of a dragon fly. Seemingly overnight, he became a demagogue on campus.

Little did he know at the time, however, that the lesson he was to learn about fame is simply and clearly this: when one arrives at the extreme summit of a tall mountain, the very next step is the first step down an inevitable decent.

The football season had come to its appointed end; his white drum major's uniform had been sent to the cleaners; his tall furry drum major's hat had been wrapped and laid in mothballs; his drum major's baton had been returned to the music department's baton sheath; and Stirling had settled into a more vigorous routine of studying, cognizant that first semester finals loomed in the near future, only two weeks after Christmas break.

Those finals had no sooner appeared than the weather turned vicious, like a hunted polar bear turning with ferocity on its pursuers. The entire campus lay blanketed beneath the thick, heavy snow. Day in and day out, students trudged arduously through a perpetual whiteout, making their way to classes to sit for exams, as if the trudging through deep snow were a defining metaphor for the drudgery of trudging through a vast body of information and feeling snowed. Applying that knowledge to the exam questions, however, both scintillated and intimidated the examinees. When the midterm exam schedule came to a conclusion, a most remarkable coincidence occurred the moment all exams had been completed: the snows ceased.

This became the ideal time to release steam from the pressure cooker, to let loose all the stress that had built to potential breaking points. As Stirling and his roommate left for dinner through the main door of their dormitory, they noticed a snow sculpture, seven feet tall, in the area in front of the dorm. It was a hand with a raised middle finger. They continued to the college commons, where they ate in silence. Returning after breakfast and passing again before the snow sculpture, Stirling's viscera churned. He felt appalled, but why should he react so? It was simply playful. Anybody could see that. It was a way to engage in harmless recreation with a few dorm mates and let off steam accumulated from a strenuous semester.

The following morning, however, Stirling left the dormitory for breakfast in the commons, noticed that the snow sculpture was still standing, and made his way through the trodden snow paths to oatmeal and toast. Perhaps it was providential or perhaps he unconsciously sought him out; whichever, he sat beside a classmate who was a pre-theological student majoring in history and was the most articulate communicator Stirling had ever met. Somewhat diminutive in physical statue, he towered over all the rest of the student body with his gigantic intellect and versatility of language. Bound for Harvard Divinity School the following academic year, he had acquired in the previous years at Bowdoin an inestimably high niche in Stirling's personal regard.

McCutcheon sat in the empty chair beside him and, following a warm greeting, asked him what he thought they should do about the snow sculpture in front of their dormitory.

"Nothing," he replied with a smile. "Why?"

"It seems rather vulgar, I should say."

"No, they were just letting off steam. It's harmless."

"I can't agree," Stirling retorted. "It makes a crude statement to everyone who passes by it."

"Stirling, you're taking this thing too seriously," he said with a laugh. "Leave it alone. It will melt in due time." With this the Harvard-bound, future theologian picked up his fork and attended to his plate.

McCutcheon returned to the dormitory, moved swiftly into his room, and removed his hanging clothes from the lead bar in the closet. Lifting the bar, he went outside to the snow sculpture and smashed it to pieces. By the time he had finished, there were chunks of frozen ice surrounding the foot of the iron pole, which had provided the spine for the sculpture.

The ensuing ingenuity of his classmates never failed—even in burning retrospect—to impress Stirling. In the half-hour interval between his demolishing the snow sculpture and his leaving for class, dorm mates had affixed a crosspiece to the vertical spine with a sign, a wordplay that read: *The damn Calvinist wins again.* Standing preoccupied before this altered pastiche, it occurred to McCutcheon in retrospect that he was standing on the precise spot at the mountaintop at which the next step began his descent into derision. From that moment on he experienced an indefinable but palpable ostracism. With the exception of his roommates, the student body— men and women alike—ignored McCutcheon. After all, they reasoned, guys in the dormitory were only letting off steam . . . it was perfectly innocent play, absolutely harmless, hurting no one.

† † †

That particular experience at Bowdoin College remained to this day a significant turning point in McCutcheon's life, not so much the turning downward from the upward ascent to the heights of fame but, rather, the turning away from a stringent Calvinism that could not relate relevantly to contemporary world mores, changing rapidly beyond recognition. By the time he left Bowdoin College and matriculated in theological seminary at the University of St. Andrew's back in Scotland, Stirling's childhood Covenanter's faith had undergone a radical revision. By that one incensed, iconoclastic act, he had pummeled his self-righteousness into the frozen fragments of an outworn belief system.

As one who, like many, has looked upon the past with an element of distain—or at least regret—McCutcheon rarely spoke of the irreversible event at Bowdoin; but when he did, he would sometimes quip that if he had it to do over again, he'd probably help to create the offensive snow sculpture rather than to knock it down. But he ceased making that quip because, at heart, he had no doubt that he never would. Even though his theology had broadened in light of the world's dramatically morphed mores, Mc-Cutcheon remained today as intransigently repelled by the symbol of a raised middle finger as he was the day he first encountered it in the snows of Maine. The only thing that had changed was his disinclination to take an iconoclastic swipe at every—or any, for that matter—raised middle finger. He could confidently attest that there remains not a shred of self-righteousness in his bones, thanks to his Bowdoin classmates; but, to be sure, he wouldn't want that to be his final gesture just before he launched off into the darkness.

In a melancholic humor, McCutcheon tapped the ashes out of his pipe, laid it in the ashtray, and wondered if there was any truth to Muggins's speculation: *Yep! He disintegrated in his own vile acid.*

8

For Good Measure

SCHOOLDAYS WERE METHODICALLY WANING, those late spring days when youthful scholars—book packs affixed to their backs on this last day—directed their lighter steps into a bright, enchanting summer hiatus. Trees—green and lush, full bosomed for months now—lined concrete sidewalks and dusty paths to and from schoolhouses. Now, this same foliage bore a hint of a subsequent season, when the luster of nature's first green fades into duller hues.

Timothy, who actually bounded with excitement to school on this last day—rushing along the tree-lined paths—also bounded home when the final school bell sounded its knell to the cessation of formal academics for yet another year. He had just turned twelve in the merry month of May, which made for a joyous occasion, of course. Twelve is an enviable age, smiled upon by women of all ages and envied by old men who would like to begin again their personal journeys precisely at that particular milepost. While the age of twelve, in and of itself, was a pearl of great price, completing sixth grade at the age of twelve made the consecutive events an unbeatable combination, a milestone most certainly worthy of a celebrative observance. Such had been planned by Timmy's parents, Thomas and Vivian, and by his older sister Esther.

A large tent was erected in their back yard and a prominent caterer was engaged; family, friends, and classmates were invited; fine food, social interchange, a few innings of softball, pitching horseshoes, and board games all marked the occasion. One could easily understand why Timmy's Jewish classmates likened the event to a secular bar mitzvah. As the party drew to a congenial close and all guests had returned to their homes, leaving the little family of four to themselves, they knew it had been a good day, for it had not only acknowledged Timmy's passage from elementary school to middle school, yet to come, but also it had suitably sealed the spring semester of his school's sanctum and flung open the door to a salubrious potpourri of summer sports, including baseball, bike-riding, tennis, kick-the-can, and hide-and-seek. There couldn't have been a more joyous conclusion to the month of June, and the world lay beautifully before Timmy, open as a gigantic door, unlocked and flung wide. On the other side of the threshold appeared the image—rife in a mind's eye—of a vibrant, robust manhood laden with utopian potentials.

Unexpectedly, malevolently, however, July became the most malignant of months. While riding his bicycle on a road near his house, Timmy was struck by a car and killed instantly, and all utopian potentials now blurred in everyone's mind's eye and disappeared from his family's vision forever. The telephone call came from the hospital to the church office midmorning. Caryn delivered it to Stirling McCutcheon with a grave, ashen countenance.

When he entered the hospital room, McCutcheon's gaze fell on Timmy's lifeless form, once in perpetual motion, now motionless, a top sheet covering his body up to the neck. Thomas and Vivian met McCutcheon just inside the door; Esther sat beside the bed and had laid her head on the mattress beside Timmy's face, her lips resting against his right cheek. Though she made no sound, her tears flowed copiously, unashamedly, probably unconsciously.

Turning to Vivian, McCutcheon asked softly, "What happened?" He looked back at Timmy and waited.

She cleared her throat, but her words came out raspy all the same. "He was riding his bicycle in the sun, which was blinding. Struck by a car. We don't know much more than that."

Thomas sought to round out the picture. "It was a neighbor who was driving the car, Stirling. He had just pulled out of his driveway, and, as Vivian mentioned, the sun was blinding. He didn't see Timmy in the glare. That's the long and the short of it . . . and that's the end of it, the end of Timmy's life and hopes and dreams . . . and ours as well." Thomas glanced at Timmy's lifeless form and—with a note of quiet bitterness—allowed his suspicions to surface and take form. "It's true. As Vivian indicated, we don't know much more than that, but, given a comment the driver made, I suspect that, while picking up speed, he was gazing to his right at the new construction across the street. But there's no way to be sure."

McCutcheon remained silent. The ensuing bewilderment was a familiar feeling, and he desperately searched for a plausible comment that would lend some sense to this senseless, needless death. The apostle contends that the Holy Spirit will give you the words in a time of trial, but nothing came. While he didn't doubt the capability of the Holy Spirit in this situation, he did raise the tacit query as to whether he was theologically tone deaf or, even worse, out of sync with the Holy Spirit. *Amen! Come, Holy Spirit. Amen! Come, Holy Spirit! Amen! Speak, Holy Spirit!* But the next words were Vivian's.

"Stirling, do you remember the first time you and Heather paid us a pastoral call?" she asked in a mere whisper.

"Yes, Vivian," McCutcheon rejoined quietly, looking intently into her eyes. "Yes," he repeated slowly, "I do. One of the surprises for us on that occasion was that the children remained around the dinner table throughout the evening. As we drove home,

Heather and I remarked how unusual we thought that was for a typical American family. We have always remembered that time with you and have spoken of it frequently."

"Then I imagine you will recall that Tom and I mentioned to you, though we are both Presbyterians, I grew up in the Russian Orthodox tradition and still have traces of that tradition in my blood. Do you remember, Stirling?"

"Yes, yes, vividly," he attested honestly.

"Then you'll remember that Timmy was never baptized."

"Yes," he said. "Esther had been baptized as a child, but, as for Timmy, you wanted to wait until he could speak the baptismal vows for himself."

Vivian's eyes welled up and tears trickled down her face. Thomas reached out and pulled her close to him. "Well, he never spoke the baptismal vows for himself," she said haltingly, ". . . and he never will."

Every tenet of faith affirming that baptism is not necessary for salvation immediately ran through McCutcheon's head in anticipation of Vivian's predictable request. And then it came.

"Stirling, Tom and I would like you to baptize Timmy," she said softly but emphatically. There was no trace of a mandate in her voice, but the request was categorically unequivocal.

Convinced by this time that the Holy Spirit was not going to provide him the words for an appropriate response—or, perhaps better stated—knowing that the Holy Spirit was undoubtedly relying upon him to offer a theologically-informed, soundly-intelligent apologetic in his own words, McCutcheon ventured a rather obvious, prosaic comment. "You know, Vivian, baptism isn't necessary."

"Necessary for what?" she asked with innocent inquiry.

"Necessary for salvation," McCutcheon replied compassionately, ready to explore the issue with a slow, deliberate pace.

This conversation was so far from the bull sessions in which he had fought so valiantly—or, rather, arrogantly—at Bowdoin College in Maine and at St. Andrew's in Scotland that it amazed him how little he cared anymore about the bloody wars of theological debate. Apparently he had heard so many stories of people's lives—real stories of real lives, of which he had been an integral part—that the passion to hold tenaciously to a theological position no longer held any attraction for him. The savory taste of the dusty tournament, or the armipotent appetite of a specific aim to draw blood for the crown of Christ, or the lingering fury with a defeated Christian opponent who challenged him to debate any theological issue . . . any and all of that had dissipated in the egregious enigmas of evil. To be sure, none of the dorm mates he had ever shouted down at Bowdoin ever conceded his point in the slightest or said, "Take me to church on Sunday, Stirling; let me meet your Master." Besides, the more he had encountered evil in the countenance of disease, abuse, rape, incest, slavery, racism, alcoholism, drug addiction, injustice, oppression, abandonment, neglect, or in his own despair, the more he was speechless; or the more he was waiting for the

Holy Spirit to provide the words; or the more clearly he saw his own sin-speckled image in the mirror. As McCutcheon looked back, how haughtily that sin-speckled image in the looking-glass—as a student at St. Andrew's—scorned what he then called stodgy pastors who returned for conferences at the seminary. Students assumed the seasoned alumni had sold out the essence of the gospel by refusing to argue for the truth. They had settled, students mocked, for the comforts that congregations could provide, serving as self-satisfied parish pastors in the safety of the Scottish Highlands, simply breathing in and out until the days their first pension check would arrive in the mail. Do they read anymore? Do they pray anymore? Do they challenge their people anymore? Or do they only nurse their smooth Scotch and ruby-red port before a warm hearth of pecuniary security!

Then came the day McCutcheon was thrust into the consuming crucibles of congregations, first one, and then the others afterwards. Soon after that initiation, he became a haunted man, sickened by his arrogance and ineptitude while donning a confident countenance. No one at St. Andrew's had warned him of this. All professors—down to the last one of them—had prepared him to enter an academic arena, as if that would be precisely where he would spend his years as a pastor. In every pastorate, barring none, he went through a brutal Refiner's fire, which burned away the chaff and the dross while looking for the gold to refine. Ah, what a fool! Ah, what a fool he had been, lamented McCutcheon. Whether the Refiner had ever discovered—even as of this time—any rare element of gold, he couldn't say. But he knew that the chaff and the dross the Refiner consumed in that caldron of crises were comprised by an aberrant, twisted conceit.

No longer was there any room for arrogance. McCutcheon no longer threw down the gauntlet in a crowded pantheon or in the Athenian Areopagus. There is no longer any room for intellectual haughtiness, and while there are rare and fleeting moments of nostalgia over the forfeiture of arrogance (which previously had fired his certainty about rigid theological postures), it was his distorted image in the looking-glass that had convinced him that he had suffered from occasional lapses of good judgment, resulting in insidious incidents of unintentional stupidity and vacuous moments of primordial myopia.

"Stirling . . . Stirling!"

It was Vivian's words again.

While in these thoughts, McCutcheon had been gazing at Timmy. He turned to Vivian.

"Stirling, are you saying that baptism isn't necessary for eternal life?" she asked more insistently.

"Yes, that's exactly what I'm saying. Eternal life is a gift, available whether we are baptized or not," McCutcheon said simply, striving to be conversational rather than didactic.

"But you're not telling us anything we don't know."

"Then why do you want me to baptize Timmy?" McCutcheon inquired as gently as he could.

"Because it would bring us comfort . . . that's all," replied Vivian as one who would clutch at straws, if straws were available.

"Vivian, Tom, we don't ordinarily baptize the dead since they are already in the eternal presence of our loving Heavenly Father, since Christ has already prepared a place for Timmy in his Father's Mansion of many rooms."

"That's true, Stirling, if you believe Jesus's words to the thief on the cross," retorted Vivian with a rising passion in her voice, "but if you subscribe to Paul's notion that we all sleep until the trumpet sounds and the dead are raised in a specified order, then Timmy isn't aware of the Father's presence yet."

McCutcheon nodded his head. "And how does that make a difference, Vivian?" he asked inquisitively.

"It doesn't. Timmy's a child of God whether he's been baptized or hasn't, and whether he's immediately in the full presence of God or will be later. It's just that we crave the comfort of knowing that he has been baptized before we lower him into the ground. After that, it will be too late, and we could regret it." Silence ensued. Esther joined them in the circle.

"Will you, Stirling?" Vivian asked, making her final plea.

"Of course, Vivian," McCutcheon assured her warmly. "Without a doubt, I will . . . and with heart."

While scurrying to leave the church office for the hospital, McCutcheon had not anticipated this request, so consequently he had neglected to bring the portable baptismal kit. He requested a silver bowl from one of the nurses, who filled it with water, over which he prayed a blessing. He knew the Rite of the Sacrament of Holy Baptism by heart and revised the usual words for this unusual circumstance. The four of them gathered around Timmy, and Vivian folded the sheet down to his waist, which revealed his chest with the mammoth bruises and deadly wounds from the massive impact of the collision. Thomas laid his hand on Timmy's right shoulder while Esther laid hers on his left shoulder, but Vivian laid her hand on his chest, caressing his deepest wound.

Standing close to the head of the bed, McCutcheon began with the words he knew so well: "Our Lord Jesus said, 'Suffer the little children to come unto me, and forbid them not, for of such is the Kingdom of Heaven.' He took them up in his arms, and put his hands upon them and blessed them. Christ's promises are for you, for your children, and for all who are far away, everyone whom the Lord our God calls. Obeying the words of our Lord Jesus, and confident of his promises, we baptize those whom God has called to be his own. In baptism, God claims us and seals us to show that we belong to God. God frees us from sin and ultimate death, uniting us with Jesus Christ in his death and resurrection."

McCutcheon then asked the first question: "Thomas, Vivian, and Esther, do you desire that Timothy Forsythe Collins be baptized?"

"We do," they replied in unison.

"At this time, in this place, by surrounding Timothy with your love and presenting him for baptism, do you confess your faith in Jesus Christ as your Lord and Savior and, in your dependence upon God's grace, do you commend Timothy to his gracious mercy and eternal care?"

There was silence. Instantly McCutcheon considered the possibility that none of the three could agree to the question.

"We do," said Thomas, choking out the words.

"We do," said Vivian, followed by Esther's "We do," which was nearly inaudible.

McCutcheon lifted the silver bowl from the night stand beside the bed and sprinkled water three times on Timothy's forehead with a triune cadence coordinated with his words: "Timothy Forsythe Collins, I baptize you in the name of the Father, and of the Son, and of the Holy Spirit. Amen." Placing his hand upon Timmy's forehead, McCutcheon prayed, "Timothy, may the blessing of God Almighty, Father, Son, and Holy Spirit, descend upon you, dwell in your heart forever, and lift you into the full awareness of God's eternal presence; in the name of the Father, and of the Son, and of the Holy Spirit."

The four stood surrounded by a blessed silence for a great space of time, looking steadily at Timmy to sear their brains with his image lest they in the future would have to strain to recall it. Then there were warm, elongated embraces among the four of them. Eventually McCutcheon left them to their final hour with a twelve-year-old boy who had been blinded by the sun of random nature and sealed in baptism by the ransoming Son of God.

† † †

It was years later that McCutcheon—quite unintentionally, while sitting in his study, sorting papers—came across an essay written by Timmy's sister Esther three years after his death. It had been McCutcheon's practice since Timmy's accident, resulting death, and subsequent baptism, to visit the Collins family every three or four months. During these subsequent years, Thomas and Vivian gave birth to another son; and on the occasion of one of those quarterly pastoral visits, Vivian—with a soft smile of relinquishment—handed McCutcheon her Russian Orthodox cross, and Esther handed him a copy of the essay she wrote in her senior year of high school: *A Place Where Dreams Die and Are Reborn.*

As he had done numerous times before, he reluctantly reread the composition . . . *reluctantly* since it caused him to weep yet again. Its pathos was so profound, he thought, it could have made blind Samson Agonistes shed tears from dry sockets while laboring at the milling wheel in Gaza.

9

Return to Civilization

WITH THOUGHTS FIXED ON the green countryside of his native Scotland, Stirling McCutcheon sat alone, nursing a neat Scotch. In the subdued light of the study, he thought warmly of his sister. She had once confided in him what she considered to be an insightful observation of the male species, which she most surely issued as an undisguised warning.

"My dear Stirling, don't be solitary," she said with the confiding tone of a ministering angel, "you ought to know that the singular man alone with his thoughts resides at the top of the list as the most dangerous of animals."

McCutcheon had laughed good-humoredly, baffled by such a graphic, sweeping generalization. "Upon what significant body of evidence would you base such a profoundly naive observation?" he retorted, amazed yet again at his sister's predisposition to assumption.

"Why, just consider all those dreadful men, any of whom might appear to be a prince of a fellow in the daylight," Bonnie blithely rejoined, "who prowl about the earth under the cloak of night like so many lions crouching, laying snares for helpless prey, driven on by an over-abundant supply of those detestable male hormones." She had set forth this conjecture as a universally acknowledged supposition, which no one, she believed—not even a doubting brother—could reasonably contest.

"And do you, my dearest sister, consider me, like all these others, to be susceptible to such propensities?" McCutcheon asked with a natural element of amused curiosity in his voice.

"Potentially, if you are too solitary, my dear brother," replied Bonnie as if apprehensive that she might find his name on some roster of infamy in a public place if he brooded too much in a solitary state. "Remember, Stirling, dark and dismal schemes are dreamt up in somber solitudes, where perpetrators of evil have no occasion to air their macabre thoughts with the mediating presence of a mollifying companion. Be wary, Stirling, and I repeat here with a proper emphasis—since I believe it with my whole mind and heart—be wary of sitting alone in the dark too long!"

Whether this doting concern had been issued to him from a bottomless well of sisterly love with a touch of bantering humor, or whether it had been articulated as an ultra-conservative testimony by an ardent Scottish Covenanter, or whether this Scottish Covenanter sister had laid a suspicious eye on his inborn loneliness and there perceived some potential danger in his pattern of inwardness, McCutcheon could not be certain. It was likely that the strange comments grew out of a combination of all three speculations. How fortunate, he thought, that his prepossessed sister resided not only in his affections but more concretely in the Scottish city of his childhood, the Town of Stirling—by which his parents had acquired his Christian name—some 5000 kilometers from Albany.

At the muted sound of a climbing jet airplane above the manse, McCutcheon raised his eyes to the ceiling of his study, dolefully looked back at his Scotch, raised his glass to the ceiling and then to his lips. "Bon voyage!" The Westminster chimes of the mantel clock, shelved majestically above the massive fireplace, struck three-quarters of an hour past ten o'clock. According to his calculations, this would be the precise time that British Airways would be rising above the manse, climbing steadily towards a lofty altitude and assuming a direct trajectory towards Heathrow Airport like a powerful Pegasus racing for his domiciliary stable after being too-long away from the stall. The distant roar of jet engines definitively marked the beginning of a second consecutive summer when Heather—like one having been interminably away from home—harnessed the three children for a return trip to Edinburgh to spend two months with her parents, comfortably ensconced in the carriage house behind their elegant, expansive mansion. Not that the harnessing had been at all arduous for their mother nor had any of the three offered any untamed resistance. Pained as McCutcheon was at the prolonged parting, he could hardly begrudge his family the spirited anticipation they evinced all the way to the airport.

Do you suppose our friends will be glad to see us? Do you think Jennie has missed me all these twelve months? Grandpa still has our horses in the stables, doesn't he, Mother? He wouldn't have sold them, would he? No, dear, he still has them. Grandpa said the horses will be rejoiced to see all of you. Thunder, in particular, has missed your daily rides, Fiona.

So animated and electric were their conversation and conjecture, their eagerness and enthusiasm, that they resembled a cage of captive, loquacious birds waiting to be released toward a sunlit horizon. And now released they were. It had been difficult, however, for McCutcheon to release them at the airport, to leave them to wait on their own at the designated gate, and then to return to the manse with thoughts too complicated to define, too scattered to amalgamate, too prickly to knead.

Fiona he held a little longer than the other two. At twelve, about to fly to a distant part of the globe, she seemed so vulnerable. A strikingly beautiful little girl with dancing, dark brown eyes, coal-black hair, and olive skin, Fiona radiated a simple, unmistakable joy at being alive, inventive, engaging, and trustful. These very characteristics were precisely the ingredients of her vulnerability and, at the same time, the features of her unwitting magnetism.

Their middle child, Annabella, possessed a composure that skillfully disguised any potential apprehension. Without question, she was the risk-taker in the family, ready to greet a new venture with an enormous optimism that overshadowed any suggestion of defeat or unwelcome inner qualm. Her uncanny ability—even at the young age of fourteen—to envision the final outcome of a major personal effort on her part caused her to appear mature beyond her years. She exuded a quiet self-confidence. Her physical characteristics reflected those of her mother's, whose figure was slender, whose hair was light, and whose skin was fair, smooth, and even milky. Unlike her mother's, however, Annabella's eyelashes appeared exceptionally long, a trait of her physiognomy that drew one into her eyes in conversation.

Tall and thin with a fine physique, Angus had a long, narrow face, handsome with finely chiseled features, a straight thin nose and dark, heavy eyebrows, unusually dark and heavy for a boy of sixteen. His skin exhibited a lighter tone than Fiona's—more like that of Annabella's—with a tint of pink in his slightly hollow cheeks. The oldest of the three, at age sixteen, he took on the responsibilities of the first-born with an indefatigable conscientiousness. Long ago McCutcheon became poignantly aware that Angus adopted a protective manner whenever his father was absent, preoccupied with the work of the church, or away on business. Who has ever understood the innate inclination of any or every eldest child to naturally compensate for the deficits of the predisposed, prepossessed father! To the best of McCutcheon's knowledge, no one had ever taught him—no one had as much as intimated—that he should step up to assume a protective role with his mother and younger siblings when fertile occasions for self-assigned duty presented themselves. The weight of responsibility could now be read in Angus's countenance as the family was preparing to part for Edinburgh. Despite the jocularity that had reverberated within the ride to the airport, Angus's present expression contained a somber, determined look, one McCutcheon had discerned on previous occurrences when they were about to depart for a prolonged period of time. With eyes that possessed the capacity to penetrate superficiality, Angus looked at the floor, then at the departures screen, then to his mother, and finally to his father, on whom he fixed his stare. McCutcheon sensed a burning, unarticulated question residing in that steady, searching gaze. Sadly he turned away. Although he was never one to elude pointed questions, either from his parishioners or from his family, McCutcheon judged rightly that this was neither the time nor the circumstance in which to entertain a query of ponderous import. After a brief interlude for self-composure, he turned back to Angus.

McCutcheon initiated the embrace. It was an extended, firm embrace, saturated with inquiry but devoid of uncertainty. So confident was he that his son would take charge of the journey to Scotland and the family holiday that McCutcheon imagined him a young oak grown to full height, invincible in the winds.

"Strong and steady, laddie!"

"Strong and steady, Father!"

Finally McCutcheon turned to Heather. "Are you certain you want to do this again? This is your last chance to change your mind," he said with a remote hope that she might bend to his wishes and remain home for the summer. Of course, he knew there was little to no possibility of such a reversal at this point. Not only would such a decision disappoint their ecstatic children but, he was reluctant to admit, Heather could not bear another summer in Albany or, for that matter, anywhere else in the States. McCutcheon stood silent, looking intently into her azure eyes, and waited for her to speak. She didn't turn away or look above his head or divert her attention in the slightest. Apparently she was prepared to say it yet again.

"No, Stirling. Most definitely, no! I need this as much as the children do." She paused, looked down, then up again to his countenance, and their eyes locked. "In fact, I need this as much as you need that church and its organizations and its committees and its relentless demands." She paused, drew in a deep breath. "I've told you before, I have to write . . . I have to go away to write . . . I have to go away to survive."

McCutcheon pulled her close to him and held her as if he might never see her again. The irrational sensation of an irretrievable loss coursed through his veins. He did everything he could not to give in to a paroxysm of fear that would betray his adopted insouciance.

"I know, Heather," he acknowledged in a soft, gravelly voice. They kissed and parted.

Now, in his study, lift-off having occurred, British Airways rising overhead, Bonnie's admonition came to mind yet again, "My dear Stirling, don't be solitary!" But he was solitary, McCutcheon acknowledged. There was no one else in the house. There was no one to come home to after an intense day. There was no familiar noise or raucous laughter or sibling quarreling. There was no love-making in the bedroom, no resting—completely spent and perspiring—in each other's arms. To be sure, McCutcheon was solitary. Solitary: the natural outcome of professional choices he had made as a driven man.

Heather's articulated contentiousness over the church came to a head six months previously, on the night of her birthday. On a Saturday, early in December, she turned forty. The children and McCutcheon had planned a dazzling party for her, which would occur after an elegant dinner that Angus, Annabella, and he would cook. Fiona was responsible not only for the party decorations but also for baking scones, which the family would enjoy at afternoon tea. All of them had purchased just the right gifts to present after birthday cake.

Before any of the plans could be executed, however, McCutcheon took a telephone call late Saturday morning. It was Jocelyn Hudson's mother reporting that Jocelyn was dead drunk, yet again, and she needed him to accompany her in a transport ambulance to Utica, where she would be admitted to a rehabilitation program at one of the hospitals. Jocelyn would agree to no one else's accompanying her. McCutcheon spoke to Heather, apologized for this dreadful interruption, and informed her that he would be back by 10:00 p.m. He would wake the children then, and they would all celebrate her birthday at that time. Heather protested, and protested when he returned that night; but he doggedly pursued his intention, woke the sleepy children, and attempted to whip up celebrative enthusiasm on everyone's part. The children did their best, but Heather's thinly-veiled pain of abandonment could not be kidded away any more than the lilting *Happy Birthday* tune could serve as a salve. After the children returned to bed, Heather and McCutcheon talked in the library, behind closed doors.

"Stirling, do you remember our days in Scotland, and the two churches in the outskirts of Edinburgh, where our children were born and grew, and where I directed the choir and taught Sunday School classes in the children's department? Do you remember, Stirling?"

"Yes," McCutcheon said, subdued and somewhat submissive.

"I was happy then, Stirling. We were in ministry together. We both had a place; we were connected at the core, and my career as a writer was gaining momentum with at least a modicum of recognition."

"I recall," he answered quietly. "Those were good days."

"I have no place in this church, Stirling. I am abjectly alone. There is no one I can call a friend. Everyone around us is a parishioner with his or her own set of expectations, many of which are categorically unreasonable. Furthermore, the people here are crude . . . rich, but crude. The television obsesses over violence . . . violence, sheer violence. I don't want us to raise our children in this environment, where the highest values are clearly those of guns, violence, and smutty talk. You can hear it on the streets wherever you walk. Children so foul and vulgar in their language, I can't imagine where they learned the filthy words. Let's go back, Stirling."

"Back where, Heather?" McCutcheon asked in stupefaction.

"To Scotland . . . to Edinburgh. To a place where there are decent sensibilities, a sense of respect for elders, an importance placed on lofty ideas . . . back to a cultivated language that abhors profanity rather than idolizes it. Stirling, listen to me! Dickens was right: he never knew what it was to feel disgust and contempt until he traveled in America, a nation of bores and boors, given over to greed, hypocrisy, appearance, and pretense." Heather abruptly left off, studied the floral configurations in the library carpet, and then pleaded, "Stirling, let's go home!"

A leaden gravity seized his heart as well as his throat. "I can't," McCutcheon said hoarsely.

"But why?" she asked insistently.

"I have an obligation here, Heather. I am committed to a ten-year term," he continued with as much emphasis as he could muster, "with seven years to go."

"With your mistress," Heather said softly, somewhat distantly.

"Mistress!" he exclaimed incredulously. "I have no mistress!"

"What I'm saying is, I'm a writer, I have a career; you're a pastor, you have a mistress: the church," spitting out her words with vehemence. "Tonight was an atrocity, a perfect example of your compulsive ministry. You're completely absorbed by your parishioners, by their demands and their needs, no matter how petty or profound. And who is left to assume the responsibility for us, your family, whom you have discarded like so many worthless leftovers? Who! Every decision about the children falls to me. Why? Because you're not here. You have crossed the children and me out of your Day-Timer and inserted another meeting—one more ridiculous, awful, boring, insidious meeting—at the price of love, at the price of intimacy. My daily disappointment begins to resemble rejection, and my rejection begins to resemble wounding, and my wounds begin to resemble dismemberment . . . and before you know it, I feel disfigured and ugly, grotesque and unlovable. Then I am bewildered! I wonder how loving someone so much and being loved so well could leave someone so pathetically disfigured! Stirling, I wasn't born a catastrophe; I became a catastrophe through love! In the most intimate of relationships, marriage, I am rejected . . . for a mistress I can't even blame. Everybody knows it's a noble thing to sacrifice your life and your love for the church. But will you sacrifice me, too? Don't I have something to say about that? Don't I have anything to say about us? Stirling, to live with you is to suffocate and to live without you is to wither!"

Frozen in his chair, McCutcheon shook his head back and forth with an element of disbelief. "How could you doubt that I love you more than anyone else, or more intimately than anyone ever?" he asked gently, all the time pushing down a rising defensiveness.

"When I walk into the worship service at Madison Avenue Presbyterian Church," rejoined Heather, "and sit in the congregation, and when you enter to lead worship, and when we exchange a look and a smile, I feel elated, but my elation doesn't last. I look around, and nearly everyone in that sanctuary loves you, even after three years here. Those who don't love you, or will never love you, can't hurt you. Those who differ with you theologically left a long time ago. As I look around, I realize that everyone wants a piece of you, to be close to you, to hear a gentle word and feel the warmth of your loving smile, your full attention and therapeutic presence. Then, Stirling, I know I haven't a chance. Your choice will always be made in their favor rather than in ours. They'll have steak; I'll have the leftovers. The mistress always gets the poetry while the wife gets the prose. So I go abruptly from elation to despair, punctuated by the biting need to weep. So many times I think I shall have to leave the sanctuary before, awash with tears, I embarrass us, or before I choke and suffocate."

Heather's eyes welled up until tears trickled down her cheeks, but she held her head in an erect and dignified pose. McCutcheon moved from his chair, approached her, sat on the ottoman in front of her, and took her hand. His eyes fell to the Celtic cross on the silver chain gracing her milky throat and upper chest. It was a cross he had given her on their wedding day, and he had told her that the circle at its center symbolized the infinity of their love, that they would never be parted, either in this life or in the next. Except on formal occasions, when it was replaced with a string of pearls or a diamond necklace, Heather always wore the Celtic cross, day and night. Often, as now, McCutcheon became mesmerized at studying it.

Her nankeen, patterned nightgown with a plunging neckline appeared fluffy beneath her open bathrobe. A deep desire suddenly awoke in him, and he wanted to take her, possess her completely, on the library floor in that very moment. But he knew she would have none of him, not at this time. McCutcheon resumed his desperate defense.

"Heather," he explained cautiously, "there are so many needs, so many people hurting, afraid and anxious. What am I to do? If I can't honestly and adequately meet those needs, I should get out of the church."

"Agreed! And you can never meet all those needs! No one can. There is only one Christ, and you are not he! But you won't acknowledge that simple fact of life. In your assessment, whatever you do is never enough. You're a driven man, as if the devil's chasing you with a red-hot poker. Stirling, the thought that terrifies me is that you will never be satisfied until you find a way to spill your blood for the cause of Christ. And Jesus!—my dear Lord Jesus!—what a waste! What a god-awful waste!" Heather paused, lifted her hand to his cheek, and asked, "What do you think, Stirling? Am I correct?"

McCutcheon's head began to pound as if it were on an anvil beneath a blacksmith's hammer. He had nothing to say.

"Silence is assent," observed Heather as she stood. She moved toward the library door and then turned to announce, "I'll be taking the children to Scotland for the summer months again after school is out. We enjoyed it last summer." She started to leave, then looked back again. It seemed an afterthought, but she said with a tone of resignation, "Besides, our visits give Mother and Dad a chance to see the children's progress."

McCutcheon nodded agreement, and—her slippered, noiseless feet upon the carpet—Heather left the library to return to bed, from which she had been roused to engage in a charade of contrived conviviality.

In the subdued light, McCutcheon moved to his desk, picked up his pipe and lit the stale tobacco. Rising with the haze of smoke were distant images of Heather and him when they were young lovers in Edinburgh, each a member of separate Presbyterian Churches situated only blocks away from each other. As a high school student, one of three tenors, McCutcheon belonged to the church choir of his home church. On Easter Sunday of his senior year, he sang in the early service, which concluded with Handel's *Hallelujah Chorus*. Without informing either the pastor or the choir director/organist, he slipped out of church before the second service to attend Heather's church three blocks from his. As his decision diminished the capability and efficacy of the tenor section for the *Hallelujah Chorus* in particular, this event—over which he subsequently felt chagrin and remorse—marked the genesis of a keen awareness of the weight of assigned responsibility, the inviolability of articulated commitment, the nature of sacred duty, and the imperative of impeccable words. As a result, whenever ecclesiastical or civic duty stood over against personal or familial desire, there throbbed within his breast a fierce, visceral conflict.

The old grandfather's clock struck midnight. He closed the study door on a blue haze in a darkened chamber and on a day that amounted to a dreadful debacle.

10

Adonis and Aphrodite

A MAN WHO IS passable in his demeanor, relatively handsome in contrast to the majority of men in his community, who strikes a dashing, stately figure in his full-length mirror in the vestibule of his own home, while brushing the lapels of his suit coat and adjusting his tie for the last time before attacking the new day with an insatiable vigor—that very man indeed may discern an identifiable confidence in his stride as he makes his way to his designated place of business or to his professional lair. He might go so far as to admit—if only to himself—to a strong sense of pride bordering on self-satisfaction. Of all the men he scrutinizes as he passes each along the street, there is not one whose deportment or physiognomy he envies or with whom he would exchange his own. The issue at hand or the subject racing about in his head is not at all a matter of value, that is, one demeanor better or worse than another; nor a matter of position, that is, one demeanor higher or lower than another; nor a matter of privilege, that is, one demeanor's suiting a man to the first-class railroad car while a different demeanor's consigning him to third-class coach. No, for this particular man, the issue is simply a matter of preference—preference without judgment, preference without conceit—that is, he much prefers his own demeanor, his own deportment, his own physiognomy, his own gait, his own hair style, his own smile, and his own sartorial taste to that of any other man he knows or casually observes.

All of this is precisely how it was for Stirling McCutcheon until the day he met Allister Drummond and his fiancée Catherine Parker. Their meeting took place at the church, in McCutcheon's study, on a magnificent spring day, with trees leafing into rich greens and yellow crocuses poking their tiny heads up through the soft earth. So resplendent the morning, McCutcheon had chosen to walk the three blocks from the manse to the office, and when he arrived, Caryn indicated that the couple was already in his study, both seated comfortably upon the loveseat, coffee in hand. The Danish she had also provided remained untouched. Caryn handed him a cup as he greeted her, and he entered the study anticipating a routine pre-marital counseling session. At first glimpse of the couple, however, he stopped and stood speechless. In all his years of ministry, he had never—literally, *never*—seen such extraordinary collective attractiveness nor matchless individual beauty as on her part and handsomeness on his. Each of them stood and shook hands with McCutcheon as they recited introductions, which made it immediately clear that Allister was Scottish and Catherine undoubtedly American.

"I'm rejoiced to meet you," McCutcheon said eagerly, surveying them inconspicuously' with an envious eye, particularly Allister Drummond. In that moment he recognized the only man he had ever met with whom he would have traded in an instant his own demeanor, his own deportment, his own physiognomy. While not diminutive in stature, neither could Allister be described as herculean or even robust; but certainly it would be apparent to anyone's eye that his physique was flawlessly proportioned with every curve clearly defined. If there were an Adonis living today, here he was, standing before McCutcheon, gripping his hand with as warm a handshake as he had ever received from any man in his recent recollection. Drummond's comely face was smooth as white marble and featured a straight, delicate nose, perfectly sized to the rest of his countenance. Later in the session, when Allister threw back his head and laughed, McCutcheon noticed that even his nostrils were finely formed and pleasingly symmetrical. Overall, his visage possessed an artistic, porcelain quality, as if it had been shaped by a master sculptor and fired in a kiln to just the right temperature and duration. Thick coal-black hair graced the top of his pate; meticulously-trimmed, dark eyebrows and a light shadow on his cheeks and chin lent a clean, masculine complement to this majestic physiognomy. Little wonder Aphrodite fell passionately in love with Adonis, and indubitably, if she were standing in McCutcheon's study now, she would be smitten once again.

As McCutcheon directed his attention to Catherine Parker, perhaps one could contend that Aphrodite actually was standing in his study. As a Christian theologian, he was not accustomed to thinking about goddesses, but were he to imagine what the goddess of love and beauty might look like, he would undoubtedly consider Catherine as the preeminent model. She could sit for any prominent painter who wished to capture the essence of Aphrodite's beauty and serve as the worthiest of subjects. The more pertinent question, however, was whether any artist could succeed in fully capturing Catherine's essence? McCutcheon, for one, knew that he would fail miserably in what would amount to a pathetic attempt to describe her classic, striking beauty; and, as he would later understand, it was her indescribable inner beauty of character that fostered her external beauty and winsome charm.

The first impression that struck McCutcheon's fancy was that, since they possessed so many common physical characteristics, Catherine and Allister could have passed for sister and brother. Catherine was the same height as Allister; had thick coal-black hair as well, though considerably longer; and matched the beauty of his countenance with her own: skin as smooth as white marble, though with an ever-so-subtle pink tint to her skin-tone, cheek bones slightly higher than his. Besides a slender, delicate, French nose, beneath her long black hair—pushed back on one side—she displayed perfect ears close to her head, her earlobes not dangling but small and elegantly attached at her upper jawbone. Catherine's thin lips called attention to a graceful chin that in turn summoned one's attention to her long, slender, milky-white neck that ended in a shallow valley at the base of her throat. A quick, furtive glimpse of the rest of her figure informed McCutcheon that Catherine was full-busted, had a slim waist, modest-sized hips, and strong calves.

"Please, make yourselves comfortable," McCutcheon said as he motioned to the loveseat on which they had been seated. "I see you've met Caryn, and she has demonstrated her usual hospitality."

"Quite so!" acknowledged Allister, "and splendidly at that."

As Allister bent to be seated, McCutcheon noticed with considerable interest a cross that dangled on a chain around his neck . . . St. Andrew's cross.

"I see you're an advocate of St. Andrew's," he observed casually as he lowered himself into the chair across from them on his side of the coffee table. "Indicative of your Scottish roots, I presume?"

"It is," rejoined Allister as he leaned forward and extended the cross in his left hand as far as the chain would allow, giving his host the opportunity to examine the icon more closely. McCutcheon leaned forward as well. Overlaid on the sterling silver St. Andrew's cross—which was characterized by the form of an X—was the Drummond crest badge, also sterling silver. Within the circular crest was a goshawk with its broad, rounded wings expanded. At the feet of the goshawk lay a small crown, which was attached to one of its legs by means of a bonding jess—a short strap. The entire effect of the crest was a pleasing display of decorous gentility, which the motto at the top of the badge underscored: *Gang Warily (Go Carefully)*.

"A lovely cross, indeed, Allister!" McCutcheon said with a note of genuine enthusiasm. "Have others from the Drummond Clan made their way to the States, or are you here on your own?"

"I'm here on my own, Dr. McCutcheon," Allister began when the former interrupted him.

"Mister," Stirling said. "Just *Mister* McCutcheon will do. Actually, I go by *Stirling*."

"Thank you, sir," joined in Catherine, "but we'd rather show you the respect you deserve." She turned to Allister for a nod of confirmation, which he gave her willingly.

"Catherine and I met at Cambridge University, where she matriculated as a foreign student six years ago," Allister continued as one who was accustomed to telling their story, "and where she remained until she completed her Masters degree in Art History. I had entered the university the same year, majoring in economics and completing a Masters of Business Administration, so we have been in lock step all the way through university. So now, we've come to Catherine's home, and I've left all the Drummond Clan in Scotland."

"In some ways, Mr. McCutcheon, it has been a difficult decision," Catherine acknowledged, picking up on Allister's narrative, "and ironic as well. It's been difficult since all of Allister's family resides in Scotland, while all of my family is here in the States. It's been ironic in that the academic work I've done in art history relates more to Britain than to the United States and suits me better for employment in the European market. On the other hand, Allister has landed a magnificent and lucrative job with Wall Street in New York City. So it comes down to my having the comfort of being with my family in Albany with my pecuniary eyes cast on the European market, while Allister has the satisfaction of working on Wall Street with his familial eyes cast on Scotland. For different reasons, we both reside on this shore with our vision extended abroad."

"Given Allister's propitious employment on Wall Street, I presume you'll make your home permanently in the States after you're married?" McCutcheon queried with his attention directed at Catherine.

"That's our present plan, Mr. McCutcheon," Catherine affirmed, "at least for the time being. I may have to travel frequently to Paris if the position I've applied for at the Louvre comes through, but most of the time I would be able to work from home."

"Will you reside in Albany?"

"Yes. As a matter of fact, we expect to buy a house in the immediate vicinity, quite near to your church," continued Catherine without any discernible excitement. "We'd prefer to live in Hyde Park, which would make the commute much easier for Allister, but my mother is terminally ill and my father is elderly, so choosing proximity to parents over convenience to work is the determining factor at this time."

With a nod of acknowledgement, McCutcheon observed with a smile, "Undoubtedly your parents are pleased to have you home . . . near them."

"Since I've been away most of the last six years, it was certainly a grand reunion when I returned. Even though we are family, however, adjusting—becoming reacquainted, accepting the significant changes that have occurred in all of us—was a momentous undertaking. For me, coming home was more complicated than a simple move across the Atlantic. It was fraught with issues of aging, illness, and loss of independence. My parents are alone, and old, and feeble, and, much to their chagrin, helpless. It isn't their fault, nor is it mine. My being back at home in Albany—living a few houses away from my mother and father—isn't a desirable state for any of us, but it's essential. They have been good to me all my life, Mr. McCutcheon . . . good and generous. This is the least I can do in return. It's more than duty . . . or responsibility. It's a yearning."

"Yearning?" McCutcheon asked.

"Yes, yearning," Catherine repeated, looking above his head as if she were searching for words of explanation on the wall behind him. "I have a deep, deep desire—an indescribable yearning—to cover each of them with a quilt of peace . . . not a shroud but, rather, a quilt of peace, and health, and strength."

McCutcheon remained silent, his elbows on the arms of his chair, folded hands beneath his chin, looking intently at her as tears welled up in her eyes.

Catherine turned to Allister, took his hand in hers on the loveseat between them. "Allister has agreed to support me in this," she said softly with an apparent affection, infectious and sincere.

"Of course," asserted Allister warmly, "given these dire circumstances, how could I not want to? Any worthy daughter would do as Catherine is doing and deserves whatever support a husband can give."

McCutcheon nodded agreement. "So, you have come to be married," he said, picking up on Allister's use of the term *husband*. "How did you happen to choose Madison Avenue Presbyterian Church?"

"As Catherine intimated, we have our eye on a house near her parents in this neighborhood," Allister commenced to explain, seeming to unfold a well thought-out plan. "A few Sundays back, we attended worship here and were delighted to see and hear a Scotsman in the pulpit. I have no penchant for flattery, Mr. McCutcheon, either to give or receive it, and we can honestly say that we responded enthusiastically to your preaching and to the worship liturgy, which is not surprising since I grew up as a young plant from Scottish Presbyterian roots. While Catherine is Episcopalian—comfortable these last six years in the Church of England—this is where we'd like to make our church home."

"I'm delighted," McCutcheon said with pleasure, "but both of you should know that membership is not a requirement for a couple to be married in this church. Unlike other churches in the city, we have no such mandatory policy. By way of explanation, the Session considers weddings a service to the community as well as to our own congregation, since such openness occasionally expands and enriches church membership."

Catherine turned toward Allister and, following a tacit agreement, she set her gaze on McCutcheon and with a look of certitude affirmed, "we understand, Mr. McCutcheon, but we're committed to both decisions, marriage and membership . . . here."

"Very well," McCutcheon replied, "welcome to Madison Avenue Presbyterian Church, your Nuptial Locus and your Ecclesiastical Refuge."

After conferring with Caryn on availability of the sanctuary on specific dates, the wedding was set for the first Saturday in August at four o'clock with a six o'clock wedding rehearsal the previous evening. They scheduled, as well, four pre-marital counseling sessions in late May and early June, and while their personal calendars were in hand, McCutcheon informed them of the two new-members classes on consecutive Sundays prior to Easter, whereupon Catherine and Allister took their leave. Much to McCutcheon's surprise at a first meeting—each of them embraced him warmly, obviously with intention.

While Milton Parker was patently elderly, he was by no means feeble, defying any assumption that old age necessarily implies frailty. When he arrived with Mrs. Parker for the wedding rehearsal, and as he pushed his wife in a wheelchair down the center aisle of the church, he actually cut a rather robust figure. Obviously, he was a man of considerable physical strength. No professional caregiver accompanied them. This would have been surprising to McCutcheon had Catherine not mentioned in one of the pre-marital counseling sessions that he did it all himself: provided all the nursing care, the dispensing of medications, gave meticulous attention to necessary hygiene . . . all of which only a devoted spouse could proffer with the expressed intent of preserving the modesty and dignity of a terminal symbiont. Evidently, Mrs. Parker had held out for this stellar day when her daughter would marry the love of her life, even as she, Gertrude Parker, had done nearly forty years ago . . . for better for worse, for richer for poorer, in sickness and in health.

It was this dastardly sickness that she resented now, which only a stalwart, faithful husband could ameliorate. Though he was considerably older than she, he was like a young gazelle in his bounding to her raw need for relief from pain, for quelling the terror in the nights, for hushing her primal screams born of heinous nightmares. She hated the ravaging of her intestines, her innards dissolving into a cancerous mush, her incapacity to process any nutrient through a cantankerous colon. She detested the insidious indignity, the aggravating inconvenience of this fetid colostomy, a foreign interloper that rendered her anus redundant. When Catherine told McCutcheon that her mother had made this startling declaration—that her colostomy had rendered her anus redundant—she said that very statement made it clear to her that her mother's anger was specifically aimed at the disease, the disease that robbed her of normal functions. It was not a crude or profane comment but, rather, a factual statement. She was simply and profoundly bemoaning the loss of what, according to her recollection, Freud had claimed to be the second most satisfying function of the human body, both physical and psychological. "So," said Catherine, "she is holding out for my wedding day, as if marriage is the only talisman that ultimately protects anyone from a maddening, crazed defeat while sinking at last into an inevitable dust."

Gertrude's point of view on marriage was no secret, even as the terminal nature of her illness was no secret. She protested any suggestion to be clandestine or simply tacit about her impending demise. The subject was consistently out front like a sharp-fanged leviathan that could not be ignored. She spoke of her condition often—never with introspective self-pity, but always with poignant rage. Surprisingly, though she experienced occasional night terrors, the principal ingredient of her rage was not fear but, rather, a cosmic objection against a scheme of things designed so that anyone or anything created had to die, that all that is created had to cease to be. Unlike the traditional existentialist—who perceives oneself as isolated in an indifferent, hostile universe, who must choose to instill meaning into a meaningless cosmos—Gertrude recognized meaning in the universe but objected to the meaning that found its essence in a pattern of random birth and compulsory dying, arbitrary creation and unavoidable cessation, inexplicable beginnings and unwarranted endings. Friends had told her to savor the moment that is fleeting but pithy, to adore the blossom when it blooms ever so briefly, to consider the butterfly whose beauty lasts only two weeks. Gertrude found no satisfaction in these words of intended comfort any more than she could discover a modicum of reassurance in Shelley's *Ozymandias*.

There had been others of her acquaintance who had given up quietly. Not her. Hers was a rage that defied benign resignations. Milton Parker implicitly observed a fierce irony in Gertrude's rage, in that it was a rage focused completely against the ravaging cancer, rather than against anything or anyone external to her need. So fierce was her rage, he thought, that were she able to transmute that rage into penetrating radiation, her cancer would undoubtedly be obliterated and her health restored. Ironic, he mused, in that one might expect her to be prickly, snarly, and querulous with those around her . . . especially with him. But not so. Catherine as well noticed that her mother never snapped at her husband or at Catherine or at anyone else for that matter. Her rage was always against the disease. Catherine wondered at times which was worse for Gertrude, the rage or the disease. This much Catherine knew for certain: there would be no typical dying process as described by Elizabeth Kubler-Ross. Her mother had never entered the stages of initial denial nor of pig-like anger against others, nor was she likely to conclude the process with acceptance or resignation. She would mount incessant protestations against an inscrutable cycle of birth, life, and its unwanted cessation to her very last breath or until the morphine drip drops her over the edge of consciousness into the bottomless abyss of that unknowable, mysterious darkness.

Weeks later—after the wedding and after Catherine and Allister had returned from their honeymoon—that mysterious darkness enveloped Gertrude soon after the doctors had administered the blessing of Morpheus. As her parents had not been attending a church for quite some time, Catherine arranged for the funeral to be held at Madison Avenue Presbyterian Church. The day before the memorial service, Catherine told McCutcheon that her mother had stopped her raging long enough to say that she could see a transom above a closed door, but as much as she stretched to see into it, she couldn't reach it . . . until at last the door opened, and when she stepped across the threshold, she discovered that, in actuality, there was no door. From that mystical observation made upon a deathbed, one could only assume that the curtain between two states of being—between two realities, one finite and the other infinite—is a curtain falsely drawn, a door falsely perceived, and ultimately one passes from one state to the other without any barrier whatsoever, either concretely solid or filmily gossamer. "There is no door," she said before she slept.

Or did Morpheus—with delicate fingers and slight of hand—simply weave a consoling hallucination by which Gertrude could slip into oblivion freed at last from the entwining tendrils of rage?

The wedding had been grand. Catherine's gown was as spectacular as any McCutcheon had ever seen, nearly as radiant as Gertrude's face when her daughter passed her pew and took the bride's place beside Allister in front of the chancel steps. According to the heritage he and McCutcheon shared, Allister wore his Scottish kilt replete with the Drummond Clan plaid, associated colors and appropriate accessories, including his St. Andrew's cross. In keeping with his request, rather than wearing clerical cassock and Geneva gown, Stirling dressed in like manner in the McCutcheon Clan kilt with its particular characteristics, though with clerical collar and Geneva tabs. By the end of that first Saturday in August, Mr. and Mrs. Allister Drummond were not only officially and grandly united in marriage to each other in the sanctuary of Madison Avenue Presbyterian Church, but they were also officially united with the church just as Catherine had intended: "we're committed to both decisions—marriage and membership . . . here."

Stanchioned outside the entrance of the church stood a magnificent white horse hitched to a black horsehead post, which had been imbedded in the pavement from an earlier era; and within minutes Catherine and Allister had fled beneath a canopy of airborne confetti, had settled ensconced in the leather seat of the regal coach, and had waved goodbye to the admiring gaggle of well-wishers. The horse and coach made for a penultimate romantic touch; and had there been snow in the air rather than confetti, the scene could have resembled that of a Currier and Ives Christmas card, summoning up all the remnants of nostalgia bred in the bone of every onlooker.

Awash with that very surge of nostalgia, McCutcheon watched until the coach disappeared down Madison Avenue, then turned and entered the sanctuary. As he retrieved his notes from the communion table, he caught a whiff of Catherine's perfume, lingering in the air. It triggered a sadness, for it was a familiar scent, and he wondered if it was the same as Heather's favorite fragrance. That, and the entire Scottish character of the Drummond wedding, threw him into a hopeless trance of homesickness. That moment was laced with a light film of finality. Not only was the wedding over and done, but there seemed a shroud over his relationship with Heather—so far away from him in so many ways—that foreshadowed a frightful demise to a living, ailing thing suffocating and gasping for air. In the shadows of that foreshadow, there was a definitive fading of an earlier era, a previous joy, now receding without even a black horsehead post to grasp as the essence of a former mutuality disappeared like a vapor into a preternatural mist.

By the time he arrived at the manse, McCutcheon had plummeted into a measureless depth of melancholy. He lit his pipe and sat until darkness settled in throughout the house. By now, Catherine and Allister were well on their way to the airport and ultimately to St. John in the Virgin Islands. He could honestly say that it wasn't jealousy he was feeling but, rather, a somber awareness. As the most mesmerizingly beautiful couple he had ever seen, they were young, vibrant, obviously in love at a depth that the vast majority of married couples never fathom. They had everything before them: a limitless horizon. The only man in the world with whom McCutcheon would exchange his own demeanor, physiognomy, and circumstances for his was Allister Drummond! The realization was worthy of the hackneyed cliché: *the world is Drummond's oyster.*

11

World-weariness

LONG BEFORE STIRLING MCCUTCHEON arrived at Madison Avenue Presbyterian Church, a prominent Chinese family had become ensconced in the bosom of the congregation. At one time Yeong Quon enjoyed widespread acclaim with major responsibilities as a medical doctor in Guangzhou, the capital city in the Guangdong Province of China, all of which came to a dismal end soon after the Cultural Revolution commenced in the late 1960s. The Red Guard infiltrated the urban hospital in Guangzhou, humiliated medical personnel, and stripped doctors and nurses of their rights to practice medicine, either there or anywhere else in the province. Those who resisted were either "reeducated," imprisoned, or summarily killed.

Given this pervasive attack on the intelligentsia of the People's Republic of China, Dr. Yeong recognized his limited options. With help from friends in British Hong Kong, he and his wife Wu Lien fled by night with their infant son Yeong Ji, wrapped tightly, muffled, and held close in his mother's arms. They remained in the British colony long enough to arrange transportation to England, and from there they subsequently made their way to the United States, all of which took the better part of four years. While in England, a beautiful little girl—whom they named Yeong Fei Yen—was born to Yeong Quon and Wu Lien. Dr. Yeong's skills as a thoracic surgeon became known both in England and the States, and he was able to support his family in each location until they settled in Albany, where they soon affiliated with Madison Avenue Presbyterian Church. Early in his career in his new location, Dr. Yeong rose to distinction as Chairman of the Department of Thoracic Surgery at the State University of New York at Albany Medical Center.

By the date of McCutcheon's aurora in Albany, the Yeong family had been grafted to this body of believers like a major branch to a towering oak, and they were deeply loved. For the previous thirteen and a half years, the children had grown up in center city Albany with an above-average school system and exceptional academic opportunities, and in Madison Avenue Presbyterian Church with an above-average Christian Education program and life-shaping occasions for spiritual maturation. Both Yeong Ji and Yeong Fei Yen tested as exceedingly bright; and at the age of nineteen, Yeong

Ji was completing his sophomore year at Harvard University while Yeong Fei Yen, seventeen, was preparing to graduate from Albany High School, her eyes trained on Wellesley College, where she would matriculate in the fall.

In a short time, due to dozens of visits to their home and chance meetings on as many social occasions, McCutcheon had come to know the family well. His opportunities to interact with Yeong Ji, however, occurred only when he was home on break from college. Yet, unlike other Madison Avenue Church students away at school—with whom communication could be characterized in no other way than as sparse—Yeong Ji and McCutcheon corresponded frequently through the written word.

Were he to ascribe a positive appellation to him, McCutcheon would term Ji *a young challenger,* who, since his sophomore year in high school, had set his sights on theological seminary. During his summers prior to college, he read John Calvin's *Institutes,* virtually all of C.S. Lewis, some of George MacDonald, most of Sören Kierkegaard, and the principal works of Dietrich Bonhoeffer, all of which was sufficient reason for McCutcheon to pay close attention to his poignant theological inquiries and exceptional powers of observation.

Following his first two years at Harvard, Yeong Ji spent his entire junior year abroad, flying home only for a brief break at Christmas. The first semester, he studied in Uganda under the auspices of the SIT Study Abroad Program: School for International Training. He ventured a second semester at the American University in Cairo in the expansive continent of Africa. In keeping with their previous pattern, Yeong Ji and McCutcheon corresponded frequently each semester; and later, when the latter had occasion to reflect on their writings, it seemed to him that all of Ji's correspondence, considered as a whole, recorded an excursion not only into the depths of the human existence of desperate masses in distant places, but also into the breadth of his own curious mind and into the vast sphere of his own passionate soul.

Two letters in particular—one from each semester—scorched the paper on which they were written and seared the eyes with which they were read.

14 November

Dear Pastor McCutcheon,

As you undoubtedly surmised from previous letters, it has been an intense semester. I'm not getting a lot of sleep, but that's fine. I've really begun to love it here. It's giving me a great perspective on development and political-science stuff, but mostly it's given me a perspective on myself. I think this semester will go a long way in telling me who I am and what is most important to me, especially in terms of vocation.

And just to give a little insight into the political situation here, East Africa is the last part of Africa right now to settle down and stop being violent. The two biggest conflicts right now are in the Congo and in Somalia. Both of these are failed states, meaning there is absolutely no government. Everyone is literally fighting for themselves.

But Uganda's violence is a little more difficult to pinpoint. In the north, the Lord's Resistance Army (LRA) has been engaged in a guerilla war for nineteen years in the bush. There are hundreds of thousands of IDPs (internally displaced persons, that is, domestic refugees) living in camps in the north, mostly near Gulu. The trick is that the LRA really isn't that big. Everyone knows that if the international community really wanted to, if Uganda had the will and the resources, the LRA could be crushed. Unfortunately, there are a number of incentives that the government has to keep the war going. In fact, we met a woman named Penny, who is an NPR journalist, who has been working in northern Uganda all summer. She believes that Museveni has been coordinating the war with the LRA.

Bottom line is this: no one knows if the IDPs would be safe if they went home. Maybe the LRA would attack, maybe not. But what we do know is that every week, hundreds of people die in IDP camps from malnutrition and disease. I mean, the death toll in this area of the world is astounding. In Congo, four million (million!) people have died in the last five years. What is most striking to me is this: people are not angry. It seems as if everyone I have talked to has needed to grow used to conflict and poverty as a means of coping.

This part of the world right now is structured to benefit the powerful who are very much enjoying the status quo. The people of Uganda don't want violence. No one is talking revolution. The rich are happy and the poor are struggling to get by. It's a very, very strange place to be in. People are living right next to the world falling apart; people buy and sell gorgeous fresh produce right next to rivers of filth and sewage; a fight broke out at the bar last night and people kept right on dancing.

Speaking of people living right next to the world falling apart, last week I visited Rwanda and made it back safely. Before I left, I read a descriptive book titled, We Regret to Inform You that Tomorrow We Will Be Killed with Our Families. It affected me a great deal. In a matter of three days there, I received the equivalent of a four-year college education, but no degree, except a substantial degree of despair framed in bewilderment.

In 1994, more than 800,000 people were slaughtered, mostly hacked by machetes, in just ninety days. The killers were mostly Hutu; the killed were mostly Tutsi. It took tens of thousands of Hutus working all day to kill that many Tutsis in cold blood. To kill someone with a machete takes serious effort and determination. Machetes don't kill people with one blow, usually. And often, people would have their hands and feet cut off and be made to crawl around before they were killed. Machetes are heavy. Arms got tired and sore, hands blistered. Genocide was tough work. And day in, day out, people slaughtered each other for three months. This was a grassroots effort. For the genocide to take place, the United States and the U.N. had to deliberately look the other way. France was even worse. They were actually arming the Hutus while they were killing the Tutsis.

When we arrived in Rwanda, we went to the hotel featured in the movie Hotel Rwanda. *There are mass graves all over the country. At the official memorial in Kigali, the capital, 200,000 people are buried in concrete terraced mass graves on a sharp, green slope down into the city. Everything about the genocide is outrageous. People in the West tend to think of the Hutu/Tutsi conflict as some never-ending tribal war. Nothing could be further from the truth. The groups lived in peace together. Hutus could become Tutsis; Tutsis could become Hutus. Then the Belgians came and used 19th century race science to demonstrate that the Tutsis were superior to Hutus. They ran around measuring people's noses and skulls, all in an effort to make an efficient system of indirect colonial rule, with the Tutsis as the divinely, Darwinly-mandated rulers.*

To be sure, the French are in no position to criticize the Belgians or any other nation for unilateral military action. During the genocide, while 800,000 were being killed, 500,000 women were being raped in a country of about seven million. The French deployed Operation Turquoise, in which their military marked off safe zones so that the Hutu genocide killers could huddle together as the Tutsi rebel army began to take back the country. Throughout the entire genocide, the French armed the Hutus, fearful that Anglophone influence in the area—namely, Uganda and Kenya—was growing too strong.

And don't put too much faith in the UN. Kofi Annan repeatedly denied supplying the force needed to stop the genocide, even though peacekeeping troops were already in the country. When the Hutus fled the country, only then the UN and the international humanitarian community stepped in, pouring millions of dollars into refugee camps for the Hutus, giving them free food and shelter to regroup and providing bases for their guerilla warfare excursions back into Rwanda to attempt to finish off the Tutsis. These camps still exist today.

While there in Rwanda, I concluded that the educational point is not only that genocide is inhuman but also that genocide is one of the most universally shared parts of humanity, especially in the 20th century. Genocide has taken place on every part of the globe: in North America, the long, systematic elimination through disease and outright slaughter of Native Americans; in Europe, the Armenian genocide (Christians), the Holocaust (Jews), the Balkans (Muslims); and in Asia (Cambodia). Genocide is not bound to a particular race, religion, or class. Human nature simply has the capacity to do the unthinkable. If I were a Hutu, I do not know what I would have done, given the structural circumstances I was in.

All this about Rwanda just goes to show the complexity of the world. Even people with the best intentions (the UN, USAID, World Vision, the Red Cross, and other NGOs) cause terrible injustice. And there is no use romanticizing the average person; he is trying to rip you off for your cab fare.

It's a lot to take in. Literally everyone in Rwanda who was there in 1994 was either killed or witnessed someone killed. In the months after, people would go to use a latrine or open up a closet that had been closed for a while and find piles of corpses. Now, when you walk the streets of Rwanda, you wonder what people were doing in 1994—holding a machete or watching their family slaughtered?

So these are the kinds of questions I'm learning to live with. Sometimes days are wildly depressing, some are wildly hopeful, most are just difficult to take in. While I very much feel privileged to experience all of this and very much feel grateful to share all this with you, it is perfectly clear to me that hopelessness is not conducive to development.

Yeong Ji

4 December

Second Sunday of Advent

Dear Yeong Ji,

Since reading your November communiqué on violence in Uganda and atrocities in Rwanda—both enlightening and shattering—I have been thinking about preaching on Herod and the Slaughter of the Innocents, though reluctantly. Each time I have done so in the distant past, it has placed a dark pall over all the congregation's previous Christmas joys. The reason why I—as well as many of my colleagues—discreetly choose a more savory pericope for the Sunday after Christmas is all too transparent.

If you could look into Herod's guarded eyes, Yeong Ji, would you trust him?

Had the Magi only known! Here before them stood a tyrannical king, through whose cold veins coursed vile, regal blood, passed down from Antipas—his grandfather—to Antipater—his father—and then to Herod. Antipas and Antipater laid the foundation of a dynasty of rulers who in various capacities had ruled all or parts of Palestine and neighboring regions since 55 BC.

Had they only known! Here before them schemed the rightful King of the Jews— though not Jewish himself—a king set on his throne by Caesar Augustus in 40 BC, Herod the Great who had reigned nearly forty years before this bad-blood encounter with the Magi from the East.

Had they only known! Here before them snarled a Roman-appointed King of the Jews who, for political purposes, had consummated ten marriages. Most of his wives he had either sent away or divorced. The one he loved most passionately—the Hasmonaean Princess Mariamne I—hated him with profound ferocity, until he silenced her protests with her execution in 29 BC.

Had they only known! Here before them stood a king—every inch a tyrant given over to inveterate temperamental flare-ups—who had murdered not only his beloved wife Mariamne but also her grandfather Hyrcanus II, as well as her brother Aristobulus. Only three years before his interview with the Magi—Herod had murdered his very own sons: Aristobulus and Antipater.

Had they only known, the Magi could have easily read the King's cunning behind his directive: "Go and search diligently for the child, and when you have found him, bring me word, that I too may come and worship him."

How close indeed is the resemblance of one tyrant to another: from a Herod to a Richard III to a Stalin to a Hitler to a Mao Zedong to a Pol Pot to an Idi Amin to a Saddam Hussein, all of whom built a society of human destiny on the bruised backs of the blameless, on the shredded lives of the scrupulous, on the senseless slaughter of the innocent. By such perpetrators of cruelty, we are forced to recognize that the world exists with absurdities.

It was an absurdity that Herod—to preserve his power and authority, his right to rule and his privilege to oppress—should have sent his soldiers to disturb the silent streets of the little town of Bethlehem, resulting in an incomprehensible portrait of an inconceivable horror. An edict by Herod—born out of a furious rage and the conviction that the Magi had tricked him—sent soldiers scurrying into the little town. It wasn't the women they wanted this time to satisfy their raging lusts. It wasn't the men they sought this time to conscript into Herod's ruthless army. It was the children they ferreted out from every corner—male children two years old and younger. Blood flowed in the streets like blood flowed in Rwanda nineteen centuries later: a river of red mingled with a tidal wave of tears. No doubt Herod's soldiers violently wrenched boy babies from their mothers' arms and dashed their heads against the rugged rocks, or hoisted them on their razor-sharp rapiers, or ran them through with their glimmering swords, until hundreds of dead children lay about eviscerated—eviscerated like a herd of baby fawns after a massive deer hunt. Reports issued from messengers paralyzed by incredulity punctuated the incessant wailing lifted into the night throughout the village: deafening lamentations of the empty-armed women, weeping hysterically for their children, refusing to be consoled because they were no more. The slaughter of the innocents. The world exists with absurdities.

It is an absurdity that the Lord's Resistance Army in Northern Uganda abducts children five to nine years old, brainwashes them, and then trains them to kill other children and their families: another slaughter of the innocents.

It is an absurdity that Hutus killed 800,000 Tutsis with machetes and even a greater absurdity to severe their hands and feet before killing them: another slaughter of the innocents.

It is an absurdity that the cries of children go essentially unheeded in Darfur, where entire villages have been wiped out, and where thousands of people have been killed due to persistent and heinous fighting among rebel groups, security forces and the janjaweed militia. Among the millions of people affected to date, more than half are children under the age of eighteen decimated by devastating hunger, ravaging disease, widespread displacement, all-encompassing fear, and violent death: another slaughter of the innocents.

It is an absurdity that the cries of abused children in the United States are muffled in complicity. Nearly 1,500 children die each year due to child abuse or neglect. More than eighty percent of children who die from abuse are younger than four years old: another slaughter of the innocents.

Of course, Yeong Ji, you—who have digested John Calvin, Kierkegaard, and C. S. Lewis—can with marked alacrity predict where this is going. You, in Rwanda and Uganda, and I, in isolated but not insulated Albany, are brought kicking and screaming face-to-face with the perennial issue of theodicy: the justification of a loving God in the face of evil in the world he created. In other words, as a Tutsi is being gradually hacked to death in indescribable humiliation by an Hutu, how do you make any sense out of a loving God countenancing such an inexplicable atrocity? If you haven't yet read John Hick's Evil and the God of Love, you'll want to in due time. Marilyn McCord Adams has emerged as an intensifying glow on the theological horizon, and her recent book, titled Horrendous Evils and the Goodness of God, disassociates evil from sin, in that the former is not—to her theological assessment—the direct result of the latter. Evil does not follow upon the heels of sin as does the night the day. Have you tasted Emil Brunner yet? In a pithy paragraph in the second volume of his Dogmatics, Brunner provides a helpful allusion to previous theologians and church fathers who offered "solutions" to the nagging issue of theodicy. Brunner's own conclusion, however, is that, since God has imbued the creatures he created with free will, human beings can freely exercise disobedience.

Assuming with Brunner that evil arises out of the freedom to be disobedient, it follows that—because of that freedom—Hutus, the Belgians, the French, Americans, the United Nations and all other world players can choose to act or can choose not to act; and only a clear glimpse of a suffering God on a bloody cross will shed any light on the mystery of impenetrable darkness.

So how can I offer a positive note (from a major chord) to such a dismal tune (in a minor key) in a sermon on Herod and the Slaughter of the Innocents? I frankly don't know yet, but I find infinite comfort and hope not only in the historical record that tyrants ultimately fall, but also in the biblical account that the Son of God, the Child of Bethlehem, ultimately rises as preeminent in God's scheme of redemption and reign of peace accomplished through unconditional love.

Carlo Menotti's inquisitive Amahl asked one of the Night Visitors if he was a real king, and did he have regal blood? King Balthazar responded that he did, to which Amahl asked to see it. King Balthazar graciously declined by attesting that it was just like Amahl's.

The Child of Bethlehem comes as Savior of the world and King of the universe with blood that is just like ours, the essence of God's incarnate love. In that Bethlehem barn, the most mysterious and extraordinary divine dynamic occurred: the three Magi found the authentic King of the Jews, the Prince of Peace, who has regal blood that is just like ours. In that Bethlehem barn, heaven and earth, the divine and the human, became embodied in this manifest infant life, in a manger in an indecipherable world.

The maddening conundrum regarding pandemic human atrocities persists as indecipherable to this very day, even as it has throughout the centuries; and we are forced to admit—even in light of all of our brilliance and advancement—that we simply do not understand the meaning in human suffering. While this maddening conundrum remains with us, so does the Christ who abides with us still. With every new atrocity I see ruefully depicted in the impenetrable darkness, I see, as well, the image of the crucified Christ as an overlay upon that brutality, which convinces me that the elusive answer to the world's suffering lies somewhere in that equally indecipherable mystery of the cross, as well as in the remnant love of Christ's remnant faithful.

Yeong Ji, there is a growing sentiment that lights have gone out in the church, that sanctuaries are dark, and that pews are empty. You were not born to live up to anyone's expectations—only your own, of yourself—but it is my undying hope that you and your inventive generation of Christian scholars and assiduous activists will keep the candles lighted in the churches—illuminating the cross of Christ—to dispel the impenetrable darkness which otherwise lies upon the earth and magnifies the cries of Rachael, the voice heard in all of Ramah, weeping for her children with wailing and loud lamentation, refusing to be consoled because they are no more.

It will be a holy night for us here at Madison Avenue Church when you deplane safely in Albany on December 16 in preparation for the holiest of Holy Nights when Christ was born.

With profound admiration,
Stirling McCutcheon

As McCutcheon led the midnight Christmas Eve Service at the church, it seemed an especially Holy Night when his gaze fell upon the Yeong Family seated in the fourth row on the pulpit side of the sanctuary. They were occupying their usual pew, in which, since the onset of autumn, only Yeong Quon and Yeong Wu Lien had been sitting during Sunday worship. In McCutcheon's eyes, the visual possessed the warm impression of a family reunion.

Other than a brief home visit the week after Christmas, McCutcheon saw little of Yeong Ji since, within days, he was off to Cairo for his second semester abroad. It was only near the end of that semester that McCutcheon received a letter from him.

1 May

Dear Pastor McCutcheon,

This is the last update! It has been a year since these started, beginning with last May on a trip to London to watch Shakespeare, then a summer of an intensive internship at Princeton's International Studies Program, a fall of living in Uganda, and a spring of living in Egypt. I've been very grateful for the correspondence I've had with you, my family, and people at the church, as I've thought about all of you a lot while I've been away! What follows are just some experiences and thoughts that have blown me away. So, for the last time, I write and project, as well as I can, the images indelibly implanted in my retinas.

On a bus coming back from Jerusalem, we went through the West Bank, and the bus driver picked up an old Palestinian woman with a middle-aged daughter and three small grandchildren. As she hobbled back, everyone told her that she couldn't sit down. No one would give her his or her seat. When I finally did, the woman next to me grabbed my arm and begged me not to let the old Palestinian woman sit next to her. The children (all small enough for a lap) and the old woman's daughter had to sit on the floor of the bus for the whole four hours, while one of them got sick and vomited the whole time.

Passengers laughed at this. Even though many men stood for most of the journey to say their prayers, not one offered his seat to a child or to either of the Palestinian women.

Four hours later, at their destination, the Palestinian family got up to get off the bus. Before they did, the old grandmother, still hobbling, approached me and placed something into my hand and, with her crooked fingers, wrapped my own around the object. I caught a cursory glimpse of it and quietly protested, "Thank you, but no, this belongs to you." She smiled, shook her head, wrapped her fingers around mine again, turned away, and hobbled to the front of the bus, where she slowly descended the steps to a dusty road and a dangerous twilight. Looking down at my opened hand, I gazed at the gift: a cross—a Jerusalem cross—which gave the impression of a circle enclosing a cross with rounded ends and four small crosses in juxtaposition to the cross pieces. I had come upon this symbol during my tour of Jerusalem—in the shops along the Via Delarosa—and the descriptions indicated that the four small crosses signify the four corners of the world influenced by the major cross of Christ in the center. How ironic that all of that should be enclosed in a circle of love which, in actuality, does not exist! Yet, for one old woman, apparently love does exist . . . and she offered it to me with a warm, sad smile.

Pastor McCutcheon, I wear her cross all the time now. The Jerusalem cross I have enclosed with this letter is a duplicate I picked up for you subsequently in a small shop in Cairo.

I walked through a checkpoint in the enormous wall that Israel is building. It looks exactly like an airplane hanger. Everyone who works there stays behind bullet-proof Plexiglas while you are herded like cattle through those rotating doors that are just metal bars. It works like prison: the light turns green and buzzes, the guard unlocks the door, the person goes through, the light turns red and buzzes, then you wait for your green light. Palestinians had to swipe an electronic ID card to get through; I could have gotten through with my Harvard ID, if I wanted. Entire communities are completely enclosed by the wall. It runs right through people's backyards. Its massive height and multitude of guard towers puts the Berlin wall to shame. People who call it temporary kid themselves.

Stories like these are as common as trips to the occupied territories. Whenever friends come back, they talk about the daily humiliations of checkpoints, the racist, segregated seating in restaurants, acts of violence. It is hard for me to imagine Americans visiting the West Bank and not feeling like they are experiencing the colonization, segregation, and ethnic oppression that so many in America's history have fought against, have died to be free of. It is just simply nonsense for Israel to both occupy Palestine in the name of Israeli security, then blame Palestinians when Israeli security is breached. Security is the responsibility of the occupier. And occupation itself is inherently oppressive.

At the same time, Arab racism towards black Africans is just as troubling. By every measure—number of displaced persons, number dead, severity of ethnic cleansing, overall poverty—Darfur far exceeds Palestine in humanitarian importance. Egyptians don't seem to care. The Egyptian government actively persecutes refugees when they arrive. It goes beyond the January massacre when twenty-three refugees were shot indiscriminately by the government while protesting outside UNHCR headquarters. At least five hundred refugees have "disappeared" into the hellish realm of the Egyptian prison system. Refugees are assaulted, denied economic opportunities . . . the list goes on. These are some of the first stories I heard when I got to Egypt, after listening in a chance encounter on a dark street corner to two refugees share their experiences.

Some of my friends have commented that since going abroad I have sounded bitter. I am bitter. After hearing these stories, after seeing the skulls in churches of genocide memorials in Rwanda, after witnessing so much poverty and injustice in Uganda and Egypt, it is easy for me to understand why Camus believed life to be absurd—not because it was so evil, but because it did not make any sense. The magnitude of darkness in the world and in others, the selfishness I've seen in myself, simply defy my comprehension. It is easy to become bitter and to despair.

But I'd like to think absurdity works the other way too. I could not understand the beauty of the open, red, and rocky desert I saw while climbing Mt. Sinai as the sun set. Nor can I explain the generosity of a poor man who pays an inept foreigner's bus fare as a welcome to Egypt. Nor the murky beauty of the Nile as it snakes its way through the human vibrancy and filth of Cairo. None of this makes sense. But this insensibility gives me hope—naked, shocking hope.

I don't know what would happen if we tallied up all the good things in the world, then put them next to all the bad things. Maybe there are more good things, and we could say the world is good. Maybe there are more bad things, and the world is bad. Maybe there are equal amounts of both, and we should all be dualists. I don't know. But what I do know is that so long as there are these wildly inexplicable good things in life, I think the risk of living is worth the adventure.

So thanks for reading to the end of this lengthy letter! I look forward to hearing from you and, in hopeful anticipation, to seeing you face-to-face within a month or a season!

Until then,

Yeong Ji

23 May
Second Day at Stratford Festival
Dear Yeong Ji,

As your semester in Cairo and Yeong Fei Yen's first year at Wellesley both draw to auspicious conclusions, I'm aware that your parents are designing intricate preparations to welcome each of you home with immeasurable anticipation, to celebrate Yeong Fei Yen's completion of her first year with unbounded pride, to exude in your safe return from Egypt, and then to sequentially see both of you happily ensconced again in your respective academic centers in the worthy and inimitable state of Massachusetts. Our hearts will be full at the sight of each of you.

Thank you, most heartily, for the Jerusalem cross you enclosed with your most recent letter! Every time I look at it, I conjure up the image of the old Palestinian grandmother with her fingers enclosing yours. I have placed it with other crosses I cherish in what I deem to be a sacred space.

As to your letter—your last update from Cairo—it was a truly disturbing document, a moving chronicle! The mounting isolation of the Palestinians—both by the erection of the temporary, impenetrable wall that will never come down and by the excoriating distain of Israelis that will never allow a burdened Palestinian mother of four children a seat on the bus—presents its wound on the scarred countenance of present history as sufficient evidence of Camus's posture on absurdity, even as you intimated. Your poignant interrogative readily calls to mind Meursault in Camus's The Stranger, *who—waiting in his cell for execution the following morning—relentlessly rails at the chaplain, ominously perceives a dark wind blowing from his future, and ultimately opens his heart to the benign indifference of the universe. Who can speak for a Palestinian woman denied a simple cordial amenity that would make her life slightly or momentarily bearable, or who can speak for any other Palestinian isolated with only his/her impoverishment and anger behind a grotesque and castellan wall? But would it stand to reason that she/he would perceive a dark wind blowing from her/his future, or that she/he would think about resigning one's heart to the benign (or not so benign) indifference of the universe, or that she/he would have stored up enough insatiable rage to rail incessantly against glib, religious sentiments that insist upon underlying meaning in an ultimately meaningless universe (as extrapolated from one's macabre set of experiences, especially when there is discernment to be deduced from the authority of experience)?*

I had promised you a copy of my Good Friday meditation, I Thirst, *Jesus's fourth word from the cross. In the first section titled* The Excoriating Heat of the Sun, *I describe the effectual impact of the sun on Jesus during those brutalizing hours, the very same sun that caused him to thirst and identify with our human nature, and the very same sun that blurred Meursault's mind and thought before he shot the Arab. In the second section,* The Debilitating Day of Hate, *it is in the hostile environment of hatred that Jesus's aspirational thirst is deeper than his physical thirst: like the psalmist, his soul thirsteth for God, for the living God. If one were to develop this Good Friday meditation into a full-length sermon, he/she wouldn't be able to ignore the implied imperative to address the thirst for righteousness, for this crucified Christ is the very same Jesus who issued the beatitude, 'Blessed are those who hunger and thirst for righteousness, for they shall be satisfied.' This is the beatitude that comes to mind at the challenging, unarticulated behest of your indicting, articulate chronicle (indicting my term). Blessed are you, Yeong Ji, when you hunger and thirst for righteousness and when you are not satisfied with glib, religious sentiments that insist upon underlying meaning in an apparently meaningless universe (in any sphere of the universe that lacks meaning).*

As I have in the past, I am studying once again in Stratford, Ontario, considering The Role of Suffering in God's Scheme of Redemption. *No one at the church was in the least surprised when I informed the Session that I planned to use study leave time and money to attend seven plays at Stratford and to look for the relationship between suffering and redemption in these literary delights. I think the term one elder used good-humoredly in reference to my choice was rationale. Because of the modest—one might even say, playful—heat I have suffered in this recurring decision, I suggested that the elder use the term irrational rationale, which I think she did with a fair measure of alacrity. Be this as it may, a man of distinguished letters, as you are, will not be surprised by my conclusion that—rationale or irrational rationale—there is considerable merit to this declared project, which deals with the essential questions as to whether literature can demonstrate any redemption apart from suffering, whether there is any redemption apart from Christ's suffering, whether the dramatic resolution achieved in most plays is akin in any way to redemption or is merely and categorically only resolution, and does the suffering of Christ—as an essential element in God's scheme of redemption—ascribe any meaning to the seemingly meaningless suffering of individuals and masses of people?*

Before my leaving Albany for Stratford, your mother informed me that you are to be in the thick mist of finals this week, no doubt an intense time for you, bringing all to a savory conclusion as you make ready to disembark from Cleopatra's heartland, where she and Antony experienced a passion so profound as to cause any other tryst to wither in the heat of theirs. I acknowledge this (your exams, not Antony and Cleopatra's passion) by way of relieving you of any necessity of responding to my correspondence before you embark for the States. I write only in response to your concluding update, free and clear, devoid of any expectation of comments in return.

As of today, I have seen two plays, the first of which was John Webster's The Duchess of Malfi, a Jacobean drama, presented in 1613. Recently widowed, the Duchess is constrained from marrying again by her two brothers, Ferdinand, the Duke of Calabria, and the Cardinal. Despite their demand, the Duchess secretly marries her steward, Antonio, secretly gives birth to his three children, secretly enjoys his low-stationed love in the joys of their connubial bedchamber. Through plotting with Daniel de Bosola, Ferdinand discovers the truth and exacts revenge upon his sister, her husband, and her children. Threats of revenge and violence pervade act two; and acts of revenge and violence—laced with ensuing madness—dominate act three. The Duchess is an independent woman with her own wealth and power. Her brothers fear her independence because it threatens the very state of nature and exposes the hypocrisy upon which their power is based. Her thought and action challenge not only her brothers but also the constraints of traditional social orders, including state and church. In the tragic end, all the principals die violent deaths with their souls pathetically shredded, and one small son ascends to authority.

Forgiveness could have figured at numerous junctures, but forgiveness was never entertained as a feasible element into a favorable resolution. Suffering abounded, but redemption deferred, and the Duchess, tragically isolated, dies alone. Written and played nearly four centuries ago, The Duchess of Malfi most assuredly could be considered—by virtue of its date—archaic and irrelevant. Present-day struggles for independence (a homeland) and the violence against self-determination lend this play an indisputable contemporaneousness.

In your Shakespeare courses, perhaps as one of the plays you saw in England at Stratford-upon-Avon or in London, Coriolanus *must have made an appearance—if only a cameo appearance—on the stage of your class study and personal scrutiny. As you will recall, the Roman general Caius Martius deftly defeats the Volscians in Corioli and, by virtue of having won the city, the rulers of the republic don him with the surname Coriolanus. Upon his return to Rome, a conqueror bearing numerous wounds of battle—which serve as pricy validation of his worthiness—the patricians nominate him for the position of consul. Tribunes who represent the common people, however, abhor his pride and turn the peasantry against him, even as he is to show his wounds to the crowd as indisputable verification of his bravery and flesh-borne credentials for exaltation to the office of consul. Pride, indeed, indomitably holds sway over Coriolanus in this matter, and he haughtily scoffs at demonstrating his dependence upon the approval of a lowly people who have unconditionally refused to go to war on behalf of Rome while unswervingly expecting the ruling class to provide food for their well-being. Coriolanus reluctantly agrees to show his battle wounds in private while goading the masses to concur with his appointment as consul without the visible evidence of prospering in battle. The resulting concurrence of the crowd is no sooner issued than it is rescinded when their fickle state of mind is malignantly tickled by the cunning of the tribunes, and the crowd reverses its previous decision. The tribunes calculatingly fuel the passion of the people, who ultimately banish Coriolanus from Rome, pronouncing such judgment that he shall never return again to the beloved city for whose honor he willingly shed his emblazoned blood. With irascible perturbation he leaves Rome only to return vengefully aligned with the Volscians to lay waste the ungrateful city of Rome.*

When it comes to my questions related to suffering and redemption in literature, it seems evident that some are born into suffering, some afflict others with suffering, and some have suffering thrust upon them. In Coriolanus, *the audience can observe all three aspects of suffering throughout the course of the play, but none of these expressions or conditions of suffering leads to redemption.*

In neither of the plays, so far, have I spotted anything akin to redemption, and, of course, that may be simply because redemption is strictly a theological term applied to the activity of God for the reconciliation of the world to himself. While acts of resolution, retribution, repatriation, and reparation variously can be described in the plays, nothing comes through as redemption.

This contrast must be cited: by Coriolanus's wounds he is exalted; by Christ's wounds we are healed.

Many ancient ascetics who resorted to self-flagellation in the early church did so in order to identify with Christ's sufferings, insinuating that pain is not only good but also necessary to achieve union with Christ. A member of our church contended, as recently as last Sunday, "pain is essential for growth." I think his conviction was issued not as a prescription to be advised, but as a retrospect from which to gain insight. I can't imagine suggesting as viable or redemptive such an assertion to the vomiting Palestinian child on the crowded bus, or to a homeless Ugandan street child, or to an Iraqi mother whose husband and children have been blown up by a U.S. mortar shell.

The horror of our times convinces us that you and I are indeed interacting with people who have experienced catastrophes that are not of their own choosing or their own design. They did not construct the crosses they are carrying, only struggling beneath their weight, often despairing over the foreseeable outcome. You and I cannot abandon them; and it is incumbent upon us to speak words of comfort and hope authentically, to tell their stories as you are telling their stories; but there is no way we can turn away or pass by on the other side of the road to watch them—from an aesthetic distance— struggle with the insufferable load of their crosses. When it comes right down to it, the only act that will reduce the horrors of our times is mutual forgiveness. Thinking about how to accomplish this in the present world scene is enough to make one fatigued. I hope you will not be afraid of being defeated in the eyes of the world, nor ashamed to be weary.

We look forward to your safe arrival home!

Yours with profound admiration,
Stirling McCutcheon

✝   ✝   ✝

By mid-June, both Yeong Fei Yen and Yeong Ji had arrived home to an expectant household, which had awaited their return with considerable anticipation and a measure of concern. Allowing a week for each of the students to settle into a summer routine, McCutcheon visited the family on a warm, balmy evening, sipping hot tea with them on their screened-in side porch. Amidst all the vintage conviviality, of which he had been a welcomed beneficiary in the past, there appeared an identifiable, an ever-so-slight *mal de siècle*—world-weariness—emanating from Yeong Ji's corner of the porch. In the twilight, McCutcheon could detect a subtle sadness that undoubtedly would mark Ji's life throughout his days to his dying breath.

The setting sun cast a soft glow on the Jerusalem cross hanging around his neck, and McCutcheon smiled. It, too, was a sad smile as he recalled the old grandmother who descended the steps of the bus to a dusty road and a dangerous twilight.

1 2

The Invisible Worm

CHARLOTTE APPEARED AT MCCUTCHEON'S study door. He looked up, and there she stood on the threshold, hesitant, apparently waiting for a permissive nod to enter. Her countenance beamed a singular radiance. Of all the distinguishing characteristics about Charlotte Humphreys, her singular radiance captivated McCutcheon, riveted his attention to her solemn gaze. Placing his pen in the inkstand on the desk, he rose from his chair and greeted her with a gentle embrace.

"May I come in?" she asked demurely.

"Of course," he said with an inquisitive demeanor.

"I won't take much of your time, Pastor McCutcheon. I simply have a question. Not a simple question," she smiled as she played with the words. "I'm here simply because I have a question."

"Please come in. I have time," McCutcheon rejoined, returning her smile with a quiet understanding that nothing at this stage in Charlotte's life resembled anything that could be construed as simple. "Please sit down, Charlotte."

"Thank you," she said almost inaudibly, as if her thoughts were dominating her voice.

"Would you prefer the door to remain open, or shall I close it?" he inquired.

"Please close it."

In the single moment required for Charlotte to make her way to the wingback chair in the sitting area of the study, McCutcheon's mind in a flash traversed eleven months and myriads of emotions, all nearly spectral now in the ghastly light of preponderant inevitability looming before her steady eyes like a suffocating shroud. Eleven months ago, at the virgin age of twenty-three, Charlotte had framed her Bachelor of Arts degree from Vanderbilt University and made her way to New Haven to hang that accomplishment on the wall of her newly acquired apartment. Her specific intention was to enter Yale and complete a two-year Masters program in social work, hang that framed degree beside the other, and then work among culturally, economically, and socially-deprived children in the poor neighborhoods of Albany. As a brilliant student, a compassionate Christian, and a woman of extraordinarily keen sensibilities,

Charlotte could envision enormous prospects before her, prospects that would inevitably contribute to opening and expanding educational vistas for deprived children trapped in what she called *valleys of labyrinthine myopia.*

Even as she was settling her apartment and preparing to enter her initial classes at Yale, she fell ill. Her living room furniture had arrived and was suitably placed, her bedroom suite situated with curtains hung for a modest vantage in relation to other windows in adjoining apartments, her study bookshelves ready to receive her collection of academic books and teaching tomes. She had everything she could possibly hanker for before her dancing eyes, everything a genuinely altruistic, beneficent, eyes-wide-open idealist could desire at the promising portal of a humanitarian odyssey. All she had to do was walk through that portal. But then, although all was ready, she couldn't walk at all, not through the waiting portal, not into the challenging classroom, not among the cacophonous streets of New Haven's poverty. So enormous the ovarian tumor, so aggressively had it grown inside her, so ravenous had been the monster's passion to devour her that Charlotte could hardly move at all, once she had acknowledged the presence of some foreign mass in her torso.

Her family arrived from Albany, appointments were made with specialists at Yale New Haven Hospital Saint Raphael Campus, extensive surgery was expeditiously scheduled, and Charlotte went under the skillful knife of a prominent New Haven surgeon for four hours of intensive surgical ingenuity at the hands of an army of medical attendants. She had lain lifeless for those four hours in order that new life might be restored to her body, in order that that future she had so methodically planned might be embroidered with hope rather than fractured like broken glass framing a torn tapestry. Then came the endless weeks of recovery, the hoping, the doubting, the wishing, the longing, the fears, the prayers, the words of certitude, the guarded assurances, the cavalier assurances, the hasty assurances, the swallowed assurance, and no assurances at all.

It was a sultry summer's day late in August when McCutcheon had received the news that Charlotte was scheduled for surgery in two days. He immediately booked a flight to New Haven and, upon arrival, rented a car and made his way to the hospital. Trevor and Gloria, Charlotte's parents, met him in the hallway outside her room and, after warm, lengthy embraces of compassion and gratitude, they reviewed their daughter's medical condition, the detailed diagnosis, and the surgical procedure the principal surgeon and his team had planned in consultation with Charlotte and her parents. McCutcheon fell silent. He could hardly think of an appropriate question to ask. He listened and searched for a positive word to utter in the face of this enormous wall of misery that blocked the sun, in light of this cloak of darkness that shrouded the future, in view of this ugly, giant troll which blocked passage through that portal to Charlotte's expectations.

In all his years of ministry, in all the years of being with those of his people whom vile catastrophe had visited in one manifestation or another, in all the years he had brought a shepherd's word of comfort to his frightened sheep, McCutcheon had seldom fallen silent. He had rarely searched desperately for words that would carry meaning while frowning upon by the distorted countenance of misfortune. There was usually a word of hope on his tongue, a word of certainty to which the afflicted could cling like the green branch with honey growing out of the wall of Tolstoy's well. But there in the halls of Yale New Haven Hospital, McCutcheon must have appeared as a mute dolt, nothing to say in the wake of wild waves of the sea billowing over him in an attitude of helplessness. When the amorphous silence had spent itself, Gloria led him into Charlotte's room; Trevor followed.

Charlotte sat up in bed as spritely as ever. A warm smile that characteristically lighted up her face appeared as naturally as it ever had before. Apparently the details of her impending ordeal had not taken her down; the wild waves that pushed McCutcheon under had not caught her in their undertow. With a steady voice, marked by an unmistakable confidence, Charlotte spoke matter-of-factly about the surgical procedure scheduled for the next day and about the recuperation planned for subsequent weeks. Her Master's program would be delayed for a year, she acknowledged, but she would certainly pick up the banner of her career goals the following fall.

Before McCutcheon left for the day, Charlotte asked him to pray with them. He did, haltingly. He did more emphatically when he returned the next morning before surgery. He did with more conviction the day after surgery before he returned to Albany. On the return flight, he recalled the deadly silence that shrouded the bitter medical revelation on that initial occasion outside Charlotte's hospital room; and he wondered that the Holy Spirit—who was suppose to provide the words—was nowhere to be found. Was he, McCutcheon, not a worthy vessel at the time?

By the end of September Charlotte was discharged from the hospital. She relinquished her apartment and returned home to Albany, where she had been receiving a consistent regimen of chemotherapy and radiation to combat the insidious cancer, the remnants of which had ceased to be remnants and had become the preponderance of her daily consideration.

"I am losing the battle," Charlotte began slowly, in a measured cadence as in a Mendelssohn *Adagio*. McCutcheon waited, said nothing. Her eyes searched his, and then she looked away . . . looked away toward Dagnan-Bouveret's *Christ and the Disciples at Emmaus* painting on the study wall. "I wish I could go directly to my resurrection now, but I have to pass through a crucifixion first. In my bleakest moments of despair, I feared that it might come to this, this endless assault on my body, this ghastly invasion by a legion of hollow-point bullets that tear into my skin and explode inside my soul. I imagine those little bullets with faces, arms and legs, in helmets and uniforms, laughing like armies of aggressors as they attack and then raising victorious shouts as I wretch and vomit anything left to spit out. I love God, Pastor McCutcheon, and I want to accept his will for my life, but there are desperate moments . . . moments when a sea of black bile washes over me . . . moments when all that poison I choke on and heave out of my stomach rises up like a ghostly specter and encircles me in a suffocating grip, and I can't get loose, I can't break free, I can't breathe, and I know I'm going to die, and I know that God is no longer in control. Some appalling apparition has won control, is in charge of my life, is in charge of the whole world." She paused, looked down at her hands in her lap, and said with quiet vehemence, "and I hate it!"

Charlotte's tall, athletic form seemed to conform to the wingback chair. She had sat all the way back on the cushion, her own back pressing into the back of the chair, her thighs close together and her legs crossed at the ankles. At this moment, she laid her head back. A light stream of tears fell from her closed eyes as she sat motion-less. Hers was a countenance of classic beauty, a slender face with pure white, milky skin, a delicate nose, ears perfectly shaped and close to her head. Her torso carried a modest-sized bosom. Her snug jeans indicated muscular thighs suited to a Lacrosse athlete, as she had been at Vanderbilt University. Even now, after numerous months of chemotherapy, Charlotte presented as a person of extraordinary health and vigor, an image that deceived.

"Around two o'clock this morning," she continued with an elegiac, brooding tone, opening her eyes slightly as if reading a vision in a distant boundary beyond the study walls, "I woke up with a start, silently screaming words that stuck in my throat, terri-fied by images that made my skin crawl and at once both hot as fire and cold as ice."

"A reaction to a bad dream?" McCutcheon inquired with a simplistic statement of the obvious.

"A heinous nightmare," she replied. "I have them all the time anymore. I hate to go to sleep."

"What were the images that terrified you this time?"

Charlotte hesitated. She closed her eyes again. Her face grew pale. She sat silently. McCutcheon waited.

"At the start of the dream, I was standing at the entrance of an enormous cave. Rather, it was more like a tunnel, what you would imagine passageways in coal mines to be, with large vertical and horizontal beams to hold up the earth. I had no idea where the tunnel led, and the passageway was dark. A gust of wind suddenly came from behind me, lifted me off my feet and carried me through the passageway. When-ever I forced myself downward, in order to touch the ground, the wind grew stronger and thrust me ahead faster. At last, the wind stopped, and I fell to the floor of a large room glittering with gold and silver furnishings." Charlotte opened her eyes and looked around the study as if she could recapture the scene. "A number of young virgins, dressed in silks of various colors, appeared. They approached me and began to remove my clothing, whispering to me that all was ready and the bridegroom was waiting. I let myself down into a warm bath. The vestal virgins surrounded me and bathed every portion of my body, singing incessantly of the ecstasy of love and the delights of marriage. All this time I could feel the riveting anticipation of a handsome groom, of a glorious wedding, as well as the thrills of a passionate wedding night.

Lifting myself naked from the bath and allowing myself to be dried with soft towels, I looked about for the wedding dress; but there was none. What I saw instead was an enormous wheel turning slowly, like a Ferris wheel over a pit of fire. The vestal virgins suddenly turned into gigantic feathered birds, which lifted me naked into the air and lashed me to the wheel of fire. It immediately started to rotate, carrying me alternately down through the raging fire and then up into the bitter cold. I counted the completed circles until I reached the twenty-third rotation. Then I lost count, for I noticed that there were rats growing out of my chest and my abdomen, each raising its head and baring its teeth at the others. Then the most astounding phenomenon occurred. There appeared at my feet a serpent . . . a snake larger than anything I had ever seen . . . a python, I think. Though terrified, I actually recall feeling hope that it would devour all the rats. That's when I woke up."

McCutcheon sat quietly, the dream images filling his thoughts, assaulting his mind's eye. It was an eternal silence.

"What does it all mean to you?" he asked hesitantly at long last.

Charlotte looked away, fixing her gaze on McCutcheon's fountain pen in its ink-stand on his desk.

"I don't know," she replied with an obvious detachment from the question.

"What was your predominant feeling in the dream?" he asked.

"Powerlessness," she answered. "I was alone and powerless."

"The force of the wind was greater than your own power?"

"Yes."

"What do you think the wind represents?"

"Fate. The inexorable directing of the inevitable."

"Do you have no choice at this time, Charlotte, over the winds of fate?"

"No. The only choice I have is to accept the inevitable, which means there is in actuality no viable choice for me."

"Is that the significance of your nakedness in the dream?"

"No doubt. I am completely and utterly vulnerable, as well as outnumbered by the hideous forces that tether me to my torturous doom, all the while tricking and tantalizing me with visions of love and matrimony. My fate is sealed, Pastor McCutcheon."

"And the rats?"

"I am being eaten alive . . . from the inside out."

"Charlotte," McCutcheon ventured. Then he paused, honestly weighing what he was about to say, tacitly assessing whether what he was about to say was actually true. He continued. "Charlotte, I would take your place . . . if I could. Yes . . . yes . . . I would take your place."

This deceptive Image of Vibrant Health opened her eyes and leaned forward in her chair. "Would you, Pastor McCutcheon . . . would you . . . honestly, would you?"

McCutcheon raised his eyes to hers, stared intently. "If I could, I would, Charlotte," he replied with quiet conviction.

She rested her head again on the back of the chair and remained quiet. Then, opening her eyes, she whispered, "But you can't, can you! I'm in this alone. Mother and Dad are devastated, and they too would take my place, I believe. But they can't either. No one can. But thank you!"

"Earlier you said that you are losing the battle," McCutcheon recapitulated, to take the conversation back to where it started. "Are you?"

"Yes."

"What have your doctors told you?"

"They have done all they can possibly do," she said with a note of final resignation. "I have a choice, to continue with this wretched regimen or to let the disease take its inevitable course."

"What hope does the doctor hold out for you if you continue with the chemotherapy?" McCutcheon asked, suspecting he knew the answer already and didn't need to ask.

Charlotte turned and looked out the window behind her. She stared for a period of time, seemingly engrossed by the children playing on the front lawn of the church. In due time, she turned back and conveyed their pronouncement. "They calculated that I could live two months more with the treatments than if I let the disease take its course . . . and the question I have been considering is whether this is actually living? Do I want two months more of this agonizing hell tacked on to this indescribable torment I'm going through now! Why would I? For what purpose!" Charlotte's voice rose continually in volume and intensity. As her voice elevated in pitch, she stood and began to pace about the study.

"Pastor McCutcheon, I am going to die! I am going to die! I am twenty-three years old, and I am going to die! Nobody can change that! Nobody can take my place! Nobody can do a damn thing to alter that outcome! Do I need to suck two more months of misery out of these undulating death-throes that scream at me in my sleep and swallow me whole when I'm awake . . . like some loathsome leviathan with its cavernous orifice? No! No! I don't need to suck sour juices from a Hemlock tree and pretend they are the milk of human kindness or some magical nectar of hope and contentment. They are death! They are rancid, sinister death! But I want life! Jeremiah says to choose life. I chose life, and I'm getting death. I thought I chose life, but I really had no choice. I didn't choose this, Pastor McCutcheon! I didn't choose this! I wanted to live! I want to live now! But there is no choice! Do you understand, Pastor McCutcheon? Do you really understand?" Charlotte fell to the floor like a stately Coliseum column that had collapsed beneath an unbearable weight, as if her spinal cord had dissolved into a hot liquid, and on her knees, hands covering her face, she sobbed profusely.

Here, kneeling before McCutcheon, wept a young woman over whose head the hangman had just slipped the noose, an innocent virgin whose abundance of immeasurable potential subsequently had been strangled by an inexplicable macabre fate.

He had no comforting explanations to offer her, no theological constructs to console a desperate destiny, no wool blanket that could wrap her despair into a rebirth of healing and hope. The amorphous silence he had experienced in the hospital hallway with Charlotte's parents nearly a year ago constricted him again. Now it was deeper, more haunting than before. He stood as a stripped, empty vessel, speechless and inadequate. While silently calling on heaven for words that could heal her anguish, McCutcheon's darkest apprehension at this moment was that heaven had nothing to offer . . . nothing. Even if he were a worthy vessel, heaven could do absolutely nothing through him.

When her sobbing had subsided, McCutcheon knelt beside her and placed his hand on her shoulder. She rose to a sitting position on the carpet and leaned her back against his desk. He offered his handkerchief, which she received, and immediately she buried her face in it, remaining perfectly still and deathly silent for an extended moment.

"I'm sorry!"

"No apology necessary," McCutcheon hastened to assure her.

"But I haven't asked the question I came to ask," she said apologetically, like a distracted woman who had forgotten why she had gone into the kitchen.

"I'm still here," he offered gently. "Would you like to sit in the chair?"

"Sure. I would."

He gave her his hand and lifted her to a standing position, at which time he was once again reminded how tall she was and how dramatically this woman of commendable stature had been brought low. Palpable regret—even momentary rage—raced through his veins like a violent fire.

Charlotte sat. Her face had taken on an ashen hue. To wit, her encounter with death-throes and the monster of the deep had taken their toll on her once again, and it became perfectly clear to McCutcheon that this was the invidious struggle Charlotte engaged in every hour of the day and every minute of the night, waking every morning, no doubt, to wish that the death knell that persistently rang in her sleep was only a dream, or a dream tone, or a tone poem . . . but nothing akin to her reality.

"My simple question, Pastor McCutcheon."

"Yes, Charlotte, what is it?" he asked, leaning forward in his chair, his elbows on his knees, his hands folded beneath his chin.

"Why did Jephthah's daughter bewail her virginity?" she asked directly, exploring his countenance for an equally-direct answer.

"Ah, yes!" McCutcheon recognized the reference immediately. "From last Sunday's sermon. You were there. I had thought about you when I prepared the sermon . . . and then as I preached it, but you must understand me, Charlotte, when I say I wasn't targeting you, or singling you out. I was thinking of all of us."

"Okay . . . sure. I'll see if I can keep that in mind," she said doubtfully, but not unkindly as though she were dressing for battle. The ever-looming contest she engaged in every hour of the day placed her clearly in the path of some perfidious foe of immeasurable dimensions, some force much larger than McCutcheon and more armipotent than an indirect application of any given sermon.

"Your first comment as you came in today was right on. This is not a simple question," McCutcheon continued, reiterating the obvious.

"A complex question with complex implications for me, I need to add," she said dryly, without passion, as if she were settling in now to receive a plateful of platitudes served up on silver trays of bland, centuries-old entrails of theodicy.

"Complex implications for all of us, to be sure," McCutcheon contended again, trusting his repetition would somehow connect the whole human condition to her specific tragic dilemma, however futile that might be in Charlotte's need for comfort in an unbearable isolation.

"My virginity has become a curse to me," whispered Charlotte through her teeth. "Throughout all my years in high school and college, I saved it for the husband I shall never have. I preserved it for the one man to whom I would give everything: faithfulness, love, spontaneous and buoyant moments, sad and melancholy days, my passions, my hungers, my shared dreams and mutual aspirations . . . and, of course, children. Most everyone I know in this congregation is married and has children or, if not married, has made love in some darkened corner of the world, in their dorm rooms, or hotel rooms, or in their own bedrooms when their parents were away for the weekend. But not me, Pastor McCutcheon! I'm a virgin, and I regret it! Just like Jephthah's daughter! Silently I go around bewailing my virginity. After worship on Sunday, I went home and looked at the passage again—Judges 11—and after her father sacrifices her as a burnt offering, the next verse says, *She had never known a man.* That's me, Pastor McCutcheon. That's me right there on the page. I have never known a man, and while Jephthah's daughter went off with her companions to wander on the mountains and bewail her virginity for two months, I have been bewailing my virginity for eleven months, by myself, afraid to admit to any of my companions that I detest my innocence."

Charlotte stopped. Her voice as before had modulated into a gradual crescendo until it was laced with a sonorous intensity. By the end of her lengthy comment, she had been gesticulating profusely. But now she rested her hands on the arms of the wingback chair and remained motionless.

"How," she queried with a vacant stare into the space above McCutcheon's head, "could Jephthah's daughter's virginity have complex implications for *all* of us? What would lead you to believe that people who are not virgins and savor their sexuality can relate to a virgin who *is* a virgin and despises her own virginity?"

"Because everyone is cursed—or blessed, as the case may be—with unfulfilled passions, Charlotte, with potentials that have not been realized, most of which may never be realized," McCutcheon rejoined with a note of melancholy. "Jephthah's daughter's virginity represents an unrealized potential. The very nature of your virginity, Charlotte, is a *potentia*, a life force that remains unrealized. The woman who has borne four children and never fulfilled her innate passion and God-given potential to sing as an operatic soprano may very well bewail her operatic virginity that was always saved for the right opportunity but was never spent. The man who possessed all the latent potential to design magnificent cathedrals or avant-garde office buildings or impressive French chalets may be working as a draftsman at General Electric while bewailing his unfulfilled architectural virginity. If the truth be known, he has been confined to this day-to-day work because he, when a young man, lost his virginity and subsequently has a fine family of a wife and three children to feed and support. There is for him, however, a virginity he bewails, an unused potential he will never unleash."

"But he has the rest of his life to work to unleash it if he chooses to," she insisted.

"I grant you, Charlotte, in contrast to these two sad accounts, nothing is more immediate or more intense than your own circumstances, but the central truth of Sunday's sermon was simply this: that there is a silent wound deep in the breast of every living soul, a wound that is never healed because a specific, clamoring *potentia* will go forever unheeded . . . just as it was for Jephthah's daughter, bewailing her virginity as she goes to be sacrificed."

Charlotte leaned forward in her chair, her head bent low in her hands, her long light-brown hair hanging down in front of her. For the first time on the occasion of this visit, McCutcheon noticed the cross that dangled beneath the ends of her thick hair, which accentuated its swinging. It was the Mayan cross he had seen around her neck numerous times before. It was her own cross. It was the cross on which her virginity was affixed as assuredly as Jesus's hands and feet were fastened to that ancient Roman torture stake. It was the cross on which her own life force was fated to ebb out into a quiescent darkness, unfulfilled, silently screaming for a sweet taste of completion. And which of us, who is not in the inferno of the *no exit,* can ever grasp how desperate that piercing awareness of the *no exit* truly is, how that moment of the shattering *anagknaresis*—that dawning comprehension—causes the utter and complete decomposition of hope, down to the very last element of hope invalidated! It is this caveat of not actually finding oneself in the inferno of the *no exit* that allows one to offer—if not glibly, at least naively—the proposition of taking the other's place in the inferno . . . "if I could," McCutcheon had said. It was a seemingly authentic offer made inauthentic by the caveat that, in point of fact, he was not in her inferno, nor could he be. This thought suddenly submerged him into a huge vat of superficiality, leaving him staring at Charlotte's Mayan cross, grateful that there was no room for him there, yet despondent that it was her own to bear when he had claimed a willingness to take her place.

"Pastor McCutcheon," Charlotte began softly.

McCutcheon raised his gaze from her cross to her searching face, her eyes moving rapidly back and forth, their pupils dilated, as if they were ready to take in some enormous portion of resolution.

"Pastor McCutcheon," she continued slowly, deliberately, "I don't want to bewail my virginity . . . I want to spend it."

McCutcheon waited, nearly breathless, wondering what she meant.

"I *intend* to spend it," she whispered with certainty, "and I am in no doubt about it."

"What do you mean, Charlotte?" McCutcheon asked tentatively.

She averted her eyes from his to the *Emmaus* painting again, as if seeking strength or willfulness or permission from the central figure there, to utter a revolutionary, moral heresy. She looked at McCutcheon again, now with a reinforced calm. "I plan to lose my virginity," she issued through clenched teeth, "tonight . . . with Jeffrey."

"With Jeffrey?"

"Yes." Rather than her ensuing silence engulfing her in an impenetrable fortress, it seemed to summon her into its vortex and draw McCutcheon down into a fathomless depth of sexual images of two young, naked lovers harnessed by fierce, gyrating passion with the blood of her lacerated virginity splashing in McCutcheon's eyes, blurring his vision, but not enough to obscure the gigantic sword hanging above their pseudo-nuptial bed with its plunging fall unavoidably imminent and tragically inevitable. "Yes," she repeated, "with Jeffrey."

"Why are you telling me this, Charlotte?" McCutcheon inquired quietly, without judgment.

"Because today I want your promise that tomorrow you will pronounce absolution for my sin," she announced without any hesitation whatsoever. She had obviously thought this through and knew precisely what she needed in her *no exit* inferno.

"Do you love Jeffrey?"

"Yes. If I had the good fortune of a future, I'd want to spend it with him. He has been through this with me from the beginning. He has stuck with me through all the soul-wrenching agony. He'll hang in with me until my dying breath . . . I'm sure of it."

"Listen, Charlotte," McCutcheon rejoined reflectively. "Presbyterians aren't accustomed to pronouncing absolution for sin. What we know from scripture is that God is more ready to forgive than we are to ask for forgiveness. He knows what we need before we ask, and you can be certain that he, who created and blessed the sexual union of a man and woman as sacred, understands your need for sexual intimacy before you die. You actually don't need absolution, Charlotte. God's grace is ever present and greater than we could ever measure."

"Pastor McCutcheon," Charlotte interrupted impatiently. "I'm already thrashing my way through the hell of this damnable disease. After I die, I don't want to wake up in some eternal daybreak to find myself slogging every timeless minute through an unbearable, endless hell of punishment simply because I didn't ask for forgiveness for the temporary joy of sexual intimacy."

"All right, Charlotte," McCutcheon responded softly, "believe me when I say you don't need absolution after what you consider to be a sin of passion. God understands! Believe me. God understands. I am not in a position to give you permission to lose your virginity with Jeffrey, but," he hesitated, "I will pronounce God's forgiveness for you *before* you lose your virginity with Jeffrey."

"Okay," she said softly. "I'll accept it."

As Charlotte sat quietly, expectantly, McCutcheon inwardly cringed at what he had just promised. In essence what he had offered was no different than what John Tetzel, Dominican Monk, had proffered to clamoring crowds in the market place of Jüterbog, Germany in 1517: letters of indulgence for the sins they had already committed, but also pardon for those sins they hadn't committed . . . but which, however, they *intended* to commit."

"Charlotte, will you kneel? Here . . . on the floor."

McCutcheon took her hands in his and drew her from the wingback chair towards him as he also moved from his chair toward the floor. As they kneeled before each other, it occurred to him—and to Charlotte as well—that they were kneeling before Dagnan-Bouveret's portrait of *Christ and the Disciples at Emmaus*. McCutcheon let go of her hands, which she put together in an attitude of prayer, whereupon he placed his hands upon her head and said, "In the name of the Father, and of the Son, and of the Holy Spirit. Amen. Charlotte, you have come to make confession before God prior to your act of transgression. You may now confess before me, your pastor in this church of Christ, sins of which you are aware, as well as the soft and life-giving sin which you are about to commit."

With her eyes closed and her hands still in a praying posture, Charlotte whispered with profound feeling, "Almighty God, I confess that I love Jeffrey, that I want to be his wife, that I intend to go to his bed this night and to enter into full sexual, intellectual, and spiritual intimacy with him as if he and I were beneficiaries of the holy bonds of marriage. Though I am not sorry for this intended sin, O God, I deliver myself into your hands, trusting in your mercy through your Son Jesus Christ, my Lord. Amen."

With the sign of the cross, McCutcheon recited these words, which were more than rote recitation, but, rather, more deeply felt in a Living Presence than he had ever known before: "Cling to this promise: the word of forgiveness I speak to you comes from God. Charlotte, by the will and understanding of the Holy Spirit, God gives you a new birth, and through the death and resurrection of Jesus Christ, God forgives you all your sins . . . those you have committed and those you are about to commit. May almighty God strengthen you in all goodness and keep you in eternal life, both now and for ever. Amen."

McCutcheon slowly removed his hands from Charlotte's head and rose to his feet, then sat in his chair, resting his chin upon his folded hands. It must have been minutes that Charlotte remained kneeling, until at last she rose, stood upright, lifted McCutcheon's hands to her lips momentarily, and then left swiftly, silently by the study door.

† † †

Shadows were descending around McCutcheon in the manse study as the evening's dark deepened into a milieu suitable for a chiaroscuro with a brilliant moonrise. He had poured a neat Scotch and was somberly musing about Heather and the children. It occurred to him that each recurring summer away from them seemed an interminably long stretch, and he wondered if he should revisit the notion of remaining at Madison Avenue Church for the full duration of his verbal contract. Who could blame Heather and the children? Scotland has always been their home. At times, including this very moment laced with a ferocious nostalgia, McCutcheon, as well, felt a poignant emptiness that only a walk in Edinburgh's moonlight could vanquish.

His roving gaze perused in a sweeping circle the hundreds of books on the bookshelves that majestically lined three of the four walls. In that instant, as his eyes focused on the fourth wall, he saw there the shadow of a cross, formed and cast by the moonlight against the crosspieces in the study's only window. How singular! As one who is intellectually bound to prophetic tradition and acutely sympathetic to mystical practice, he wondered what particular significance the shadow of a cross on his study wall could hold.

The telephone rang. Ten minutes past nine.

"Stirling, I'm sorry to call so late." It was Trevor Humphreys's voice, which sounded weary and beleaguered. "But we have just admitted Charlotte to Albany Medical Center, and she has asked if you would come to see her tonight. Could you possibly?"

"Of course, Trevor," McCutcheon rejoined without hesitation. "I'll be there directly. Give me half an hour."

"Thanks, Stirling! She's in Room 402."

McCutcheon sat back in his chair and looked at the fourth wall. The shadow of the cross was still there, however the cross was no longer perfectly shaped but was now twisted with the moon's adjusted angle.

It had been six weeks since Charlotte had visited him at the church study seeking absolution for a sin she was about to commit. Subsequently, each week, he had visited with the family in their home and noticed a steady decline in Charlotte's emotional vigor and physical health. Jeffrey was invariably present. While nothing was ever mentioned about the sexual engagements between him and Charlotte, it became apparent to McCutcheon that Trevor and Gloria had accommodated Charlotte's need for an acceptable arrangement between her and her lover. Jeffrey had taken on a husbandly role with Charlotte and the pseudo identity as a son-in-law to her parents. Nothing tawdry characterized the entire affair but, rather, something tender and routine as nightfall. Despite the cancer's swift progression and ravaging effect, an inviolable contentment shone in her demeanor, the obvious result of a sacrificed virginity on God's High Altar of Mystical Union.

Now came the phone call McCutcheon had dreaded. No surprise. His most recent visit with the family two days ago took place in Charlotte's bedroom. Her relentless pain hovered at an excruciating level. Her eyes remained closed most of the time he was there, and she had only enough strength to lightly squeeze his hand following the prayer.

McCutcheon dressed quickly, picked up his small New Testament, prepared his portable communion set, and drove directly to Albany Medical Center. When he arrived on the fourth floor of the hospital, Trevor was waiting for him.

"She's going down fast, Stirling. The doctors have put her on a morphine drip to manage the pain. She's in and out. Sometimes I think she recognizes me, and then she says something far out as if I'm someone else . . . Jesus, or John or somebody. Once I think she called me *Jephthah*, or something like that."

"It's all right, Trevor," McCutcheon answered with as much reassurance as he could muster. "It's perfectly normal at this stage of the disease. Undoubtedly the morphine is causing a degree of hallucination. I know she knows you and loves you. Nothing could be more self-evident."

"She asked for you. I hope she'll be lucid," said Trevor as his voice began to quiver, modulating into heart-wrenching sobs; and his body shook uncontrollably. McCutcheon reached for him and with a firm embrace held him close . . . man to man, a duo of the tormented, whose mutual sorrows and gushing wounds merged into an ineffable propinquity.

After moments in this state, after a concerted exertion to regain control, Trevor pulled away, smiled weakly, and pointed down the hallway.

"Room 402, Stirling. I'll be along shortly," he murmured, struggling to gain control.

Upon entering Room 402, darkened for patient composure with only a soft light emanating from the adjoining lavatory, McCutcheon observed Gloria at one side of the bed and Jeffrey at the other, each holding Charlotte's hands as she lay motionless. Saline and the morphine drip were the only ministrations sustaining her in these final hours. Gloria approached McCutcheon and greeted him with a warm embrace, a gesture that seemed to cry out for an answer. She and McCutcheon had talked at length about this before, searching for a justification of God's way with Charlotte, and they both had concluded that there was no intelligible explanation.

"Thank you for coming, Stirling," she said with a tone of virulent resignation. Gloria had arrived at the hospital prepared to spend the night: the long, dark night of her own soul; the long, dark night of her daughter's departure into an unknown realm. "She asked for you as soon as we admitted her. Your being here is timely." She took McCutcheon's hand and led him to the bedside. "Pastor McCutcheon is here, Charlotte."

Charlotte opened her eyes and managed a weak smile. She squeezed his hand and attempted to speak. Jeffrey, intuitively recognizing every need, reached for a glass of water and a straw, placing it between Charlotte's lips. She drank, cleared her throat and, with a renewed effort, again attempted a few words.

"I had another dream, almost identical to the one I described to you," she began.

"Can you tell me about it?" McCutcheon inquired, speaking softly and with riveted attentiveness.

"It was the same tunnel entrance into darkness, the same dominating wind that carried me to the large room with glittering gold and silver furniture, the same bath in which I washed, and the same vestal virgins attending to me; but this time there was no wheel of fire and no grotesque rats and no enormous serpent, no transformed gigantic feathered birds, just the beautiful attending virgins who clothed me in the white wedding gown and lifted me into the air." Charlotte stopped, closed her eyes, and smiled. Her pale, gaunt countenance—previously so full and radiant and salubrious—in this instant acquired a beatific aspect.

Perceiving what he suspected to be some new-found divine contentment, McCutcheon asked, "Then what, Charlotte?"

She lay motionless, still as death—still as the death so imminently present, waiting, lurking, but which she no longer feared—and remained silent, until at last she said, "The virgins lifted me high into the air, where I joined them dancing. We danced and danced and danced. What a joy! What an ineffable joy, dancing so freely and unencumbered! Then I noticed a kingly figure, dressed in garnet and gold; and beneath his right foot lay an enormous serpent, crushed and motionless."

At this point she opened her eyes and looked meaningfully at McCutcheon.

"What, Charlotte?" he urged gently.

"Pastor McCutcheon," she continued. "I felt an enormous compassion—not pity . . . no, not pity—for the lovely ladies dancing with me in the air."

"Why?" McCutcheon asked.

She turned her head toward Jeffrey and smiled with dancing eyes. "Because they were virgins. I wondered if they had ever known the warmth of a human embrace."

Every word Charlotte spoke now was formed with a strenuous effort.

"I've brought communion. Would you like to celebrate it with your family?"

She closed her eyes and nodded almost imperceptibly.

It seemed that all the words of the communion liturgy possessed a nuanced authority, infused by a divine *peripeteia*. "The body of Christ given for you. The blood of Christ shed for you. Do this for the remembrance of me." Never before had the words been so penetrating, so transformative. All of them received the bread; all of them received the wine; all of them chose to drink from the same cup. But only Charlotte ate the bread and drank the cup with a profoundly complete, existential, empathic identification with the sufferings and sorrows of the Christ.

She motioned to Jeffrey and pointed to the nightstand drawer. Jeffrey opened the drawer, selected an object, and passed it to Charlotte, who clutched it, kissed it, and handed it to McCutcheon.

"Pastor McCutcheon, I have cherished my Mayan cross, which I purchased on the mission trip I took with Professor DuBois two summers ago. Please take it . . . keep it . . . and when you touch it, please think of me. I do not want to enter that vaulted cave unknown or unknowing."

McCutcheon closed his fingers around the necklace with the Mayan cross, bent down slowly, and kissed Charlotte on the forehead. "None of us will ever forget you."

At the very moment of this promise commenced the genesis of Charlotte's final struggle. Her pain elevated dramatically, her breathing became noticeably labored, her verbal communication ceased completely. McCutcheon relinquished his proximity with Charlotte to Trevor and Gloria, who—inseparably with Jeffrey—watched silently by her side into the early morning hours.

Shortly after 2:00 a.m. nurses entered the room, checked her vital signs, and gave everyone the option of leaving for home with the assurance that each would be called if Charlotte took a turn for the worse, but no one chose the offer. Wait and watch. Wait and watch. *Could you not watch with me one bitter hour?* rang over and over in McCutcheon's ears like the pendulum of a church bell repeatedly sounding its doleful tolling. Within the hour, Charlotte became agitated, opening her eyes and searching the room with a distant gaze. McCutcheon walked to the head of her bed and, from behind her, placed his hands on either side of her face. The others encircled her, holding hands.

"Charlotte, look there, at the Emmaus table," McCutcheon said quietly. Her agitation ceased. "Can you see the Christ . . . the Risen Christ? His arms are open. His hands are reaching out to you. Can you see yourself moving toward him? He's beckoning to you . . . to come to him. He is receiving you to himself. He is now enfolding you in his arms, and all is well. All is perfectly well. All is pure peace. And there you will be forever . . . safe and complete and totally loved."

At the word *loved,* Charlotte's muscles relaxed and her breath ceased, and the spirit of divine discontent had found its resolution in a dramatic manumission of her spirit—what the Greeks call *metempsychosis.* Jeffrey bent down, laid his face in her neck, and wept silently.

✝   ✝   ✝

In the three years McCutcheon had served as Pastor of Madison Avenue Presbyterian Church, he had never seen the sanctuary filled with so many people, overflowing into the aisles, the narthex, the balcony, as well as into an antechamber adjacent to the worship center. Two busloads had arrived from Vanderbilt University, Charlotte's alma mater, including the Dean of Students and the Dean of Alumni Affairs, the former who had known Charlotte while a student and the latter who had conversed with her frequently since her graduation. Numerous people from the medical community appeared for the memorial service: the surgeon from Yale New Haven Hospital with an entourage of nursing staff who had attended to Charlotte, as well as medical personnel from Albany Medical Center, where she had received treatment since her return home. He couldn't think of any member of the church who wasn't present on that occasion for the celebration of her life. Of course the most conspicuous segment of the congregation that day sat as a group in the middle section of the nave. They had composed the immediate aspiration of Charlotte's future plans: the disenfranchised children from marginalized Albany, where Charlotte had tutored the summer before her senior year. The plan that took shape in her mind's eye, and that she held close to her bosom, now lay dormant in the modest casket positioned in front of the chancel steps.

At the appointed hour, the Cassavant organ began a composite prelude of J.S. Bach pieces, the final selections being *Jesu, Joy of Man's Desiring* and *Sheep May Safely Graze*. Vested in black robes and white stoles—appropriate for witnessing to the Resurrection of our Lord Jesus Christ and for the Celebration of Life—Marcel DuBois and Stirling McCutcheon led Charlotte's parents and Jeffrey to the front pew pulpit side, entered the chancel, reverenced the cross on the communion table, and took their designated seats.

Because the mission trip to Peru, organized and led by Professor DuBois, had been a life-shaping, transformative experience for their daughter, Gloria and Trevor had requested Marcel to co-officiate at the service and offer Remembrances of Charlotte in Peru. DuBois presented his tribute eloquently, threaded as in a magnificent tapestry with a strong fiber of sentiment but without a trace of sickly sentimentality. It is hardly an overstatement to compare Marcel's skillfully crafted encomium to Michelangelo's portrait of God's reaching out to Adam with the spark of life. He verbally painted vivid images of Charlotte as a seraph serving in the trenches of Peruvian poverty, a seraph who became the embodied representation of the Presence of God in the depths of deprivation and despair; a seraph who, by her own presence, cried out: *Holy, holy, holy is the Lord of hosts; the whole earth is full of his glory;* a seraph who sought to convince the desperate ones that they were not beyond the reach of God's glory and blessings.

Marcel concluded with a brief account of their last day in Peru, when they visited the expansive catacombs beneath the magnificent San Francisco Church at Plaza de Armas in downtown Lima. It was reported that over 25,000 people were buried there, and their bones were arranged in aesthetic configurations. Unlike many of the students who reacted to the scenes with horror, Charlotte expressed sadness for each person who had lost an individual identity in this mass grave. Before the group left the San Francisco Church at Plaza de Armas, Charlotte purchased a Mayan cross, which she said she would wear every day to remember those who went to the grave unknown and unknowing.

Following Marcel DuBois's remarks, the congregation stood to sing a hymn that Charlotte sang quietly to herself during her last days in hospital: *Jesus Christ, My Sure Defense.* But the people did not sing quietly as Charlotte had but, rather, robustly. The church's vaulted ceiling could not contain the rhapsodic refrains of faith-filled voices or the doxological strains of an unleashed Cassavant, all of which rose gloriously heavenward.

> Jesus Christ, my sure defense / And my Savior, ever liveth!
>
> Knowing this, my confidence / Rests upon the hope it giveth,
>
> Though the night of death be fraught / Still with many an anxious thought.
>
> Jesus, my redeemer, lives; / I, too, unto life shall waken.
>
> He will bring me where he is; / Shall my courage, then, be shaken?
>
> Shall I fear, or could the head / Rise and leave his members dead?

Emboldened by this hymn, McCutcheon climbed the steps of the pulpit, read three passages of scripture: the first from II Samuel 6, the second from I Corinthians 15, and the third from Luke 24. Then to an utterly silent congregation—as silent as the moving spheres at the edges of the hushed universe—he preached Charlotte's memorial sermon titled, *Her Dance before the Lord*. Like King David's dance before the Lord, McCutcheon contended, Charlotte's dance before the Lord also served as a defining metaphor for her life and passion. After the statement of this theme and its development, he concluded with the Apostle Paul's affirmation that God gives us the victory through our Lord Jesus Christ . . . and Charlotte's dance goes on.

†   †   †

As night settled upon the cemetery adjacent to the church, McCutcheon sat alone in the manse study and thought about the shadows descending upon a fresh grave. He took the Mayan cross from his suit coat pocket, held it tightly in his hand, thanked God that Charlotte had not gone to the grave unknown or unknowing, and summoned up a mental image of her dancing in the air. Could it be possible? Of course, he thought . . . actually, irrefutable. He opened the box of crosses on his desk and laid the Mayan cross gently, reverently alongside the others.

The rising moon shone in the study window. He looked at the fourth wall and saw only a reflection of light. He picked up his pipe, filled it, lit it, and settled back in his chair. His thoughts fled to William Blake:

> *O rose, thou art sick!*
> *The invisible worm*
> *That flies in the night,*
> *In the howling storm,*
>
> *Has found out thy bed*
> *Of crimson joy,*
> *And his dark secret love*
> *Does thy life destroy.*

Then the image of Charlotte's gazing at the portrait of Christ at Emmaus came to mind. She could not move directly to her resurrection as she had wished; she had to go through the cross, not around it. But now McCutcheon could envision her seated with the Christ at the Emmaus table. *Did not our hearts burn within us while he talked to us on the road . . . ?*

13

Legacy of a Stone Statue

GAVIN DAVIES STRUCK AN impressive Welsh figure: tall, slender in appearance beneath his black cassock, his neck white-collared, and his waist cinched with a wide, black-fabric belt connected at his side with two broad strands, fringed, draping down his left hip to knee-length. His facial features seemed well-defined by a thin, straight nose, medium-high cheekbones, a slim, longish face, deep-set brown eyes, an ample forehead graced by a shock of thick black and gray hair representing a dense, salt and pepper mane. His ears were pinned close to his head, but unlike the right one, which possessed a natural curve at the top, the top of his left ear revealed—when exposed—an ever-so subtle indentation. Even though this irregularity was modest in its aspect, the Reverend Mr. Davies apparently considered this flaw a serious imperfection and chose to conceal it with a copious layer of his abundant salt and pepper attribute, meticulously styled to disguise nature's defect.

While not the first time for McCutcheon to spend his study leave at Gladstone's Library in Hawarden, Wales, unbeknownst to him at this moment, it would be the most unforgettable, principally because of Gavin Davies. This ecclesiastical paradigm of clerical appearance took his place on the chancel of St. Deiniol's Chapel with its high-vaulted, octagonal-shaped ceiling and multidirectional beams. Nearly thirty retreat guests had gathered for evening vespers and Holy Eucharist. Stirling McCutcheon among them. The Daily Evening Prayer: Rite Two began with several sentences of scripture followed by confession of sin and assurance of pardon, psalter and readings of the lessons. The Reverend Gavin Davies read with a modulating, soothing, yet distinct and compelling voice, which reminded McCutcheon of a doleful mourning dove's call, which he, as a boy, had heard at Dunsapie Loch near Edinburgh. Following the designated Lessons, Davies stepped down from the chancel and seated himself in a chair facing the small congregation. He referred to the four-by-six-inch card everyone had received on entering the chapel, the Prayer of St. Teresa of Avila:

> Christ has no body now on earth but yours,
> No hands but yours, no feet but yours.
> Yours are the eyes through which must look out

Christ's compassion on the world.

Yours are the feet with which he must go about doing good.

Yours are the hands with which he must bless men now.

Davies asked everyone to pray St. Teresa's prayer in unison. Once concluded, all sat quietly in a reflective period of meditation. He turned to Paul's *First Letter to the Corinthians* and read from chapter 12, beginning with verse 12: *For just as the body is one and has many members, and all the members of the body, though many, are one body, so it is with Christ.* All the way to verse 31 Paul was making a compelling case for the church as being one with Christ and, in point of fact, actually being the body of Christ. With that, Davies transparently introduced his theme for the seven evening vespers during this week at Gladstone's Library, St. Deiniol's Retreat Center: *The Body of Christ: Evening One, the Hands of the Body; Evening Two, the Feet of the Body; Evening Three, the Eyes of the Body; Evening Four, the Ears of the Body; Evening Five, the Mouth of the Body; Evening Six, the Unpresentable Parts of the Body; and Evening Seven, the Head of the Body.*

"Having a thorough go at this extraordinary image of the church as the body of Christ," continued Davies, "initially we'll consider the *Hands of the Body,* keeping in mind the concluding line of St. Theresa's prayer: *Ours are the hands with which he must bless men now,* the term *men* being both generic and perfectly acceptable in her sixteenth century ecclesiastical milieu but meaning in essence blessing *all people now.* Before we get into the intricacies of the hands of the body, however, a word of introduction regarding Paul's passage in I Corinthians 12 is essential to our overall theme. Verse 27 contains an implied imperative, which is that we are required to understand that the church of Jesus Christ today is in actuality the body of Christ. Paul does not use the image of the body of Christ as a simile or a metaphor or an allegory. *Now you are the body of Christ.* It is our identity as the church. We are not like the body of Christ, nor are we similar to the body of Christ, nor are we a symbol of the body of Christ. Rather, we are equated to the body of Christ. We *are* the body of Christ. *Christ has no body now on earth but ours.* In other words, we are his body in this world."

McCutcheon sat transfixed by the notion of *actuality,* that is, the church is in actuality the body of Christ. He had read the *Corinthians* passage numerous times and had preached on it frequently, but Davies's presentation of the concept struck him in a singular way that seemed he had never heard it before. There welled up in him a new and profound sense of responsibility as a member of the body of Christ who suffers whenever another member suffers.

How could McCutcheon account for the insightful nuance he had just experienced? Undoubtedly the Holy Spirit had spoken through Gavin Davies. McCutcheon was convinced of it, and fortifying that conviction was another: that Gavin Davies was a pure instrument, an attractive, compelling, mesmerizing instrument of the Holy

Spirit, who conveyed fresh, authentic understandings of scripture unencumbered by personal biases or theological slants.

The remainder of the evening—including Davies's presentation on the *Hands of the Body* and the celebration of Holy Eucharist—served to underscore McCutcheon's initial impressions. He intuitively perceived the vivid presence of the Holy Spirit as mediated by Davies's quiet charisma.

Even though Gavin Davies acted as chaplain for the entire week, it wasn't until the fourth day that he and McCutcheon experienced a significant encounter, when they sat together for dinner in the refectory. As the community of retreatants gathered, remained standing, and bowed, Chaplain Davies returned thanks for the meal, crossed himself, and looked for a vacant chair.

"May I?" asked Davies as he motioned to the seat beside McCutcheon.

"Please do," responded McCutcheon as he moved his chair a little to the left to make more room for Davies.

"Are you here for Joshua Cummins's seminar on *Evil*?"

"Yes," said McCutcheon.

"Josh is a close friend," Davies admitted with a broad smile and a note of warmth in his tone. "I usually refer to his course as 'the Evil Seminar' and suggest to him that it must take an evil person to present an evil workshop. Then he counters with an attack on my Chapel Talks as an obsession with body parts, insisting that it must take an incurable sensualist to focus on parts of the body for seven nights sequentially. Then, of course, what can I say?"

McCutcheon smiled benignly, amused at the implied camaraderie in the friendship of the two retreat leaders. "Probably not much, although you could make a case for your subject being more tangible, therefore more substantive than any contrived answer to the question of evil."

Davies laughed quietly. "That's the lance thrust I'll use in the next joust. Thank you! It's McCutcheon, isn't it?"

"Yes. Yes, it is. Stirling McCutcheon."

While extending his hand and shaking McCutcheon's, he said, "I'm Gavin Davies," stating what he knew was already known.

"Yes, of course. I believe we're all up for your take on the *Ears of the Body of Christ* this evening."

"You're from Scotland, obviously. To quote that well-known accusation leveled against Peter in Caiaphas's courtyard, *your accent betrays you*."

"Yes, originally; but presently I'm serving a church in the States, in Albany, New York."

"Extr'ordinary! Which one?" Davies inquired somewhat intently.

"Madison Avenue Presbyterian Church . . . quite appropriately located on Madison Avenue," matching in kind Davies's previous statement of the obvious.

"Isn't Albany somewhat close to Rhinebeck?"

"About fifty miles north. Do you know Rhinebeck?"

"Only by way of a friend. I've never been there in person."

"Charming town!"

"To be sure, from what I've heard! I'm to understand that it's as picturesque as the most beautiful village in Wales." Davies paused, stared at the brilliant tapestry on the refectory wall—Raphael's depiction of St. George's slaying the dragon—and remained reflective. "Well, actually," he continued, "to tell the truth, I can't think of any Welch town that can compare with the reputation of Rhinebeck."

McCutcheon noticed Davies's brief descent into deliberation. "Then I'd suggest you come to see it . . . in person; and while you're there, visit us in Albany. What our city lacks in Rhinebeck beauty we certainly compensate for with unsurpassed hospitality."

"Well, thank you, Stirling. I have no plans presently to do so, but if I do, I'll certainly consider your offer."

"Good. We have ample room for you in the manse."

Both men ate slowly, reflectively, as if each were sensing simultaneously a strange bond—an unanticipated chemistry, an instantaneous dynamic—that riveted two souls together by a mystical force external to the will of either. Neither had ever experienced this with another man. McCutcheon could not classify it. Davies could not describe it. But both recognized it. Davies broke the silence.

"Stirling, setting all jesting aside, what drew you to Cummins's seminar on *Evil?*"

McCutcheon had finished his meal. He pushed his chair away from the table and turned it slightly towards Davies. "To answer that honestly, Gavin, I'd have to admit that I'm a driven man."

"Driven. How so?"

"Much like the Dutchman in Wagner's *Flying Dutchman,* cursed by his own choice and assigned to a state of restlessness . . . or, perhaps, more like Ponce de León, searching for the fountain of youth that doesn't exist. In my case, it's searching for an answer that's forever elusive and never found. But I'm driven to find it."

"Answer to what? What's the question?"

"Why an all-loving, all-powerful God allows an all-pervasive evil to abound in an otherwise beautiful world?"

"Yes, of course."

"The age-old question of theodicy, the burning question since Job lamented his plight, the gargantuan problem that every credible theologian has examined but none has solved. And now your friend Joshua Cummins is rising to the challenge as well."

Davies nodded ascent and continued nodding wittingly. He smiled and admitted, "Seriously, Stirling, I know Joshua is not evil; perhaps foolish, but not evil. More likely, I think, courageous. It's one thing to climb Mt. Everest because it's there, but quite another to climb a mountain that literally has no summit. There is no resolution for the aspirant in this matter . . . only an eternal alpinism; but one has to admire the courage of the alpinist who keeps at it despite the Sisyphean futility. Granted, Stirling, no one has ever found the answer that is universally true, but God forbid we should ever stop asking the question, '*why evil?*'"

"I need this seminar to work for me."

"What do you mean?"

"I don't need Cummins to provide the answer—that elusive, invisible, inconclusive answer—but I need him to help me understand the redemptive constructs necessary to stay faithful to my calling and resolute in my understanding that God is both all-loving and all-powerful, while the people of my congregation are decimated by wanton, senseless suffering. Is this too much to expect of Cummins?"

Davies looked down at his empty plate and remained silent, his eyes narrowing to mere slits, until at length he said, "I don't know, Stirling. Perhaps." He raised his head, turned his chair toward McCutcheon. "My suspicion is that those redemptive constructs will emerge more from your inviolable experiences with your people than from seven days of discussion on the subject of *Evil*. But I would never underestimate Joshua Cummins's impact on his seminar attendees."

"To be sure?"

"To be sure," attested Davies. "I sat in on his seminar here two years ago. It moved me in a way I hadn't anticipated. As a matter of fact, I was bemused to realize that by the conclusion of the discussion on evil, the intense question about suffering in the world had lost its global, theoretical quality and had shrunk to a personal dimension: namely, evil in my life and my own culpability as an agent—both witting and unwitting—of malevolence. In point of fact, for the very first time, I recognized myself as an instrument by which others had suffered at my hands by my mindlessness, or simply through poor judgment on my part. It was a grotesque awakening, Stirling, one of the necessary stumbling stones on a rocky, endless path to redemption. No, I certainly could not underestimate Josh Cummins's influence on the people who take his seminar seriously."

"How do you account for the focus narrowing from global to personal, Gavin?"

"Without our realizing it at the time, Cummins forced us from an abstract theoretical hypothesis to a categorically experiential conclusion. He waited until the third of seven sessions—after each participant had spouted his or her theories on theodicy—and then he predicated that history has less to do with universal abstractions than it does with personal, concrete experiences. The key words here were *abstraction* and *history*. Cummins's worldview, as it became clear, acknowledged both the violent, global interactions of world cultures throughout the centuries, as well as—and more importantly for our purposes—the cruelty in our own personal histories in the brief span of our lives. He advocated our moving away from abstraction and narrowing our focus on the specificity in our own experience. It was from that day that I stopped asking *why* and began inquiring *whom*: that is, whom had I violated, or manipulated, or betrayed, or ignored, or abandoned? Then the malicious specters in my own heart rose up to overwhelm me."

Davies paused, then looked at his watch. "I should set up the Eucharist for this evening, McCutcheon. What do you say to a nightcap in my apartment after vespers?"

"Surely, but of course! See you soon," said McCutcheon as he rose with Davies. The two men hesitated, each inclined to embrace the other, but understandably reticent, they shook hands and separated.

†   †   †

As with every previous evening, McCutcheon felt lifted by Davies's Chapel Talk and celebration of Holy Eucharist. In this particular discourse on the ears of the body of Christ, Davies adroitly bifurcated his theme into two streams: the Indispensability of Every Member of the Body with reference to verse 16: *And if the ear should say, 'Because I am not an eye, I do not belong to the body,' that would not make it any less a part of the body*; and Suiting Action to the Word, referring to Jesus's words in Mark 4:9, *they who have ears to hear, let them hear* . . . and Luke 6:46, *why do you call me 'Lord, Lord' and not do what I tell you?*

After a suitable interval, McCutcheon made his way to Davies's second-floor apartment, decorated with a rather elegant old world motif. The living room was graced by a myriad of books on floor-to-ceiling bookshelves lining three sides of the chamber.

"Come in, Stirling. Welcome to these temporary quarters of mine," said Davies warmly. "Actually, to say *mine* is not quite accurate, but *temporary* is correct. Come in, come in."

"Thank you," rejoined McCutcheon as he shook Davies's hand. "Quite splendid, indeed, whether temporary or permanent! Do you mind if I have a look?"

"Quite to the contrary. Have a go at it. Drink it in," encouraged Davies.

McCutcheon moved slowly around the room while examining the books on a vast variety of subjects, including history, theology, science, medicine, political science, and European and American literature with a predominance of Russian novelists.

"Gladstone must have been an extraordinary scholar," interjected Davies into McCutcheon's archival tour. "Besides all the countless number of volumes here in the main library of his home, there are these hundreds of books in this space as well."

"And you prepare all your Chapel Talks in this setting, surrounded by all this inspiration?" McCutcheon queried.

"Right! It's only a week each year that I serve as chaplain; but it's one of the best weeks of my year."

"Truly impressive, Gavin!"

"I'm delighted you can spend this time with me, Stirling. There are times it seems a little too solitary and the week seems long. Will you join me for a bourbon?"

"Yes, thank you!"

Davies poured as McCutcheon approached the loveseat on the other side of the large coffee table, on which a substantial plate of cheese and assorted crackers had been placed.

The two men raised their glasses as Davies offered a toast. "Cheers, Stirling, and to the church universal: may the body of Christ prosper throughout God's weary world!"

"Cheers! To the body of Christ!"

The clink of the fine crystal sounded a reverberant ring that marked the genesis of an evening so profound that neither man would ever fail to recall its significance.

"Will you visit Scotland before you return to the States, Stirling?" asked Davies as he sat and sampled the cheese plate, gesturing to McCutcheon to follow suit.

"I have another two weeks before I fly back, and I'll spend those visiting family in Edinburgh."

"Parents and siblings?"

"Parents, one sibling, wife, children, and in-laws."

"That will be a lovely fortnight, no doubt."

"Yes, I fully intend it to be."

"So, your wife and children have gone on ahead of you?" inquired Davies innocently.

"Oh, to be sure. From the beginning of the summer. Heather takes the three children and spends the entire summer with her parents in Edinburgh, which is delightful for all the relatives in Scotland. While it affords me the opportunity to visit my Scottish roots, I find myself less delighted than all the other family members."

"How long have you been in Albany?"

"Three years July first."

"How did you happen to land a pastorate in the States, Stirling?"

"Actually, I went to college in the States, and seminary back in Scotland. Then, fifteen years later, after serving two congregations in Edinburgh, I was called to Madison Avenue Presbyterian Church through the reference of a college classmate who had settled in Albany and was serving on the Pastor Nominating Committee."

"Sounds a bit unusual! As you know, we Anglicans invariably move around only within our own dioceses."

"Granted, it's a bit out of the ordinary as well for us Scottish Presbyterians, but the church I serve has been accustomed to pastors from the United Kingdom. My immediate predecessor was English and the one before him was Welsh Irish."

"Apparently it's more common than I imagined."

"It's not common in American Presbyterian Churches, Gavin, but the pattern is common at Madison Avenue Church. There's something about the nature of this congregation—perhaps a wistful association with the Tories in the early revolutionary days or a riveting fascination with their Scottish roots, perhaps a deep longing for a scholarly ministry or sheer intellectual sophistication—whatever, that unnamed proclivity historically sends every one of their pastoral search committees across the Atlantic to British soil to pluck a ripe prospect from our ecclesiastical tree of life. Of course, it's fine with me. I'm a direct beneficiary of such a practice. There's not the slightest doubt in my belief system regarding this call to ministry among the people of Madison Avenue Presbyterian Church in Albany. The congregational constituents comprise a fertile vineyard, rich in human resources, boundless in compassion." McCutcheon paused, looked distantly into his clutched bourbon, and finally said, "but the needs, Gavin, are infinite. Never before have I encountered such voracious, dissipating unmet needs of people who deem there should be more to life than loneliness and ennui. Resultant choices some of them make leave them finally in emotional ruin and irretrievable despair. In some of these cases, they are swept far above and below the usual vicissitudes of normal living. Thrown about, as it were, by external tempests, but also by the winds of the wars they tacitly declare against themselves." McCutcheon sat quietly, again distant until Davies broke the silence.

"What's your stake in all this, Stirling?"

"Somehow this call has riveted me there. They are all a beautiful people. Many of them have a fractured beauty, and that's my stake in this."

"That matters to you . . . their fractured beauty," Davies observed.

McCutcheon nodded. "Yes."

"Is Heather with you in this . . . what shall we say . . . contract, or divine agreement with the church?"

"I had thought so, but an honest answer would probably be 'no.' Undoubtedly, she will find every opportunity she can to visit Scotland. She considers Americans crude and violent, a sentiment she admits is a sweeping generalization but not one she believes is either crass or unfounded."

"Will you eventually return to Scotland, Stirling?"

"Ten years. I am committed to a ten-year term in the States. Seven more to go. Then we'll return to Edinburgh, but clearly, according to Heather, seven years is a very long time to wait . . . too long!"

Davies raised his glass slowly to his lips, took an ample mouthful of bourbon, which he savored before swallowing, nodded his head thoughtfully, and smiled. "You're swinging on the horns of a dilemma, aren't you, Stirling! And the hell of it is that the dilemma is divine, and each horn is divine. You have a divine call to ministry . . . a divine covenant, to be sure; and your covenant as a husband is sacred as well."

"Yes," acknowledged McCutcheon.

Silence ensued. Davies refilled their glasses.

"Gavin, at dinner this evening, you indicated that Cummins's worldview took into account both the violent interactions of world cultures, as well as the cruelty in our own personal histories, and then you intimated that you examined the evil in your own heart."

"Yes, yes. That's exactly what I meant."

"We're peers here. I have no reason to ingratiate myself to you, so I'd want you to take what I say as an honest comment, a true observation of what I have perceived you to be during these last four days. From the first evening of the first Chapel Talk, I have been convinced that the Holy Spirit has spoken through you. Absolutely certain of it. I believe you are a pure instrument—and I repeat: I need you to take this in the right way—an attractive, compelling, mesmerizing instrument of the Holy Spirit, who conveys fresh, authentic understandings of scripture unencumbered by personal biases or theological slants. My perception is incongruous with your notion that you have to examine evil in your own heart. I don't need to know anything more about you, Gavin. I only need to tell you what I have observed. It's an observation. That's all."

"Stirling, I know you understand that we have all sinned and fallen short of the glory of God. So, to state the obvious, there is evil—or, at the very least, the capacity to do evil—in everyone's heart."

"Understood."

"But the evil to which I was referring earlier this evening has its origin in a personal experience in a specific time in my life. For me to talk about it, I'd have to admit that I have never mentioned that experience to anyone—with the exception of one person."

"You needn't go any further, Gavin. I have made my observation. That's all I needed to do," said McCutcheon, sensing that he had unwittingly probed a dark perplexity.

"No, no. If you'll allow me, I want to continue."

McCutcheon raised his hand to his forehead, deliberated, considered what dark corridors of Davies's mind or past he, Stirling McCutcheon—a veritable stranger prior to glasses of bourbon shared across a coffee table on opposite sofas—might traverse in the ensuing moments . . . or hours.

"Surely, Gavin . . . if you wish," attested McCutcheon.

"True, the Holy Spirit undeniably uses pure instruments. But, if what you say is true, the Holy Spirit also uses impure, flawed instruments, as well. Despite appearances, I harbor an invisible restlessness that has never abated—even for a moment—since those enigmatic, malevolent days when my choices were self-serving and my mindfulness was clouded. It is a restlessness that is different in kind than that which St. Augustine cites when he contends that *our hearts are restless until they find rest in Thee.* No, the restlessness I know is the inevitable result of having espied the countenance of evil, of having looked evil in the eyes and accepted its invitation to consciously choose the wrong. My restlessness is the outcome of knowing the good—what is right—and electing not to do it. Then that restlessness is significantly compounded by the unavoidable realization—when, like the prodigal son, one comes to himself—that the choices one has made cannot be reversed, and the indelible harm one has caused others cannot be erased, and that there are more unforgivable sins than the one to which Jesus refers . . . or that all the unforgivable sins towards others are gathered like evil children under the umbrella of that one unforgivable sin Jesus identified: blasphemy against the Holy Spirit. There is no forgiveness, Stirling, for unforgivable sin, despite what we say to console the desperate one."

McCutcheon sat motionless, intent on every word, fully understanding every nuance.

"When I was a young priest at St. Mary's Church, a small Anglican church in Overton, Wales, one of my elderly parishioners approached me one afternoon on the main street of the village. He was perhaps in his late eighties and still operated a sweet shop in the center of town. He said, 'Pastor, I have a question for you, and perhaps only you can answer it. One of my long-time friends, a married man, when he was younger, had an affair with a woman whom he adored, and his wife, even to the very day of her death, had never found out. Now, in his declining years, he is smitten by guilt and fearful for his soul. Looking back on his clandestine tryst, he is afraid that he will be condemned to the fires of hell. He asked me to ask you if there is any hope for him to be received into heaven in spite of his adultery.' My parishioner's eyes welled up, and I was certain he was using the old ploy of attributing to a fictitious friend his very own confession. 'What should I tell him, Pastor?' Stirling, I said that he should assure his friend that with God nothing is impossible, that in Jesus Christ we are forgiven the most grievous of sins we can possibly imagine. His friend need only ask Christ to forgive the sin he names, and he will be forgiven. Tell him that, I said, and his heart and soul will be at rest."

"Was your answer reassuring to your parishioner, Gavin?" McCutcheon asked quietly.

"Sure. A few months later I officiated at his funeral in the church, presided at the table, and commended him into God's hands, trusting in God's mercy. I felt certain at the time that he also, at long last, trusted in God's mercy."

"And you?" McCutcheon asked.

"My answer to his question was straight out of the pastoral care volumes we studied in seminary. It worked for him . . . it doesn't work for me."

"Why? What's different? I don't think the nature of God's mercy has changed in the intermittent years between Overton and Hawarden, have they?"

"No, it's the magnitude of the matter."

Davies filled his glass for a final time, drank, and placed it on the coffee table.

"Nearly five years ago," he said, "an American couple attended St. Deiniol's Church. They were both very impressive and stood out in the congregation. As they greeted me before leaving, they indicated they had rented a flat in Hawarden and would remain in Wales on business for six to ten months. Later in the week, upon their invitation, I visited them at their apartment and learned that he was an executive with IBM, the Vice President of Acquisitions. His job was to acquire the various facilities of businesses that had failed and to establish IBM branches throughout the country. Obviously, very bright. Obviously, very well off financially. Brett and Laura

Coverley, two of the most engaging people I have ever met in my life. Their home in the States was Rhinebeck, that charming town we mentioned previously, Stirling. All the while Brett spoke about his IBM mandate, there was a nearly palpable burning in my chest as Laura trained her eyes on me—wondering, inquisitive eyes. At the close of the evening, they stated that they would be attending St. Deiniol's Church during the duration of their stay in Wales and would like to be involved as fully as their time would allow them. I offered a prayer of thanksgiving for their safe arrival in Wales and a blessing on their new, though temporary, home, and I left.

"The following week a telephone call came from Laura Coverley, in which she requested a pastoral visit. When the predetermined day had arrived, she suggested that I stay for lunch. It was a chilly day with a substantial bite in the air. When I entered the apartment, I noticed Laura had laid a welcoming fire in the drawing room and had prepared tuna salad on wick, wrapped in foil and heated through by the fire. As we sat on the floor at the hearth and attended to the carefully-prepared lunch, there was little I could identify that characterized this as a pastoral visit. Even the most mundane question or the least self-disclosing answer seemed to chart a mutual path toward an unintended union, or if not unintended, at least not consciously plotted. A casual hand on mine to emphasize a point, or a wry smile to soften a derisive reference to her husband, or a demure glance over her shoulder as she cleared the dishes from the floor . . . every gesture, every expression pointed me to metaphorical wrist shackles into which I would choose to slip my hands and lock them. My choice. In those moments, I could choose to make a bet with Mephistopheles and consign my soul to Sheol just to satisfy that raging fire in my chest, or not. And I did."

"You did?"

"I did. Imagine, if you will, Stirling, what such a salacious salutation to evil does to a man's soul."

"Aye."

Both men sat pensively searching the depths of their bourbon, McCutcheon slowly swirling his, Davies grasping his tightly as if it could be coaxed with persuasion to deliver up an answer to his remorse.

"From what deep wellspring did her unabated passions arise? I had never before experienced anything like it. We were one soul, one flesh, moving in and out of the other's sacred space, soaring to a peak where the air was too thin to breathe, falling and then soaring again, nearly to the point of losing consciousness, until spent, we lay in a silent union of indelible betrayal. Who could have articulated it in that moment? Neither of us, but in that moment a new, impassioned allegiance was bought at the immeasurable price of a fatal betrayal of familial loyalties.

"As we lay quietly, intertwined, Laura admitted what she would enunciate numerous times in the future, that she felt the same craving as the Black Widow Spider: to make love with the male and then consume him, to devour him to the last fleshly morsel. This entire scenario, concluding with the same declaration, found its repetition frequently throughout the ensuing months . . . almost on every occasion Brett traveled on business. All the other times Brett was at home, we engaged in the charade of pastor and parishioner.

"There came a day weeks into the affair that I could no longer endure the duplicity. I informed Anwen, my wife, that I needed time away from her and the children to sort out my identity, which led her to believe that it was a gender issue. She inquired as to whether I was actually gay or bisexual. 'No judgment,' she said. 'Just tell me.' I said I didn't know, but I needed to work it out on my own. Anwen agreed. We told the children on a Sunday afternoon, the worst day of my life, barring none. I took a flat in Hawarden, showed it to the children, and, despite the upheaval, we had some excellent times there.

"Taking a flat in Hawarden, however good it was for the children and me, raised suspicions on the part of members of the congregation and the bishop. One strictly evangelical member of the church wrote me, saying that undoubtedly there was a problem between my wife and me. She cautioned, 'If you are thinking of divorcing your wife Anwen, you will decimate the congregation and disillusion adults and children alike. I urge you to think carefully about this matter.' I kept the affair to myself, however, and continued stating that I simply needed time to think through my marriage. The inevitable day arrived when the bishop called me into the Diocesan Office, informed me that he would give me six months to work this separation through to a conclusion, and, depending on my decision, he would decide what to do with me professionally. In the meantime the bishop expected me to perform my duties at the church and to make my decision carefully, first and foremost, keeping my wife and children—their well-being—in mind.

"Perhaps it was five months into the affair when Brett returned from one of his extended trips, actually abroad to Greece as I recall. He brought back a gift for me, an object that he thought might hold some religious cultural interest. It was a small, carved, reddish porcelain statuary, which stood not more than two inches high. It was a representation of Medusa, one of the Gorgons with a tangle of snakes for hair and eyes that turn people into stone. Brett informed me that since I was in the business of religion and spirituality, he thought a priest might find this interesting as an icon that supposedly kept away evil. 'The natives of the Greek island hand it to anyone,' he explained, 'whom they deem is evil or possesses an evil spirit with the ability to harm them. This little icon protects them from evil.' It was long after the Coverleys left Wales to return to Rhinebeck when I realized that Brett perceived me as a threat and gave me the icon to keep me away from his wife. The passion never diminished, and the icon didn't work . . . at least for some time.

"I had given Laura a gold cross pendent in the form of an Ankh, which, as you know, is the Egyptian cross, the crux ansata, a symbol of life, even eternal life. My meaning was to declare that ours was an eternal, inseparable union. As often as I thought that she and I were in an inseparable union, however, there were still mysteries—seemingly indecipherable mysteries—about Laura. At times she would withdraw so completely that I couldn't reach her—any part of her—no matter what approach I employed. I could only assume that, during those times, she was exploring those internal, vast wastelands and was lost . . . not alone and bored, but, rather, lost and unloved. And I wondered at those empty spaces in Laura's gestalt. One day, as I recall vividly, I discovered a missing piece.

"Her mother and father had come from the States to visit the Coverleys. Laura and her father went shopping, and while in one of the stores, her father suffered a severe heart attack. He was rushed to hospital. Laura called me and asked me to pick up her mother at the flat and bring her to the hospital waiting room, all of which I did. What I saw I shall never forget. Her mother entered the waiting room. Laura rushed to meet her, threw her arms around her, and held her firmly, kindly, lovingly. But her mother never reciprocated. She stood like a stone statue, her arms riveted to her side. Nothing. No emotional response. No love, no affection, no intimacy for her daughter. Venus de Milo—without arms—could have offered more reassuring comfort. Laura's gestalt was filling in.

"Her parents' extended stay complicated matters. We seldom saw each other except on two or three occasions when she stopped by my flat. It was on one of those occurrences when I explored options for our future together. I told her I was ready to divorce, to face the professional consequences, and marry her. She grew sullen. 'Certainly not, Gavin! It's unthinkable. How would you support us?' She left that day, making crystal clear the nature of her investment in our relationship. Another part of the gestalt fell into place. There was no way to compete with an IBM executive. Like many other females, she had looked over available males and chosen to marry one with the largest caches, like the African Village Weaverbird who enters the male's flamboyant nest, examines it for its high quality, and makes her choice for the only male who makes a superior nest with superior resources.

"Soon after this encounter in my flat, our relationship deteriorated rapidly. I heard from her less and less. Neither she nor Brett attended church regularly. Laura had no intention of separating from her husband and staying with me in Wales. The affair concluded a month before the Coverleys returned to Rhinebeck.

"I last visited Laura and Brett the day before the Coverleys departed for the States. In the course of the conversation, I apologized for any intrusion I may have made in their lives while in Wales. Before I left, Laura covertly handed me a key to a baggage locker at the railway station; and when I left, I thought all was well. The following day, however, before they headed to the airport, I received a telephone call from Laura.

"She told me in no uncertain terms: 'You really know how to screw up people's lives, don't you!'

"I was confused. 'What do you mean?'

"'Brett took your comment on *intruding in our lives* as a confession that you and I were lovers.'

"'I had no intention of intimating that.'

"She emphatically insisted that I never contact her in the future: 'I can never see you again. The problem is that I still love you, Gavin, and I can never see you again.'

"I swore to her that she would never see me nor hear from me, ever again. 'But before you hang up, Laura, I'll tell you whose lives I've really screwed up, to use your term. I've screwed up Anwen's life and my children's lives. I didn't do it alone, but I certainly did it!'

"The following day I went to the railway station, found the locker that corresponded to the number on the key, opened it, and discovered all the greeting cards and love letters I had sent her, as well as a book titled, *The Legacy of Stone*. There in the railway station I sat and read the book, then lingered—interminably, it seemed—on a key sentence she had underlined: *I ask, if my parents can't love me, who can?*

"Inside the last page and the back cover was the gold Ankh on the gold chain . . . obviously, there was nothing eternal about it. I left the station, went to my flat, read all the cards and love letters, set them on the fireplace grate, and struck a match. The book I placed in a sacred space.

"The six-month period the bishop had allowed me to work through the separation with my wife had come to an end, and the bishop had arranged a meeting. Days prior to my appointment with the bishop, I reconciled with Anwen, telling her the truth, sought her forgiveness, and reestablished a commitment to mutual trust. She was pure grace, a marvelous woman of the highest noble nature, but who had been hurt to the point of indelible scarring at the foundation of her once convivial spirit. What had I done to her? And why?"

Davies lifted his glass to his lips and swallowed deeply.

"You said you have no plans to travel to Rhinebeck, Gavin," McCutcheon said after a long silence.

Davies nodded assent.

"I understand."

"I've kept my word. Until my last breath, I'll keep my word."

"But do you still struggle with Laura's edict to stay away, to disappear, to blot out your mutual past?"

"Yes."

Davies turned his gaze to the hunt board across the room, and at the foot-high statuary of Jules Dalou's *The Bather* sitting there. Laura's graceful form flooded his memory, but it proved to be only a memory, a fading memory at that.

"Do you find yourself thinking of her still?" asked McCutcheon, following his glance toward the hunt board.

"Her emphatic insistence keeps me at bay, but her final words keep me hooked."

"Which words?"

"She said, 'the problem is that I still love you, Gavin.' What am I to do with that?"

"What *do* you do with it?"

"I ride the tempestuous, relentless winds."

"What do you mean?"

"I'm sure you remember that the Second Circle in Dante's *Inferno* is designated for people who were overcome by lust. They are punished by being blown about incessantly by turbulent winds; and, accordingly, they find themselves in an eternal state of restlessness. Two of the most tragic lovers found there are Francesca di Rimini and Paolo Malatesta, both of whom are killed by Paolo's brother Gianciotto, who is married to Francesca. Subsequently, Francesca and Paolo were buried in a common tomb and endured a common fate, being blown about eternally by unforgiving winds. But, Stirling, here's the most poignant parallel: they could have been at rest—the winds would have ceased—if they would only repent and give up their love. They stubbornly refuse, and persisting in their adulterous love is the very source of their perpetual agony. You see, Stirling, how haunting the sentiment, 'I still love you, Gavin'!"

The silence grew more profound.

"Will you ride the winds to your grave, Gavin?"

"I don't know. I can't determine whether my restlessness is due to an ongoing love for Laura—which is impossible for me to express and for her to return—or whether it is perpetuated by sheer eviscerating guilt. In the first consideration, I identify with the Byronic hero, who willfully engages in a passionate love that—though he is fully cognizant of its implausibility—is categorically impossible to bring to fruition. Consequently, he endures an endless torment and is thrust about by lacerating winds of craving."

"And your second consideration, Gavin . . . restlessness due to sheer eviscerating guilt?"

"I can't get beyond it, Stirling. As I mentioned, years ago I was able to give comfort and reassurance to my old parishioner who cheated on his unsuspecting wife. With God, nothing is impossible; our Savior forgives the most heinous of sins. But there is no way I can apply that to myself. Since I messed up the Coverleys's lives, I have never felt a modicum of forgiveness . . . even during those utterances in the sacred liturgy when either I declare—or another announces— *in Jesus Christ we are forgiven.*"

"I don't understand, Gavin. The word of forgiveness applies to everyone else, but not to you? Is that what you're saying?"

"Yes."

"There are some who would contend that that is the apex of arrogance, that you are so above God's forgiveness that it can't reach you, or that you are so mired in your guilt, so low at the extremity of sin that God's grace is rendered impotent."

"I know. I've heard it before. But that's not it. It's not arrogance."

"Then what?"

"It's betrayal. In my case, betrayal is the cause of messing up other people's lives, and mine. Every kiss in my relationship with Laura was a kiss of betrayal. Every other kiss on Anwen's lips was a kiss of betrayal compounded by destructive duplicity.

Stirling, listen to me. You can accept it as truth when I say I believe irrefutably that betrayal is the unforgivable sin. You know as well as I that there are biblical scholars who contend that Judas Iscariot was the foreordained designee of the means of God's salvation. Redemption by way of the cross could not have happened without Judas's act of betrayal. The conclusion to this argument is that Judas is not only forgiven as an essential part of God's plan, but that he enjoys a special place in the heart of God. On the other hand, there are other biblical scholars who maintain that Judas's kiss of betrayal earned him a unique place in the bowels of hell, a prime space in everlasting outer darkness. My conclusion to the argument is that betrayal is the unforgivable sin; I hold with those who believe Judas is a hopeless, irredeemable outcast."

Davies raised his glass and drank deeply. "If only the porcelain Medusa could have effected its influence sooner!" he whispered hoarsely.

McCutcheon kept his eyes on Davies throughout an ensuing interval of silence, until a question finally occurred to him.

"Gavin, did anything good come from your relationship with Laura?"

Davies set his glass on the coffee table, leaned back in the love seat, and folded his arms. He had raised the same question to himself numerous times in the past, but now considered it with a probing, self-analytical inquiry.

"Yes, I think so," rejoined Davies reflectively, then assertively said, "I'm rather sure of it. From the hospital waiting room encounter with her mother, it became clear to me that she couldn't have felt loved by her parents . . . even as her underlining that very part of the book she left for me conveyed, attesting that she was never good enough to have her parents' love. If there was anything she could not deny in our relationship, it was that she was loved . . . probably as she had never been loved before . . . especially if part of her motive for marrying and staying married to Brett was to keep his gilded nest. In that gilded nest, she fell into a maddening state of loneliness and ennui, into an inexplicable loneliness. Until their arrival in Wales, I suspect she had never known an all-consuming passion, the very passion we experienced mutually in our love. Despite the shameful atrocity of the dishonest circumstances, to have experienced the concrete reality of an authentic love is an undeniable good, even the *summum bonum*. It's what all the crooners sing about but only a few are fortunate enough to discover."

McCutcheon nodded affirmatively. "And what about you?"

"A couple with three children are susceptible to ennui as well, or, better said, to connubial complacency," asserted Davies. "Speaking of falling into an undesirable state, Anwen and I had comfortably descended into that connubial complacency. Nothing was wrong, but, by the same token, nothing was exciting, nothing was new, nothing was exhilarating. Everything for her was about maintaining the household, where the children and I looked to her on all household operations in the everyday drama of life. On the other hand, for me, I was completely consumed by ecclesiastical commitments, which left little energy or interest in romantic encounters between the sheets of our nuptial bed. The good that emerged from the bad was a revisiting of a former life force. My tryst with Laura awakened an old passion I have subsequently put to use in my revived love with Anwen. Whether Anwen understands this dynamic as the result of an illicit assignation or has simply thought of it as my attempting to make up for my frightful infidelity, I can't say. I don't know. All I know is that it's very good for us now."

"There are times," rejoined McCutcheon, "when, in retrospect, I feel overwhelmed with regret: regret about poor choices that inevitably result in dire consequences. Then it occurs to me that everyone I know has suffered the same dynamic of cause and effect. Not that I find any comfort in the old adage that misery loves company but, rather, that God brings us up short on our Damascus Roads and redirects our passions into his purposes. You could tick off as well as I in a matter of minutes a hundred people from scripture who travelled their own self-directed, misdirected roads, only to be brought up short by that blinding light: including King David mired in concupiscence, Saul of Tarsus steeped in vengeance, Elijah hiding from Jezebel, James and John seeking privilege, Peter cowering in denial. On and on. Any of us with an ounce of integrity would admit that at some point in our journey we ignored the compass—either the practical or the moral compass—and rode like the wind in the wrong direction. Such acts of willfulness have played a prominent part in our personal—even clandestine—histories and are likely to play a significant role in our personal futures. It's not the turn in the road we miss that's lamentable, but, rather, it's the road we fatefully choose and then—upon a doleful discovery—regretfully acknowledge as the willful road, one that seemed enticing enough, even romantic, with an adventurous lure or carefully calculated with limited information or inadequate experience. It might have been indeed a calculated choice that later for some reason—for any reason, for a twist of good fortune gone bad, or an unexpected turn of circumstances—changed direction and turned sour. For whatever reason, that road was a willful road, a mistake, a miscalculation that required a turning back or forging a new direction. For whatever reason we chose the enticing roads in the first place—whomever we have hurt along the way, whoever has made the personal sacrifices to help us survive, whatever we have learned in the course of our blunders—God uses the blinding light in our darkness, brings us up short, and sends us back into his design."

Davies moved to the edge of the love seat. "Agreed, Stirling, but the regret for being so long on that willful road, so invested in the misdirected road! The regret, Stirling! Perhaps—given what you've said—you have tasted that biting, stinging, rancid regret that lingers in your mouth, oozes out of the pores of your soul, and makes the air around you fetid . . . absolutely foul. Believe me, it rots the soul!"

McCutcheon stood and moved to the hunt board, turned and answered intently, "Yes, but aren't you now in God's new design for your life? Intellectually, Gavin, you know the good news of the gospel: in Jesus Christ, we are forgiven. For Christ's sake— and for your own sake—own it! Believe it! Accept it!"

"Then grant me Christ's absolution, Stirling! I need to be absolved of this sin that seemed so beautiful and pure, but was so cunning and captivating. I want to be released from these miserable manacles into which I inserted my wrists!"

"I can't. Christ's forgiveness has already been given. But one thing's missing," said McCutcheon softly.

"What? . . . what's missing?"

"You haven't forgiven yourself. It's only your forgiving yourself in conjunction with Christ's forgiveness that invalidates your original pact with that Mephistopheles to whom you referred . . . or deferred," McCutcheon contended as he seated himself again on the love seat.

Davies sat with his head in his hands, interminably, it seemed.

"All right. You're right. I haven't forgiven myself, but I'm willing to acknowledge that God has used the wrong road I have taken to bring me to the right place I'm in now . . . and I forgive myself. I forgive myself. In Jesus Christ I am forgiven, and I forgive myself."

Davies moved to the hunt board on which a crucifix was centered. He knelt, and he prayed: "Have mercy on me, O God, according to your loving-kindness: in your great compassion blot out my offenses. Wash me through and through from my wickedness, and cleanse me from my sin of infidelity and betrayal."

McCutcheon moved behind him, laid his hands on Davies's head, and asked, "Gavin Davies, do you believe that the word of forgiveness I speak to you comes from God himself?"

"Yes. I believe," responded Davies.

"God is merciful and blesses you. By the command of our Lord Jesus Christ, I, a called and ordained servant of the Word, speak to you Christ's word of forgiveness, which absolves you of your sins in the name of the Father, and of the Son, and of the Holy Spirit. Amen. As you are forgiven in Christ, and, in light of his forgiveness, as you have forgiven yourself your transgressions, may you go in peace to serve the Lord, living in his grace and in his boundless love."

Davies rose to a new height, a liberated man, a newly-purified instrument of the Holy Spirit. He reached for a small wooden box on the hunt board, opened it, and pulled out the gold Ankh, which he placed in McCutcheon's hand.

"Please," he said. "It holds no value for me."

Gavin and Stirling embraced . . . a long, firm embrace filled with resolution; and McCutcheon left.

14

The Lure of Farquharson

McCutcheon's train from Chester pulled into Waverley Station promptly at 3:15 p.m. The week of study leave at Gladstone's Library had been an extraordinary experience, and parting from Gavin Davies had affected him more than he had anticipated.

In all his years of ministry in the church, as often as he had read the books of First and Second Samuel, until now he could never fully understand the force—the élan vital—of the covenant formed between David and Jonathan, who claimed that he was knit to the soul of David and that he loved David as his own soul. There had been no point of reference in all McCutcheon's experience that could potentially rivet a vow in him to a claim such as Jonathan's. Such deep love between two men eluded his comprehension. When Jonathan was killed in battle, David's lament—that *Jonathan lies slain upon thy high places . . . I am distressed for you, my brother Jonathan; very pleasant have you been to me; your love to me was wonderful, passing the love of women*—was as an ethereal, esoteric refrain from an invisible cloud. There had never been a sterling propinquity of that description in McCutcheon's life . . . until the previous week.

By the time the Chester Express had come to a complete stop, passengers were standing in the aisles ready to detrain. He waited pensively for the aisle to clear before he lifted his luggage from the rack and made his way to the door, down the steps, and onto the platform. Heather was waiting with a broad smile and a ready embrace, sustained and firm, filled with all the longing for resolution that their mutual separateness had fostered since the day they parted at the Albany airport.

"Hello, Darling," she whispered audibly, "welcome home!"

They kissed with little deference to anyone who might be observing their reconnected solitudes.

"Hey, my lovely lassie! Good to be home with you!" said McCutcheon, refusing to release his hold on her, until at last he placed her at arm's length to gain a full view of her. Tall and stately as ever, though a bit thinner, she was wearing a summer outfit that complimented her exquisite form and caused her inherent beauty to shine in the sunlight. Her Celtic cross hung gracefully from the chain on her neck. "Are you losing weight?" McCutcheon picked up his valise and they headed—her arm locked in his—toward the station and baggage claim.

"No," she said, "but if I am, it wouldn't hurt anything. I could stand to give up a few pounds here or there."

"No, yourself, Heather! You're perfect just the way you are. I don't want to make love to a beanpole," he retorted, smiling.

"Oh, now, there's my answer. I didn't know whether you wanted to make love at all or not . . . don't you know, after all this time," she said, easing his arm closer to her torso.

McCutcheon searched her eyes for a deeper meaning behind her gentle quip, then took it at face value. "*Especially* after all this time, my love!" he said genuinely and opened the door to the station for her.

"Walter is waiting at the car in front of the station," Heather said. "He'll pick up your luggage if you give him your claim check."

"Good afternoon, Mr. McCutcheon," Walter said with a deferential bow, respectable but not obsequious. Walter did not remove his chauffeur's hat, a gesture he reserved for greeting only women. "Was it a pleasant trip from Wales, sir?"

"Quite, thank you, Walter!" McCutcheon answered. "Very good to see you again! I trust the Chisholms are well."

"Yes, indeed, sir. Spitting images of robust health! I daresay they could model for any of the Edinburgh health journals and be mistaken for ten years younger than they truly are."

"Good news, Walter!" McCutcheon said, searching his billfold for claim checks. "Mrs. McCutcheon intimated that you would pick up my luggage. I have the claim checks here."

"Glad to, sir!" acknowledged the congenial chauffeur as he opened the door to the rear seat of the Rolls Royce. Heather and McCutcheon settled into the luxuriant comfort of this living room on wheels.

Turning to her, he asked about the children: where they might be, what they're up to these days, how they are enjoying the summer, whether they miss any of their friends in the States? All of her responses comprised exactly what he expected to hear, except in regards to the last question.

"As to missing any of their friends in the States, Stirling," she admitted reluctantly, "they don't . . . not actually. Perhaps they reminisce about their Albany classmates when I'm not around; but, to be perfectly honest, they haven't mentioned a single one of them in my presence. Not one."

"What about their friends here?" he queried, fully cognizant that old Scottish friendships were winning the day with his three children, which potentially portended a poignant inner struggle for all of them come the scheduled day of their return to the States at summer's end.

"It's as if we had never left. Their bonds of friendship are strong."

They heard Walter open the boot of the car, lift the luggage into place, and within minutes, having left the congested city traffic behind, they were moving along the motorway towards the Chisholm estate. The countryside seemed unusually lush for this time of year. Apparently an inordinate amount of rainfall had washed the earth immaculately clean so that the verdant meadows along the motorway shone with a sparkling iridescence more luxuriant than McCutcheon could recall ever seeing previously. In places along the way, Birnam Oaks, like so many Scots Guards, lined either side of the road. In the distance, the rich lavender of Flora Heather covered the graceful hills, and between the Birnam Oaks saluting the motorway and the Flora Heather waving from a distance, McCutcheon spotted occasional dwarf shrubs of Bell Heather and Scottish Primrose. Every sensory perception informed him incontrovertibly that he was back in his homeland, the bonnie realm of Scotland.

Walter drove into the circular driveway and brought the car to a gentle halt in front of the mansion. For a matter of minutes, Heather and McCutcheon stood beside the car and gazed silently at the vast stretches of land around them. Virtually everything in sight composed Farquharson Heights. A poignant ambivalence rose like searing heartburn in his breast, for as much as the soothing contentment of standing again on Scotland's soil brought a peace and rest to his soul—long beleaguered by the crucibles of his American parishioners—he felt the ravaging inadequacy of his financial impotence in the face of this expansive affluence. While Heather would one day inherit all of this that surrounded them and filled their purview, McCutcheon would never be in a position to provide for her and the children as her parents have in the past. And every current act of generosity on their part only served to accentuate the disparate chasm between Farquharson Heights and the Madison Manse.

"Magnificent, isn't it, Stirling!" Heather whispered as she took in the riveting splendor of the *mise en scène*. "Are you glad to be here?"

"I am," McCutcheon rejoined, consigning his reservations and aforesaid ambivalence to silence.

At that moment, the front door of the mansion opened and Heather's parents emerged, sporting broad smiles and offering open arms. A giant of a man, Ainsley Chisholm towered above his wife by at least eight inches. Not that Inghean was a diminutive woman by any stretch of the imagination, but her husband reached at least six feet six inches on the charts and undoubtedly weighed in at two hundred and twenty pounds. He had a round, ruddy face with a well-groomed red beard, a brighter red than his thick head of hair of a deeper crimson tone muted by grey hues at his temples. His was a high forehead that rose nobly into his front hairline, and while he wore his hair slightly over the tops of his ears, it was a magnificent mane, in which every hair knew its place and employed obedience to it wearer's will. His nose was long and straight, his cheekbones high, his eyebrows also thick but obviously attended to; and his dark brown eyes danced in their sockets when he spoke. Even a cursory study of the man would note that one is quickly drawn to his unusually thick neck and massive, broad shoulders, straight and powerful. The barreled chest tapering down to a well-defined waist completed the image of a man who has maintained his extraordinary, immaculately-groomed, military physique into his early sixties. Everything about Ainsley Chisholm's appearance intimated perfection, and, to be sure, the only imperfection of which McCutcheon was cognizant was quite invisible: Chisholm's anosmia.

His military career in the Scots Guard had been one of personal distinction and acknowledged accomplishment, resulting in the high rank of *General* by the time of his retirement six years ago. During a three-year tour in India, however, Chisholm had contracted malaria and, for three months, had lain critically ill in a British hospital near Calcutta. While it appeared that he had made a full recovery, it soon became clear that he had subsequently lost his sense of smell—anosmia—and, as a consequence, his sense of taste as well. But, looking at him now on the front porch of his massive mansion, who would know? He cut the figure of an absolutely perfect human specimen, one who possessed a talisman for eternal vigor, one who demonstrated the indefatigable verve of a Herculean colossus.

"How grand to see you, Stirling, my lad!" It was first a bone-crunching handshake, then an engulfing embrace so forceful that it undoubtedly left, for an instant, his body imprint on McCutcheon's smaller form.

"Marvelous to see you as well, sir . . . Ainsley!" McCutcheon responded hoarsely, wondering if his lungs had collapsed in the embrace. For years he had called Chisholm *sir* but finally had taken his corrections to heart and resorted to addressing him as his equal: *Ainsley.* To be quite direct, however, from the day of his marriage to Heather, he had never felt the actual sense of equality in his relationship with her father. Perhaps his height and massive figure sabotaged any hope of that, or perhaps his inestimable wealth and military accomplishments caused his Christian name to stick in McCutcheon's throat.

He recalled the day it all changed for him, the day Chisholm and he sat in Farquharson Heights drawing room. Over a glass of sherry, he told McCutcheon he would give up all of his wealth—every last thing he owned—if he could have the faith McCutcheon had, if he could believe that there is more to life than *having,* if he could be certain that there is a life beyond these few short years on earth.

"Stirling," he said, "as you know, I've been a Covenanter all my life, but the one uncertainty that torments me is that about the actual reality of eternal life. To be sure, the likelihood that there is only nothingness after death consumes me. For the three months I lay in a hospital bed in Calcutta, Inghean constantly at my side, I experienced a mental anguish I never want to envision again . . . ever again. I knew there were hallucinations caused by the fever, but there were also visions created by the fear of nothingness."

From that very moment—from the day Chisholm became vulnerable with Mc-Cutcheon, when the realities or the possibilities of non-existence eclipsed his rich garners—McCutcheon acknowledged a mutual, egalitarian footing and accepted his invitation to address him as a peer. In that drawing room, on that day, for McCutcheon, his humiliation—once forged and tempered before an incalculable prosperity—turned into simple humility at the acknowledgement of a common humanity.

When Chisholm left off from the robust greeting, Inghean stepped in to extend her impeccable hospitality with warm embraces and familial kisses. "My dear Stirling, it has been such an intolerably long time!" Inghean exclaimed with an emphatic, earnest tone, each principal word accentuated with a note of genuine benignity. "It has been heavenly having Heather and the children here! There is nothing like it in all the world . . . nothing that brings Ainsley and me greater joy than being surrounded by our family . . . except . . ." Here she stopped with an obviously calculated aposiopesis and then, with the gesture of a judge striking her gavel on her high desk, repeated her last word with uncanny force, ". . . *except* . . . when we have the entire family together! Now, Stirling, our joy is absolutely complete!" She took McCutcheon's arm in hers with a most decisive grip and marched him to the front door. "Come in, come in, come in, dear boy, dear son!" she ejaculated like a town crier. "We shall kill the fatted calf and ignore all the jealous cavils of the elder brother!" Adopting a playful whisper, she put her mouth to his ear and murmured, "as if there were any elder brother around here." With this, like a barmaid in a London pub, she let out a resounding peel of laughter, which, they all knew, served to spread yet another layer of Gilead balm over the gaping wound in her lacerated heart.

Indeed there had been an elder brother. Laughter ultimately took his place when it became certain that he would never return from the deep, when it became known that he had bobbed about on the heaving waves for endless days before he slipped exhausted into the deep, "there to sleep," Inghean had moaned over and over, "there to sleep while I weep . . . no, no, while *we* weep, while we weep . . . his pilot wings, his little metal badge of courage on his airman's coat, could not lift him up from off those avaricious waves that readily swallow innocent, unsuspecting boys . . ." Inghean had prattled on unintelligibly day-after-day, having begun to prattle on the very day the piercing blow had struck her in the heart. Then it was weeks and months. Now it is years, but no more prattling. Laughter now fills the void. It isn't an easy laughter; nor is it an empty laughter; it is an imitative laughter. It is the sound and tone and timbre of the laughter that characterized their son's mirth. His hilarity once reverberated through the cavernous chambers of Farquharson Heights, waves of bacchanalian laughter that later succumbed to waves of an implacable submission. Ultimately, Inghean had to choose. Going on as a willowy shadow without substance, devoid of essence, was not optional. She must either join her son in the dark deep or replace him with the resounding laughter that embodied his preternatural spirit.

"Inghean, my dear Mother Inghean," McCutcheon said as they walked through the foyer and into the gargantuan, ornate living room, "to be sure, there is an elder brother around here. There will always be an elder brother around here, but he will never carp at our killing the fatted calf, for he is remembered in such joyous revelry, and his presence is never felt so warmly as when there is such joyous revelry and unbounded laughter."

Inghean was still walking with her armed looped into his; and, upon hearing this comment, she pulled his arm closer to her with almost a desperate grip, as if she were attempting to pull something from a vast distance into her proximate body. Stirling could feel the shape of her right breast just above his left elbow as she clung to his arm.

"You are right, dear boy!" she said with a sad smile. "You are right! There is an elder son here, and now his dear younger brother has returned." She stopped, leaned toward him, and kissed his cheek. How warm! How welcoming! How familial! How nostalgic! No son-in-law could ask for more from a set of affectionate in-laws. What was more remarkable to McCutcheon was that the very fabric of this hospitality displayed by both of Heather's parents contained the threads of intrinsic acceptance, devoid of unarticulated expectations. Of this he was certain, for during his entire visit to Farquharson Heights, neither Inghean nor Ainsley—either together or separately—pressed him to return to Scotland and reestablish their home in Edinburgh. Certainly they must have known of Heather's discontent in the States . . . or perhaps they didn't. Perhaps Heather spared them the acidic distaste she felt at heart for her circumstantial exile in Albany. As McCutcheon revisited the thought, undoubtedly their daughter considered the heaviness her parents carried and disguised every waking moment regarding her brother's death and, in light of that, remained tacit about her own *fin de siècle*—her own world-weariness. Certainly the Chisholms wanted their daughter and grandchildren near them but, for whatever reason, they adopted and maintained a stance of non-interference, never forced the issue . . . never so much as broached the subject.

Ainsley and Heather—also on her father's arm—followed Inghean and McCutcheon into the living room, where they sat for afternoon tea. Inghean rang for Edana, who promptly appeared with a large tray of tea, tea sandwiches, scones and cakes. When it came to maids, butlers, chauffeurs, and other household servants, there was hardly ever any turnover among the Chisholms' personnel. All of these McCutcheon had known since Heather and he began courting nearly twenty years ago.

Edana greeted Stirling warmly as one well-known. "Good afternoon, Pastor McCutcheon. Welcome home to Farquharson Heights, sir," she said with a broad smile and a slight bow of the head.

"Good afternoon to you as well, Edana," McCutcheon rejoined with identical warmth. "I trust you have been well this past year?"

"Quite well, sir, thank you. It is a pleasure to have your family with us these summer days . . . and an added delight that you have come as well."

"I'm sure we shall enjoy every minute of the holiday," he assured her . . . or was it he himself whom he was assuring? Edana made her gracious exit and within minutes all of them had settled into a comfortable conversation over tea.

Inghean directed her gaze intently across the tea table at McCutcheon. Heather was sitting beside her father on the sofa to Inghean's left. Without including Heather in her gaze, she trained her eyes on McCutcheon. "The children are growing splendidly, Stirling. Wouldn't you say so?"

"Quite," he readily affirmed. "You must realize, Inghean, it's Heather's doing."

"Surely not entirely!" Inghean exclaimed. "I can see your hand, as well, in the whole business of their blossoming. Clearly there are two imprints on each of them."

"Perhaps," McCutcheon acknowledged, "but I'm sure you would agree that, customarily, in the home, the woman exercises the greater influence on the household regarding norms of behavior. She sets the moral standards, models the principles of kind and considerate interaction among family members, and encourages individuals' pursuits of self-expression. In point of fact, she is the exemplar of love's indelible effects. That's how it is in our household, Inghean."

"Granted, Stirling, that's the quiddity of the matter. The most pertinent question, however, is whether the children can grow without you?"

McCutcheon at once felt his vessel's being commandeered, wrested from its moorings, and headed out to deep waters.

"They could, if need be, Inghean, with Heather's vigilant guidance. But, to be sure, there'll be no need of it."

As mused earlier, neither Ainsley nor Inghean had ever pressed him to return home to Edinburgh to live. At least up to this point. Could the current be changing? A warm, accepting expression on Inghean's countenance, however, indicated that this was a friendly discussion, perhaps an exploration of familial waters previously uncharted, previously avoided.

McCutcheon reached for his ship's wheel to take control of the direction of the dialogue and to avoid the rapid current.

"Unless there is some unforeseen misfortune, dear Mother Inghean, the children need not grow without me. Though Heather is perpetually there for each of them, while she occupies the supreme position in the home, I remain at the helm."

During this verbal exchange, Ainsley and Heather had remained silent, though neither had looked away for an instant. Her father's daughter in this regard, Heather rarely pulled away from a verbal encounter. Ainsley usually welcomed a joust, friendly or hostile, though a preferred friendly joust in the family allowed for greater opportunities to insert humor, comic relief, if necessary.

Inghean nodded ascent. "Just as I thought, Stirling," she said, her words emitting an aroma of affirmation, and a smile. McCutcheon noted it was a sad smile all the same.

Edana entered the room to freshen the tea and scones. "Will there be anything else, my lady?"

"Thank you, no, Edana."

As Edana disappeared through the archway, Ainsley addressed McCutcheon. "It's a matter that is simple to explain and simple to grasp. You are a son to us, Stirling. The interminable intervals between visits create an inextinguishable yearning. Heather and the children mollify that greatly, but, as you might suspect, we want it all," he laughed heartily, somewhat apologetically. "We realize that that proclivity is a bit crass and enormously greedy, but you are the missing X factor in the equation."

"It won't be like this forever, Ainsley," McCutcheon ventured to explain. "A few more years will fill the bill."

"We know, laddie. It's an important work you do. No expectations on our part, believe me. Just to tell you our thoughts."

"Noted," said McCutcheon, "with thanks!"

Stirling glanced at Heather. Her face was a *tabula rasa*, her motionless figure a *tableau vivant*. The one person in his life he had known so well appeared in that instant an inscrutable enigma. There was no conceivable justification for deeming Heather a stoic; nor could she be found at the other extreme among women who are lachrymose. To McCutcheon, ordinarily, she was characteristically readable. But not now. Not in this venue. Not in this opulence. Not on this stage. Not on that sofa next to Ainsley.

Inghean poured more tea for McCutcheon, and then for the others. He split a scone, discreetly smothered it with clotted cream and settled back again for the remaining repast, waiting for the next ill wind on his billowing sails. But the sea went calm, the winds reneged. McCutcheon let down his guard. Conversation morphed into successive vignettes about the three children, their riding and jumping feats on their respective horses, as well as the plethora of activities among their friends, with whom each had fallen into lockstep as if never having been away for a day. McCutcheon laughed heartily as the three adults regaled him incessantly with gleeful accounts of the good life at Farquharson Heights, in Edinburgh, in Scotland . . . all the while shrouding the invisible nausea that nearly impaled him on that incriminating extreme among women who are lachrymose.

The door burst open and in flew the three children, like a trio of swooping peregrine falcons. Annabella and Fiona landed upon McCutcheon with notable exuberance, embracing and kissing him before he could rise from his seat, while Angus waited impatiently for him to get to his feet, then greeted him with a manly embrace and kisses on each cheek respectively. All of this left little doubt in McCutcheon's mind that he was both loved and missed by his children, an affirming notion that laced his heart with both joy and remorse.

Now began the incessant chatter with each of the three taking turns plying their father with their summer adventures, excursions, sports, their daily horseback rides, and the undeniable melding of all three with each of their Scottish cadre of friends. What pierced McCutcheon like an arrow into Saint Sebastian's heart was the poignant realization that none of the three children ever mentioned Albany. Except for summers, all of them had lived together in the Madison Avenue Manse for three years, had participated in the life of Madison Avenue Presbyterian Church for three years, had moved among their fellow students in school and youth groups for three years; but not a word about any of it.

"Angus," Ainsley said as the chatter diminished, "tell your father about your summer course at university. I should think he'd be interested in that."

"Sure," said Angus, addressing McCutcheon. "It's great. Aunt Bonnie told me about it since she receives all the notices from her alma mater. She saw that Professor McLaughlin would be teaching a summer course on Greek Mythology and Drama, designed for secondary school students. No credit, just reading and discussing the great Greek plays and related literature. It's all in a symposium setting, limited to a class of twenty-five. Aunt Bonnie asked, I said *yes,* and she submitted my name; and, I think, she put in a good word for me to Professor McLaughlin. And now, this week, we're reading *Prometheus Bound* by Aeschylus and Shelley's *Prometheus Unbound.*"

"Marvelous!" exclaimed McCutcheon. "Is it engaging?"

"Yes," answered Angus. "Today, for example, Professor McLaughlin suggested that we place ourselves in the scene where Prometheus is bound to the rock and the eagle or vulture is eating his liver, only to be regenerated overnight so that the eagle can eat it again the next day. 'There you are watching this wretched scene,' he said, 'and you are overcome by pity or, if you think *pity* is too condescending an emotion, let's say you are overcome by compassion. I don't want you to identify with Prometheus; that is, I don't want you to put yourself in his position but, rather, to be yourself in the scene, on the spot, so to speak. What would you do? What would you think? What would you feel? How would you show what you feel? To what action would that thought or feeling drive you?' So we had ten minutes to write our responses to his questions. And then we read them to the rest of the class. Some said they would drive the eagle away, while others said they would pull at Prometheus's chains in an attempt to free him, in spite of the futility. Those who said that justified it by saying that attempting the impossible is better than doing nothing."

"And what did you say, Angus?" asked Heather, enthralled by his account of the assignment.

"I said that I would hold Prometheus by his ankle. Driving the eagle away was impossible since it would either return or attack me as an interloper. While pulling at the chain by which he is bound to the rock would be an option, as previously admitted by others, it would accomplish nothing, which would lead to helplessness and despair. But holding Prometheus by his ankle would cause him to realize that he was not alone at that rock, that someone else was fully present with him. It would be an action that could convince him of our commonality . . . or the realization that at some time in all our lives, each of us is devoured by time-limitation, our finitude."

"Angus!" said Fiona, "that's disgusting."

"No, it isn't," responded Angus, "it's Greek."

"What I don't understand," said Annabella, "is why you would hold his ankle rather than his hand."

"Because his hands are shackled to the rock by the wrists; only his feet are accessible. If I hold his ankle, he will know, but the eagle will not."

Everyone fell silent, each thinking about McLaughlin's questions and Angus's answer.

Annabella broke the silence.

"I would hold his head or put my arms around his neck."

Edana reappeared. She conferred with Inghean as to the time for dinner, and it was set for seven. As the initial preparation for such, the children and Heather led Mc-Cutcheon to the Carriage House behind the Chisholm Mansion. In variance only by its rustic lure and diminutive size, the Carriage House was in every way as charming and comfortable as the Manor.

And so began the two weeks at Farquharson Heights, a beginning that possessed in its quiddity—as Inghean would say—a nearly irresistible lure as intense as the siren's song resounding enticingly from the Island of the Sirens. McCutcheon first heard that alluring song on the second day, when the three children had gone with their grandparents for a four-hour outing. Heather and Stirling stayed behind to make love in the afternoon.

Though for two months neither had had the occasion for intimacy—since occasion for such lay on the opposite Atlantic coast—their respective passions were easily summoned, and a small spark burgeoned into an immediate and intense flame—a flame that burned without consuming, a desire that lasted well beyond exhaustion, a craving that had been deprived of expression. At last, fully spent, they lay upon the bed, breathless, separate. Eventually Heather moved to McCutcheon's arms, looked up into his face and said, "Annabella would hold Prometheus's head or put her arms around his neck." They laughed quietly. "That's what she would do, Stirling. She's definitely a modern-day woman. I think that's what I would do as well."

"No, I think you would make love to him in the afternoon. That would certainly help him get through the rest of that horrible day," he teased affectionately. "And, by the way, that belligerent eagle would be looking on with a smoldering envy."

"Well, maybe. Whenever we have rendezvoused in the afternoon, it helped me get through the rest of the week, actually . . . playing mother to the children, writing the pages I want to write, publishing books I want to publish, putting up with missing you when you're off bandaging someone else's tattered heart."

"Heather, tell me why you like to make love in the afternoon."

"I've told you before."

"Tell me again."

"I like to make love with you in the afternoon, Stirling, because I like to see your face, your eyes sparkling first with anticipation and then with pleasure. I like being in the light, where I can see us together—our bodies, our lives—moving in harmony.

Then when we careen into space, I look for the lines in your face to deepen. I want you to lose control and—in a single fleeting moment—to be vulnerable. In that moment, you have no choice but to trust me."

McCutcheon's eyes twinkled. He asked tauntingly, "How do I know it's not because you want to control me?"

"You don't. You have to trust me."

"Believe me, Heather, I trust you," McCutcheon said slowly with a measured emphasis.

"And I also like making love with you in the afternoon because it was in the afternoon we first made love. Do you remember, Stirling?"

"Yes."

"For a long time now, nothing in our lives has been predictable. There are always emergencies, demands, interruptions, irregularities, surprises. I can hardly ever count on anything; rarely can we make plans with even moderate certainty. When we make love in the afternoon, however, it occurs to me it is something we have done before, a hint of repetition, a pattern, and, to be straight with you, that makes me feel secure."

"Secure! Since when have you had the need to feel secure, Heather? As long as I've known you, you have been like a lighthouse in the storm, giving off the light rather than needing it."

"Perhaps you haven't been listening, or noticing, or haven't been around enough in the last three years to understand my needs . . . or worse yet, to even care what they are. Security may be a foreign word in your vocabulary or a flower of little beauty or worth. I know that reliable routines and planned patterns mitigate your spontaneity, but for me, at times, on those rare occasions, shall we say, security, routine, and patterns feel awfully good. Such as here, Stirling. The kids and I thrive on routine and feel safe in the large arms of Farquharson Heights. And that's why I want you to stay."

"What do you mean, *stay?*" asked McCutcheon for clarity. He could hear the siren song's first few measures, the lure of Farquharson Heights, calling him towards the jagged rocks of an opposite coast.

"I mean, call Caryn Corrigan and tell her to inform the Session that you are not returning. They can pack up your books from both studies and your belongings from the manse and ship everything here. We'll pay them whatever it costs."

McCutcheon sat up, moved to the edge of the bed, and sat there staring at the wall ahead of him. He subsequently turned and said, "No, Heather, I can't. I promised them ten years, and it's been only three. I have seven more to go. When you and the children return at the end of the summer, I'll have figured out a way for all of us to spend more time together, and for you and me to keep the same closeness we have this afternoon."

"Stirling, the children and I are not going back."

McCutcheon sat motionless, staring again at the bedroom wall decorated with an elegant wallpaper of large prints of lavender Flora Heather on a cream background. "Well-suited for Heather's room," he thought sardonically.

"All right, Heather, I'll think about it carefully," he said softly, affectionately, but inwardly unstrung.

They dressed in silence and made their way to the living room. McCutcheon poured white wine for Heather and Scotch for himself. He moved to the screened-in porch, lit his pipe, and looked out across the vast legacy which lay in Heather's future . . . and, he just learned, in her undaunted present. It could be extremely comfortable for him here if he would only acquiesce to a full life with his wife, three children, Heather's parents, and his parents and sister in close proximity. Heather interrupted his musing.

"Bonnie just rang up and wondered what time we'd be arriving this evening. Dinner could be as early as six thirty. What do you think?"

"Let's say six. Say we'll arrive at six."

It was a splendid evening with McCutcheon's parents and sister Bonnie. The children had come as well, and the occasion marked the first of numerous visits back and forth between the McCutcheons and the Chisholms during the course of McCutcheon's two-week stay in Edinburgh. While Heather referred to her stated expectation frequently throughout the fortnight, McCutcheon's standard response was that he was thinking about it . . . seriously. Remarkably, however, the dangling irresolution didn't interfere with their passionate lovemaking until the day before his scheduled departure. It was love in the afternoon again, and they were alone in Heather's bedroom. They had engaged and were moving rapidly towards the mountaintop when Stirling detected Heather's detachment.

"Do you want me to stop?"

"Yes," she said, and he disengaged. "I can't go on in this uncertainty," she continued when he sat up again on the edge of the bed, again staring at the lavender floral print on the cream background. "I need to know."

McCutcheon turned and searched her lovely, sad face. "No, I can't stay here and let my people in Albany flounder and have to start over with a new pastor whom it would take two years to locate. It would be wrong of me. It is wrong of you to require this of me. If you have to stay here with the children for all of you to be happy, I understand. I'll come and visit as often as I can, perhaps as often as every three or four months, but I can't abandon my people."

"But you can abandon your family," Heather retorted bitterly.

"No, we were in ministry together."

"No, we *were* in ministry together . . . *here* . . . here in Scotland; but we were never in ministry together in Albany . . . *there* in Albany, in the States where people are violent and crude."

"They are people with needs, just as Scots are people with needs," McCutcheon rejoined defensively.

"No, they are people with guns and foul mouths and a zero level of sophistication, and I don't want our children growing up in that dumbed-down milieu."

"Heather, if you want to be here at Farquharson Heights with your parents, and you want our children to have an Edinburgh education, fine; but admit it! That's what you want. You needn't project the blame on a congregation that cares about us, about you and me, about our children."

"Think of it anyway you want to think of it, Stirling. My mind is made up."

"All right. I'll visit as often as I can."

Heather stood up and put on her robe. "No," she said. "I'll be going for a divorce."

That evening McCutcheon spent his time constantly with his children, playing games, laughing at their jokes, and hearing their selected short stories of great writers. Heather played the role convincingly and seemed a full participant in the evening's activities. After a family breakfast in the morning, the three well-groomed equestrians and McCutcheon enjoyed a last ride on well-groomed horses.

Walter appeared with the Rolls Royce precisely at 10:00 and, after appropriate *goodbyes* all around, Stirling McCutcheon climbed into the back seat. Heather had embraced him and sent him off with a kiss on the cheek, but as she did so, she had slipped the Celtic cross—the silver cross he had given her years before—into his hand. Walter drove out of the driveway and pointed the Rolls Royce figurehead in the direction of Waverly Station. McCutcheon opened his hand and sadly examined the cross. He had little doubt that the cross signaled an approaching crossroads at which Heather would choose to travel her road without him.

As the car sped along the motorway, the lone passenger looked out the window at the iridescent countryside. The Birnam Oaks were saluting like Scots Guards; the lavender Flora Heather was weaving in the breeze among the Bell Heather and the Scottish Primrose. McCutcheon saw none of it.

15

Aphrodite's Disillusionment

THAT NIGHT MCCUTCHEON'S INTERCONTINENTAL sojourn concluded at 11:05 p.m. at the Albany Airport, and by 11:55 p.m. he was sleeping mindlessly in his own bed *. . . in Heather's former bed,* he thought when he slipped beneath the covers. When the morning sun intruded on his somber sleep, he made his way down the stairs to the kitchen and prepared coffee. He noticed his suit coat hanging on the back of a kitchen chair, where he had left it when coming in from the airport. Still dazed from events from the previous day, he reached into his side pocket and pulled out the Celtic cross, sat down at the table and held it while the coffee perked. A wave of sadness washed over him.

With coffee in hand he adjourned to the study, lifted the lid of the box of crosses on his desk, and laid Heather's cross in among the others. Apparently the blazing sun hid behind a passing cloud, and the natural light dimmed to near darkness momentarily in the study.

When he entered the church office, Caryn rose and gave him an enthusiastic embrace with a verbal greeting that warmed his heart. After inquiring about Heather and the children, as well as extended family, she waited until he settled at his desk and then, equipped with coffee for both, entered to brief him on all that had transpired during his three weeks away. At the end of a forty-five minute update, she pointed to his accumulated mail on his credenza and brought his attention to the small box on top of the pile.

"Stirling, I believe that little box is related to the voice mail you received two days ago from the sergeant at the Ballston Spa Jail. You may want to listen to that right away."

"All right, Caryn," said McCutcheon. "Thanks for managing all of this while I was gone!"

He picked up the telephone, selected the voice mails, and found the one from the sergeant. *Hello, Mr. McCutcheon. This is Sergeant Meadows from the Ballston Spa Jail. I understand you have been working closely with Jocelyn Hudson for some time now. Your secretary informed me that you have been out of the country for a couple of weeks. I'm calling to report to you that while you were gone, Jocelyn fell off the wagon, as they say, violated the terms of her bail, and was placed here in our custody. When she arrived, however, she was recovering from a horrendous case of pneumonia, which apparently worsened last night. The doctor was called, but she died before he arrived. According to her mother, there's to be no funeral or calling hours. Her body will be cremated and the ashes given to her mother. Jocelyn gave me your business card and told me that if anything happened to her, I should send you her gold cross. I am mailing that to you today by United States Postal Service. Thank you, sir. If you have questions, please feel free to call.*

McCutcheon placed his head in his cupped hands. Heather's *Medea's Bitter Anguish* rushed to mind. Jocelyn was far from a bad woman; she was an abused, abandoned woman, who wanted little more than to love and be loved. Is that really too much to expect in an affluent neighborhood? He turned to his credenza, opened the small box, and lifted out the little gold cross he had first seen dangling between her naked breasts and then weeks and weeks thereafter in the local coffee shop, a symbol of agony . . . of longing and loneliness.

†   †   †

It was barely two weeks following the wedding and the Drummonds' return from their honeymoon when Gertrude Parker took residence in the heavenly city. McCutcheon noticed that Catherine was uncharacteristically subdued when she returned from St. John. He was quite certain that her mother's illness was weighing heavily upon her, contributing to a doleful, low-grade withdrawal. If this had not been her emotional state while in the Caribbean, it certainty had become so upon her return. Understandably so. Who wouldn't fall into such a vortex of inevitability pulling one down, down, and yet down further at the sight of a diminishing presence, wasting and diminishing, diminishing and wasting, so emaciated that certainly she would eventually become invisible before one's very eyes?

When Caryn informed McCutcheon subsequently that Catherine Drummond had wished to see him, and that she—Caryn—had made an appointment for her on a Monday afternoon, he was hardly surprised. It was now approximately three months after her mother's funeral, and in the few times McCutcheon had visited Catherine and Allister since then, there seemed to be that fatal aftermath that hung tenaciously in the air of their home, dogging their nuptial joy. Catherine's spontaneity and conviviality had dissipated; tears came quickly on several occasions; she clasped her hands in her lap as if clutching at something she feared to lose. This was hardly the same Catherine who had appeared in his office the very first time with her gallant fiancé a number of months ago. Apparently the tragic loss of her mother had metamorphosed this young beauty into a hollow woman who struggled to cling to the meaning of her relationship with her mother, even now, as memory of her mother's images were fading faster than smoke rising into a northerly breeze. McCutcheon began to rehearse the old clichés about loss of a parent, about the gift of time that heals wounds, about the new road that lies so invitingly before the two of them as a newly-married couple who has so much opportunity ahead of them. Knowing better than to resort to answers that have been glibly recited in the past, he blotted out all of these platitudes in his mental exercises and resolved to listen.

The appointed time on the designated Monday afternoon arrived, and so did Catherine. She greeted McCutcheon with the customary embrace, this time a little more tentative than usual. She refused Caryn's offer for coffee, albeit graciously, and sat in the loveseat where she had first sat the day he had met her. McCutcheon sat across from her, also as he had on that first day, but it was obviously not the same. So many major events had occurred in the meantime, enough to make one think it had been a lifetime since the beginning of their relationship, but it had been only a few months. A lifetime showed on her face, however, and in her eyes. She wore no makeup. Her hair was disheveled. She had obviously been crying as recently as entering the church.

They remained silent for a long time until at last McCutcheon broke the silence with what he would call in retrospect an *inanity*, betraying a vast system of assumptions he had been making tacitly in the immediate past. He said softly and with the utmost sincerity, "Catherine, I realize that your mother's death has been utterly excruciating for you. I'm deeply sorry." Catherine remained motionless, looking down at her hands folded tightly in her lap. He continued. "I wish there were something I could do to bring her back . . . in good health, of course . . . and that you could have the relationship you once had when everything was good for you and your parents."

"No, Stirling, no!" Catherine interrupted. For a few months now, Allister, Catherine, and McCutcheon had been on a first-name basis, and though it was a troubled, insistent *Stirling*, it was like a welcomed melody to hear her use his name in such a despondent moment. "No, no, no, no, Stirling!" she hoarsely whispered shaking her head back and forth. "It's Allister. It's Allister."

McCutcheon waited, completely unsuspecting. He had no earthly idea why she referred to Allister. As one surprised by a night intruder in the house, he sat still as death, waiting.

"Allister?" he queried at last. "What about Allister?"

"I don't know," she replied, almost vacuously. "He isn't who I thought he was." She paused, gained control again, and then said, "as you know, we had been so happy for so many years at Cambridge. I would have laid down my life on a wager that he was the most transparent of men, that everything he appeared to be he was in essence, and everything he was essentially was absolutely congruous with his appearance. Though a deep person and a profound thinker, there was absolutely nothing nefarious hidden in those depths. I would have sworn to it, Stirling. As one of his own countrymen, you have given assent to his character. I have heard you speak admirably of 'this impeccable young Scotsman.' That's how you said it, Stirling. I remember distinctly. There was a time when that very approbation brought me deep joy, an immeasurable pride as his bride-to-be." Catherine began to weep more profusely. McCutcheon waited until she composed herself again.

"Yes," he concurred. "Yes, Catherine. That's true; to my knowledge, that is still true . . . unless something has changed."

"We left the church on our wedding day and were bursting with joy, virtually weightless as if we could fly. Any other mode of transportation seemed redundant at the moment. But we took the horse-drawn coach to the hotel, and then a limousine to the airport, and then an airplane to St. John. The first night could be characterized in no other way than as sheer bliss. What a phenomenal lover Allister is! When I'm in his arms and he's in my body and in my psyche, his love carries me to an explosive height in which all the best of who I am as a woman, as a lover, as a person, sits on the pinnacle of actualization. Life could have come to an end in that very moment, and I swear, Stirling, it would have been complete."

"Marvelous, Catherine!" McCutcheon exclaimed quietly. "Marvelous!" Heather came to mind . . . Heather and those afternoons together in bed in the Carriage House at the Chisholm Estate in Farquharson Heights. "To be loved so completely, Catherine, is a rare thing!"

"Completely, Stirling, but not singularly."

"What do you mean, 'not singularly'?"

"All the following days we sat on the beach, Allister read pornographic magazines: *Playboy, Hustler, Penthouse* . . . blatantly, in plain sight, in front of me. And when I was in the hotel room waiting for him to come to me . . . aching for him to come to me, he remained on the beach reading those damnable magazines. It was quite apparent that he couldn't get enough of them. He was insatiable. It wasn't that he couldn't get enough of me—which for me would have been the ultimate delight of Eden—but he couldn't get enough of different images of naked women in every conceivable pose anyone could imagine and in every compromising position anyone could contrive. I screamed, 'Allister! Here I am, Allister! Look at me, naked in my need! What? Have I suddenly become invisible? Don't you see me? When you see me, don't you care? Don't you want me? Why, instead, these paper sirens with their siren song calling to you from the cliffs of Anthemusa?' Can you imagine what he said, Stirling? . . . No, no, I'm sure you can't! He said, 'I have you. You're in my reach, and I can have you anytime I want; but these are out of my grasp; therefore, I want them.' We planned all these years . . . for what, Stirling? For me to become invisible? For me to have no voice? Or for my voice to be drowned out by some sleazy siren's song?"

McCutcheon kept his gaze on Catherine as she wept again, his heart constricted by a raw empathy—*raw* as in *bare* and *bleeding*. How had he missed Allister's character flaw in their conversations, the four pre-marital sessions in which they had delved deeply into their relationship. It had appeared to McCutcheon that both of them—and he himself when they had made personal inquires—had engaged in an exceptionally large measure of self-disclosure, freely sharing their individual and mutual life stories. He had married the two of them without the slightest reservation, convinced that they—more than any couple he had ever married—would succeed splendidly in the art of love and marriage. JoHari's Window came to mind, the fourth quadrant in particular, in which there are aspects of ourselves known only to ourselves, and those aspects may reside completely curtained until the day we choose to disclose them . . . if ever. McCutcheon never detected a hint of that part of Allister's behavioral pattern. In all her six years with him, neither did Catherine . . . until Allister had the marriage license securely in hand.

"Catherine, I had no idea," McCutcheon began apologetically. "I'm sorry I failed to see it in Allister."

"How could you? He is a master impostor. You know that we have lived together for years. We were nearer to each other than breath. I could attest that our breathing at night on our pillows was synchronistic. We walked the streets of Cambridge, and invariably we were in lock step with each other. I had thought that there wasn't a minute of our days when we didn't know what the other was doing or where the other was located. Now I have no idea what Allister was up to while he was at class, or engaged in research, or at the library. Stirling, I literally do not know the man. How could I expect you to pick up on a pattern so carefully disguised for so many years?"

"Males should have a sixth sense about these things, I suppose, Catherine," McCutcheon offered reflectively. "Perhaps I was blinded by the light. I didn't suspect any deviant patterns whatsoever."

"I know," Catherine said softly, staring at the floor as if in a trance. The wind outside was picking up with a hint of growing ferocity. It was now the beginning of December, and the usual chilling introduction to the winter cycle had made its appearance. During the silence between them, McCutcheon listened to the wind whipping about the church like the growing storm in the Drummonds' marriage.

"What will you do now, Catherine?" he ventured, then waited attentively.

"If it were only a matter of paper pin-ups, Stirling, I'd learn how to live with his obsession. Since we returned from the honeymoon, we have discussed the issue from every angle, the how and why and what of it all. I've made it abundantly clear that I don't like the image of his drooling over pages of these naked exhibitionists. All he can say is what he said by way of explanation when we were in St. John. And he can't help it. It's part of who he is as a male, he said. So, if it were only this, I'd compensate, Stirling, even though I wouldn't like it."

"Certainly! I understand," McCutcheon responded, perhaps with more feeling than complete objectivity would have suggested.

Catherine raised her eyes to his, paused an interminably long space of silence, and finally confided, "But that isn't all."

McCutcheon's throat tightened. He remained motionless, maintaining with some difficulty his gaze as she scrutinized his countenance.

"What, Catherine?" he inquired. "What else is there?"

"It all came out last night. As you know, we had come to the service yesterday morning. It was a quiet Sunday afternoon, and then we took my father to an early dinner at Salvatori's: lots of good food and plenty of hearty, red wine. After we dropped Dad off at his house, we settled in at home. Allister opened another bottle of red wine, which he was knocking off at a fairly rapacious pace. I asked him how the job on Wall Street was working out and whether he had any regrets about our having come to Albany. Actually, I was setting the stage on which to air a thought I had been mulling over, namely, to take Dad and return to Scotland to live, say, perhaps in a year or so. Since Mother is gone, there is nothing to hold us here except Dad and Allister's work. Before I had time to introduce the idea, Allister threw his head back, consumed the remaining wine in his glass, and then answered my question. 'It's going swimmingly,' he said with a sonorous note of certainty. 'I love the work. Every day is an adventure. I thrive on beating those jackals at their own game.' He began slurring his words, and I became aware that he had more wine than he could comfortably handle. 'I love New York. It's a deliciously wicked city with every virtue and vice one could ever want to taste.' And do you? I asked. He smiled a rye smile and said, 'Sometimes.' What vices do you mean? I probed carefully. By this time Allister's eyes were heavy and his head nodding ever so slightly. 'Catherine, my love, since you say you don't really know—even after all these years—I'll let you in on a little secret. Sometimes I use my lunchtime to walk a few blocks from the office. I go down into a large, lavish, subterranean lounge. There I consult with a lady named Dominick. I'm not sure that that's her real name, but it certainly fits her because she's a dominatrix. We adjourn to her particular workout room, so to speak, and within minutes she has undressed me completely, lashed me to a life-size X cross and for half an hour applies her sadomasochistic talents to my body, something you have never been able to do for me.' Now Allister was virtually nodding off. Riding the crest of a rising rage, my urge to scream with a primal thundering and my passion to tear out his eyes gave way to an hysterical realization that here before me—not more than twelve inches away from me—sat a man whom I not only didn't recognize but also whom, as I eyed the St. Andrew's cross around his neck, I deemed a human matrix of incongruity. Shaking Allister firmly but carefully, I asked him about the meaning of the cross around his neck and how that was consistent with his Christian beliefs and his metropolitan visits to Dominick. He laughed and mumbled, 'Oh, the St. Andrew's cross! That has nothing to do with Christianity. It's a sign to anyone who sees it that I am ready for a round of S&M.' He stood up and made his way, with considerable difficulty, upstairs to bed."

Concentrating in the immediate present suddenly became an insurmountable challenge for McCutcheon. An involuntary flashback carried him back to the first time he set eyes on Allister Drummond. He vividly recalled thinking that in that moment he recognized the only man with whom he would trade in an instant his own demeanor, his own deportment, his own physiognomy for Drummond's. Now, with this heinous disclosure, how accurate the recollection but how erroneous, how repugnant the sentiment! McCutcheon's envy upon their first encounter and the somber sadness he identified in his darkened study on the night of their wedding fell away from him like soiled clothes consigned to the incinerator, leaving him naked on a bath mat hankering for the cleansing waters of purification. He had been taken in by Allister's St. Andrew's cross. Now, he looked deep into his own soul. What shame does he, McCutcheon, employ—wittingly or unwittingly—to cover himself with a convincing pretense of righteousness?

"Stirling." Catherine's voice summoned him back to the present moment. "Stirling, I know you cherish your relationship with Allister. I don't want anything to ruin that, but I must decide what to do."

"Where is he now?" McCutcheon asked blandly.

"He went off to work this morning as if we had never had the conversation last night. I think he was so inebriated that he doesn't recall telling me about the dominatrix. What should I do?"

"Hide nothing. Confront him cautiously but tenderly. Recount your conversation with him from last night. Then see if he'll talk with me. In the meantime, Catherine, since you are an extraordinary woman in your own right with your own voice, remain impeccable with your words and vibrant in your demeanor. You have every reason to be disheveled now, but don't let his moral wretchedness shatter your inner beauty. If you feel yourself heading toward the edge, call me. We'll talk it through. It'll be temporary."

Catherine rose from the loveseat, nodded her head. "All right," she said softly, then reached to embrace McCutcheon. He stopped her, took her hands in his.

"Catherine, in the Byzantine Catholic liturgy there is a rubric called *Passing the Peace*. As each person embraces the other—first to the left, and then to the right, and then back to the left again, one says first: *Christ is present here,* and the other responds: *he is, and he always will be.* The other then says: *Christ is present here,* and the first responds: *he is, and he always will be.* May I?"

Catherine nodded assent.

They embraced left and right and left again. "Christ is present here," McCutcheon said.

"He is, and he always will be," Catherine responded. Then she left.

16

Lethal Scissors

THE RICH, DARK, PURE tone of the oboe pierced the summer air. Its sustained 4-40A brought the anticipatory audience to an expectant silence. Three times it sounded that hypnotic note—once for brass, once for woodwinds, and once for strings—that every instrument would be perfectly pitched with every other orchestral instrument. Twilight had settled in beside each anticipant, like a welcomed guest who had heard the oboe's mesmerizing summons—as distinctive and compelling as an Islam call to prayer—and responded to the lilt of its resonant singularity.

The Overture to Adolphe Adam's *Giselle* commenced with a definitive statement by the violins; lights rose on the dimmed scene, and presently—only minutes into the ballet—Daphne Astor, the principal ballerina, took center stage at the Saratoga Performing Arts Center on a pleasant July midsummer's evening. By her request, Stirling McCutcheon was her guest.

It wasn't a long trip from Albany, only twenty-five miles north. The Performing Arts Center had been a favorite concert venue for the McCutcheons before Heather and the children returned to Scotland. Strange, though, how McCutcheon hadn't been here since their departure. Actually, maybe not so strange! Sitting, waiting, gazing about at the crowd—comprised mostly by couples—brought only painful recollections of the extraordinary times they as a family had enjoyed there on previous occasions. To be sure, this present occasion differed considerably from all of the other occurrences here, for never before had McCutcheon been invited by the starring performing artist to attend as her guest.

In May, a note postmarked *New York City* arrived at the manse. Much to his surprise, it was from Daphne Astor and included a ticket to *Giselle* for this particular July Friday evening performance. Although Daphne was a daughter of the congregation—having faithfully attended Madison Avenue Presbyterian Church all the years she grew up in Albany—McCutcheon had never met her; she knew Sinclair Chamberlain well, was fiercely devoted to him as her pastor, apparently was devastated by his accidental death, and had moved to New York City for her advanced ballet training before Stirling arrived at the church. Her note read: *My dear Rev. Mr. McCutcheon, please be my guest at the New York City Ballet's performance of Giselle at the Saratoga Performing Arts Center on Friday, July 12, 8:00 p.m. A complimentary ticket is enclosed. I would be deeply honored if you would meet me backstage following the performance. I must speak with you privately. Merely present the enclosed business card to the backstage personnel. If it is impossible for you to be present, please drop me a note at my address on the card. Otherwise, I shall look forward to seeing you on the twelfth. Thank you for your kind consideration! Sincerely, Daphne Astor.* There was only one ticket enclosed with the note, which seemed to indicate that either Daphne wanted to see McCutcheon alone—clearly her prerogative as a member of the church—or she was aware that Heather had returned to Scotland, which of course obviated the need for a second ticket.

Spellbound. *Spellbound* is the most suitable word for his captivated state during the ballet. Daphne had certainly mastered her craft. Given the peculiar circumstances of this particular evening, and given their pastor-parishioner relationship—existing until now *sans* a face-to-face encounter or a formal introduction—McCutcheon had to admit to a biased proclivity towards this ballerina. On the other hand, he was more likely to subscribe to an objective assessment that Daphne Astor was a phenomenal ballet dancer, and her performance of Giselle was nothing short of brilliant, inspiring, passionate, flawless in its precision. Her leaps carried her high into the air, where she seemed to be suspended for an immeasurable time, as if time would stand still, or as if the air, itself, were palpable enough to support her indefinitely. As a case in point, the *pas de deux* in the second act—performed with the principal danseur—exhibited just such suspended animation and brought all in the audience to their feet at its conclusion, which foreshadowed the long standing ovation for Daphne after the blackout at the end of the ballet.

Moving upstream against the exiting horde, McCutcheon made his way arduously toward the stage. He showed Daphne's business card—inscribed with her words of invitation—to the usher guarding the front of the stage and inquired about the appropriate way backstage. The usher examined the card carefully—somewhat suspiciously—and pointed to a receded doorway to his left. At the top of that hidden staircase, McCutcheon encountered another man, considerably more amiable, who looked at the card as if it were a common artifact.

"Ms. Astor. Yes, of course," he said warmly, raising his eyes to the inquirer with an intense, benign look of inquiry. "Are you a relative, sir?"

"No, my good man, I am not," McCutcheon rejoined good-naturedly. "I am an acquaintance, and after this evening's performance, I'd say that I am an acquaintance of good fortune."

"Yes, sir! A masterful performance indeed!" he acknowledged. "And who, may I say, is wishing to see Ms. Astor?"

"McCutcheon is the name, sir! Stirling McCutcheon. She is expecting me."

"Pleased to meet you, Mr. McCutcheon!" He returned Daphne's business card and explained, "At the present moment, Ms. Astor is autographing programs on the other side of the stage and will then go to change. If you would be so good as to be seated in this waiting area, I'll inform Ms. Astor that you are here."

From a seated position, McCutcheon watched the backstage sentry turn slowly, methodically, with a ceremonial air—not unlike a member of the Queen's Guard at an official royal residence—and stride along the back of the cyclorama still hanging as the final scene's backdrop. From the rear, he seemed broader in the shoulders than he had face-to-face, and McCutcheon mindlessly gazed at his forest-green blazer with SPAC insignia and his sharply creased black trousers until they disappeared into a pulsating sea of well-wishers.

Forty-five minutes passed before the forest green blazer and black trousers emerged again, this time leading Ms. Astor to the waiting area McCutcheon occupied with an uncharacteristic measure of patience. All that time, recollections had been swimming in a wave of recurring images of Daphne's leaps; simultaneously, speculations as to why she needed to talk with him in private soared out of control. A fertile imagination steers its wandering bark down every eddy that emerges on its conceptual horizon.

"Mr. McCutcheon," the forest-green sentry said with an adopted formality, which seemed perfectly suited to both his role and to the present occasion, "Ms. Astor, sir."

"Thank you, sir," McCutcheon said with a tone of gratitude as he rose immediately to greet Daphne.

Extending her right hand, she spoke first. "How lovely to meet you, Mr. Mc-Cutcheon, and how good of you to come this evening!"

One can always be fooled by appearances. If there was anything that struck Mc-Cutcheon right away upon this first meeting, however, it was her warmth, her *genuine* warmth. He detected no airs, no assumed guise designed to impress. She seemed completely devoid of pretense. Not only had she developed her craft to the penultimate of perfection, but she had obviously accomplished that without a trace of guile, at least according to McCutcheon's initial impression. Certainly he should not rush to favorable judgment or give way to a hasty blend of naiveté and impulse, for within the next few moments or hours he could discover quite another side to Daphne Astor, which would render his first impressions ludicrous, if not insidious. For the present, however, McCutcheon took comfort in her warmth and counted on a lasting first impression.

Like anyone else—the common man or the common woman unaccustomed to stage lights—Daphne was a complex repository of opposites. In this moment she was as gentle here, backstage, as she was powerful out there on stage. She was as down-to-earth and real here as she was esoteric and fantastical there. As regards to similarities in her complex repository, she was as beautiful as she was talented, as feminine as she was genteel. Her light brown hair, which she wore tight and in a topknot for the performance, now fell loosely in full, long tresses upon her shoulders, that is, upon the shoulders of her grey, lightweight, waist-length summer jacket, which she wore over a lavender silk blouse with a high collar. Black dress slacks completed her outfit, all of which lent her a striking demeanor.

"Truly, Ms. Astor," McCutcheon responded with heart-felt enthusiasm, "it was an unparalleled delight for me to find myself in the audience tonight, thanks to your kind initiative! Your performance was genuinely extraordinary. What an exquisite ballerina you are! You have certainly made a name for yourself . . . and so young!"

"God has been good to me, Mr. McCutcheon."

"God, undoubtedly, in conjunction with an indefatigable discipline and passionate effort on your part . . . undoubtedly. Indeed, Ms. Astor, I'm honored to know you."

Daphne looked around and concluded that they were essentially alone. "There's a restaurant on Broadway that's open late: Druthers Brewing Company, 381 Broadway. It's my favorite, and we can have a table that's relatively secluded. I've made a reservation. The other members of the ballet company usually go back to the Gideon Putnam for drinks, so we'll probably not see anyone we know, unless, of course, you frequent Druthers on a regular basis." This last she said with a smile in her voice.

"No, I haven't been there at all," McCutcheon laughed quietly. "I trust we'll be sequestered as much as you want. Would you care to ride with me?"

"Thank you, but my car is in the performers' lot, and I'll need to drive on my own."

Were McCutcheon to extrapolate from that brief interchange any conclusions about Daphne's personality traits, he would first register with himself no surprise that she had achieved the great heights in ballet performance that she had at this nascent age. There was not a trace of ambiguity to be detected in her words. She had made prearrangements, didn't ask her guest's advice or seek to know his wishes. There were no add-ons to her sentences, such as, *381 Broadway, I think . . .* or *right?* or *you know?* or *is that all right with you?* Definitive, decisive. McCutcheon supposed that any ballerina—cursed with uncertainty—who hesitates before the next prescribed move will be crushed beneath the oppressive weight of precise timing. Why would Daphne, who consistently makes the exact move, on an exact note, at the exact second, wait for McCutcheon to weigh in on a place to meet? Definitive, decisive.

By the time they were seated at the reserved table in a secluded nook at Druthers, it was passed eleven o'clock. Arnaldo, their waiter, knew Ms. Astor by name, implying that Daphne was a steady customer when in Saratoga. They ordered light fare along with tea and Irish coffee. After the exchange of a few pleasantries—such as the ease of finding parking on the street at this time of night rather than during the day and McCutcheon's confessing to the frequency of his visits to Saratoga Springs and her indicating when she first performed ballet at the performing arts center—Daphne moved right into her agenda.

"Mr. McCutcheon, I apologize . . . "

"Please call me *Stirling*."

"Agreed, Stirling! Thank you! And, of course, I go by *Daphne*."

"If I could digress only briefly, I want to say that *Daphne* is such a lovely name . . . one that we seldom hear anymore, which lends it all the more charm for its being so rare."

"It wasn't all that charming as I grew up, especially in middle school where cruelty and bullyism have their day."

"I can imagine."

"Indeed, as you could guess, words such as *daft* and *deef* and *dwarf* all fit well into one clever taunt after another. It was something to endure, but then every middle school kid had to endure something."

"No one escapes it."

"But when I realized that cruelty grows out of weakness, every taunt became encased in a protective perspective and ultimately lost its power to hurt. By high school, I began to appreciate my name, and have grown to wear it with an element of pleasure."

"As you know, I see your parents often at church," McCutcheon said as Arnaldo brought their order, placed it before them, inquired about further wishes, and retreated. "Your parents have spoken of you frequently, but I never asked how they happened to name you *Daphne*."

"Since you know my parents, you probably know that my father teaches the classics at State University of New York in Albany. One of his favorite Greek myths is that of Apollo and Daphne. In brief, Apollo falls in love with Daphne and chases her with the expressed intent of making love to her. As she runs with all her might, and when she espies the river ahead of her, she prays to her father, who is the river god. Her father hears her prayer and changes her into a laurel tree just as Apollo reaches her. Devastated, Apollo realizes that all he can do is to embrace the trunk of bark on the laurel tree, and—from her leaves—make laurel wreaths to crown the heads of victors. And there you have it, Stirling. *Daphne*." She poured a little milk in her tea, stirred it, and took a sip before she concluded, "and if there is a time you can't find me, search among the laurel trees, and there you'll discover me in my alternate metamorphosis."

They both laughed heartily. "I love it," McCutcheon declared. "Great story! Beautiful name!"

"And how about yours?" Daphne queried. "How is it that *Stirling* is spelled with an *i* instead of an *e*? No doubt you've had to answer that question hundreds of times since you've come to the States."

"No, no, hardly that many! It's rather a simple answer. There's no intriguing story behind it," McCutcheon replied after wiping Irish coffee whipped cream from his lips. "I'm named after a bridge. If you don't like that answer because it would seem that I could be walked on, or over, or across, then I could tell you that I'm named after a castle. I should hope that you would think that I was king of the castle, but since I came to live in the United States, I either gave up my title or I wasn't king of the castle in the first place. So, then, I would have to admit that I was named after a city, the city in which I was raised. It has become a common practice of the Scots to name their children after cities or towns or villages. Stirling is a lovely city that boasts of a lovely castle and a lovely bridge. And there you have it, Daphne. That's all there is to it."

She smiled benignly, warmly, a non-verbal acknowledgement. A quiescence fell upon the table between them. She leaned back, her eyes trained on her teacup. McCutcheon leaned slightly forward, his forearms positioned on the table's edge.

"Daphne," he ventured with a steady voice, "my apologies! I interrupted. You said in your note that you must speak with me privately."

"Yes." She paused. McCutcheon waited. "There are only two people in the world who know what I need to tell you. Obviously," she smiled, "I am one of the two. I'm asking you to mark this conversation *confidential*."

McCutcheon nodded. "Certainly," he promised. "It will stay with me. Since it's not my story to tell, no one will hear it from me."

"Thank you, Stirling. The other thing I need from you beside your confidentiality is your help in offering a perspective on the subject . . . something akin to what I said about middle school taunts that can be encased in a perspective—a *protective* perspective—and thereby become powerless to hurt."

"I'll do my best, Daphne," McCutcheon said reflectively.

Daphne looked up at him and held her gaze without words for a pregnant interval. Then she spoke softly without shifting her eyes away from his.

"Before I get into the issue that's been haunting me, you should know that I was enthralled by Sinclair Chamberlain. From my childhood on, he was the only pastor I knew at Madison Avenue Church, and I adored him. Even as a little girl, when I was too young to understand his sermons, I loved hearing his voice. When other children went off to Children's Church, I begged my mother to let me remain in the worship service. I sat mesmerized Sunday after Sunday. Then as I grew older and comprehended his thoughts, his theology, his prayers and sermons, I understood that this was a truly great preacher. Then that Good Friday arrived, that horrible Friday when he was once again performing Claudel's *Morte de Judas*. As usual for Easter break, I was home from the conservatory, sitting there through the masterful, intense monologue . . . and then his going to the tree, climbing up on the hidden stool, placing his neck in the noose . . . and then the awful accident. We all saw it. We had all seen it before. When the lights would rise at the end, he was always out of the noose; but not this time. There he hung, as dead as Judas on his original hanging tree." Daphne waited a little while, until she gained her composure, which had been gradually slipping away. "I remained for Easter, as planned . . . a chaotic Easter it was. No one could think about resurrection . . . only about death: Sinclair Chamberlain's death. Ironic, isn't it, Stirling! The Easter message was identical to the Good Friday theme. We were all stuck on Good Friday; stuck in time and couldn't move beyond the smell of death, as if the stone had been rolled away from the tomb and Jesus was still lying there, inside the tomb, on the rock slab, dead and decaying. No one on that particular Easter could embrace the Easter story. It was, for sure, *an idle tale,* as one of the gospels uses the phrase. I returned to the conservatory on Easter Monday and have never been back to the church since."

McCutcheon nodded with understanding. Why wouldn't he understand? Freda Chamberlain had described the accident in vivid detail; Marcel DuBois, as well, had related the tragic occurrence; their descriptions, along with Daphne's, conjured up a critical incident that could never be erased from a congregation's historic memory.

"When the episode I'm needing to share with you happened, I longed for Sinclair Chamberlain to be alive, so I could divulge it to him; and if he were, I would have gone to him. I'm telling you this because, in all honesty, I'm glad he is not here—not that I wouldn't love to have him alive—but, if he were, I wouldn't have the joy of knowing you . . . authentically. I would have ingratiated myself to Dr. Chamberlain, idolized him, and swallowed his elixir—whatever it might have been. I would have cared too deeply what he thought of me as a result of my action; and if he approved of me, I would have been worthy, but if he showed disapproval, I would have been worthless. But, Stirling, already I can tell that there is no hero worship here. There you are: caring, compassionate, authentic, and insightful, all of which I know from seeing you and from your humble reputation at our church. I take comfort in your being here with me. I take comfort in your being there at Madison Avenue Church with my parents and all the other members of the congregation. Stirling, all I'm saying is: I'm glad it's you. Thank you!"

McCutcheon sat back in his chair, smiled warmly, and lifted the Irish coffee to his lips for the last swallow remaining.

"Thank you . . . more tea?"

"Yes, please."

It was already a late night. While he didn't think he would need any more stimulation than their conversation, McCutcheon signaled Arnaldo and requested more tea and another Irish coffee.

"How long have you been carrying this episode around with you, Daphne?" McCutcheon asked gently.

"A little over a year. It was a year ago last May."

"And you've spoken to no one about it, you said?" he inquired with the intent of confirming what he had heard her say earlier.

"No. That's correct," she nodded with a wry smile, a sad smile, which wasn't a smile at all, not in the sense that smiles usually come to one's lips because of a pleasant thought or remembrance.

Arnaldo returned, served them, and turned away.

"As I said, Stirling, it was a year ago last May, near the end of the New York City Ballet's season at the David H. Koch Theater in Lincoln Center. Our final ballet of the season was Prokofiev's *Romeo and Juliet,* and I had the privilege of dancing the part of Juliet. The Friday evening performance had come off well . . . to rave reviews by the critics, who, as you know, can be ruthless, even savage when they spot flaws or cultivate a distain for a particular interpretation that differs from their preferences. But we were fortunate. There were two more performances—Saturday night and Sunday afternoon—and then the season would come to a rather glorious conclusion. All that remained was an annual gala, scheduled for mid-June, to raise funds for the ensuing season. The gala was always supremely formal, the biggest fund-raiser of the year, and if the current season had been a smashing success, the fund-raising was that much easier since it played off the high enthusiasm of the contributing ballet patrons.

"It was after ten-thirty that Friday night, and I was walking—as I almost always do—along Columbus Avenue, but this time intending to go beyond my own apartment to a gathering of a few friends for a few laughs and a nightcap. About a hundred yards before my apartment, there is an alleyway between two buildings. As I was passing it, I was suddenly grabbed from behind, a hand over my mouth, my right arm twisted behind my back. His upper body strength was obviously enormous. He forced me to the ground, succeeded in deftly slapping a strip of duct tape over my mouth, pulled my hands together and tied my wrists with a cord in front of me. That evening I had worn a skirt rather than slacks, which was ideal for the predator. A slight reflection of light from the main street showed me that he was wearing a mask of some sort . . . such as a ski mask . . . so I had no idea who my assailant was. Like a madman in a psychotic episode or a prowling lion in heat, he tore my blouse, ripped my bra, lifted my skirt, and yanked down my panties. Obviously he had prepared himself. He threw off his overcoat and came at me like a crazed Neanderthal. He violently pushed my thighs apart. In the very instant he thrust himself at me, I wrapped my legs around his waist, locked my feet behind his back, and so vehemently yanked him toward me that I broke his back, snapped his spinal cord at waist level. His yelps were like a dog's that had been hit by a car. I pushed him off me, ripped off the duct tape with my restricted fingers and undid the knots on the cord with my teeth. He was writhing on his back, completely helpless, moaning in excruciating pain. I dressed myself as well as I could. Then I bent over him and said, 'When I want to lose my virginity, it won't be to a sleazy lecher like you.' With that, I yanked off his facemask. To my utter dismay, I recognized him. Here—with a broken back—was one of the most generous ballet patrons the New York City Ballet had ever cultivated . . . CEO of a multinational corporation headquartered in New York. I had seen him numerous times at the ballet and always at the annual gala. I stared at him, bewildered beyond belief."

Another quiescence fell upon them. They sat in silence for an eon, it seemed. Her hands were resting on the table, on either side of her teacup.

"What happened after that, Daphne?" he eventually asked, softly.

"Nothing," she responded, barely audibly.

"Nothing?"

"No, nothing. And that's precisely the issue. You see, Stirling, I just went home to my apartment. Left him lying there; didn't call an ambulance; didn't call the police; didn't even call my friends to tell them I couldn't come for a nightcap. I just went home and stared at the wall, which seemed to have this rich patron's face all over it, grimacing, pleading for help. But I didn't help him. I suppose he could have died."

"Did he?" McCutcheon asked solemnly, a solemnity that disguised as best it could a rising internal rage. If he were to enter a confessional at that very minute, he should have to confess that he was perfectly indifferent to the CEO's fate; or, to be more accurate, he should have to admit that it would have been all right with him if that prowling lion-in-heat had died in that dark alley, writhing on a bed of concrete. McCutcheon should also have to confess that he didn't like that about himself, that is, thinking a thought such as that while affirming the intrinsic value of all human life.

Daphne raised her eyes. They possessed an inscrutable aspect. "No, he didn't die."

"Do you know what became of him?" McCutcheon inquired with a managed calm.

"Yes," she answered. "I saw him at The Ritz, at the annual gala three weeks later. He was dressed to the nines in his formal dinner attire: tuxedo or tails, I couldn't tell which since he was sitting in a motorized wheelchair—accompanied by his beautiful, diamond-studded wife—and carrying on with his usual *savoir-faire*. The explanation that had made the rounds was that he had been dragged into the alleyway by a mob of ruffians, who had robbed him and then broken his back to keep him from contacting the police. Supposedly he had lain there until morning when his chauffeur, who had been searching for him throughout the night, found him in a state of extreme agony. The aura that surrounded him at this gala, therefore, was one of veritable heroism: a victim that had experienced a grave injustice at the hands of young criminals, yet a hero who had valiantly suffered through a long night of debilitating pain. He was in hospital for two weeks following surgery. Now, with the aid of his faithful chauffeur, he was able to go about his usual business activities, but not his tennis, racquetball, or golf. I wondered, Stirling, what exactly he told his chauffeur . . . and what exactly he told his chauffeur not to tell."

"I suppose you'll never know, Daphne," McCutcheon said without expression. "Those unholy alliances are usually cemented together by big money . . . or blackmail."

"His chauffeur was with him at The Ritz that evening, standing near him like a loyal bodyguard," Daphne continued, picking up the thread on the chauffeur. "There were a few of us dancers who had performed three excerpts from Tchaikovsky's *The Sleeping Beauty* on the stage in the ballroom and had then changed into formal wear. As we were mingling among the attendees, the chauffeur approached me with a message from the confined patron, who, he said, would like a word with me at my leisure. I looked across the room and smiled at him demurely, appealing to his façade and playing into his social veneer. 'Ah, our gracious patron! How sorry we all are for your terrible misfortune! It must have been a horrific ordeal!' I said to him as I gave him a ballerina's curtsy. The patron dismissed his chauffeur with a wave of his hand, leaving us out of earshot from anyone else in the ballroom, and smiled wryly as he said, 'my dear Miss Astor—or should I say *Dis-aster?*—how unfortunate that this past season was your last as a ballerina, either on this stage or anywhere else. This season of your life is over, I dare say. I certainly will see to that!' I stood motionless for a moment, then pulled a nearby chair into juxtaposition to his motorized conveyance. 'That certainly is curious, my dear patron,' I said, speaking not more than twelve inches from his face . . . a face that, needless to say, I detested. 'Curious indeed, patron, for I have not received a termination notice or submitted a letter of resignation. How do you come by this intelligence—which apparently pertains to me—yet about which I have heard nothing?' Since my eyes undoubtedly resembled lurching flames, he drew his head a little to his right . . . away from me. His square jaw jutted out, and his lips tightened as he said through clenched teeth, 'It's all in the works. I've spoken to the artistic director, and he knows that it's either you or my annual gift of $800,000. And upon your departure, the gift will increase to $1,000,000. Now, which do you think the ballet company will choose? It's a no-brainer, isn't it, my dear Miss Astor—or shall I say, *Dis-aster?*' I glanced around the room, saw no one nearby, and placed my hand on his left thigh. 'I suspect, dear patron,' I said pseudo-compassionately, 'that you have no feeling in this leg or in the other. Gang of hoodlums, you say! Only you and I know how this accident occurred. I can assure you that the rest of New York City—even the rest of the multinational world—would love to know the truth about this horrible . . . oh, shall we say, *disaster*! You had better hope, my friend . . . or shall I say, *my fiend?* . . . that my ballet career prospers here at the David H. Koch Theater, or everyone, including *The New York Times* and *The Washington Post* will hear about every sordid detail of that demonic night.'

"While he dared not raise his voice, he snarled distinctly through clenched teeth, 'Who would believe you, Miss Astor? No one would take your word over that of a renowned philanthropist—especially since you have no proof.' I pulled my hand away from his thigh and then leaned into his left ear and whispered, 'Where, dear sir, is your ski mask with some of your white hairs, each of which contains your unmistakable DNA? And are you aware that your ejaculate—containing your unmistakable DNA—is on my skirt? You ask, how could that happen since you didn't come inside me? Shall I compare it to the experience that young adolescent boys have when they intentionally hang themselves to have an orgasm just before losing consciousness, but release themselves from the noose in the nick of time? Your back cracking at a high pitch of passion undoubtedly gave you a release you weren't counting on. It's all over my skirt. And where is it now, dear patron? Of course, it's with the ski mask. Give me cause, sir, and I'll do thirty pirouettes into the courtroom with a soiled skirt in one hand and a ski mask in the other; and your phony façade will disappear. It would be for you, to be sure—shall we say?—an Astor disaster!'"

After a brief pause, Daphne excused herself to go to the Ladies' Room. Arnaldo came with the check; McCutcheon paid it and included a generous tip as rent for their settling into his table as if they possessed squatter's rights. He glanced at his watch: twelve-fifteen a.m. Daphne returned.

"I'm good for all night, Daphne, but I know you have to dance tomorrow. Are you all right with continuing?" McCutcheon asked out of respect for the demands on her physical energy, although he had concluded early in their conversations that she could certainly take care of herself and make her needs known.

"I'll need to leave at one, Stirling," she said matter-of-factly, "but I'm good until then. Besides, I need to continue." She emphasized the word *need.*

"Sure. What is it you need?"

"I need resolution, perspective. I can't carry this around much longer, Stirling," she retorted emphatically. "I broke this guy's back. He's a paralytic, who will never walk again. I left him there, helpless. Had I called the paramedics, he might have had a greater chance at a better quality of life."

"Then it all would have come out. Everyone would have known, and instead of his being an aristocratic paralytic, he would have been a pauper paralytic. He would have lost everything in addition to the loss of the use of his legs. Do you suppose he would say now he'd prefer the truth to the lie?"

"I don't know! But I know I broke him a second time. When he expressed his emotional torment in the threat of my dismissal, I played all my aces to trump his hand, leaving him helpless yet again. What kind of inveterate succubus am I?"

"You're not!"

"Stirling, listen to me! I am responsible for his broken back. How could I know there was so much power in my legs? They are like a lethal weapon. I am responsible for his broken back, and I am responsible for leaving him there alone. I can't carry it anymore! I dream about it every night. I see his contorted face. I hear his bitter moaning. Do you hear me, Stirling! Do you hear me? I am responsible. I don't want to beat myself up anymore, but I can't go back and do the right thing . . . I can't make it right!"

Daphne began to cry, softly, silently. McCutcheon sat quietly with his elbows on the arms of his chair, his folded hands beneath his chin, nodding assent . . . up and down in little vertical motions . . . nodding assent.

"I think I understand, Daphne . . . at least this much, that you can't go back. And now you're looking for perspective. You didn't say *perception.* The most aggravating cliché I know is that *perception is reality.* There is so much perception that is wholly false, something quite contrary to reality. You said earlier you need perspective on this issue. You already have a *perception* of the events that occurred a year ago May and June. I firmly believe that that perception is absolutely erroneous and is not to be confused with the reality of that demonic night—the very phrase you used in your conversation with the patron: that *demonic night,* which is the reality but not the perception. Your perception, Daphne, is that what occurred on that night is your responsibility. That's erroneous. We want to put that demonic night in perspective, like the taunts encased in a protective perspective, which ultimately become powerless to hurt you. Here's the perspective: evil ultimately devours itself. What this means, of course, is that evil, sooner or later, turns upon itself and is forced to bear the dire consequences of its own evil action.

"The image this conjures up for me is that of a snake that recoils back upon itself and, beginning with its own tail, swallows itself, becomes self-fed and self-consumed. Daphne, I'll be so bold as to suggest that what you dream about every night—his contorted face, his bitter moaning, his writhing upon the ground, helpless—is both the manifestation and the outcome of the evil that seized you from behind. Your virtue was assailed, but ultimately it cannot be hurt when that evil is encased in a protective perspective. The evil of that demonic night has recoiled back on itself; that's the perspective. The consequences belong to him; that's the reality."

Daphne sat quietly, her attention trained on McCutcheon, her mind on a dark alleyway near her apartment in New York City. The image there that had haunted her incessantly for months slowly dissolved and disappeared from view. She nodded knowingly, rose from her chair, bent down, kissed McCutcheon on the cheek, and left the restaurant. He sat, lost in thought . . . caught Arnaldo's eye and ordered a Scotch.

17

If He Says Nothing

FRANCESCA CALLED TO SAY he's depressed. "He won't get out of bed, Stirling. Says nothing. Won't open his eyes to look at me."

"Since when, Francesca?" asked McCutcheon seriously. He picked up his desk pen to make notes.

"This is the second day. I've called my psychiatrist to request an appointment for him, but Keith refuses to go."

"Does he know?" rejoined McCutcheon.

"No. I don't think so. I'm desperate, Stirling. As you know, he's been down before, but never this long . . . certainly never this deep."

"I'll be right over. Just stay with him so he doesn't do anything foolish."

McCutcheon put on his suit coat, picked up his car keys, and informed Caryn where he was headed. It was a fifteen-minute drive to the Harlansworths' house. Since that unforgettable evening at the Schumanns' dinner party three years ago, McCutcheon had had numerous conversations with the Harlansworths together, individually, and casually at church meetings and special events. They had become close friends and, prior to Heather's return to Scotland, the two couples had often found themselves at the same social engagements. The McCutcheons had entertained them in the manse on various occasions, and one thing was consistently true—whether at the manse, or the church, or any other setting—Keith presented as Dostoyevsky's *man without a personality,* just as DuBois and he had observed that evening at Schumanns'. Always a mystery. One could read Francesca like a neon sign. She was incessantly talkative, sharing her most minute thoughts with anyone next to her and wearing her emotional spectrum on any of her blouse's long-sleeves. But in contrast, Keith Harlansworth remained consistently tacit. Francesca was the predominant theme in a Beethoven symphony; Keith was the grand pause. It had never been a challenge for McCutcheon to be with Francesca; mostly, he had only to listen. But with Keith, he continually struggled to engender meaningful dialogue. The fierce paradox, however, was that Keith was phenomenally brilliant, a graduate of M.I.T. with a BS in Chemical Engineering, a highly valued chemist with Bayer Corporation in Albany. After many early, unsuccessful attempts to penetrate Keith's reserve barrier, McCutcheon had devised the approach of tapping their common interest: tennis. As a result, these two men had built a strong rapport upon a mutual avidity and a paucity of words.

As McCutcheon entered the bedroom, Francesca greeted him warmly, relinquished her chair to him, and left the two alone. McCutcheon sat.

"Keith. It's I, Stirling." Harlansworth remained still, unresponsive, his back to McCutcheon. "Francesca said that you're down . . . deep down, she thinks . . . is she right?" McCutcheon's voice framed words that apparently were an inaudible fragment of a dim unknown. If one could see through Harlansworth's eyes, one might recognize McCutcheon's mouth moving without sound, words ejaculated from his lips but scattered without form or order into endless space. Whatever the nature of McCutcheon's address to Keith's stoic senses, all was meaningless.

McCutcheon sat, waiting, silent, perhaps for a full half-hour.

In due time, Harlansworth, stirred, turned, and looked at McCutcheon.

"What?" he asked nearly indistinctly.

"I've come to pick you up for a set or two of tennis. What do you say? Shall we?"

Harlansworth pushed down the covers, sat up on the edge of the bed, selected his tennis clothes, and changed in the bathroom. Within minutes they were on their way to the club, where McCutcheon removed his tennis racket from his locker and dressed accordingly to take on his worthy opponent. He couldn't recall Keith's ever before having played with such vigor and determination, as if he were awash with anger. Having won a set each, they adjourned to the clubhouse for drinks.

After a toast to the spirit of friendly competition, McCutcheon asked, "What's going on, Keith?" Not at all optimistic about receiving an answer, he persisted. "Why are you so far down?"

To McCutcheon's surprise, Harlansworth spoke with a deliberate intensity but without inflection. "Do you know?"

"Do I know what?" rejoined McCutcheon.

"Do you know that Francesca is having an affair with her psychiatrist?"

In point of fact, McCutcheon did know but had been told in confidence by Francesca herself. "What makes you think she's having an affair, Keith?"

"I heard them on the phone together. She had answered the phone in the kitchen but then went to the study to talk privately. She apparently thought she had put the kitchen phone on hold, but she hit the wrong button and it went to speakerphone. It was such a clumsy mistake that I wonder if she wanted me to know. If so, why would she want me to discover the affair? Why not just tell me straight-out . . . face-to-face?"

Any other man in Harlansworth's state of mind, thought McCutcheon, would be shouting—perhaps shouting obscenities—or throwing his wineglass against the stone fireplace, but not him. His voice was intense but measured, deliberate but modulated.

"Did you confront her, Keith? Talk with her about the affair?"

"No," answered Harlansworth with a palpable sadness. "When they finished their intimate conversation, I hung up the phone and returned to the kitchen table."

"You said nothing to her?" McCutcheon asked incredulously.

"No."

"Why not?"

"I never do."

The two men sat in silence for minutes, McCutcheon staring at Harlansworth, who was staring into his wineglass.

Harlansworth raised his head and fixed his gaze on McCutcheon. "Stirling, at the beginning of my senior year at M.I.T., selected seniors were welcoming freshmen to the university and orienting them to college life on campus. Part of the week-long orientation was the IMUR sessions in the gymnasium with numerous circles of eight freshmen and two seniors getting to know each other. The seniors would introduce themselves, beginning with *I am*, then relate their backgrounds, turn to a freshman and say, *and you are?* I was one of the two seniors in our circle. The other senior—an articulate, self-confident philosophy major who was planning to go on to Yale for a PhD—started the introduction with his *I am* followed by his biographical sketch. When he had finished, he pointed to me and said to the group: *This is Keith Harlansworth. If he doesn't say anything, you'll like him.* With everyone else, I laughed, but I never laughed it off. It wasn't my classmate's fault that I went under and inward from that moment on. Undoubtedly, his was simply a playful quip. No harm intended. I was the one who attached a cynical meaning to his witticism, assuming it was an accurate assessment of my personality, of how I had come across to classmates during the previous three years. Just as surely as *Honi soit qui mal y pense* has stood for centuries as the motto of the Order of the Garter, *if he doesn't say anything, you'll like him* became the defining maxim of my life for decades . . . from then until now. So, Stirling, you ask, *why not?* Why didn't I say something to Francesca? Because the maxim is indelibly ingrained in my psyche. The irony, however, is that it hasn't worked. I don't say anything, but still I am not liked . . . not loved . . . married, but to one who loves someone else."

"Keith," McCutcheon responded somewhat emphatically, "I know you're brilliant. I've known that ever since I met you three years ago. How could you let that salty, frivolous—undoubtedly a self-aggrandizing quip from some cocky philosophy major—wisecrack define you?"

"I know . . . I know. I've reproached myself thousands of times. *You can't let someone else define you,* I say to myself, but it never works. The thunder of that insidious remark drowns out my admonition and intensifies my sensibilities."

"Listen to what you're saying, Keith! Listen to how articulate you are! How could anyone *not* like you! Besides, what if someone *doesn't* like you? So what? Was that cocky little philosophy major likeable? If he amused himself by belittling others, what's to like? . . . Can you let it go? What would it take for you to let it go?"

Keith took his last swallow of wine, held up the glass and examined the residual coating of Cabernet Sauvignon. "That same year at M.I.T.," he said reflectively, "my history professor wrote a comment on the last page of one of my papers. He scribbled these words: *I can't help but believe there is so much more depth to you than what you show me.* It's like this fluted wineglass, Stirling, cloudy, hazy. No one can tell what's inside—either the nature of the contents or the amount, whether empty or full. Ever since those days, I have never been adept at self-disclosure . . . perhaps I never was."

"What about your history professor? He looked into that cloudy wineglass and suspected contents of a vast potential, unrealized," observed McCutcheon with a quiet, exploratory intensity in his voice. "Did you follow through with him?"

"Yes. You just now used the term *brilliant.* How ironic! I made an appointment to see him in his office, went there with my paper in hand, and asked him what he meant by his concluding comment. He said, 'Harlansworth, why don't you show me what you have? From what I've observed, you have a cache of brilliance . . . *constipated* brilliance. Enormous potential . . . *blocked* potential. I don't see your life force shining through . . . your *potentia.* Why don't you show me what you have? I need you to put yourself out there—engage, ask questions, risk suppositions! We're all in this educational excursion together, exploring a vast world of thought, inquiring into any and every aspect of this limitless universe. Nobody's suppositions have to be tried and proven before stated or theorized. Take the risk, Harlansworth!'

"I told him that I never had . . . or that I had, but never again after that. 'What do you mean?' he asked. Then I related a childhood incident at Kaydeross Park, the amusement park near Saratoga Springs where I grew up. My aunt was the accountant on staff there, so whenever my brother and I visited, we could go on rides for free. My brother and I especially liked the merry-go-round and the challenge of pulling the rings from the long black sleeve as we passed it on our favorite oscillating horses. 'If you're on a free ride, never go for the brass ring,' my aunt had told us. One day, I didn't realize that the ring I reached for was the brass ring. I thought it was a regular black ring, and I grabbed it, only to discover that it was brass. My aunt didn't reprimand me, but I was aware of her embarrassment and displeasure . . . as if I had deliberately disobeyed her. She reiterated the rule: since she worked as the staff accountant at the amusement park, and since, therefore, my brother and I could ride the merry-go-round free as often as we wanted, we should leave the brass ring for those who pay and who, if successful in grabbing the brass ring, could have the next ride free of charge. Ever since that day, I never went for the brass ring . . . in fact I never went for any ring on any ride for fear I would mistake brass for black and pluck the coveted object from its beckoning sleeve, that shiny object to which I was not entitled. From that day on, I never went for the brass ring. I never went for the gold.

"My history professor listened, remained silent, as if something in the story resonated in his soul. He looked away, glancing at the picture of a young woman on his desk, then back at me, and said, 'Damn it, Harlansworth! Go for the blasted brass ring!'

"Stirling, I went for the blasted brass ring when I married Francesca. Now I have discovered it wasn't brass after all. It was one of those regular black rings. Apparently, I wasn't entitled to the gold."

As they returned to Keith's house, the two friends rode in silence. The noises of inquiry, however, were anything but silent in Harlansworth's head, leaping around in a thicket of doubt like so many laughing hyenas: *what would it take for you to let it go? What if someone doesn't like you? So what? Why don't you show me what you have? Constipated brilliance!*

"Call me tomorrow morning, Keith?" McCutcheon asked as Harlansworth reached for the door handle. "I'll want to know how you are."

Harlansworth nodded, stepped out of the car, and headed towards the house as McCutcheon drove away.

"How was the match with Stirling?" asked Francesca dispassionately as she looked up from her writing desk.

"All right," rejoined Keith. "Two sets, one each."

"Feeling better?"

"Not really."

"Sorry to hear it."

"I'm sorry to hear you are having an affair with Dr. Lattimore."

"Where did you hear that?" inquired Francesca, wondering if Stirling McCutcheon had betrayed her confidence.

"From you. Three days ago . . . when you put his call on hold but hit the speaker button instead. I couldn't hear a thing through the study doors, but your amorous words were broadcasted throughout the kitchen."

Francesca looked away, first to the door with a fleeting thought of leaving the room, then down at what she had been writing. She shook her head sadly.

"Why, Francesca? Why? . . . and how long?"

"Three months . . . I need something more, Keith. It's so utterly dead around here. I feel like some aristocrat's handmaiden buried alive with her in a musty tomb, starving to death, when suddenly there's the possibility of new life in a new relationship." Francesca's voice rose steadily in pitch and volume. "You're vacant, Keith . . . non-responsive. You don't talk to me. You don't tell me anything significant! I don't want to hear about chemical formulas or evincible equations. Do you have any visions, any aspirations other than sitting in that chemistry lab and gazing into a microscope forty hours a week? What in heaven's name do you want? Or don't you know? I'd insist that you tell me what you need, but I don't think you know!"

Keith stood quietly, staring at Francesca, as if she were a woman whom he had never known.

"I know what *I* want, Keith! I know precisely what I want. I want to seize that possibility of new life. I want to be free. I feel like a frantic butterfly, barely alive, whose wings are pinned to a display board of white cotton cloth under glass, in a wooden frame, whose life is seeping out of her. I need the pins out of my wings. I need to fly free." Francesca picked up the book in which she had been making notes and hurled it against the study wall. "I don't want to decay and putrefy in this feckless crypt! Do you hear me? Do . . . you . . . hear . . . me!"

Francesca stood, threw her head back, ran her hands through her hair, then sprinted from the room. Keith stood like a stone statue for countless minutes, his eyes altogether as vacant as Francesca had intimated. When at last he summoned the energy to move, he made his way to his desk in their shared study, sat at his computer and searched the Internet for available apartments in the area. Within minutes, he had made his selection, sent his credit card deposit, and left the house to scrutinize his new accommodations.

18

The Fragrance of Christ

"STIRLING HERE."

"This is Allister, Stirling."

"Allister! Good to hear from you! Where are you?"

"I'm in the city . . . at work."

"It's been forever, it seems."

In point of fact, McCutcheon hadn't seen Allister for nearly a month, and it had been two weeks since Catherine had been in his office with the unseemly revelation about her husband. Since then, a shroud of silence covered the Drummond affair, and McCutcheon had waited to hear from either one of them as previously agreed upon with Catherine. Now Allister was calling him on the manse phone at night. McCutcheon glanced at his desk clock, which read 10:15.

"I've been reluctant to call," continued Allister. "Apparently Catherine has spoken with you, and, consequently, it hasn't been easy to lift the receiver and ring you up."

"I understand, but I'm here for you if you wish."

"I suppose we should talk. Do you have time this weekend . . . perhaps Saturday morning?"

"I do. Where would you like to meet? The church study should be quiet," McCutcheon offered.

"Anywhere but the church, Stirling. Right now it feels a bit strange to enter that building. How about some place public with a table in a corner somewhere?"

"What would you say to the Coffee Shop in Hampton Plaza, State Street? Ten o'clock?"

"That works. See you then." Allister hung up.

Bewildered, McCutcheon thought about calling Catherine to understand what had transpired since their last conversation but then thought better of it. If she had wanted to contact him, she undoubtedly would have picked up the phone or stopped by. He resolved to trust that she was all right and that she had confronted Allister with the facts as she knew them . . . indeed as he had unconsciously disclosed them to her on that fateful night.

Three days later McCutcheon met Allister as planned. The Coffee Shop was bustling with Saturday morning coffee conclaves, but before Allister arrived, McCutcheon found a small table perfectly ensconced in a little alcove. As soon as he appeared and sat down, McCutcheon apologized for the busy crowd—as if he were responsible for the ebb and flow of the shop's clientele—but Allister was actually pleased at the throng of people, which made their meeting all the less conspicuous. Someday McCutcheon would get over the assumption that he was personally accountable for everything that transpires in the universe . . . but obviously not today.

Neither of them knew where to begin, so they sat and nursed two large lattes.

"It was after ten when you called on Wednesday," McCutcheon finally initiated, "and you said you were in the city."

"Right. I'm no longer commuting during the week . . . at least for the time being," Allister rejoined, looking down at his latte, stirring it aimlessly with a latte swizzle stick.

"Was that a mutual decision?" McCutcheon asked, searching Allister's face for warmth, or worry, or sadness . . . any emotion that he could read, any visible indicator that he was feeling anything at all.

"No. I decided."

"What brought you that decision, Allister? What has it been? A little more than four months married? How could all of this have gone so awry?"

He clenched his teeth and, for the first time, looked McCutcheon in the eyes. "You know perfectly well how this marriage has gone awry, Stirling!" he said emphatically enough for him to hear but well beneath the ambient noise. "I understand that Catherine visited you at the church and told you everything. *Hustler* on the beach and Dominick in the city."

"Yes," McCutcheon answered warily.

"I went volatile, stormed out of the house, and two days later took an apartment in New York. I come back now only on weekends."

Simultaneously, as if scripted in the playbook, they both turned sideways in their chairs, leaned their backs against the wall and scanned the crowd. They said nothing for an extended time. McCutcheon turned back, sipped the latte, and looked at Allister.

"How can I help?"

"I have no idea," he said. "I thought you could tell me. Somebody has to have an answer. I certainly don't."

"Answer to what, Allister? What are you looking for? What answer?" McCutcheon asked in rapid succession.

"How can I have both? I don't want to lose my marriage. Contrary to what you may think now, I love Catherine more than anything. But I'm so far into S&M, I see no conceivable way of climbing out of that miry pit, of abandoning that murky world Catherine wants nothing to do with. This is my answer, Stirling! To have Catherine join me in the S&M dungeon. I know that once she has tried it, she'll revel in it. We'll be there together. It will meet both our needs."

"What does she say to the idea when you suggest it to her?"

"It's a resounding *no!* She says she'll return to England before she would ever consider that way of life. But you see, Stirling, it *is* a way of life for me. I cannot imagine ever denying myself what brings me the greatest pleasure sexually and the greatest sense of empowerment psychologically. Why would I? How could I?"

"How are such disparate views going to sustain your marriage?" McCutcheon asked, knowing full well that it would be impossible to merge two intransigent positions on a wide spectrum of sexual posturing. "Two incompatible expressions of human sexuality!" he continued with greater emphasis. "It will be worse than two ships passing in the night; it will be two ships in the night on a collision course. Perhaps it is already. If each of you refuses to move to center, to a negotiated mutuality, your marriage can never be more than two solitudes riveted in bitter isolation, never touching each other until you choose to collide."

Allister looked down at his porcelain mug, lifted the residual dregs to his lips, and asked if McCutcheon wanted another. He handed Drummond his cup and sat motionless until he returned with more coffee and two biscotti.

"Thanks!" he said warmly.

"Tell me how to change, Stirling," Allister queried softly. "Catherine won't. It would have to be up to me. How can I change?"

"I don't know," McCutcheon replied seriously. "I can't say that I understand the sadomasochistic passion well enough to know, or whether yours is a genetic disposition or a learned behavior. Undoubtedly, you have at least dabbled in the medical literature enough to know its genesis for the S&M community or, more specifically, its origin for you. I'd be reluctant to quip, 'Physician, heal thyself,' but I suspect you have a better understanding and see from a clearer vantage point than I. What do you know?" The ambiance buzz in the busy bistro had diminished substantially, which caused the silences between Allister and McCutcheon to seem more pronounced. McCutcheon waited, then repeated, "What do you know . . . about yourself?"

"When Catherine and I first met you, I told you that I was born and raised in Scotland, but I never mentioned which town. It was actually a small village on the northern coast of the highlands: the Village of Macduff, Aberdeenshire, quaint and earthy, peopled with men and women of hearty stock, ones who are seasoned and accustomed to handling the perpetual pounding of the North Sea with its gigantic waves crashing against the rocky coast, sending up sea spray as tall as New York skyscrapers, savage winds screaming and howling day and night with razor-sharp blades that can cut through a man's coat and chill his heart to stone in a matter of a fleeting minute."

"Forgive me for interrupting, Allister, but I am profoundly incredulous that, as a Scotsman, I never inquired about your hometown. It would be the most natural question two Scottish expatriates would proffer at the very inception of an acquaintance.

My apologies!" Of course McCutcheon knew the accountable reason for his omission, which was simply that he had been absorbed by Allister's fetching handsomeness. Yet, even when Allister was out of sight, or when McCutcheon thought of the couple together, the question of his Scottish locale never occurred to him.

"No apology necessary, Stirling!" responded Allister. "I never inquired about your birthplace either. Scotland—dear, dear Scotland—is all we need to know." With a broad smile, Allister repeated, "it's Scotland, bonnie Scotland! It's all we need to know."

"True," McCutcheon said reassured. "That's true, but, for sure, your home was in Macduff, Aberdeenshire, by the sea?"

"Yes. My father was a prominent barrister in the village; so we avoided the daily dread of so many, who repeatedly perched themselves in the proverbial widow's walk and waited for the first sign of their husbands' and fathers' fishing vessel. I am the youngest of three, with two older sisters who cared for me as if they were mothers. My actual mother was one to whom you could apply the positive appellation *old fashion*. The aroma in our house everyday was literally captivating, for there were smells of fresh-baked doughnuts, breads, rolls, pies, poultry, beef, and pork. Ours was a good life in this little village. We were one of the families on whom good fortune had smiled perpetually, while other families had been dealt steely death blows by devastating fates on unforgiving seas. As you know, Stirling, we are Presbyterian—I at least ostensibly so—and the principal ministrations of the Presbyterian Church in Macduff were first and foremost to families whose loved ones had been swallowed by the sea. It was a sad, sad sound of the church bell that reverberated across the moors with its doleful message that yet another had succumbed to the icy waves."

"Aye, to be sure. To be sure," McCutcheon said softly.

"My two sisters were three and four years older than I, respectively," Allister continued. "I was hardly into the business of dolls and playing house or dressing up. In those matters, I was hardly more than an observer, refusing many sisterly invitations to play the role of baby and later the role of father of the house. But ten or eleven houses down our street there was a girl my age, actually a classmate in our elementary school. Unlike my sisters, Nairne Roy liked to play games of guns and army, and what people in this country would call *cowboys and Indians.* The summer that Nairne and I turned ten years old, we played together nearly every day: army, guns, cowboys and Indians . . . never any games related to fishing on the high seas. We learned how to capture each other, and how to tie up the other, and how to carry the other off to a prisoner's camp with imaginary, insurmountable walls. There the victor tied the loser to a tree and kept him or her there until the prisoner swore to make some kind of made-up concession that would give the victor that dominant sense of triumph. One day I was the victor, she the prisoner; the next day she was the victor, I the prisoner. This went on day after day, all summer. It was the best summer I could ever remember. One day, midway through August, it was her turn to be the victor and I the prisoner. Rather than taking me tied to the imaginary prison with imaginary, insurmountable walls, she took me to the camping tent that had been set up in her back yard and tied me to the center pole in the middle of the tent, then zipped the tent door closed. After all the make-believe dialogue we spontaneously composed as we acted out our parts, she came close to me and unbuttoned my shirt, down to my bare skin. She unbuckled my belt and unzipped my trousers. An electrifying sensation—heretofore never felt—coursed through my body at what she did next. Even the pulsating pain seemed an immeasurable pleasure. Then she whispered into my left ear, 'I am the victor, and you are my captive.' As had been our past pattern, it was my turn to be the victor the next day. The roles were reversed. I had captured Nairne, taken her to the tent, and lashed her to the center pole. The dialogue of make-belief was shorter now. There seemed to be an urgency in getting to the dominance of victor over prisoner. I followed the very same steps Nairne had prescribed the previous day and, in a matter of minutes, she was as exposed as I had been during the preceding encounter. I applied the same pressure to the corresponding places, and while she pretended to scream, she actually moaned with sounds I had never heard before but which, I suspect now, she had heard somewhere else."

McCutcheon concentrated intently on Allister's words, never looking away, though fiercely inclined to do so. There had been no time in his years as a pastor that he could recall feeling embarrassed. He received any and all comments, circumstances, and confessions as an integral part of the multifarious schemata of life as he knew it. When anything seemed bizarre, even unseemly, he simply mentally relegated whatever it was to the colorful fabric of life, or as an unusual ingredient of the human condition. By the same token, never before his time with Allister that Saturday morning had he ever felt the inclination to look away, to lower his eyes and cover them, or to cringe with a twinge of embarrassment. Undoubtedly, in his lifetime McCutcheon had heard something worse . . . perhaps the atrocities of the lascivious guards in Hitler's concentration camps. Surely Allister's revelations couldn't approach the heinous quality of those diabolical minds. But there was something—something he couldn't describe—that sent the blood to his face, causing a blushing he hadn't felt since a child in fifth grade when he bungled a rather simple recitation of Macbeth's soliloquy. Perhaps his blushing was slight enough so as to avoid a comment by Allister. McCutcheon resisted looking away and trained his gaze steadily in Drummond's eyes. Why the embarrassment in the first place? Allister, for sure, was not referring to atrocities. Undoubtedly, for an entire segment of the world population, what he was describing was perfectly legitimate, a natural way to express sexual pleasure. Suddenly McCutcheon realized that he was caught in a violent vortex of bias, a marked prejudice laced with a self-righteous, judgmental insinuation. Earlier in their conversation, Allister had described this behavioral proclivity as "a way of life." Clearly, it was a way of life for him. Was McCutcheon to judge that? Was he to put that down as a perversion in contrast to strict, conventional sex he believed to be the only acceptable medium of sexual expression in the eyes of God? God—speaking of God—look where that has gotten him . . . Heather in Scotland to stay, and he? Here sat McCutcheon on this side of the Atlantic, forced to adopt an unwanted celibacy. Come to think of it, how sick was that!

Allister looked around the room, as if he were about to disclose a secret, and to see if he recognized anyone in the coffee shop now. He continued, "this rhythm—this going back and forth alternately between victor and prisoner—continued for the remainder of the summer. Each of us thought up various approaches to what I now understand as S&M. Sometimes, when the sessions became too intense, when the pain became apparent and actual, the victor eased off. We never left identifiable, damaging marks on each other, which was an indication that we both cared deeply for one another, a bond that grew closer and deeper with every intensifying episode. Besides, we had no interest in having our parents or any other member of our family raise questions about a suspicious blemish.

"At the end of the summer, Nairne and I regretted seeing the tent taken down and stored away until the following year. We remarked to each other that we were fortunate indeed that no one ever surprised us in the tent. Our secrecy continued. At school, we pretended to hardly know each other. We never spoke in the hallways or by the lockers, and it wasn't until the following summer that we picked up our game again . . . and the summer after that . . . and the next summer after that. It was always the same. Outside the tent—wherever that might be—we acted as strangers. Inside the tent—invariably—we were S&M lovers. This continued for a total of five summers. Nairne and I turned fifteen the same month, and our bodies had been developing in ways that surprised each of us, especially each of us about the other. Because we both had summer jobs now, we couldn't be together every day. The upside of that restriction, however, was that because of my summer job, I could not go on holiday with my parents and sisters, and they left me alone to work and tend the house for a week. It was then that I built a life-sized St. Andrew's cross in the basement, and every evening Nairne and I played our old game of *The Victor and the Vanquished*. By the time my family was due home, I had dismantled the cross and restored the boards to the lumber pile. But on that last evening, as Nairne was strapped to the cross, I kissed her passionately, a kiss she returned with an equal fervor, and I slipped a silver St. Andrew's cross on a silver chain over her neck, then showed her mine as well. 'Every time I pass you in the school hallways,' I whispered, 'I'll know that we are bound together and bonded to each other.' She smiled, kissed me again, and said, 'Yes.' I released her from her bondage; she dressed and left. A week later her summer job concluded in time for her to go on holiday with her family the last week in August. On Saturday, Nairne and her family boarded a ferry to Stornoway, located at the northern most point of the Isle of Harris. In the middle of the night the boat took on water, sank, and everyone on board was lost."

There was nothing to say. McCutcheon had no words. Not a single cliché came to mind. Allister placed his head in his hands, and his body shook shamelessly with a syncopated rhythm that intoned a devil-may-care moan regarding who might be watching him. It was literally minutes before he lifted his head.

"We never said *goodbye*. Catherine claims I am an imposter, whom she doesn't know. I am an imposter, true, but not for the reason Catherine surmises, not because she suddenly knows I read *Hustler* and visit a dominatrix. I'm an imposter because I'm married to Catherine while Nairne is imbedded in my bone marrow."

"Was Nairne's body ever recovered?" McCutcheon asked quietly, suspecting the likelihood that it wasn't. "I know the North Sea doesn't readily give up its treasures."

Allister looked solemnly at Stirling's tie, averting his eyes from his. "No," he replied, shaking his head slightly. His word was barely audible. Then more forcefully he explained that the bodies of her parents, her brother, and sister were retrieved, but not Nairne's. Seventy-four other passengers, out of more than two hundred, were never found either.

"One has only to draw the simple conclusion that there was never a closure for Allister," thought McCutcheon. "It takes no renowned psychiatrist to understand that."

McCutcheon put the question to him. "Allister, does all this mean you still want Nairne?"

"Yes. Do you think she's still out there?"

"No, I don't. But wait, Allister, let me restate that. Yes, I do. She's still out there for you, but she isn't alive. Nor is she out there for anyone else. She's dead. She drowned in a capsized ferry years ago, and she's the jewel of the North Sea now. She's not coming back."

"I wish you hadn't said that, Stirling."

"I know."

"I didn't want to hear that, Stirling."

"I know." McCutcheon waited and then said, "why don't you say *goodbye? Goodbye, Nairne!*"

Allister's face began twitching. McCutcheon could feel the floor shimmering ever so slightly as his right leg was moving up and down rapidly. He sat staring into his coffee mug as if searching for Nairne in the tempest. Then, in an instant, his face stopped twitching, and his leg ceased its shaking . . . and he said, "Goodbye, Nairne."

Leaving their coffee mugs on the table, McCutcheon went for a third round of lattes, all the time furtively searching for a Men's Room sign. When he returned to the table, lattes in hand, Allister was sitting up straight, no longer leaning over the table.

"Are you ready for a final round, or do you want to call it quits?" McCutcheon asked whimsically.

"Do you have time?"

"I do."

"I need resolution with Catherine."

"What kind of resolution do you want?"

"I know I still want a life with her, but I haven't the foggiest notion now how to go about achieving it. We're in a stalemate."

"What if you told her that?"

"I could, but I think she's as confused as I am. She's absolutely certain about two things: that my reading *Hustler* offends her and she won't submit to S&M games."

"Then I have two questions for you, Allister," McCutcheon said without hesitation.

"All right."

"The first is: have you needed S&M for sexual fulfillment, or have you needed Nairne?"

"I thought I needed S&M. To be sure, whenever I visited the dominatrix, it was akin to a séance with Nairne Roy. It was as if she were with me again, just like we were when we were kids. But the end result was never the same. There never has been an S&M high like there was with Nairne."

"Then what do you think? What's you answer?"

"Stirling, I know the answer. It isn't S&M I needed. It was Nairne I wanted, and I couldn't have her."

"I have a second question, but first I want to share what Catherine told me you said to her by way of explanation regarding *Hustler* on the beach. Reportedly you said, 'You're in my reach, and I can have you anytime I want; but these are out of my grasp; therefore, I want them.' My second question is this, Allister: those paper nudes were out of your reach, so you wanted them just as Nairne has been out of your reach, and you wanted her. Is the pornography beyond your reach simply another manifestation of Nairne's being beyond your reach? Obviously, you can't have either."

Allister sat motionless. "Yes. I think so. Perhaps I don't need or want either any-more. Naine was whom I wanted. I've said *goodbye* to Nairne. It's what I needed to do. It's what I've done."

"When it comes to *joie de vivre*, Allister," McCutcheon said, "when it comes to capturing the unadulterated joy of living, there's a very simple secret: passionately desire what you already have and let go of the insatiable craving for what you cannot have."

They sat silently for another long interval. Then Allister lifted his hand and re-moved the silver chain from around his neck and the St. Andrew's cross from beneath his shirt. He set it on the table and pushed it toward McCutcheon.

"I can hardly wait to see Catherine, Stirling," he said with a look of anticipa-tion McCutcheon had never seen in his face. "If I'm not mistaken, I have new bone marrow."

"Before you leave, Allister, I want to tell you about a Ukrainian Catholic bishop I met at a retreat center a few years ago. He was speaking to a gathering of Byzantine Catholic priests on their annual retreat. He spoke about dwelling in the fragrance of Christ. If you go into a perfume shop, he said, or merely pass through the perfume de-partment of a large department store, or especially if you spray a few perfume samples on your wrists, when you leave, you carry that magnificent fragrance with you. Then he referred to his being raised on a farm and indicated that there are times when one fails to watch where he or she is stepping, and the results are foul-smelling. He then drew the conclusion that we carry the aroma of those with whom we associate or of those practices in which we engage. His concluding admonition was to remain in the fragrance of our Lord Jesus Christ.

"Allister, when you and Catherine recessed out of the sanctuary on the day of your wedding, Catherine had left her fragrance behind her—in the air—in the chancel. I caught a whiff of it when I returned to pick up my prayer book. I can't condemn anyone's method of sexual enjoyment or fulfillment, but I'd like to say, Allister, that if I were you, I'd much rather spend the rest of my life surrounded by Catherine's fragrance than that of the S&M dungeons of New York City."

Allister rose from his seat. McCutcheon did as well. It was no surprise this time when Drummond drew him close and embraced him with the force of a man with healthy new bone marrow, and with the gratitude of a man on the edge of a new day dawning. He hurled himself toward the door.

† † †

Early the next morning, when McCutcheon arrived at the church, Trudel Swenssen handed him an envelope containing a note. He opened it to discover it was from Catherine and Allister, apologizing, for they would not be in church for services that day. Their explanation was simple. They had left for New York City early that morning, and Catherine would be working from there for the foreseeable future. They would be returning occasionally to check on her father, for whom they had found an extraordinary live-in cook, housekeeper, and caregiver.

Three weeks later the Drummonds appeared in McCutcheon's office with coffee and Danish for the three of them and for Caryn. They seemed more radiant—if that could be possible—than the first time he met them as they drank coffee together on that familiar loveseat. Caryn left them alone and closed the door.

"It has been only three weeks, Stirling," Catherine acknowledged, "but we have the promise of a full and joyous life together. Thank you!"

"You're welcome, Catherine, but tell me, how did it all work out for you two?"

"It's all clear to me now, Stirling," rejoined Allister. "I've let go of my past—including Nairne—of what I can't have and, frankly, genuinely do not want . . . and passionately desire what I already have."

Catherine smiled a wicked grin. "Forgive me, Stirling, if I tell you something a little too intimate, but I have offered Allister some kinky sex ploys that could resemble a dominatrix's touch, but over and over he refuses. At times, though, he's still insatiable, but now it's always for me. And he says, 'How lovely your perfume, Catherine!'"

19

A Bargain with God

THE OLD GRANDFATHER CLOCK struck six the very moment McCutcheon appeared at Helga Wenzel's ornate, mahogany front door. As the door opened to a short, stocky woman with crimped white hair, a full round face, and a broad smile, the dinner guest felt a surge of nostalgia and familiarity as if he were walking into his parents' home in Edinburgh. Over the past three years, he had come to know Helga well, he thought, and privately valued her as one of his favorite parishioners. He and Heather had sat at her dinner table numerous times to drink in light-hearted, spirited warmth and cordiality. This occasion, on this particular evening, marked her eighty-first birthday.

"Come in, come in, Herr Pastor," Helga exuded with her rich German accent.

"Happy Birthday, my dear Lady!" McCutcheon exclaimed. He embraced her, gave her the large bouquet of flowers he had been holding by one hand and the bottle of Johannesburg Riesling from the other.

"Right on time, sir!" she remarked as she turned down the hallway toward the kitchen. "Come. Come with me to the kitchen, and we'll give these beautiful flowers a comfortable residence in Helga's favorite vase. And why not start on the Riesling!"

"Of course! To celebrate this distinguished lady's birthday!" rejoined McCutcheon.

McCutcheon opened the wine, Helga produced the glasses, and—the colorful nosegay ensconced on the dinner table—they adjourned to the living room with glasses in hand.

"Please raise your glass, dear Helga, for this is your evening. To Helga! As the years pass with more fleeting resoluteness, and as your life takes on fuller form with each ensuing year, may you celebrate what your life has been and what your life will be with its contrasts of light and shadows, of what is bright with what is dark, of what is clear in contrast to that which is obscure—all the contrasting aspects that are necessary for the complete life portrait. May this, your eighty-first birthday, be filled mostly with light and that which is bright: may this day and the coming year be filled with love, laughter, friends, and fullness in Christ! To Helga! Happy birthday!"

"Yes! Dankeschön, Herr Pastor!"

They touched glasses lightly together, drank the smooth German wine, and attended to a coffee table of elegant hors d'oeuvres.

"How have you spent your day so far, Helga?" asked McCutcheon. "Lunch with friends? Opening birthday cards?"

"Well, I opened my eyes at six forty-five this morning and then immediately closed them while I prayed a prayer of thanksgiving to God for giving me so many blessings in these eighty-one years. Lunch at the Corinthian Club with Babbs Schumann, Chantal DuBois, and Glynnis Vandeusen. A lovely time! And yes, lots of cards! Then I spent the rest of the day looking forward to our time together."

"It's actually immoral," began McCutcheon with a smile, "to be cooking on your birthday. You really should have accepted my invitation to dinner out."

"Of course, but so many people out, so noisy, and so public, Herr Pastor. I much prefer a peaceful room so we can talk."

"Helga, after three years, we know each other well enough for you to call me *Stirling*. Please do."

"Oh, no, I couldn't. That would seem so disrespectful."

"Then I must call you *Frau Wenzel*."

"Oh, no, no, no! That would be worse."

"Then you must agree to call me *Stirling*."

"All right . . . Stirling," she said awkwardly. Then she laughed. "I've said it only behind your back, never to your face."

"Now's the time—on your eighty-first birthday—to come clean and say *Stirling* to my face."

"All right! But never in church," she said, acquiescing.

"All right! But never in church. In church it will be *Herr Pastor* and *Frau Wenzel*."

They erupted in laughter.

"Stirling, thank you for your eloquent toast!"

"You're welcome!"

"You spoke of contrasts. You referred to light and shadows, to what is bright and what is dark, clear and obscure. How apropos, for there are many shadows in my past I have never shared with you . . . or with close friends here in Albany. But I have been thinking about them continually this afternoon."

"Today, more so than other days?" inquired McCutcheon.

"Yes."

"I wonder why today?"

"I suppose I have finally acknowledged the eighties as the decade of the penultimate, the time before the end or before transition into the unknown. I find it to be days when there is more looking back than looking forward. In looking back, there's an ever-looming sensation of an ever-present sorrow. So many have gone, so many much younger than I," Helga said pensively, "and, without losing even a modicum of faith, I wonder about the meaning of it all . . . losses, tragedies, atrocities, and, above all, the deep, immeasurable longings I have to see them all again, to sit at kitchen table with my mother and father with coffee and homemade doughnuts and hot freshly-baked rolls . . . to touch August's hand again in my lap or press my thigh against his as we sleep. There is so much I have never told you."

"I'm sorry, Helga," McCutcheon said softly.

"There's no need to apologize."

"What I mean is that I apologize for my assumption that after all this time as your pastor, I supposed that I knew you well, but I didn't probe the depths of your past. I know that before I arrived here at the church, you had given the communion set we use on communion Sundays . . . in memory of your husband August, but admittedly, I don't know the circumstances surrounding that magnificent gift. Helga, what is it that I don't know about you?"

Helga sat quietly, staring at her gnarled hands folded in her lap, hands that had seen many years of hard work and selfless giving.

She raised her eyes and said, "Stirling, dinner is ready. Shall we talk at table?"

"Certainly," said McCutcheon as he rose from the sofa and led Helga to the kitchen.

Handing him a large soup tureen and ladle, she led him to the dining table where, following grace, they enjoyed their first course, soup.

"This is called *Hochzeitssuppe*. I trust a bona fide Scotsman will allow an old birthday lady the pleasure of her heritage on this one occasion, Stirling," she said with a droll smile and tilt of her head.

"Come, come, Helga! Heather and I have had your authentic German food numerous times here at this splendid table . . . and it wasn't on your birthday. This bona fide Scotsman has no complaint. Believe me!"

Soup cleared, Helga brought on Bratwurst with options of sauerkraut, red cabbage, and hot German potato salad with bacon bits.

"You mentioned *shadows*, Helga," McCutcheon said, intending to resume their previous conversation.

"When August and I married in Zurich in 1948, each of us was only nineteen years old. We had grown up together in Frankfort—childhood sweethearts, I suppose you could contend—and when the Nazi regime was at its height in fervor and malevolence, and when their demonic machinations were finely tuned and systematically devastating, August's parents and mine were fervently enmeshed in the underground resistance efforts. There was a clandestine passage for Jews out of Germany to Switzerland. For nearly three years, our parents worked with other Christians, who refused to honor Hitler's National Church, to implement the escape of hundreds of Jews—individuals and families—from tyranny to freedom. Though we were exceptionally young to be involved, both August and I worked side by side in this covert operation. We were eyewitnesses to the terror that was occurring openly in our region as Jews felt the brutal Nazi hammer pulverizing their lives. And then we saw first-hand the great elation and relief other Jews experienced as they walked from the shadows of certain death into Switzerland's sunlight and liberty . . . in that moment for each of them, a new life had begun.

"Then came the dreadful day when the Gestapo discovered the escape route to Switzerland. They shot August's father on the spot. August wrapped his arms around his mother to shield her from a bullet, was wounded and left for dead. His mother was deported to Dachau where she was abused and subsequently died. It was their vigilance and quick responsiveness that saved the day for the rest of us. Somehow word had come to them that the Gestapo was onto us and the operation had been compromised. They sent that intelligence to the rest of us with a rendezvous time to meet at the departure point. Their intention, of course, was that all of us would make our way out of Germany into Switzerland. The six of us were among the last to leave. My parents and I made it into the tunnel just before the Gestapo arrived. The Wenzels didn't. When they didn't catch up, my parents and I returned to find Mr. Wenzel dead, Mrs. Wenzel gone, and August wounded. The Gestapo had left. Within a couple of months we learned of Mrs. Wenzel's fate."

It seemed disrespectful to McCutcheon for him to continue eating during so personal and profound an account of Helga's background. Neither had finished dinner. Both had rested their forks on their plates. McCutcheon listened; Helga continued.

"When you spoke of shadows and light, what is obscure in contrast to what is clear, Stirling, it is true that all these contrasting aspects are essential to the whole life portrait. While I continually wish it could have been different, the distorted faces of corpses lying unattended in the streets of Frankfort—men, women, children of all ages, gays and disabled—they all are principal actors of a darkness in my spirit, a shadow so enormous, so overpowering that I can't imagine how superficial my life would have been without it. I would to this day give anything I own, anything I am, for their lives to have been free of fear and oppression and death. I also know that it was that darkness, that looming shadow that gave meaning to bright Jewish faces lifted to the brilliant light of the Switzerland sun. These opposites weave a conundrum so bizarre that I have no plausible way to solve it. Why? Why? Why? I don't know, Stirling. All I know is that those distorted faces—some known, most unknown—still visit me at night and before waking to the daylight."

McCutcheon remained silent, his eyes trained on Helga, his eyes imperceptibly moist.

"And August?" McCutcheon asked after a few moments of utter stillness. "Did August ever indicate that he was visited by similar images?"

"Whenever we spoke about it, he said that for years he envisioned them lying there, brutalized. But they never came to him in the night. In the day. It was always during the day, when he saw some icon or monument, or a market square similar to the one where they had been lined up and shot, or a balcony that resembled one from which a disabled person confined to a wheelchair had been pushed to a cruel death.

The daytime. It was always in the daytime. His nightmares were invariably reserved for his parents. His father's being shot to death, his mother's being whisked away, his failure to save either of them. These were persistent and recurring themes played out over and over again, night after night, year after year. Finally we came to a tacit agreement—though neither of us ever articulated it—that we wouldn't speak about these shadows anymore. Not that that dispelled them. The silence simply drove them deeper into our souls while we pretended to embrace resolution. It was at best a fabricated resolution."

"What happened after the war, Helga?"

"August, my parents, and I settled in Zurich after our escape. Both of my parents had been professors in Germany and found teaching positions at the University of Basil . . . adjunct professors in medicine and anthropology respectively. August and I enrolled in school and, by the age of nineteen, we were prepared to enter university. August was already like family and lived with us from the time we arrived in Zurich. So, it was perfectly natural for us to marry at that young age. We matriculated in university together and graduated from university together. As the saying goes, neither of us could remember a time we had not known each other. We continued with graduate studies, and by the mid-fifties we had earned advanced degrees in architecture and psychology. Germany was being rebuilt. There were many opportunities for an architect to help raise the phoenix out of the ashes, as well as for a psychologist to address the issues of trauma and guilt associated with acquiescence to the evil of a demonic regime. We moved to Hamburg in 1955.

"A new beginning," McCutcheon observed quietly.

"Yes. August was a magnificent husband with a gentle, creative spirit. It would have been a great joy to have produced a little August or a little Helga, but because of his wound, courtesy of the Gestapo, we were never able to have children. We had each other, however, and that was quite sufficient."

"How was life for you in Hamburg?"

"Mostly it was a beautiful life for us, but for all of Germany it was a long road back to magnificence and economic stability. As you know, Stirling, the German people are an industrious lot, and in the decade after the war, great strides had been made to develop a new infrastructure. Because the market was ripe for our particular fields of endeavor, we were blessed financially within a short period of three years. We enjoyed a good life in an elegant apartment. For all intents and purposes we were happy. My parents remained in Switzerland where they continued to teach, but the absence of August's parents left a vacuum that could not be filled . . . for either of us. So, while we were given the good life, it was only the lingering shadows that tormented us."

"I assume there was no way to dispel them, to put them to rest?"

"No," said Helga reflectively. After a pause, she continued. "But there was a mitigating factor . . . or I should say a *mitigating person* who helped us to acquire insight into the atrocities of the Nazi's Jewish pogrom. Actually, Stirling, you remind me of him . . . your preaching, I mean, reminds me of his."

McCutcheon smiled. "Do tell, Helga!"

"We arrived in Hamburg soon after the Reverend Dr. Helmut Thielicke became the Rector of St. Michael's Church. He had been through interrogations by the Nazis because of his ties with the Confessing Church. But, unlike Martin Niemöller and others of the Resistance, he was never incarcerated for his anti-Nazi stance. August and I joined St. Michael's Church six months after we settled in the city. The first service we attended was on Christmas Eve—with my parents, visiting from Zurich. In that Christmas Eve sermon, he dealt with the truly radical mystery of God's taking on flesh and dwelling among us in the incarnate form of the Christ Child, an infant born in an obscure village of Bethlehem. He examined the far-reaching implications of the mystical reality of *Immanuel—God with us*.

"As you might imagine, Stirling, having been through what we had endured and having seen the atrocities played out before our very eyes, August and I had questioned whether God was actually with us, or, if he was with us, what earthly difference did it make in the Nazi state and the world's crumbling culture of the early forties. There was something about Thielicke's apparent faith and resounding proclamation, however, that made the issue of God's interaction with the world he created worth examining after all. Perhaps God does intervene in history, or at the very least reside in some mystical capacity with a chaotic world that saunters along in its own hubris and folly.

"That Christmas Eve made a deep impression on August and me. The insights offered in Dr. Thielicke's sermon were not derived by an outsider but, rather, by someone who had witnessed the same atrocities we had seen in the marketplace. Resolution for us came only a few months later, however, when he preached on the parable of the Good Samaritan, in which a lawyer puts Jesus to the test, asking, 'Teacher, what shall I do to inherit eternal life?' Dr. Thielicke spoke about secular refuters, who engage in endless arguments in order to keep Christ at arms length and cultivate a moral alibi for their unbelief. It was after that sermon that August and I realized that we had been using Nazi atrocities as arguments to put God in Christ to the test, to attack our very own faith, to justify our incensed doubts and nurse our unarticulated despair. At last, we chose faith over explanation."

"And the shadows?"

"Mollified . . . to a degree at least."

McCutcheon reached out for Helga's hand, squeezed it affectionately, and held it for a moment.

"When did you and August come to the States, Helga?"

"It was in the late seventies . . . 1978 to be precise. August had made his mark in Hamburg by the late sixties. He had acquired great respect in the reconstruction of large buildings in Hamburg and other German cities. A prominent American architect was attending a conference in Hamburg, learned of August's work, and offered him a position with his firm here in Albany. We agreed, he accepted, and we made our way to another new life in what has now become our home . . . our home far away from home."

"I regret that I never knew August," said McCutcheon thoughtfully.

"Yes. Yes. You would have liked him . . . and he you. He also would have found your preaching thought-provoking, faithful, insightful."

"Has it been five years now that you've been without him?"

"Five years. But we had years we had not counted on . . . extra grace, you might say.

"Two years before his death, August was critically ill. As you might suspect, I was frantic. I was not prepared to lose him. So I bargained with God. Stirling, I know that God isn't one who bargains, but I was desperate, and I prayed: *if you will spare August his life, I will do something wonderful for the church.* And yes! August recovered; and because God granted my request, I bought the entire sterling silver communion set that we use on communion Sundays at Madison Avenue Presbyterian Church—all the bread trays, the wine trays, and the beautiful chalice. God came through, and so did I. After that, August was robust and the healthiest he had ever been since his arrival in the United States. For two years he was healthy and happy, and we had marvelous times together, traveling about the world, attending theater, ballets, operas, both in Europe and here in the States. Then, unfortunately, he suddenly acquired an infection. Septicemia set in, and in three days he was dead; but I shall always be grateful for those two robust years we had together. Who says that God doesn't take us up on a bargain? Have you ever known God to pick up on a wager?"

"To be honest, Helga, only in literature," he confessed with a smile.

"For me, it happened once before . . . when we were active in the resistance, and I was very young, and I possessed a childhood's faith. Perhaps it was a month or two before the Nazis discovered our escape route to Switzerland. One night a Jewish family—parents with three children—was set to make their escape along with eight other people. Somehow—probably by way of a Nazi informant—the storm troopers learned of their intent, raided their home, and shot all except the youngest child, eleven years old. We arrived and looked in the window just as the gun was pointed at his head. The others lay dead on the floor. I remember praying to God that if he would spare the boy's life, I would give up whatever I valued most. At that instant, the Lutheran pastor from the local parish of the German Evangelical Church—the *Reichskirche*, who had capitulated to Hitler's nationalizing the protestant churches—appeared at the door and shouted at the storm trooper to stop. He flung the boy across the room, holstered his gun, and left. At the time, inexplicable! We later learned that the Nazi soldier was a member of the pastor's church. That certainly explained the soldier's obeying the pastor's demand, Stirling, but why did the pastor appear right at that moment?"

"Did God answer your prayer, Helga . . . take you up on your bargain?"

"He certainly did. Not that I realized it then. We retrieved the eleven-year-old Jewish boy—Adar Bieber—and connected him with another of the Jewish families who escaped that night. On the way to the point of departure, he and I sat together in the vehicle, and I held him as he wept long, quiet sobs. We exchanged names and embraces, and he left."

Helga paused, obviously moved by her retrospective, then continued.

"Stirling, earlier this evening I said that it would have been a great joy to have produced a little August or a little Helga. To be honest, that was a considerable under-statement. The truth of the matter is that having a little August or a little Helga was my most passionate desire in all the world. It was what I craved most in life . . . to bear August's children. God accepted my wager, however, spared Adar Bieber's life, and accepted my offer to relinquish what I valued most: children."

"Do you really think so, Helga?"

"Yes, Stirling, I really think so. I *believe* so."

"For sure?"

"For sure! But not without an immeasurable reward in the bargain. This is how I know. Two years before August and I came here to the States, there was a knock on our apartment door in Hamburg, and we opened it to a young, handsome man of a similar age to us. It was Adar Bieber. He had tracked us down, said his family was in the car, and asked if it was a convenient time for them to visit us. Of course! Of course! We embraced. He brought up his lovely wife and their three small children, each of them named after himself, his sister, and his older brother. Stirling, do you see! These are my children. August's and my children . . . what I had valued most in life—chil-dren—these children stood before us, and they had life and freedom due to a bargain with God one dark night in a world of atrocities."

Helga stood and made her way to the living room sofa end table and returned with a small box. She drew her chair a little closer to McCutcheon's, sat and placed her hand lightly, affectionately on his. "Stirling, I want to give you something . . . some-thing dear to my heart, even as you and Heather are dear to me." She opened the box and took out a cross. It was the Iron cross the Nazis adopted as their central symbol during World War II. It was black with a white outline around its edges. All four arms were equal in length, and each arm grew from the center into a flared end.

"Helga, you say this Nazi cross is dear to you?" McCutcheon inquired somewhat bewildered.

"Yes. You see, that evening years ago in Hamburg, when Adar Bieber and his family visited us, after coffee and cake, Adar reached into his pocket and pulled out this cross. He held it tightly in his right hand, as if it were imbued with some sacred element. Again I say, *completely inexplicable*: a persecuted Jew holding a Christian symbol, the cross that had been bastardized by the Third Reich. Inexplicable . . . at first blush anyway. But then he told us what we had not seen on the tragic night of his family's brutal deaths and his escape. He said, 'After the pastor commanded the storm trooper to cease, and after I had been thrown across the room and my assailant left, the pastor rushed to me, opened the neck of my shirt, lifted this cross from off his own neck, placed it around mine, and told me, *Wear this cross. It will keep you safe during your escape to Switzerland.* Now, Adar said, I want to thank you, and I want you and your husband to have it.' Stirling, as repugnant as this cross could be as the symbol of a diabolical force for evil, this cross—this particular cross—tells a story that is ultimately beautiful and redemptive. Perhaps every cross has a story to tell."

There was nothing for McCutcheon to say. He looked down at the cross, back up at Helga, and smiled a long warm smile.

"Please take it, Stirling, and keep it safe. On this birthday, at eighty-one, I'm not convinced that I have many years left. There is no one who will care for it as well as you."

Helga placed the Iron cross in McCutcheon's right hand. She held his hand affectionately as he nodded sadly and whispered, "Thank you, dear Lady!" A sudden urge welled up in McCutcheon's breast, and he bent down and kissed Helga's hand that still embraced his.

The dear lady finally rose from the table, heated their remnant food in the microwave, and they ate in silence. The meal concluded with German chocolate cake.

"Stirling, I listened to your announcement in the worship service last Sunday. I'm truly sorry about your pending divorce. I have loved Heather dearly ever since the two of you came to Madison Avenue Church. With August, I have known loss, but I have never known the loss of a marital union. Please be certain that I shall continue to love you both. I wish to know nothing more than to know that you are both all right . . . and will be well, apart or together."

"Thank you, Helga!"

"This house is your house, a haven, if you wish . . . to sit quietly or read or enjoy a home-cooked meal. You will be safe here . . . and no expectations."

As the large, ornate, mahogany door closed softly behind him, he breathed in the balmy air of the tranquil night that engulfed him. There was no traffic on the road. He slowly descended the steps of Helga's front porch. The streetlamp across the street shone as a singular beacon in the darkness, casting shadows of moving leaves onto the sidewalk before him. Shadows. He clutched the Iron cross in his coat pocket and began his walk home. He had his own looming shadows now to mollify. But at the moment, they were as haunting as a heinous, unappeasable specter that showed no inclination to bargain.

20

Wednesday's Child

The telephone rang three times before McCutcheon awoke to reach for it.

"Hello, Stirling McCutcheon here."

Silence.

"Hello. Are you there?"

McCutcheon detected irregular breathing at the other end of the telephone line.

"Can I help you? . . . What do you want? . . . What can I do for you? . . . Who is this?"

There was a click and then a dial tone. McCutcheon looked at the clock. 2:12 a.m. He examined the caller ID on his handset, but the number was unfamiliar to him. He hurriedly dialed the number, but to no avail. He let it ring a dozen times, but there was neither an answer nor a recorded voice greeting. He lay back upon his pillow, his hands folded behind his head, his eyes wide open as he stared at the ceiling. At 2:20, unable to dismiss the phone call and return to sleep, McCutcheon got up and pulled on a sweatshirt over his sleepwear. A gleam of moonlight shone on Heather's side of the bed, accentuating its vacancy. He moved through the dark hallway to the stairs, down the stairs to the study, into the study to his leather chair. The same gleam of moonlight softly illuminated his north wall, so that it seemed to him that he was surrounded by that luminous darkness, of which Howard Thurman had written in the early sixties. He fixed his attention on the wall-hanging lighted by the moonlight and recalled the day one of his parishioners in Edinburgh walked into his office before he and Heather were to leave for the States and gave him this farewell gift. It was a magnificent etching of Heidelberg by Reynold Weidenaas, with gold design on white matting and an antique gold frame. Beneath the intricately detailed etching was inscribed in Old English lettering the introduction of the Heidelberg Catechism, beginning with the poignant question, *What is your only comfort in life and death?* Remembering his former parishioner with both gratitude and admiration, McCutcheon recollected that he was the same man—Reginald—who told him that he thought the most brilliant beginning of any novel he had ever read was that of Melville's *Moby Dick:* "Call me Ishmael."

"And then there are Ishmael's words much later in his narrative," continued Reginald, "words, born out of an hypnotic state, that are so profound: *There is a wisdom that is woe; but there is a woe that is madness.* What do you make of that, Stirling?"

"Ah, good question! One could make a case, I suppose," McCutcheon had ventured, "that that succinct statement sums up the human condition, at least from a philosophical perspective akin to Kierkegaard's—that unrecognized genius, who had come to know thoroughly, as he claimed, the appalling lack of character in humanity and an expansive feeling of anxiety in himself."

All of this somber retrospective was particularly pertinent since McCutcheon had been working on his sermon on Jeremiah for Sunday next, titled, *Wednesday's Child, Full of Woe.* He lifted it from his desk and read his unedited first draft, editing as he read to the end.

McCutcheon laid the manuscript on his desk, looked up at Weidenaas's etching of Heidelberg, and considered the question, *What is your only comfort in life and in death?* The poignant answer seemed especially pertinent in McCutcheon's present frame of mind: *That I, with body and soul, both in life and death, am not my own, but belong unto my faithful Savior Jesus Christ.* The sound of the telephone on his desk punctuated this catechetical consideration. 3:30 a.m. This time he recognized the caller ID.

"Stirling! This is Francesca. Keith is dead."

"What are you saying, Francesca?"

"We were at a party together . . . at the home of mutual friends. He left me off at the house around eleven thirty and went to his apartment. Both of us had had numerous glasses of wine, and I was concerned that he would have an accident along the way or get slapped with a DUI. But he made it to the apartment. He must have taken medication to sleep. He called me about two thirty. I couldn't understand a word he was saying. I drove to his apartment, let myself in, and found him on the bedroom floor. The medics said it was too late. There was nothing they could do and took him to the hospital. Stirling! Stirling! I didn't want it to come to this! I didn't! I didn't! Believe me! I didn't!"

"I know, Francesca. I know," said McCutcheon with conviction. "I'll be at your house in a few minutes. Do you need to go to the hospital?"

"Yes."

"I'll take you. Sit tight. I'll be there directly."

Drew Lattimore had arrived at Francesca's house shortly before McCutcheon pulled into the driveway and made his way to the front door. When the door opened, Lattimore was standing behind Francesca in the foyer. His drawn, somber face carried a dazed demeanor, which struck McCutcheon as an inscrutable mystique. Was it of grave concern, or was it of hidden culpability, or was it of genuine remorse, or was it of benign indifference?

Francesca reached for McCutcheon's hand, drew him into the foyer, and embraced him tightly, laying her head upon his chest. "I can't believe this has happened, Stirling," Francesca said tearfully. "What was he thinking? How could he let this happen? Why?" She released McCutcheon and stepped away into the living room. "You know Dr. Lattimore, my therapist, don't you, Stirling?"

"Actually, we have never met. Hello, Dr. Lattimore. I'm Stirling McCutcheon."

"Yes. Yes. How do you do! I just came by to offer support. Francesca seemed understandably distraught when she called to tell me. I decided I should see her. But now that you are here, I'll be on my way. Thank you, Rev. McCutcheon!" Lattimore approached Francesca. They embraced warmly.

"I'll call you when I get back, Drew," she said. "I'm sure I'll need to talk this afternoon, if you have the time."

"Just call Rachael, and she'll fit you in," Lattimore replied with an urbane, businesslike tone. With that, he nodded to McCutcheon and left.

"Am I to surmise that he doesn't know that I know?" queried McCutcheon with a sardonic frown as his gaze turned from the front door to Francesca.

"No. I have never told him that you know about our affair," confessed Francesca. "He has assumed that no one, including Keith, has ever known about our liaison."

McCutcheon and Francesca sat opposite each other, McCutcheon in the chair across from the sofa, Francesca on the edge of the sofa, leaning forward, her face buried in her hands. This was the first and only occasion McCutcheon could recall when Francesca failed to fill all the surrounding space with unremitting words, seemingly endless sentences, incessant paragraphs. He waited, tacitly acknowledged the silence until she looked up, shook her head in small, rapid shakes of bewilderment . . . or remorse . . . or regret . . . or furor. What? Which? Who could know? How could she get in touch with that unfathomable, fathoms-deep gnawing at the base of her soul, where everything that resided seemed to be rotting, and where everything that was recorded there during the past few months was written in permanent ink, indelible and irreversible.

"It's a paradoxical agony, Stirling!" she ventured, attempting an explanation of her incapacitating confusion. "I wanted to be free, and now I am free, and now I don't want to be free. I wanted Drew, and what drew me to Drew was his voice. He spoke. He related to me, and now I can't hear his voice without visceral spasms. I didn't ask him to come tonight. I just called to tell him. I didn't want to see him. What is happening to me, Stirling? I'm decomposing. It's as if I've had an abortion . . . an abortion of a marriage, and there that aborted marriage lies bloody on the lid of a trash can, and I want that aborted marriage back in my empty womb again, and it never will be. Has God damned me, Stirling?"

Francesca laid her face in her hands again as she sobbed. McCutcheon sat motionless, afflicted again by the Holy Spirit's silence. He couldn't say that God had damned her. He thought of saying that she had damned herself, but he didn't believe that either. It occurred to him that perhaps there was a crass element of demonic justice here, an element so ironic that the thought of it nearly nauseated him: that Francesca also had gone for the gold—to which she was not entitled—and the ring in her hand had come up black, not brass. And the merry-go-round goes round and round, utterly indifferent to the disappointments and despair of all those riding plaster horses.

"No, Francesca," he said. "You are now engulfed in what others have named *the tragic vision*, which they claim is a more profound vision of human life than the comic. Who can blame you for wanting more? For wanting to ride the winds of intellectual exhilaration, to engage indefatigably in verbal discourse with an insightful seer— Drew Lattimore—into the intricate regions of the human mind? Now, I believe for the first time in your life, you have experienced the catapulting force of the tragic, and you are being propelled up the rocky path to Golgotha while carrying your own cross. No, God is not damning you, Francesca. God is confronting you. If you can see beyond the tragic vision, you will encounter with your wounds the wounds of the Crucified God of Golgotha: wounds to wounds, face to face. Your ultimate determination, Francesca, will be to transform this tragic vision into a vision of the wounded Savior."

"Forgive me, Stirling, I just can't get my mind around all of that . . . not yet anyway."

"But of course," apologized McCutcheon. "All I meant to say is that God's mercy endures forever. Condemnation is not an ingredient of his grace."

Francesca nodded affirmatively. "I can understand that, Stirling. Thank you."

"Do you need to identify Keith's body?"

"Yes, and release him to the funeral home."

"Albany Medical Center?"

"Yes."

"I'll drive you there and bring you back."

Francesca rose from the sofa. "Before we go, I need to tell you that I don't know if Keith intended to kill himself. I want to believe that he inadvertently mixed sleeping medication or tranquillizers with more wine when he got to his apartment after the party. But . . . I found a sheet of paper on his desk after the medics took him to the hospital. It seemed like a blank page from a journal with just one sentence at the top, which said, *I am so weary of asking why.*"

"What do you think he meant?" asked McCutcheon with an intent expression.

"I don't know for sure, but I assume it has to do with the day he returned from playing tennis with you and confronted me about my affair with Drew Lattimore. He asked me two questions: *How long? And why?* Both of those questions I answered. I told him how long and I told him why, but he must have still been asking himself, *why?*"

McCutcheon stood and faced Francesca. Conflicted by the need to reassure Francesca and at the same time to honor the confidence Keith had placed in him,

Stirling said, "I believe Keith's question *why* has less to do with your affair with Lattimore than it does with his own internal struggles about his own personality. Without getting into the intricacies of his restlessness, I think it's possible he was asking why he couldn't brush off negative comments that he had allowed to shape his behavior, or why he couldn't show more of who he was, or why his was a constipated brilliance, as someone had flippantly remarked, or why one experience on a merry-go-round had deterred him from taking significant risks in life. I suspect those are the *whys* he was wearied of asking. Why you had an affair in all likelihood was much more understandable to him because of all the other *whys* he couldn't answer. During the bi-weekly tennis matches he and I played, and during the numerous visits with him in his apartment, the *why* I kept asking him was, 'Why won't you tell Francesca what you have told me?' Apparently he never did. By virtue of that fact, Keith denied you the rare opportunity to know his true essence. Francesca, in my view, this is the deepest tragedy: that had he allowed you, you could have ridden the winds of intellectual exhilaration, to engage indefatigably in verbal discourse with the brilliant mind of Keith Harlansworth—if he had only let you . . . if he had only disclosed himself to you. Decidedly, Drew Lattimore would have been dispensable."

Slowly, Francesca reached inside her dress pocket and pulled out a cross. She examined it carefully, longingly. She handed it to McCutcheon who looked at it closely. It was a sterling silver cross on a sterling silver chain. In the center of it was a blue butterfly where the vertical and cross pieces came together.

"That horrendous day—when Keith came home from tennis with you and confronted me about my affair with Drew—I told him I wanted to be free, that I felt like a butterfly whose wings were pinned to a board, and I wanted a chance at a new life. A week after he moved out and had settled into his apartment, he gave me this cross with a note that said, *My precious Butterfly, I know you must be free.* I don't want this cross, Stirling. I don't even want to be free of Keith. I know that now, and I know it too late."

Which of the two, wondered McCutcheon, *was Wednesday's Child—Keith or Francesca?*

† † †

Four days later, following Keith Harlansworth's memorial service and burial, Francesca met McCutcheon in his office and informed him that she had broken off the affair with Drew Lattimore. Three months later, Francesca met McCutcheon in his office and informed him that she had broken the lease on Keith's apartment, had sold their house, and that she was moving to Billings, Montana, within the week. "I need open spaces, Stirling. Please wish me well."

As McCutcheon warmly embraced Francesca, and as each gave the other a kiss on the cheek, McCutcheon thought of the Butterfly cross, which he had sadly placed in his box of crosses. He wondered if Francesca would see beyond the tragic vision to the countenance of the crucified Christ in the open spaces of Montana; or will the merry-go-round continue to go round and round, utterly indifferent to the disappointments and despair of all those riding plaster horses?

21

Pas de Deux

5 December

Dear Stirling,

My apologies for remaining so inexcusably quiet since your last visit to New York in early October for the opening of Swan Lake! *Dinner with you following the performance was an utter delight, and our conversation, as usual, caused me to continue thinking of new ideas for weeks afterwards. You are such an antithetical thinker, exploring any subject from every one of its multisided angles!*

But, dear Stirling, shall I forgive you, or shall I not? At that time, I had no idea whatsoever—and how should I if you refuse to share said information with me?—that Heather and the children had planned to stay in Scotland and never return to Albany. It was only when my parents informed me of your announcement following worship on Sunday, October 15, that I realized Heather and you are to divorce. I am deeply and sincerely sorry, Stirling, and wish you strength of purpose (whatever it may be) and clarity of mind (though you always seem to possess it, whatever the circumstance) as you and she move through the proceedings.

Of course I should have written before now, but, quite frankly, I had not wanted to appear opportunistic, for I do care about you as a dear friend, which must not be read, if you please, as anything resembling a proposition. Actually, the term proposition *brings me to the next point, the fuller purpose of this letter. As is the custom every year for the New York City Ballet, we are performing* The Nutcracker *throughout December. Once again, I shall be dancing the part of the Sugar Plum Fairy, and should very much like to have you come to New York for a performance of your choosing. If you are willing, I shall send you a ticket, meet you at the train, and entertain you as royally as I am able, including after-theater dinner . . . on me this time.*

When you came for Swan Lake *in October, you undoubtedly recall that I reserved a room for you at the hotel near the ballet theater. Please do not read anything into this next offer, but my spare bedroom is available and ready to accommodate you in the most innocent of milieus. Or, if you prefer, my dear Stirling, I shall be glad to reserve a room for you in the same hotel.*

I await your response, with anticipation.

Sincerely,
Daphne

P.S. The wealthy ballet patron of whom we have spoken numerous times never greets me with a smile, but only a sneer from his wheelchair. But, of course, who could possibly blame him?

McCutcheon read the letter a second time, laid it on the desk and picked up his Day-Timer. He quickly deduced that Friday, December 15, would be the best date to make his way to the Big Apple. He lifted the telephone receiver, dialed, and left a voice mail.

"Daphne, this is Stirling. Many thanks for your lovely letter and for your good wishes regarding Heather, the children, and my divorce proceedings! Actually, Heather wanted immediate results, so the divorce is already final. More when we speak face-to-face. Yes, I shall plan to arrive at Penn Station at 10:50 a.m. on Amtrak 236 Empire Service on Friday, the fifteenth; and, since you know the universal reputation of frugal Scotsmen, I shall take you up on your offer to bed down in your spare room. Looking forward to the dance . . . your dance, Daphne. See you soon!"

Having left the message for Daphne, McCutcheon set to work planning both the second Advent vesper service for Wednesday evening the thirteenth and the sermon for the seventeenth, Third Sunday of Advent. He felt an adrenalin rush, as though he were a college student again, and the scintillating image of Daphne's commanding the stage as the Sugar Plum Fairy invigorated his thoughts and set his fantasies ablaze. It had been a few years since he last attended *The Nutcracker,* and this would be the first he would see Daphne in that dazzling role. This Christmas ballet is all fantasy—sheer fantasy, McCutcheon mused—and it substantiated his belief that fantasy plays an essential role in faith by transporting the audience via imagination to the highest aesthetic plain, to the spiritual summit.

Amtrak 236 Empire Service arrived promptly at 10:50 a.m., precisely on time. As McCutcheon entered the enormous waiting room, Daphne ran to meet him, light on her feet, swift as a snow goose. Immediately McCutcheon envisioned Daphne in the role he had seen her in October—the Swan Queen Odette from *Swan Lake*—and smiled warmly as they embraced firmly.

"I'm rejoiced to see you, Stirling. Thank you for coming!" Daphne said rhapsodically. "Your train was right on time!"

"I can't think of a better way to lean into this marvelous season than to watch this Sugar Plum Fairy do her dance. So! Thank you for inviting me, my dear Daphne!"

McCutcheon lifted his portmanteau, which he had set down when he saw the Swan Queen flying towards him. Daphne took his arm as they made their way to Penn Station's elegant egress to hail a taxi.

"You have never seen my apartment, Stirling."

"No. No, I haven't."

"Well then, we shall go there directly. I've prepared a simple lunch for us, and then you may settle in as you like. If you need to work, there is a small desk in the spare room . . . a charming little desk that was my grandmother's. She was an excellent correspondent, who wrote so many wonderful letters to her children and to all of us grandchildren. That little desk is a great symbol of a unique love. It is a brand of love that all of us in the family would choose to emulate if we could. Oh, there! Taxi!"

The yellow cab pulled to the curb, and Daphne and McCutcheon climbed in.

"Two Lincoln Square, please, 60 West 66th Street," Daphne instructed with a New York City veteran's confidence.

"Your grandmother's love, Daphne," said McCutcheon, alluding to her previous comment, "you referred to it as unique, a unique love that all of you would emulate if at all possible. What, pray tell, characterized it as unique?"

Daphne sat quietly, pondering for a moment or two. "For years, Stirling, I have attempted to define it; and if I couldn't define it, I wished at least to describe it. All of us have wondered how such a precious stone could be replicated, so to speak, or how even to depict the beauty of that precious stone. But even the likeness of a precious stone is not analogous to her love since her love, unlike a precious stone, was intangible. All of us know this, and all of us believe that any description of such a love falls short of the true essence of that love. Yet, we desperately want to know how to love in the inimitable way she loved. Here is my feeble attempt at saying it as I'm seeing it in my field of precious memories of her. Her love was tailor-made, fitted to each family member whose life she touched. Any of us who has talked about it has agreed with all others that she undoubtedly possessed a prescience regarding every member of our extended family. Speaking only for myself, Stirling, long before I could walk, as my grandmother held me in her arms, she told my mother that ballet would reign supremely in my life—that, in all likelihood, there is nothing else that would be more important as a vehicle for full expression of my essential nature. Then, from that moment on, she loved me as Daphne . . . and she also loved me as Daphne, the ballerina. Every letter she wrote to me began with this inscription: *To my beloved granddaughter Daphne, with my best love and adoration.* Then she would address any and every issue or concern that was occurring in my life . . . not anyone else's life . . . just mine, fitted only to me. When other members of the family finally conferred, it was the same for everyone else: love suited to each individual, fitted precisely to that person, with the same inscription: *To my beloved* whomever, *with my best love and adoration.* Stirling, it was—beyond the shadow of any doubt—a best love."

"Do you love that way, Daphne?" asked McCutcheon gently.

"No. I don't think so," she responded sadly.

"I suspect you do and don't know it," said Stirling with a tone of conjecture.

"Two Lincoln Square," announced the cabby. He pulled to the curb.

Daphne paid the fare, adding a generous tip, and stepped to the sidewalk as Mc-Cutcheon held the cab door.

It was a swift elevator ride to the sixth floor, then a short walk to apartment 620. Daphne unlocked her door and opened it to an elegant hallway that led to a long, narrow—though spacious—living room with high ceilings, hardwood floors, and large windows that offered an expansive view of Central Park. At the far end of the living room was an ample dining area furnished with traditional Stickley furniture, tastefully arranged and suitably compatible with complementary Stickley furniture throughout the rest of the apartment, all of which appeared to McCutcheon as vintage Farquharson Heights. In point of fact, had McCutcheon never been introduced to a similar elegance at Farquharson Heights, he would likely have been bowled over by the remarkable refinement of these sophisticated surroundings. This is not to say, however, that he wasn't struck by a bold inconsistency of what he saw now with what he had anticipated previously, namely an image of the modest apartment of a ballet dancer who struggles to make ends meet in an inestimable, enormous city. How could a ballerina's salary support this grand accommodation—finely appointed—in New York City's Lincoln Center Cultural District? No sooner had the question occurred to him, however, when her surname came to mind as well. *Astor.* Could it be—but of course it could be—that part of the Astor fortune had filtered down to Daphne?

"Stirling," came her voice mid-thought, "let me show you the guest room before we sit for lunch."

"Lovely!" exclaimed McCutcheon. "Your apartment is absolutely lovely! You must truly enjoy standing here, taking in this extraordinary panorama of the city."

Daphne moved toward him, stood beside him, and silently gazed into the distance. "Yes, I do, Stirling," she said thoughtfully. "There is an identifiable pulse to everything one sees, to all that's moving perpetually, but even to all that's seemingly still. It's all an integral part of that beating pulse that's keeping time with the beating of your heart or, to be overly dramatic, with the rhythm of the universe—spinning spheres and orbiting planets. Quite extraordinary . . . and actually impossible to adequately describe."

They stood looking at the vast world, and, as they did so, a union was tacitly suggestive to each—perhaps a growing bond, somewhat akin to the bond that had developed with such certitude between McCutcheon and Gavin Davies at St. Deiniol's; but this was different, all encompassing. This feeling seemed not only spiritual as nurtured by the Holy Spirit; it was spiritual as in the body as spirit or flesh purified.

"Come, Stirling, I'll show you around."

The grand tour of each room concluded with the guest bedroom, where Daphne had previously set down McCutcheon's portmanteau and hung up his overcoat.

"Lunch will be served momentarily, Mr. McCutcheon," she said playfully with a grace that becomes a prima ballerina and with a charming bow as she exited the bedroom, making her way to the kitchen. McCutcheon entered the bathroom adjacent to his room, washed, and emerged as one who had just found his way out of a desert, one who had thought he was living with a heart that no longer beat, one who had become accustomed to the wilderness as a way of life. How could he identify this feeling that seemed completely foreign, yet vaguely familiar, like the return of an old college friend who had reportedly died in the war?

"Would you care for anchovies on your Caesar salad, Stirling, or do you prefer it without?"

"Anchovies please," said McCutcheon.

Daphne asked him to return thanks after they sat. He complied, and prayed with deliberation, a feeling forgotten and now recalled. She had her back to the great window. When McCutcheon raised his head, however, he could see for miles across the city skyline, beyond Central Park.

"Do you ever tire of the view from here, Daphne?"

"Not really. Of course one becomes accustomed to it, but I don't think I have ever taken it for granted. It continually causes me to wonder how a city so expansive, so densely populated, so diverse in a multiplicity of facets manages to function so incredibly smoothly day after day." She gave a little laugh. "If indeed it does."

"I have often had a similar thought about Edinburgh. But that's hardly comparable since Edinburgh seems barely more than a quaint village in contrast to New York . . . and Albany smaller still."

Daphne uncovered warm, homemade rolls, poured seasoned dipping oil in respective saucers, dished up the salads, and administered the anchovies evenly to each. They ate slowly amidst a rapid interchange of words.

"Speaking of Albany, what time do you have to return tomorrow?" she asked.

"I'll take the 3:15 p.m. Ethan Allen Express out of Penn Station. I'm sure you have a matinee to perform, so I'll leave late morning by cab, look around the city a bit, study my sermon notes over lunch, and head north by mid-afternoon."

"All right. But you don't have to rush off. I'm not dancing tomorrow afternoon . . . only the evening performance. It's a school children's matinee, and Sophia Greisen is dancing the Sugar Plum Fairy."

"Then I'll stay a wee bit longer," McCutcheon said with a warm smile and a decisive nod of his head. He set his fork on his plate, paused, leaned back a little in his chair, and said, "Daphne, in my message on your voice mail, I intimated that I would share more about the divorce when I saw you face-to-face. Let me assure you upfront that I have no interest or intention of laying my issues on your back, or at your feet, or in your path. I am perfectly capable of dealing with those issues on my own."

"I understand, Stirling, and actually there's no interest—and certainly no intention on my part—of prying into your affairs . . . into your private life," reassured Daphne. "I'm only concerned that you're all right throughout all of this."

McCutcheon smiled again with a warm recollection. "I read the question in your letter as lighthearted scolding: *But, dear Stirling, shall I forgive you, or shall I not?*"

"That's precisely how it was meant . . . my dear Stirling."

"I could have shared it all with you in early October, but I wanted only the pure experience of *Swan Lake* . . . no obstacles to the transcendence I was anticipating in your performance of the Swan Queen Odette. And there was none. There was only transcendence. I wanted to get out of myself and soar. Thanks to you, I did. It's true I could have told you during our late-night dinner together, but a high for me remains a high only if I allow it to sustain the reverie. I couldn't introduce the dross of my circumstances or the dudgeon in Heather's intransigence knowing that, by virtue of such a conversation, I would relinquish the . . . what shall I say? . . . relinquish the otherworldliness I was savoring. Sorry!"

"No, no apology necessary, Stirling."

"The two weeks I spent in August with Heather, the children, and her parents were exhilarating . . . at least until the end. Heather and I reconnected, talked incessantly, rode horses with the children every afternoon, enjoyed formal meals with her parents every evening. The family and I spent a long weekend in Edinburgh proper with my parents and sister—a thoroughly delightful time—and they all came to dinner at Farquaharson twice the second week. It was the night before I left that Heather leveled with me. Intermittently during the fortnight, she had been alluding to my returning to Scotland, but it was the night before my departure that she became adamant and, as I said, intransigent. I told her I needed seven more years at Madison Avenue Church to fulfill my promise to the congregation of a decade-long tenure; but she wouldn't hear of it, insisting that the children would all be grown and on their way, and we would miss everything precious in their growing up, and how could I be away from all of them and be happy! 'Then, come back to Albany,' I said. It was at that point in the conversation that she informed me in no uncertain terms that she and the children would never set foot again in Albany, rehearsing once more her repugnance with America's vulgarity and violence. Then she set down the ultimatum, that is, if I did not stay in Scotland and simply inform Madison Avenue Church that I would not be returning and they could send my books and possessions, then she would seek a divorce . . . an immediate divorce. There would be no contesting from her standpoint since she wanted nothing from me, since the children would certainly choose to stay with her, and since she had her own financial independence, which indeed is quite substantial."

"And you think she was dead certain?"

"Oh, without question! My departure the next morning could be characterized as loving with the children, warm with her parents, and ostensibly civil with Heather, like a lovely veneer covering cold marble. By the end of August, I had received divorce papers for my signature, and by the end of September I had received the official notification that the divorce was final, all of which I kept to myself until my announcement to the congregation on October 15."

"How do you think the congregation received the announcement, Stirling?" she asked sadly. McCutcheon had resumed eating and tacitly considered Daphne's question while dipping bread in oil and savoring an anchovy.

"I can't be sure. I suspect that most were stunned but that others had surmised my family's absence bore some significant implication or other. Many have been nothing but encouraging, expressing moral support for both Heather and me, as well as the three children. Your parents in particular have been truly gracious . . . the Schumanns as well. Helga Wenzell has been like a dear mother. Marcel and Chantal DuBois have been extraordinarily attentive. I think Freda Chamberlain, on the other hand, is struggling with the divorce. Following the announcement after the service, she didn't greet me as invariably she has done every Sunday in the past. Her attendance pattern has changed, absent occasionally and obviously more distant. I've called to set up an appointment to visit her, but she hasn't returned my calls. She sent me a note early this month—a short note, perhaps curt, but I can't be sure—saying that she was leaving on an extended holiday to England, traveling to Italy and Greece, picking up a tour tracing the Apostle Paul's journeys through Asia Minor. I feel certain she is quite put off by this ill-fated development in my personal life. Why wouldn't she be? It's entirely out of her control."

"Yes, why wouldn't she be? I doubt that divorce from Dr. Chamberlain would ever have occurred to her, even if there were any element of just cause for it in their marriage. So one can't really blame her, Stirling . . . not that you do."

"No, of course, I don't."

"As I was growing up in the church there, and as I was cultivating a career for myself, it often occurred to me that Mrs. Chamberlain had only her marriage in which to invest—her marriage and the church . . . no children, no profession . . . just her marriage and the church. I have no idea how she felt about your children—whether she ever suffered a twinge of jealousy, or what she thought about Heather's writing and publishing—but I do know that her marriage and the church consumed her days. There again, why wouldn't she be put off by the turn of events in your life? Undoubtedly, it is something she would never allow in her own."

McCutcheon sat quietly, looking down at his salad bowl, nodding slow nods of agreement . . . sad, slow nods of agreement. Never had it occurred to him either that he would be considering divorce, or, rather, would have gone through the crumbling of the institution of marriage, like so much crumbled blue cheese on top of Caesar salad. But, after all, could the truth of the matter be that he had never invested in his marriage the way Freda Chamberlain had devoted herself to hers?

"Stirling," interposed Daphne, "what would you say to a tour of the David H. Koch Theatre?"

"Splendid," said McCutcheon as he stood and took his dishes to the kitchen.

"Give me a moment to get ready," she said, following with hers. "I'll need time to warm up, so I'll stay there." She reached for a small envelope on the kitchen counter.

"Here's your ticket and a key to the apartment. The doorman knows you're my guest, so you can come and go as you like and arrive in time for an eight o'clock curtain. After-theater dinner tonight, my dear Stirling, at the Plaza Hotel."

"Bonnie, lassie! A rare excursion, this!" exclaimed McCutcheon with a warm smile.

He cleared the remaining dishes from the table and loaded the dishwasher, as if he were in his own kitchen.

It was a short walk to Lincoln Center. Until now, the only perspective McCutcheon had had of the David H. Koch Theatre stage was from the auditorium balcony, seat B110 in the First Ring. Entry into the back stage opened to him a vast new world of magic, that is, an intricate display of mechanisms that make the magic happen. This was Daphne's world, a sphere in which she was comfortable and continually felt a keen sense of belonging. It was plain to McCutcheon that she was highly regarded by her fellow dancers, stagehands, lighting technicians—everyone to whom she introduced him as her pastor. She showed him her dressing room, equipped with make-up mirror, table and lights, as well as her Sugar Plum Fairy costume.

"It strikes me that this is a world within a world, within a world, within a universe," said McCutcheon as they sat and he gazed about the room, "and I can only imagine—but never comprehend—the complexities of scenes within your worlds from one ballet to the next. How do you memorize the moves and keep one move distinct from another?"

"My dear Stirling, how do you keep one sermon idea distinct from another? That's as puzzling to me as my distinctive moves are to you, no doubt. As for me, the explanation lies principally in the body. The old cliché applies here: *the body remembers*. And as to *worlds*, I think you are often off in a world of your own . . . even a world within a world, within a world, within a universe; or, should I say, ultimately within the City of God. I suspect there are times when no one can reach you there in one of your remote worlds . . . do you think?"

"Perhaps. But, I assure you," said McCutcheon, indicating the entirety of the theater, "I have no world quite so imaginative as this."

"Maybe that's true," rejoined Daphne with an intent expression, "but, I assure you, I have no world as mystical as Madison Avenue Presbyterian Church, nor as compelling as your pulpit."

"Touché, my dear Daphne!" conceded McCutcheon as he rose to leave. "May you have a brilliant performance this evening. I understand that *break a leg* is not a suitable wish for dancers."

"No, believe it or not, it's *merde!*"

"*Merde?* The French word for *shit?* Seriously?"

"Yes, I kid you not, Stirling!"

"How did that come about?" asked McCutcheon with piqued curiosity.

"No one seems to be absolutely sure. The dance teacher Jennifer Mabus said she thought it originated in Paris, and that if the ballet performance had a good audience, there would be much *merde* outside from all the carriages. Therefore, the wish for *merde* is a wish for a good performance."

"Then, *merde,* Daphne!"

They embraced, and Daphne led him to the street exit.

As he set foot on Columbus Avenue, it occurred to him that—in his sphere of influence—there was much *merde* in church politics, but he could not imagine using the term as a means to wish anyone in ecclesiastical power well . . . or a brilliant performing of one's role. But maybe he should. "I'll have to think about that," he said to himself.

McCutcheon strolled about until he found a flower shop, where he ordered an elegant bouquet for Daphne and had it sent to her for a seven-thirty arrival in her dressing room. He returned to the apartment, let himself in, and lay on the guest-room bed, where he fell into a deep sleep laced with disjointed dreams.

He awoke with a start a few minutes before six, checked his watch, and hurried to the bathroom. By seven fifteen he had shaved, showered and dressed formally, and by seven forty-five was seated in the First Ring, Seat B110. When the curtain rose on Christmas Eve at the Stahlbaum home, McCutcheon was instantly caught up in the fantasy, which persisted throughout the dramatic first act. Act II opened with the arrival of Marie and the Prince in the Kingdom of Sweets, ruled by the Sugar Plum Fairy. Then began a grand festival in honor of Marie, who had saved the Prince's life in the previous act; and her bravery was celebrated by dancers from many lands. The festival of dances culminated with the magnificent *pas de deux* by the Sugar Plum Fairy and her Cavalier, danced exquisitely to Tchaikovsky's heart-stirring *adagio*. When the house lights came up, McCutcheon remained in B110 until Daphne appeared beside him.

"My dear Stirling," she said softly.

"My dear Sugar Plum Fairy," responded McCutcheon. "How lovely! How perfectly exquisite!" He smiled warmly. "But shall I tell you the absolute truth . . . the absolute, inexplicable truth? Or will you take it wrong and detest me as yet another Apollo in heated pursuit?"

Daphne gave a soft, affectionate laugh. "I don't know, Stirling, but now you have piqued my curiosity. Do tell. What is the absolute, inexplicable truth?"

"I am jealous of your Cavalier."

"Stirling, you can't be serious!"

"I am serious. I sat here wondering what it would be like to hold my hands at your waist while you twirled, and what it would be like to lift you in the air, and what sensations I would feel while holding you as you leaned backward . . . and where I would feel those sensations . . . in what parts of my body . . . or what stirrings in my soul would enchant me. Then I remembered that Apollo wanted the mythical Daphne and nearly caught her in the chase when she prayed to her father, god of the river, who answered her prayer by turning her into a laurel tree, leaving Apollo with only a handful of laurel bark. Then I wondered how you and I could dance a *pas de deux* throughout the rest of our lives."

Daphne sat very still for a long time, looking down at her hands. McCutcheon stared at the stage. Minutes later, she slid her hand into his hands and raised her eyes to his.

"I wonder, too, my dear Stirling."

The Palm Court at the Plaza Hotel bustled with theatergoers. Daphne had reserved a table for two, where the maître d' seated them, and then spent the next twenty minutes graciously acknowledging admirers who approached her. To a select few, she congenially introduced McCutcheon as a dear friend from Albany; and to the others, she simply allowed them their own contrived speculations.

"How do you decide which?" McCutcheon quietly inquired with a gentle grin.

"Which what?"

"Which ones you allow to speculate and which ones you decide to answer their obvious inquisitiveness?"

"Those I know as gossipers, I leave you to their imaginations. As with the others who have a genuine interest and tight lips, I share you."

"Now I shall be able to identify which is which," McCutcheon quipped as he searched the room to spot the two types . . . only momentarily, however, before he trained his attention on Daphne.

The wine list, a bottle of choice red wine, the menus, appetizers, and the main course, but desserts waived . . . it all constituted an epicurean delight. As McCutcheon helped Daphne with her coat, he expressed his hearty appreciation for the lavish meal as well as the *Nutcracker* ticket. Snow had accumulated on the walks, and large flakes filled the sky, wet heavy snowflakes falling on the two of them as they meandered to the apartment. Daphne placed her arm through McCutcheon's, and they walked in silence, each sensing that prognosticated union they had intuited earlier in the day while standing side by side, looking out the apartment windows.

They sat on the sofa nursing Harvey's Bristol Cream Sherry for nightcaps. Daphne had removed her shoes and drawn her legs up beside her. McCutcheon had taken off his shoes at the door—as he usually did when entering the manse—had removed his tuxedo coat and untied his black bowtie. He slouched, his legs stretched out in front of him. Daphne laid her hand gently on his shoulder, moving her fingers tenderly.

"Stirling, how do you see our dancing a *pas de deux* throughout the rest of our lives?"

"I realize it sounds atrocious . . . a sheer fantasy! When Marie cannot decide in the *Nutcracker* whether she has dreamed it all or whether it all was real, that's when I identified my feelings for you as real, not mere fantasy. It may well be that wanting a *pas de deux* with you, so to speak, is mere fantasy. But what if it were real for you as well? What if the feelings I feel are identical to feelings you may have? Here I am coming off of a divorce four months ago. What business do I have of speaking to you like this? I know you are thirty-three years old, and I am forty-four—eleven years difference. I know you will never give up ballet. I wouldn't ask you to make that sacrifice. But neither would I ever give up the church. What if we had a secondary love relationship that were equally essential to us as our primary love relationships, seizing every mutually available moment together?"

Daphne set her glass on the sofa end table, put her arm around Stirling's neck, and laid her head on his chest.

"It's true," she acknowledged readily. "My love affair has always been with ballet. I would never give up that love affair for another. The question for me is whether I can possess two affairs of the heart simultaneously. I have been schooled in the belief that a prima ballerina cannot have both passionate romance and impassioned ballet. *The Red Shoes* is the case in point. Vicky Page cannot hold both her passion for ballet and her love for Julian in the same spinning sphere without that sphere's cracking, splitting apart. But it's true. I want you, Stirling. I have never wanted any other man before."

McCutcheon retired his glass as well, turned her face to his, drew her fully into his arms, and kissed her. He then lifted her from the sofa and carried her toward the guest bedroom.

"No," she said, "my room. I want to remember us in my room."

He changed directions, carried her to her bed.

"So this is what it's like to lift you, to hold you, to touch you, and to feel the passion rush through my body, for my soul to spill over with *élan vital.*"

They lay on Daphne's bed and gently moved rhythmically in a *pas de deux* of unprecedented intimacy. They lay back, exhausted, until Stirling pulled Daphne close again. She laid her head on his chest and mounted her leg across his body. Their breathing was synchronized. Their hearts' pounding began to slow, moving them into a state of rest.

After a profound, prolonged savoring, Daphne said quietly, "Stirling, I would never ask you to give up the church for me. I know your love affair is with the church. Is that what Heather asked you to do?"

"No, not the church *per se.* Madison Avenue Presbyterian Church . . . to give up the church in Albany and return to a church in Scotland."

"Why couldn't you do that? Couldn't you have a congregation in Scotland . . . as you did before?"

"Yes, of course. But I had already been touched by the people's pathos at Madison Avenue. They had already become my people. How could I walk away from them before I had fulfilled my commitment to a ten-year tenure with them?"

"Pathos, Stirling? Is there that much pathos at Madison Avenue Church?"

"Yes," he said reflectively. "There's a common notion that everyone has a cross to bear. I've heard numerous people say it: *it's my cross to bear.* What I've realized is that every cross possesses its own mystery, its unique story to reveal, the story of the one on whose back that cross is carried. And most of the time there is a deep, profound pathos disclosed by each of those stories."

"Is that why you're sad at times?"

"Yes, I suppose it is."

"What do you think about in those sad times?"

"A loving God in a cruel world. It seems so paradoxical. I've wrestled with that paradox incessantly for decades. It's what theologians call *theodicy*, but there has never been a suitable answer that everyone can subscribe to universally. Whenever someone wants to know *why* God allows one tragedy or another, I have no satisfactory response. To tell you the truth, Daphne, I feel helpless in those moments, as if the Holy Spirit, who is suppose to give us the words to utter in those occasions, has forsaken me . . . or, to be less dramatic about it, has simply left me on my own to devise an acceptable, understandable retort."

"Have you devised one?"

"No . . . Well, yes, but it isn't one that makes sense to anyone in the cascading throws of devastating grief."

"What is it?"

"I've concluded we'll never know the answer to the paradox: *if God is good, human suffering is evidence that he is not all-powerful; if God is all-powerful, human suffering is evidence that he is not benevolent.* So I've just recently accepted a nuanced variation on theodicy to include the dynamic of *encounter,* namely, *the wound is the sign of the blessing.*"

"What do you mean by that?"

"The notion has come from my thinking about Jacob, who wrestled with the angel of the Lord, which is to say, he wrestled with God himself. Three dynamics are particularly telling here: Jacob's tenacity, indicated when he declares to the angel, *I will not let you go unless you bless me;* then the angel's asking Jacob's name and refusing to give him his own name but blessing Jacob with a new name—*Israel*, which means *He who strives with God*; and God's wounding Jacob in the hollow of his thigh, which causes him to limp throughout the rest of his life. Jacob's blessing of his new name and his wounding occur virtually in the same moment, in the very same encounter—contest, wrestling—with God. Jacob's wound is nothing other than the sign of Jacob's blessing derived from Jacob's encounter with God."

"Hence, your conclusion that the wound is the sign of the blessing implies—*ipso facto*—an encounter with God," observed Daphne, who was listening intently to grasp McCutcheon's full meaning.

"I'd say that it implies—*ipso facto*—at the very least the opportunity for an encounter with God. Whenever any person wounded by tragedy of any sort asks the question *why, God?*, the dynamic of the encounter has already occurred . . . as with Job. When Job asks, *why, God?* and seeks vindication as a righteous man, he doesn't receive vindication but, rather, the profound awareness of an inimitable divine-human rapport between God and him. In other words, Job has been encountered by God, and his wounds—his losses and afflictions—and his question *why, God?* compose the sign of the blessing. So, whenever any of my people—on whose back a cross has been laid—asks that question, that person has come face-to-face with God."

"But, as you intimated earlier, you can't tell that to a person who is sinking in a vortex of horrific grief. Is that it?"

"Otherwise, it comes off as cold and esoteric, or—worse yet—as irrelevant theological rhetoric. Hardly pastoral."

"Have you tried?"

"Once . . . recently . . . but I should have known better. The result was similar to an experience I had years ago."

"What happened then?"

"When I was serving as a seminary intern on a large, center-city, church staff in Scotland, in the dead of winter, I went with the pastor to a family's home when they had received word that their thirty-three-year-old daughter had been killed on her way to work that morning. Her car had careened on ice and smashed into a utility pole, killing her instantly. Principally, the pastor engaged in the conversation with the parents, but at the end of the visit, I assured them that God certainly understood their pain since he too had lost a son on Calvary. They were furious . . . and understandably so. It had been a theological comment, not a pastoral one. While the thought was theologically sound, it was pastorally bankrupt . . . given the timing. Perhaps they would never be able to hear it and accept it, but, for sure, there was no hearing it at that moment. The pastor, my mentor, expressed that opinion pointedly—albeit kindly—in the car on our return trip to the church."

"It has to be chalked up to the cost of learning, doesn't it, Stirling?" Daphne observed. "There have been many-a misstep on the way to principal dancer, and the ballet masters are quick to correct, some vociferously and didactically, others quietly with a nurturing tone. At the least basic level, corrections are given in the interest of safety; at a higher level, however, corrections are made in the endless pursuit of precision and perfection."

"I suppose in any endeavor, one is fortunate to learn from the masters."

During this involved interchange, Stirling and Daphne had been lying on their sides, facing each other as they conversed. Now McCutcheon rolled to his back, and Daphne laid her head on his chest.

"Stirling, do you remember the night we first met in Saratoga Springs, when I told you about the wealthy ballet patron who attempted to rape me?"

"Yes. Speaking of pathos, there's no way I would forget that evening," rejoined McCutcheon compassionately, pulling her closely to him, then relaxing the embrace. "Why?"

"I told him, 'When I want to lose my virginity, it won't be to a sleazy lecher like you.' I wasn't sure at the time that I would ever lose my virginity. Actually, I felt quite certain I would always be a virgin. My dear Stirling, as of this moment, I can tell you exactly what I have gained and what I have lost . . . and what I have gained tonight—at this precious loss of my virginity—is an experience of love so far more transcendent than anything I have ever known before . . . in all my life."

McCutcheon pulled her even closer so they blended into a single being. They kissed fervently, turned out the light, pulled up the covers, and slept soundly, contentedly, amid the soothing sounds of the city that never sleeps.

† † †

During the ensuing months, elements of the previous scene occurred repeatedly . . . at reasonable intervals, always in New York City, usually on opening nights of Daphne's ballet performances. In February it was Tchaikovsky's *The Sleeping Beauty* and Ludwig Minkus's *La Bayader (The Temple Dancer)* in April. Daphne danced the principal role in Sergei Prokofiev's *Cinderella* in June prior to the New York City Ballet Company's appearances at the Saratoga Performing Arts Center, where the company mounted Prokofiev's *Romeo and Juliet*.

The passion and devotion that grew steadily between Daphne and Stirling throughout these months appeared to challenge the basic premise of *The Red Shoes*: that one cannot hold both passion for ballet—one's principal love—and passion for a lover in the same spinning sphere without that sphere's cracking, splitting apart. While holding fiercely to their principal love affairs—Daphne to ballet and Stirling to the church—the passion of their secondary love for each other grew to a commensurate height and significance equal to the respective dominions that reigned over each.

When not together in New York City, they wrote letters of love and affection, which recorded their mutual commitment and enduring loyalty. When Daphne visited her parents in Albany, she gave McCutcheon the most circumspect consideration, making appointments through Caryn to see him at the church office. Never did they give either her parents or other members of the congregation any tangible cause to suspect a growing alliance between them.

Following Daphne's opening night of *Cinderella* in June, however, the requirement of circumspect consideration altered significantly. The maître d'hôtel seated them at their usual table in the Palm Court, and following glowing greetings from devoted admirers, McCutcheon stood and seated her one last time before they ordered wine. On this occasion, however, the waiter brought champagne rather than their usual red, popped the cork, and poured the bubbly into their respective glasses. Stirling raised his glass and said in typical Presbyterian fashion, "If the way be clear, and if the prima ballerina concurs, I propose this toast to my future wife and to our eternal union bound together by our—to quote your grandmother, the lovely connoisseur of love—to our eternal union bound together by our *best love and adoration*. Will you say *yes*, my beloved Daphne?"

"Yes!" she responded rhapsodically. "Yes! Yes! Yes, my beloved Stirling!"

They touched their glasses together and drank to their future. McCutcheon pulled from his tuxedo vest pocket a gold ring topped with a marquise diamond. He slipped it onto her finger.

"My dear Daphne, I understand you will not be able to wear this on stage, but it is a symbol of my love for you, one for you to wear whenever feasible."

✝   ✝   ✝

The ballet company made its annual transition from David H. Koch Theater to Saratoga Performing Arts Center by the end of June, ready to perform Prokofiev's *Romeo and Juliet* on July 1. Before she took residence in the Gideon Putnam Hotel, however, Daphne stopped for an overnight at her parents' home in Albany. She had asked McCutcheon to come by in the afternoon for tea and share in the unveiling of their engagement to her mother and father. Her parents' astonishment at their announcement served only to verify the discretion Daphne and Stirling had used in their nascent relationship. As animated questions about how it all happened filled the conversation, it became apparent that the degree of the parents' joy was equivalent to the level of their initial astonishment.

Daphne and Stirling had set their wedding date for fourteen months hence, on the second Saturday in August following the ballet's season at SPAC the month before their wedding. They swore her parents to secrecy until McCutcheon had the opportunity to inform his congregation by mail . . . *four weeks from today*, Daphne said.

Looking first at her husband Carl and then back to Daphne, Marian said, "I'm sure your father and I would very much like to have an engagement party for the two of you. Would you be willing?"

"Yes, I'm sure we would . . . wouldn't we, Stirling?" answered Daphne.

"Of course. We'd appreciate that . . . quite," McCutcheon responded with a note of reservation in his voice.

"Does that put you in an awkward spot, Stirling?" asked Carl, sensitive to the ordeal McCutcheon had confronted the previous October: the divorce, having to inform the session and the congregation, and having to face the fallout in the aftermath.

"Well, no. Not really. We have spoken about the need to be inclusive of the congregation as we both pass through this transition. Both of us could be delighted to marry this summer, but we believe the congregation needs time to get use to my being divorced and then moving into a new relationship with Daphne. We need time to assure them that I'll still be wholly committed to them as their pastor and that Daphne will be fully devoted to ballet, which means she will be away from the manse a good share of the time, which negates her performing the traditional minister's wife's role."

"Would it be better, Stirling, not to have an engagement party for you two?" asked Marian quietly.

"No, Marian, I'm not thinking that. I wonder if you and Carl would mind making it an engagement reception following a church service in August? That would include anyone and everyone in the church, who would want to attend."

"What do you think, Carl?" said Marian as she turned a broad smile toward her husband.

"Splendid idea!" Carl said with a stentorian affirmation.

†   †   †

The first Sunday in August arrived at Madison Avenue Presbyterian Church with the appearance of four deacons setting the communion table for the celebration of the Lord's Supper. This was also the designated Sunday for Daphne and Stirling's engagement reception following the worship service. As planned, McCutcheon had sent a pastoral letter to all members of the church, informing them of his engagement to Daphne Astor and the wedding date they had selected a year later. Included in each letter was an invitation to the engagement reception sponsored by Marian and Carl Astor in the Great Hall of the church.

Throughout the month of July—while Daphne danced the part of Juliet in Prokofiev's ballet—McCutcheon's mind danced about from one contention to another, contending first that in his sermon for the day he should be straightforward with his people, but then, backing away from that approach, contending that he should simply ignore the topic of divorce and remarriage and let his record as a loving pastor tacitly stand for itself. The final outcome of this oscillating dialectic ultimately favored the direct approach, and he prepared and preached a sermon titled *The Sin behind the Sin*, based on Mark 10:2–16. The sermon acknowledged straight-out that divorce is a sin; then referring to Barth's notion that any cruelty in marriage is an act of adultery, McCutcheon contended that we all come under the judgment of God and must rely upon his mercy, his forgiveness, and his *kairos*—God's timing and invitation to new life. Concluding with the assertion that it is the hard-hearted writing off of others that leads to the great divorce among people and ultimately adulterates God's intention for his world, McCutcheon turned to the communion table in the center of the chancel and declared: "no one is ever written off at this table, the table of our Lord Jesus Christ."

Daphne met him in the Great Hall, took his hand and said, "You're no coward, my dear Stirling! In the spirit of Luther, here we stand. I'm proud to stand with you, my Love!"

"Ah, it is a *best love* you give, Daphne. It is that very *best love* I shall reflect throughout our days together . . . throughout our magnificent *pas de deux.*"

One parishioner after another greeted Daphne and Stirling with genuine, warm-hearted wishes for long life and happiness together. Those who were opposed to this unfamiliar manifestation of pastoral matrimony either didn't attend the reception at all, or they avoided the couple's stream of salutations . . . but with one exception.

The previous week Freda Chamberlain had returned from her extended stay with relatives in London and her tour of the Apostle Paul's journeys throughout Asia Minor. She waited until the Great Hall was nearly cleared of church members before she approached McCutcheon, who now was standing alone.

In a low voice, she said with a somber tone, "Stirling, there is no place for divorced clergy in the pulpit of Madison Avenue Presbyterian Church, whether you remarry or you don't. I shared with you some of the serious aspects of my marriage with Sinclair. There were times, as you suspect, that I could have chosen to divorce him for his stand against having children in the manse or for his melancholy that weighed with a profound preponderance on his mood. Undoubtedly, you have surmised correctly that I was miserably lonely, but never . . . and I mean *never* . . . would I have ever considered divorcing Sinclair Chamberlain, for as much as you can rationalize *the sin behind the sin,* as you said, *divorce . . . is . . . a . . . sin.* Beside that, Stirling, what makes you think that a second marriage will be any more successful than the first? Bright, literary Scotsman that you are, surely you remember Chaucer's *Prologue* to *The Canterbury Tales,* the precept the Parson practiced: *If gold rusts, what will iron do?*" With this, Freda turned and walked decisively into her own sequestration.

Daphne approached McCutcheon, placed her hand in his at his side and watched Freda leave the Great Hall. "What was that all about, Stirling?"

"I think . . . I think it was a manifestation of the sin behind the sin."

†   †   †

One year later to the day, on a Saturday afternoon, the month following the New York City's ballet season at Saratoga Performing Arts Center, Daphne and Stirling recited vows to take one another as husband and wife, *for better, for worse, for richer, for poorer, in joy and in sorrow, in sickness and in health, as long as we both shall live.* Their formal *pas de deux* had officially begun.

22

Feet of Clay Suspended

THE NIGHT CAME EARLY those winter days. By four thirty, the afternoon clouds hung unusually low above the city, and darkness settled like a thick blanket over the neighborhood surrounding the church. Trudel Svenssen, the industrious sexton fondly known as the Great Dane, would have been finished for the day and on his way home except for the deep snow that had covered the city streets and sidewalks during the past two days. The final Advent vesper service was on the church calendar for the next evening, and he worked tirelessly to plow the parking lot and shovel the sidewalks all around the church building to stay ahead of the storm's generous offerings. He had just completed his work for the day, had dropped by McCutcheon's study to bid him a *good night* before checking the doors and heading off into other snow drifts. McCutcheon returned to his reading.

Within minutes of Trudel's leaving the office area, gunshots reverberated through the hallways of the church. McCutcheon jumped to his feet and ran in their direction. Bolting into the sanctuary, he caught a glimpse of a figure fleeing through the main sanctuary doors. Looking about the room anxiously, he noticed that the gold Celtic cross was missing from the communion table and on the floor in front of the table lay the Great Dane. McCutcheon knelt beside him to see if he was still alive. His breathing was labored, but he was conscious.

"I tried to stop him," he said with effort, "but he was too fast. Surprised me. Couldn't get to him before he pulled the gun."

"Sh-h-h-h, Trudel!" McCutcheon cautioned him. "Don't talk. Save your energy. I'll call an ambulance."

It seemed an eternity before the ambulance arrived, but in real time it was only minutes, commendable actually in light of the heavy snow. In the meantime, McCutcheon stayed with Trudel, encouraging him to conserve his efforts. When the ambulance attendants appeared, they succeeded in stopping the bleeding, and lifted him into the emergency vehicle.

"With this blinding snow," said one of the attendants, addressing McCutcheon, "my partner and I should both be in front. "Would you mind riding in back with the patient? We have him on oxygen, and the bleeding has stopped. He should be all right." McCutcheon climbed in and sat beside Trudel.

"Stirling, I'm sorry," he whispered arduously.

"Trudel, it's all right," McCutcheon answered reassuringly. "It couldn't have been helped. No one could have stopped him so long as he had a gun. Don't talk now. It will sap too much of your strength. We just need to make sure you get well again."

"But what if I don't?"

"You will."

"I need to tell you something, just in case I don't," Trudel said haltingly. He looked furtively around to make certain they were indeed alone in the back of the vehicle.

McCutcheon leaned closer, placed his hand on the Dane's shoulder, and waited. Even though the ambulance attendant had reassured him that Trudel would be all right, he felt an escalating concern that their progress along snowy, icy roads was slow, methodical, and treacherous. At this rate, it could be an unduly long time before they reached the hospital.

"Stirling, you know that I have been sexton at the church for nearly ten years, thanks to Sinclair Chamberlain. I loved the man dearly. He is the one who gave me my chance here in America, and I have always been grateful to him for treating me well all the years I knew him."

"I recall this from our previous conversations."

"On the day of Glynnis Vandeusen's accident, everything changed. I lost my respect for him," Trudel murmured with tears welling up in his eyes, "because I alone know the truth."

Trudel paused. McCutcheon waited for him to gather more strength to continue. "What truth, Trudel?"

"Sinclair Chamberlain did not have another crisis to attend to that day."

"How do you know that?"

"The emergency telephone call came at noontime, when Caryn was at a business lunch with the ladies study group, and I was covering the telephone in her absence. The urgent call came, I answered it, and the person on the other end described the circumstances of the accident, indicated that Glynnis was under the teetering bus, and that she had asked for Dr. Chamberlain to be contacted to come and hold her hand and pray. I said that I would get Dr. Chamberlain immediately. His study door was open, and I told him that there was an urgent call for him. He picked up his phone, listened to the caller's message, and then said that he was in the midst of another emergency but would be there just as soon as he could. I had been sitting at the secretary's desk, out of Chamberlain's line of vision. I heard everything he said. He then closed the door and, to my knowledge, never came out the rest of the afternoon. Stirling, there was no other emergency. For some unknown reason, he lied. He left Glynnis Vandeusen to fend for herself beneath a teetering bus . . . and, on that day, in spite of my deep love for the man, I became disillusioned with the Reverend Dr. Sinclair Chamberlain." Trudel drew in a deep breath and rested momentarily.

"Did you ever talk to him about your disillusionment?" McCutcheon asked conciliatorily.

"No. I distanced myself from him, and my indignation grew day by day," Trudel answered, laboring all the more now to breathe freely.

McCutcheon's anxiety was mounting, and he encouraged Trudel to close his eyes and take deep breaths, to postpone his story until another time. He refused. Some force beyond McCutcheon's perception was apparently compelling him to continue.

"Stirling, you must understand that I have never approached Glynnis Vandeusen with anything other than respect and kindness, but I have always—since the very first day I set eyes on her—I have always admired her, loved her as a brother, and would love her as a lover were she ever open to my adoration. But no, though she has never said anything of the sort, she is way out of my class. She has been for me the Laura on the passing train, the image of beauty beyond belief, the vision of feminine perfection beyond a man's reach. None of this have I ever said to her. But you can understand, then, that when the distressed caller portrayed her helplessness beneath a hovering bus, I was beside myself; and when Chamberlain closed his door and refused to go, I took off in my car and drove to the scene of the accident. By the time I arrived, however, there was already someone with Glynnis under the bus, holding her in his arms."

"Who was it? Do you know?" McCutcheon asked, knowing the answer already.

"Honeysuckle . . . the town idiot. How I longed to be him in that very moment," Trudel said wistfully. "I waited until the rescue workers pulled her from danger, lifted her into the ambulance, and drove off. Then I returned to the church. Dr. Chamberlain's door was still closed, and there was no sign of him the rest of the day."

"Trudel, I understand your disillusionment," McCutcheon said. "But you know, perhaps better than anyone else, that ministers are not perfect people. You have worked with ministers day in and day out. Like anyone else, we make poor choices at times, let people down, fail to meet people's needs, sometimes those we love most dearly. I'm sorry you had to experience that first hand."

"I understand, Stirling, but that was no small matter. Something I can't explain was going on for Chamberlain, and I'll never know what it was. What I *do* know, however, is that my resentment grew by the day. The love and gratitude I had felt for him dissipated, was replaced by bitterness, anger, and antagonism. I hated his duplicity. How could anyone who turned his back on a parishioner's pain and brokenness subsequently stand in the pulpit Sunday after Sunday and proclaim the love of God with a stellar call to Christian commitment! I detested him for it."

"Consistency is not everyone's long suit, Trudel," McCutcheon retorted somewhat defensively.

"Granted, but he himself changed after that day," Trudel contended. "Not more consistent but morose, withdrawn, edgy. I think he drank more . . . the months passed, and every day was an effort for me. I had loved going to work; now I detested it. Finally the season of Lent arrived, and then we moved on toward Easter. The church calendar was packed as usual during these weeks. Chamberlain had decided to present his dramatic monologue of Judas again that Good Friday. For all of those presentations, I worked behind the scenes for him, whether at our church or some other church in the area. That night was no exception. Since I had worked this play with him many times before, I knew the cues by heart. Everything that night went as we rehearsed it, except that, when he came to the final speech, when he had slipped his neck into the noose, and as soon as the lights went out, with a long pole—a hook on the end to open the upper windows in the sanctuary—I yanked the stool from beneath him. I disappeared into the back room, and from there I heard all the confusion when the lights came on and he was swinging from the tree limb."

McCutcheon became rigid. Beads of perspiration formed on his forehead and dripped into his eyes. There was no way for him to find his voice, and he simply remained staring at Trudel, this great big man, who had the largest heart of anyone McCutcheon had ever known. How could he be capable of such an act of retribution! Waves of incredulity washed over him as he formed the words silently in his mind: *not suicide, homicide*. Momentarily he found the strength to squeeze Trudel's shoulder affectionately as the ambulance came to a stop in front of the medical center.

Hours dragged on as McCutcheon sat in the waiting room, anxious to hear a report about Trudel. Doctors apparently removed three bullets from his torso, one of which had lodged in his spleen. By the time Trudel had undergone surgery, had bided his time in the recovery room, and had settled in his room on the sixth-floor Intensive Care Unit, it was 2:30 a.m. McCutcheon spent a few minutes with him, prayed, gave him a reassuring embrace, and left for home by taxi.

It was a fitful sleep after that. Horrid dreams haunted McCutcheon's REMS, until the telephone rang beside his bed at 4:30 a.m., just twelve hours after the shooting. "Dr. Stevenson calling," said the voice. "Mr. McCutcheon, I'm sorry to say that Trudel Svenssen just died. Undetected massive internal hemorrhaging . . . Mr. McCutcheon, are you there?"

"Yes . . . yes, I'm here."

"Is there any next of kin I should notify?"

"No, sir. He lived alone."

"Then shall I send his personal belongings to you at the church?"

"Yes . . ." said McCutcheon ponderously. "Yes, and the church will arrange for his funeral and his medical expenses."

"Very well, Mr. McCutcheon. Goodnight."

Dazed, McCutcheon stumbled to his study and sat at his desk. He reached for the box of crosses, opened the lid, and lifted out the Lalibela cross. In the dim light of the desk lamp, McCutcheon studied this intricate symbol, wherein lay DuBois's onerous secret: that Sinclair Chamberlain had intentionally hanged himself while playing Judas. But that secret was not *the* secret.

The secret went with the Great Dane to his grave following a magnificent memorial service in his honor at church. It was *the* secret known only thereafter to McCutcheon and Trudel's lapel pin of the Danish red flag with a white cross, safely ensconced in the box of crosses.

23

As in Gorky's Lover

ON A FAIR SPRING morning, McCutcheon—now a considerable distance from Fraquharson both in years and in miles—was intrigued to have received a letter marked *personal* with an Edinburgh postmark. At first blush, he thought it to be from Heather. Rather than placing it in his mail cubicle, Caryn had handed it to him directly. The return address, while not Fraquharson, he recognized immediately, though it had been years since he had visited that apartment on that street: Heritage Drive.

Dear Stirling,

I have been thinking of writing to you for some time. Actually, I've been thinking about it since I was forced to retire last April. All this time alone for the past year has given me much time to think about many things, but most especially about the mistakes I have made.

By far, the biggest mistake of my life was "making" you get out of my life because I was hurt. I want to apologize for that. Whether or not you accept is, of course, entirely up to you. I certainly can't blame you for not accepting my apology.

You were the closest friend I ever had, and I truly regret the loss of your friendship in my life. No one could have been kinder to me than you were. It all started the day of Dad's memorial service when you asked how I was. You were the only one who cared how I was. That caring continued through the next several years, until I was stupid enough to destroy it. I was hurt and couldn't face it, so I hurt you back.

Now I know all too well what I did—there was no one in my life who cared as truly as you did—you were such a wonderful friend. I could tell you anything and you were never unkind or judgmental to me in any way, even when you disagreed with me.

I am so terribly sorry that I hurt you. I wish I could have your friendship in my life again, but I'm sure that's something that can't ever be, and I'll regret that for the rest of my life. Even though you are far away, we could have written letters to each other and talked on the phone occasionally.

My illness and the subsequent loss of part of my sight have strangely brought this to a clearer perspective. I was so wrong and I cannot forgive myself. The last year would have been better with your friendship. I deserve what I got.

Anyway, I had to write this and tell you how very sorry I am for what I did. I do thank you for the years of friendship that we shared. You were incredibly generous to have been my friend.

I wish you well for always—all ways.

Lenore

P.S. Thank you for reading this. Please excuse the writing. My vision problem hinders me somewhat. I want you to know that I still treasure the St. Thomas cross you gave me, reminding me that once, when filled with doubt, I actually believed at heart. I hold it when I pray at night.

Once again McCutcheon perused the envelope, noting that it had been postmarked over two months ago. True, it had been sent from Scotland, but obviously it had been lost or detained somewhere along the way. Slowly, deliberately, McCutcheon folded the letter and inserted it into its envelope and then into the left breast pocket of his suit coat. Lenore Lomharach. Virtually the last person in Scotland he expected to hear from after their last encounter.

He kept to his calendar, the day's appointments, pastoral visits, hospital calls, and meetings. By the time he returned to the manse in the evening, it was nine fifteen. Helga Wenzel had left him a plate of food to be heated in the microwave. He ate in quiet and then adjourned to his study, lit his pipe.

Lenore had been on his mind throughout the day. He removed her letter from his coat pocket and then removed his coat before he sat in the burgundy leather Queen Anne chair across from his desk. He read the letter again . . . and then again, hearing her voice each time in his mind's recollection. Each time he read her words, a deeper sadness fell upon him. Here her tone was softer, more supplicating than he ever recalled its being face-to-face.

A member of his second parish in Edinburgh, Lenore was one of the most unforgettable people McCutcheon had ever known. She used words that could make a seasoned sailor's green parrot turn a flaming scarlet, even while talking to a pastor—or perhaps only while talking to the one pastor with whom it was safe to do so, with one who would not judge her or flinch or turn a back on her flagrant impropriety. By the same token, McCutcheon doubted that he was the only one so designated—targeted—with a volley of spicy profanity, for all those colorful phrases had been woven into the fabric of her demeanor since years past. She regaled him with stories of her interactions with colleagues at work, and, if her accounts of work-a-day dialogues were at all representative of those she related, she had assimilated and put to common use the most disreputable expressions to be found in the shadows of impolite society. And by these, loaded in a cannon of volatile temper, she attempted to control people around her with anger and with threats of anger, never reluctant to stoop to the lowest art of name-calling. Needless to say, she pushed people away. Those who related to her remained leery of approaching her, while those who observed her from a distance remained at a distance. How could she wonder at being lonely, isolated, despondent!

Though a member, confirmed as a teenager in the church years before McCutcheon had been called as pastor, Lenore and her family rarely attended worship. Indeed, consistent with his recollection, "It all started the day of Dad's memorial service when you asked how I was." Her father, Robert Lomharach, had been diagnosed with pancreatic cancer, and within three months he was dead. McCutcheon had visited him numerous times during those months, had come to know his wife Marilyn but had never crossed paths with Lenore at the Lomharach homestead. The first time he remembered talking with Lenore was after the memorial service at the reception in the Lomharachs' home. She was sitting by herself on the front porch, coffee in one hand and a plate of food untouched on the end table beside her.

"How are you, Lenore?" McCutcheon had asked.

"How do you think I might be, pastor?" she had responded curtly.

"Sad, no doubt."

"More than sad, I can tell you that without a damn bit of self-analysis!"

"What more?"

"Angry!" she answered vehemently.

"Angry at whom? God?"

"No. I don't even give God a thought. I haven't for some time. He has never done much for me, never will."

"But you're angry at someone. Is that true?"

"My father was a fine man, a decent man, the only man in my life I could say that about. All the other men I have ever known are asses, looking for only one thing. But when he got sick three months ago, I came to see him time after time . . . many times each week, but during the last month, my mother wouldn't let me in to see him. She said that he needed quiet. I told her I could do *quiet*. Even the last days, when everyone knew he was at the end of his life, she kept me out, saying he didn't want to see me . . . or, no, saying that he said he didn't want me to see him like that."

"Like what?"

"Sick and gaunt and in pain."

"And you took it personally, I suspect."

"How else should I take it? Wouldn't you take it personally? Crying out loud!"

"So when was the last time you saw him?"

"Like I said, over a month before he died!"

"So you're angry."

"That cantankerous mother of mine! She kept him to herself, as if there was no one else in the world who loved him."

"Do you think that that exclusion was directed at you alone? How about your brothers? I see you have two."

"They saw him."

"During the last month?"

"During the last month, the last three months, during the last week . . . as many times as they wanted. I must be the bastard child! Why does she hate me so?"

McCutcheon, knowing he had no answer for that vehement exclamation and that poignant question, remained silent, looking with compassion at her. Lenore finally broke the silence.

"Why are you looking at me like that?"

"No reason . . . other than I'm concerned."

"About what?"

"About you."

"Well, you needn't be. No one else is. I get by all right on my own, thank you very much!"

"Would you like to talk further sometime?"

"What's the use?"

"You will recognize these words as clichés, Lenore, but they bear some truth: the church is a beacon in the night, a harbor in the storm. You could find some comfort in the very place you were baptized and confirmed."

"All right. I'd like to talk further, but not at the church. I don't want people to see me as weak, as one who needs pastoral counseling at the church office . . . Do you make house calls?"

"Sure," replied McCutcheon. "It's a common practice."

"Sunday evenings are my best times."

"A week from tomorrow evening then. I'll come to your apartment at seven."

Lenore's facial features seemed to relax. "Thank you! And thank you for the service this morning."

This encounter was the genesis of a long-term pastoral relationship with Lenore Lomharach, lasting for nearly three years, marked by one-hour visits every other Sunday evening. Even though, eventually, she returned to Sunday morning worship, she never relented on the location for their meetings . . . always at her apartment. It became customary for McCutcheon—the very moment he knocked on her door—to breath words from Proverbs: *A soft word turneth away wrath; but grievous words stir up anger.* As much as he schooled himself in soft words and in not taking personally any of the wrath she spewed out, the slings and arrows she hurled about the room invariably felt too close to deem innocuous.

Lenore's apartment was adequate but not spacious, occupied but not cluttered, decorated but not classic, apparently adorned by what suited her tastes. While there are those who would characterize her wall-hangings as little more than kitsch, there hung on the longest wall of her living room a framed print of Peter Paul Rubens's seventeenth-century Baroque painting, *The Rape of the Daughters of Leucippus.*

For the initial visit, Lenore brewed a pot of tea and had made a batch of molasses cookies to sweeten the occasion, no doubt a little chagrined at her first conversation with McCutcheon on her mother's porch.

"My grandmother's recipe," she said as she passed the cookies.

"I can never turn down molasses cookies," he rejoined warmly. "Thank you!"

"The old saying that *the way to a man's heart is through his stomach,* in my opinion, is too general. I think it is more that the way to a man's heart is with cookies in the man's stomach. Not that I am attempting to get to your heart, Pastor McCutcheon."

"Well, if you were, you could count it a direct hit."

Lenore smiled. It seemed to McCutcheon a benign smile, without guile or calculation. He had seen no trace of such benignity that funereal day on the porch. She set down the plate of cookies within McCutcheon's reach and, with a bit of effort, seated herself on the sofa beneath the Rubens print. For some inexplicable reason, it was in that moment that McCutcheon realized how enormous a frame Lenore carried about, moving slowly when she walked, laboriously rising and sitting whenever she stood or sat. He couldn't determine why he had not taken note of her size before, but now it was clearly obvious. When she had opened her apartment door, it had registered with him that she was nearly his height. But only now did he appreciate the similarity of her muscular, corpulent body with those of Rubens's women, only Lenore's form was far more substantial—not only muscular but qualifying as obese. Though she possessed a very large, protruding bust, her midriff as well as the flesh beneath her waist extended beyond her bust-line. The greatest paradox McCutcheon perceived about Lenore was that she presented as one with a beatific, cherubic face and, simultaneously, a devilishly profane tongue. Yet, in spite of the latter component of the paradox, McCutcheon learned within that first hour in her home that Lenore Lomharach was at heart a good woman, a caring woman, a lonely woman, a hurting woman. When Mc-Cutcheon stood to take his leave, Lenore also stood and moved carefully towards him.

"May I have a hug before you leave?" she asked softly. "An innocent hug?"

McCutcheon hesitated, but for only an instant. What flashed through his memory was Maxim Gorky's short story titled, *Her Lover,* in which a Russian student mistakenly believes he is being coyly propositioned by a powerfully-built brunette named Teresa—another tenant in his rooming house—with a bestial gleam in her dark eyes. But then it dawns upon him that alongside of him, not three feet away, lived a human creature who had nobody in the world to treat her kindly, affectionately. Here McCutcheon was, in a remarkably similar venue. Not three feet away from him stood an enormous woman who had no one to love her. McCutcheon reached out and embraced her . . . an innocent embrace.

During the next two-and-one-half years, McCutcheon faithfully kept his bi-weekly appointments with Lenore Lomharach, with Earl Grey tea and extraordinary molasses cookies, though occasionally reticent to listen to her vituperative rants. During those years he examined with her the impact of her father's death, her being cut off from him by her mother, the deep wellspring of her anger, her poor self-image, and her perception of being exploited by others. Her basic philosophy, she contended, was that people have to use the cards they are dealt—obviously a deterministic position—but, she said, "I don't have to like the cards that were dealt to me." While she insisted that she didn't have much to do with God, or did she give him much thought, she had some sense that there existed an eternity in which her father continued to live on as a twinkling star in the universe, quite perceptible to the naked eye. When her grief at his death persisted for longer than six months, her mother castigated her, maintaining that Lenore's tears were keeping him from entering heaven for an eternal rest.

It was well over a year of these pastoral visits when Lenore finally admitted how she felt about her obesity.

"Stirling, why do you think I have this Rubens print of *The Rape of the Daughters of Leucippus?*"

"I don't know, Lenore. It certainly is a classic."

"For me it's more than a classic. It's a reminder that there are other fat women in the world, and they are desirable to some men . . . even to the gods! But believe me, Stirling, in this Twiggy-minded culture, I can read the disgust in the faces of most lascivious men I meet: "she's so disgustingly fat, I wouldn't be seen in the same hemisphere with her." But Rubens's women! They're almost as fat as I am. It brings me a little comfort."

"How deep is the pain?"

"Too deep to measure. I wonder if that's why my father said he didn't want to see me—or my mother said my father didn't want to see me. Were they ashamed of me? Is my mother ashamed of me still?"

"Could you ask her?"

"I could, but I won't. I don't want to hear the answer."

"Perhaps it could open a door in your relationship."

"A door better left shut! But speaking of doors and fat women and lascivious men, there is one man I trust you have never met."

"Yes? Who's that?"

"He's a constable in a neighboring precinct to ours. He likes fat women . . . naked fat women, and he comes by here when he's in the area . . . parks his police car down at the end of the street and walks to my apartment. He knocks three knocks and then one more on the door, and his greeting never varies: 'I'm a humble servant in search of the lower gate to the holy city.'"

" Is he a man you'd like to marry, Lenore?"

"Sure, but he's already attached . . . a wife and two kids. He just likes a fat woman, and I fill the bill. A fetish, I guess."

"Don't you feel used?"

"But it's no worse than being one of Leucippus's daughters."

"Is there much difference?"

"No, but look around, Stirling. Do you see any other men coming to my door?"

Every session ended with an innocent embrace . . . until one Sunday evening, McCutcheon could feel in her arms an expectation for something more. She clung to him and wouldn't let go.

"Come to bed with me, Stirling," she whispered.

" I can't. I need to go."

"There's plenty of time. Stay with me. I need you."

"I can't."

"Why?"

"Because I'm married."

"So what? So is my constable friend."

"I know. But I love my wife and am faithful."

Lenore broke away as she shoved Stirling in the chest and went into a tirade that made all of her previous expletives seem like Hallmark greetings.

"Get out! Get out, you saintly, self-righteous clown! Get out and never come back!"

McCutcheon turned and left without words. It was the last time he ever saw her or heard from her . . . until now. He set down his pipe in the ashtray, looked at the clock and, calculating the five-hour time difference, concluded that it would be 4:00 a.m. in Edinburgh. He checked his file to find the directory of his last Scottish parish and discovered Lenore's name and telephone number. He would call in the morning.

It was a restless night. At 7:00 a.m. he lifted the receiver. He felt dryness in his throat, drank water, and dialed. There was a call forwarding message, indicating that the number he had reached was out of service, and his call was being forwarded to another number. A male voice answered, "Ian Lomharach here."

"Hello, this is Stirling McCutcheon in the States. Is Lenore available?"

"No, Mr. McCutcheon. This is her brother Ian."

"Yes, I remember you, Ian. And how are you and your family?"

"We're all well . . . except for Lenore."

"What's wrong with Lenore?" McCutcheon asked cautiously.

"She's dead now, by about a month. I know she wrote to you to inform you about her diminished eyesight, but then the doctors discovered a growth behind her left eye. They thought it was operable, but when they went in to remove it, it was too massive. She died on the operating table."

McCutcheon remained silent.

"I know she missed you, Mr. McCutcheon," he continued slowly. "We all wished you were here to conduct the service, but we knew that wasn't even a wee bit feasible."

McCutcheon made all the appropriate condolences without recalling later a single phrase he used. *If onlys* flooded his brain: if only the letter hadn't been lost or detained somewhere for more than two months; if only he had inquired about her before he left Scotland the last time; if only he had been in touch with her before he had moved to Albany . . . if only . . . .

He wondered what ever became of Rubens's corpulent women, *The Rape of the Daughters of Leucippus*. So many Sunday evenings, not more than three feet away from him stood a woman—a Rubens woman—with nobody in the world to treat her kindly, affectionately . . . no one in the world to love her. Innocent embraces. Could anyone blame her for wanting more?

24

The Darkest Depths of Woe

THE MORNING BEGAN AS a stifling introduction to a sultry summer's day, one that would portend a searing indelibility by nightfall. Lawrence Montgomery's invitation to an early breakfast at a quiet table in the air-conditioned dining room at Hampton Court seemed irresistibly attractive. Lawrence, the congregant who issued the invitation, had scheduled his retirement for the last day of the year and was exploring ways of investing volunteer hours into service to the church. He met McCutcheon at the door. They walked into the spacious dining area, delightfully cool, where they were immediately seated and efficiently served.

They had no sooner consumed the first morsel, however, when a man from a nearby table assertively approached them, stared at McCutcheon, and inquired, "Aren't you so and so?" The person he mentioned was a nationally known celebrity, who had supposedly dodged the draft and had allegedly paid someone else to go in his place to Vietnam. Before McCutcheon could respond to his interrogative, he sat down and accelerated the interrogation: "How was it? How did it feel to have someone else go in your place, especially when so many were dying on foreign turf?" The questions—which implied a poignant judgment—hooked McCutcheon's Thespian inclinations; so with little thought about unforeseen consequences, he grasped the implied challenge and decided to play the part. McCutcheon began to answer his questions as if he were the draft dodger the interloper accused him of being. With a certain swashbuckling *joie de vivre*, he cleverly crafted his answers in such a way that they carried an unmistakable verisimilitude—that they were absolutely convincing—every answer marked by rich feasibility. This role-playing masquerade continued for at least half an hour, until after Lawrence and he had finished breakfast. By the time their self-imposed friend had returned to his table, their plates were empty, their coffee cups filled for the last time, and the bill lay in the center of the table.

It was a stellar performance, quite extraordinary, a dramatic victory, worthy of any professional stage in the northeast . . . but there followed a defining moment of profound misfortune.

"What was that?" asked Lawrence with a trace of rancor.

"A case of mistaken identity, I guess," rejoined McCutcheon with a wry smile.

"But that's not you, Stirling . . . or is it?"

To be sure, McCutcheon had lost all personal authenticity with Lawrence. For him it was as if McCutcheon had placed a veil over his face, or as if he had adopted a different face altogether, a visage to which he could not relate at all. The inevitable, indelible tragedy of that theatrical tangent was that McCutcheon never fully recaptured that opportunity for authentic interchange with Lawrence—never, ever again. After Lawrence laid a few dollars on the table, he picked up the breakfast bill and stood to leave. He reiterated his singular interest in volunteering at the church, curtly indicated that he was scheduled for a routine blood test, and left stage right, so to speak, after stopping at the cashier's counter on his way out.

The full impact of the hideous charade gripped McCutcheon's heart as it lay like a lead anchor in his chest or was constricted like an iron mask compressing his countenance. With a bitter taste of self-recrimination thickening his tongue, he furtively scanned the breakfast room for the interloping interlocutor, intent on speaking a clumsy, caustic word or two to him, but he too had left. He sat motionless; the waitress filled his coffee cup yet again, and he stared brooding into the little vessel of black java, feeling small enough to drown in it. He had seriously violated—albeit playfully—a fundamental tenet of pastoral care: authentic being allows no room for pretense. The regretful ramifications not only shattered the foundation stone of Lawrence and his relationship but also laid it to irreversible ruin.

Upon leaving the restaurant, McCutcheon walked briskly up State Street hill, hoping that an exercise of self-exertion would clear his cluttered mind and release a constricted conscience. Subsequently he thought about other matters, such thoughts fleeing to Daphne as they often did these days when consolation was so sorely wanted. He thought also of Heather and their children happily and securely ensconced in the Carriage House behind their grandparents' mansion. While their happiness induced happiness in him, he was forced to recognize a wistful element in his every thought, a sad note in his every word, an unrealized yearning in his every silence. Could it be that the abominable pretense he orchestrated at breakfast was nothing more than the logical extension of the repugnant pretense he harbors in his avowed self-sufficiency? After concluding that a visit to Scotland was imperative for him and Daphne, he turned around, walked down State Street hill, found his car and drove to the office.

By the time McCutcheon arrived at the church, it was ten fifteen. Caryn greeted him warmly and waited for him to settle in. She then entered his study with a note, which she placed on his desk blotter.

"Margot Winthrop called to request an immediate visit. I told her you were at a breakfast meeting and due to arrive after ten o'clock. I promised that I would have you call as soon as you came in. 'Don't bother,' she retorted, 'I'll be dead by ten o'clock' and hung up." She directed McCutcheon's attention to the pink note on the desk. "There's her telephone number, Stirling."

His day's packed itinerary flashed before his eyes. There was a report that he needed to finish before a trustees' noon business meeting at the University Club. From there he was due to make three hospital visits, two of which were to the Coronary Care Unit, all followed by a scheduled four thirty home communion. There was no way he could afford another lengthy hand-holding hour or two with Margot Winthrop while predictably, having emptied another fifth of whisky, she would issue sequential series of rants that rose from a vile, poisoned well of childhood abuse.

Caryn remained standing. "Shall I get her on the phone, Stirling?" she inquired.

"If she's to be dead by ten o'clock, Caryn," McCutcheon quipped with a note of irony, "there's no point in calling her."

Obviously caught off guard by this uncharacteristic response, she rejoined skeptically, "I suppose not," and returned to her desk.

McCutcheon leaned back in his chair. Everything around him seemed rancid. Every sentiment he felt carried with it a sickly sensation, as if there were some imperceptible tick that had bored into his psyche, eating his sense of well-being. More than ever, his recurring mantra that *ministry is messy* sounded its doleful tune. His head ached with a flagrant self-dissatisfaction, a nagging discontent at poor decisions, at flippant remarks. *This isn't who I am; or is it? Speaking of authenticity, what is true, what is genuine? Could I possibly be so insensitive as to write Margot off as one who cries wolf but would never take her own life?* Involuntarily McCutcheon walked to his locked closet, opened it with a key, and looked at the sealed box on the highest shelf. It was still there as he had suspected, and he recalled the day Margot had brought it to him at the office. "If anything untoward ever happens to me, Stirling," she directed, "I want you to open this box, read the letters enclosed, and then burn them."

With some inexplicable comfort derived from the sight of the box, as if there were a reassurance that as long as the box was visible Margot was alive, McCutcheon closed the closet door, locked it, and returned to his desk to write the pressing report for the trustees' meeting. His powers of concentration waned, however, and his thoughts were flooded by images of Margot, clad only in her nightgown and duster, sitting on her living room sofa, then standing and pacing about the room like a she-jaguar in heat, roaring and ranting in her unmet need and in her present volatility programmed by her violent past. It was her father who had violated her and her mother who had permitted it. Her older brother Brian had been her only haven, as much as his child's bravado could exert. He had had broken bones that testified to his noble attempts to shield her from their father's virulent wrath. He had cat-o'-nine-tails bruises as thanks for his valiant efforts at protecting her.

"McCutcheon," she would scream, the whiskey glass in her hand, "do you have any idea what is it like to be cornered in a small room with an irrational brute, passing himself off as a caring father, standing in front of the only door, wrapping a wide leather belt around his hand, and instructing me to remove my clothes, obviously so the impact of the belt against naked skin would bite like a snake, obviously because he derived some lurid pleasure from a child's naked form writhing beneath his lash! As I grew older, he seemed to enjoy it more. As my tender breasts implied an approaching womanhood, his eyes glistened as he leveled his blows adroitly at the objects of his desire and abominable lust. I hated the ruthless blackguard! Not only because of his immeasurable cruelty but mostly because of his disgusting duplicity. At home he was a perfidious tyrant. In the community he was known as a God-fearing, eloquent-praying, law-abiding, love-dispensing elder of the First Presbyterian Church."

Margot would stop pacing, cease ranting, set her whiskey glass on the fireplace mantel, and stare into the empty fireplace, empty except for a pile of ashes beneath the grate. McCutcheon would remain silent. Eventually she would return to the sofa and sit down again beside him. Though her hands would tremble—either from too much liquor or too little love—she would sit quietly, speak softly, as if from a distance.

"But there came a day, Stirling," she would begin and then pause, " . . . but there came a day for the inversion of power, when my brother had grown taller and heavier and stronger than that bedeviling old man. One day the worthless wretch ordered me into the small room, but before I entered it, my brother appeared behind our father, swinging the cat-o'-nine-tails, which he wrapped around my father's neck, yanking him backwards all the way into the back yard, down into the horse corral. With the force of a madman gone wilder and the accumulated anger of eighteen years of subjugation, my brother lifted the old man into the air and dunked him into the huge watering troth for the horses. He held him under water, pulled him up, and submerged him again, repeatedly until at last he pulled him out and threw him to the ground, where he lay on his back choking, coughing, sputtering. My brother knelt down, placed his knee in the old man's chest, and drew a knife from his belt. With the knife at the old man's throat, Brian told him through clenched teeth, 'If you ever, ever lay a hand on Margot or our mother or on me . . . ever, ever again, I will slit your gurgling throat and laugh raucously at your spurting blood. Mark my word, you old rotter! Mark my word!'

"He never touched us again. Instead he went into a shell of silence . . . then drank himself to death. When nearly a hundred members of the church and community attended his funeral and nodded their heads in agreement with the ebullient eulogies, Brian and I sat in the church anticipating the last shovel-full of dirt being tossed on top of his casket."

For McCutcheon, this was a recurring retrospective. With few variations, with a little more elaboration here or there, it was the same story issued with the same vile content vomited out with the same vitriolic distain for paternal exploitation and the same primal screams for a parental love she had never known. With all candor, McCutcheon could admit to himself that his patience never grew thin. At the very least her past misuse warranted current concern, an attentive ear, a listening heart. He couldn't change her past or reward her for her long-suffering. No one could. But he could listen, listen with an empathy that would vouchsafe a common human bond . . . except today, not today. He had listened time and time again . . . frequently throughout the last three years. Whenever the telephone call came to the office or at home, and Margot's strident voice threatened suicide if he didn't come right away, he'd first seek to soothe her and, that failing, would set out to visit her . . . and listen. Her psychiatrist charged her too much; her husband disappeared too often; her children had never been born; and her emptiness had never been assuaged.

There had been a time a year ago when the church had set out seeking an additional pastor. When they issued the call to Mark Winslow to become the Associate Pastor for Congregational Care, Margot—in a veritable rage—called McCutcheon the following morning, accusing him of hiring another pastor who would take her off his hands. "Mark my word, Stirling," she ejaculated, "that damn Mr. Winslow isn't going to bury me!" As much as he reassured her that her fears were unwarranted and that she would always be his parishioner, her suspicions persisted. At every subsequent visit, she raised the question, apparently clamoring for reassurance that McCutcheon would not desert her, undoubtedly an uneasiness born of her husband's intentional absences. Ironically, to Margot's delight, Winslow didn't accept the call.

Margot had married Stanley soon after she fled from home with her brother. She and Brian had made their way to the Capital District, where he had been offered a position with General Electric in Schenectady. He was twenty-two, and Margot was only nineteen. She had cultivated her aptitude for mathematics, quipping that she kept herself sane by adding up the seconds between blows, the minutes between expletives, the hours or days between beatings. With this native talent for arithmetic, she scoured the tri-cities for a suitable job and had landed an accountant's position at a small business in Albany. So Albany was where they settled in a two-bedroom apartment on Pine Street, and Brian commuted to Schenectady each business day. Margot contended that these were her happiest years. Even though undulating waves of anxiety plagued her, unshakeable fears of abandonment infiltrated her nightmares, and fluctuating moods characterized her waking hours in the apartment, thoughts of suicide seldom occurred to her. Brian was the faithful constant in her life. He was attentive to her every need. As one who manifested wisdom beyond his years, he understood Margot's mood swings, her frightening flashbacks, her bursts of anger at the hint of fraternal scorn or at the shadow of a crooked smile. Then, while attending with her brother a General Electric cocktail party in honor of the new Vice President of Operations, she met Stanley Winthrop.

Margot happened to feel particularly outgoing and congenial on that specific evening. She possessed a winning smile and proffered a genuinely warm hand upon being introduced to Stanley. How could Stanley have known—while receiving the touch of an unintentionally deceptive warm hand—the severely scarred person who resided behind this radiant, gregarious appearance?

Her warmth inspired a longing in Stanley, who invited Margot to the balcony of the Country Club. It became immediately apparent to him that here was a bright and charming woman of infinite grace and keen intellect. A man of twenty-six and never-before married, Stanley felt smitten for the first time in his life. Of all the women he had known or dated or worked with, he had never felt the stirrings in his viscera that he experienced in that very instant. Silently he admitted to himself that here was the woman he would someday marry. Conversation flowed unimpeded. Her charm increased with every new expression of thought. Before the evening came to a close, Stanley asked to see her again, whereupon Margot said, without answering his question, that it was late and that she needed to be going.

With a laugh, he exclaimed, "You're like a Cinderella. I don't know you yet and you have to leave before I know where to find you."

"Ask my brother Brian. He works in your department. He'll tell you." And with this, Margot left the balcony, joined her brother in the main ballroom, took his arm and disappeared.

A year of unsuspecting courtship—characterized by active planning, intellectual but superficial interchanges, and the ever-present, camouflaging mask—occurred from that night until their wedding night twelve months hence. Like the ship's captain aboard the Titanic, Stanley—for the entire year of preparations—was absolutely certain that their voyage together was destined for a resplendent port of marital joy and personal fulfillment. But also like the Titanic's captain, Stanley had not seen the fatal iceberg beneath the sea's surface.

During the course of their subsequent years of marriage on relentless stormy seas, Stanley had come to McCutcheon's study countless times, seeking a safe harbor during a domestic tempest, the nature of which he had experienced over and over again.

On one such visit, Stanley initiated the conversation with a quotation from *Psalm* 13. "Stirling, this morning the psalmist articulated it for me: *How long, O Lord? Wilt thou forget me forever?* I feel certain that God no longer hears me, that God has hidden his face from me, while my enemy taunts me. My enemy isn't Margot, Stirling. It's her state of mind. One minute she loves me like no other possibly could. In the next, she lashes out at me as if I were her inveterate tormentor. She's up, then she's down. She's sober, then she's drunk. She's clinging to me, then she's pushing me away. She draws me close to her with pleas to never leave her, then she's telling me to get out of the house and never come back. She declares that she could never live without my love, then she's accusing me of never having loved her at all, that all I wanted was to use her. In one of her fits of self-loathing, I asked her, 'who do you think you are to tell me to get out of the house and never come back? Just who do you think you are!' Tears filled her eyes; sobs broke out like ghosts released after centuries from a locked chest, and she shouted, 'I don't know! Don't you know? I don't know! I don't know who I am! I don't know who I am . . . to ask this or to ask that . . . or to ask anything, or to think anything, or to say anything! I . . . don't know!' I held her. For a long time I held her until the sobs subsided and she fell asleep in my arms."

Stanley sat dejected in the wingback chair.

"I think I understand, Stanley," McCutcheon offered after a time of silence. "You may not think so, but I'm sure I understand."

Stanley looked up, having run his hands repeatedly through his hair. "Then you know why I go to the hunting lodge in the Catskills every chance I get . . . most every weekend and on holidays?"

McCutcheon nodded sadly, though empathically. "Yes," he said, barely audible, still nodding.

† † †

Caryn's appearance at the study door interrupted McCutcheon's recollections of the Winthrops' years of undulating torment. "Here's the packet you need for your meeting with the trustees this noon, except for your own report. Is there anything else you want at the moment?"

"No, thanks, Caryn," McCutcheon responded pensively. "I'll have my report ready for you to type in a few minutes."

Caryn turned to leave, but McCutcheon called her back.

"Caryn, I apologize for my comment earlier. I'm sorry. It was flippant."

"Sure, Stirling, I understand," Caryn said with a gracious smile. "I knew it wasn't like you. It's okay." She left the room and closed the door quietly behind her.

The remainder of the day proceeded as planned: the trustees' meeting with its usual challenges of dealing with financial shortfalls, budgetary constraints, endowment interests, stewardship campaign planning, and committee reports; then the three hospital visits followed by the 4:30 p.m. shut-in home communion, for which McCutcheon was ten minutes late. By five forty-five he had finished for the afternoon and returned to the church office. Caryn had left for the day, but not before stacking a few telephone messages on his desk. He leaned back in his chair to read them and to set a priority for return calls. The telephone rang. He answered it.

"Stirling!" It was Stanley's voice, trembling.

"Stanley, are you all right?"

"Margot is dead . . . when I arrived home from work, I found her in the garage, the garage door closed, the car engine running."

McCutcheon's throat tightened, his tongue thickened, his eyes watered. "What time, Stanley?" he asked somberly, eking out the words dryly.

"It must have been sometime after three o'clock," Stanley answered. He sounded bewildered, incredulous. "I discovered a note on the nightstand beside our bed with today's date, and the time she wrote was 3:00 p.m. She was still alive when I found her, but she died in the ambulance on the way to the hospital."

Stanley's voice trailed off into a detailed account of the suicide, the scene in which he discovered her, her state of unconsciousness, attempts to revive her, the ambulance ride to the hospital, and her final breath—none of which McCutcheon could repeat verbatim. His mind had become preoccupied with a choice he had made after a cruel quip: *if she's to be dead by ten o'clock, there's no point in calling her.*

†   †   †

Weeks passed, and McCutcheon stood on the threshold of autumn, staring at the forthcoming launch of the ecclesiastical program year. It was late Saturday afternoon, the day before Rally Sunday, the appellation with which his church had traditionally tagged the first Sunday of the church school year, which begins after Labor Day. All was ready for the next morning: teachers selected and trained, Rally Day notices sent out, adult education arranged, the worship service planned, his sermon written, and communion organized. Margot came to mind. Margot Winthrop often came to mind, usually at times when he least expected a thought or an image of her to appear. Stanley had been moved by the memorial service, even though afflicted by an irresolvable paradox: simultaneously he was devastated and liberated. "How can this be?" he asked McCutcheon, mystified.

"How could this not be?" McCutcheon rejoined knowingly.

Though occasionally on the brink of self-disclosure with Stanley, he had never related to him his offhanded comment to Caryn the day Margot died. Nor did he ever divulge to Stanley that Margot had called him that morning. Night and day McCutcheon wrestled with these omissions, thinking that such self-disclosure could help Stanley understand his dilemma and McCutcheon's identifying with his paradox. But guilt invariably won over, and McCutcheon remained private.

The box. McCutcheon thought of the box. Numerous times since that fateful summer's day McCutcheon had thought of the box. Numerous times since her death, McCutcheon had unlocked the closet with the fanciful notion that the sight of the box would reduce her death to mere rumor. "How naïve," he'd say, close the closet door and lock it yet again.

Unlike most frenzied days in the office, it was quiet there on this particular Saturday. There was less likelihood for an interruption than any other time he could imagine. Overcoming a phlegmatic state, he slowly rose to close the study door and then unlocked the closet. He lifted the box from off the top shelf, carried it to his desk, and cut the packing tape. An initial glimpse calculated as many as two hundred handwritten letters. He was surprised to spot the one on top addressed to him. Using his desk letter opener, he unsealed the communiqué:

Dear Stirling, I trust you will not be alarmed or in the least bit surprised by the contents of this box since, in a recent conversation, I revealed to you my intimate and intricate relationship with Sylvia Wilbur, my lesbian lover of the past six years. Whenever Stanley retreated to the hunting lodge—successive weekends, minor holidays—I found solace in Sylvia's bed, in her firm embraces, in her passionate lovemaking. As you know so well, I have sought a genuine love all my life, first with my parents, then with my brother Brian, with numerous men before Stanley, and finally with Stanley himself. All either misused or abandoned me. Brian was the most faithful until seven years ago when he took the General Electric promotion in Seattle and settled in the Northwest, way beyond my reach and ultimately out of touch. As for Stanley, he said that I tested his mettle every day and he needed weekend reprieves. Abandoned, yet again. It was only Sylvia who remained. We saw each other every weekend and holiday that Stanley escaped to the hunting lodge, and in between times we corresponded by mail frequently during the week. The weekends and holidays were filled with an insatiable physical passion while our lengthy letters served as poetic interludes. Etudes, as it were, of longing, aspiration, union, and hope. Sylvia's was the only love I have ever known that filled my soul, honored my muliebrity, savored my feminine sexuality, actuated my legitimate lusts . . . all at the same time, without exploitation. Until recently.

Lately, during our weekends together, in our lovemaking, she became rough and hurtful, inexplicably biting or scratching. Often she drew blood. The pain would initiate instantaneous flashbacks of my father's swinging the belt with a brutish force. When I protested, pulled back, or questioned her motive, she laughed derisively and taunted me with infantilizing barbs: "Such a baby!" she'd exclaim in disgust.

Last month the postman delivered this box to my door, including all the letters and cards I sent to her during the past six years. I have added the correspondence I had received from her, so that all evidence of our relationship is compiled in one place and can be immolated on the same funeral pyre of a rare but dead relationship. The loss is immeasurable, and it raises the reverberating, incessant question as to whether there is anyone in the entire world who could love me . . . as I am. The answer is clearly no. I became convinced of that the day I stopped at Sylvia's house unannounced and found her with another woman. Obviously they had been in bed. Since then, the only consolation I have found that eases the pain is the determination to follow through on the threats I have made so often that no one could take them seriously.

You will find in the bottom of this letter's envelope a cross . . . the cross of Lorraine, which Sylvia and I both wore as gifts from each other. As you undoubtedly have known and will of course see here, there are two parallel horizontal crosspieces and the vertical piece. Sylvia and I agreed that these represented our parallel lives that were connected by the vertical aspiration toward God, toward heaven, toward an elusive love, toward some ultimate meaning in our lives and relationship.

Do with it what you will, Stirling, and think of me now and then.

Sincerely,
Margot Winthrop

Looking in the envelope, McCutcheon discovered the cross of Lorraine, just as she had indicated. He took it in his hand and studied it. Then he tightened his grasp upon it, intent on gaining a tactile sense of a life he had encountered but not really known. It occurred to him that Margot Winthrop had gone to the *grave unknown and unknowing,* the very fear that Charlotte Humphrey had wanted to dispel for herself.

Well into the late evening McCutcheon read the letters and cards in the box, the outpouring of love and affection of two women, each to the other. There were detailed descriptions of their intimate expressions of lesbian sexuality, but none of it seemed in any way lewd or repulsive. Quite to the contrary! Any vivid depiction of sexual intimacy had been beautified by the embrace of two authentic beings and tempered in the furnace of divine discontent.

As McCutcheon placed the cross of Lorraine in his shirt pocket to be transported to the box of crosses on his manse study desk, he thought of Margot's benighted father and of how desperately everyone craves for a loving father who, by his love, guides his child to the full awareness of who that child is. Without such a father, how can one ever discover the precious essence of his or her own identity?

Darkness covered everything as McCutcheon made his way to the manse. He entered the living room, the box of letters in his arms, and opened the fireplace doors. With mixed emotions—for his inclination to retain the letters conflicted with Margot's final request—he heaped the letters upon the grate and struck a long fireplace match. As the *funeral pyre of a rare but dead relationship* roared into a hungry blaze, he fancied he heard Margot's words: *the only consolation I have found that eases the pain.*

For McCutcheon, there was no consolation to be found.

269

25

The Silent Wound

"I can't think about it, Mr. McCutcheon, except in fleeting moments. Then I have to dismiss it as quickly as it occurs to me."

Stephanie Statler sat fingering a letter in her right hand, savoring the touch, the texture of the missive. Clearly the document was well-worn—though well-preserved, not tattered—certainly not a correspondence recently acquired.

"What's the worst of it all, Mrs. Statler?" McCutcheon inquired, attempting to get at the source of her discomfort.

"But that's just it, Mr. McCutcheon, I can't bear to recollect the worst of it long enough to lend it a suitable description. On the other hand, I can go on at great length about the best of it."

"Would you? I'd like to know."

Mrs. Statler remained silent, obviously meditative, gazing at the letter in her lap, then raising her eyes to the light streaming in the only window in her miniscule room, equipped simply with two easy chairs, a twin bed with bedrails, and a small night stand.

"Knowlton Williams and I were lovers at a young age in the late 1930s. I had just finished four years at Sarah Lawrence College—class of 1940—when Knowlton graduated from Annapolis and received his orders to serve at the naval base in San Diego, at that time called the *U.S. Destroyer Base*. I had been approached by the dean of faculty at Sarah Lawrence to remain as a teaching assistant in the Classics Department; but within a month of his arrival in San Diego, Knowlton proposed to me in a letter, which included a one-way bus ticket to California if I planned to say *yes*. I did, and I went."

"San Diego? Sight unseen?"

"Sight unseen. I could be anywhere with Knowlton, so long as I was *with* Knowlton. We used to declare to each other that we could go through anything—indeed the worst of circumstances—so long as we were together."

"Did that prove to be true, Mrs. Statler?"

"Yes, I believe so. But unfortunately, the worst of circumstances occurred when we were apart."

"Apologies! I veered you off track. You were speaking about the best of circumstances."

"I travelled to San Diego, and it was an inimitable blessing as profound for me as Dante's *Paradiso*. The glorious sunshine of every day was to me as brilliant and as redeeming as that deep light that Dante saw with its three circles and three colors of one identical magnitude. I took it for a sign of promise . . . the light, I mean. *Providence*, I said. I took it for a sign of divine providence, a glint of future prosperity, replete with an unbounded joy of marital bliss, a husband I adored and children I could conceive—both literally and visually. Actually, Mr. McCutcheon, I *mis*took it for a sign."

McCutcheon tacitly identified this as a sacred moment and remained silent. Mrs. Statler's eyes returned to the letter in her hand. She appeared to be absorbed in it, as though she had submerged beneath a vast sea of billowy waves.

" Knowlton and I were married soon after I arrived in San Diego. It was a magnificent military wedding on base, the Navy chaplain officiating. With three day's leave, we toured the Napa Valley wine country. Unabashedly, Mr. McCutcheon, I admit to an inveterate single-mindedness, since for three days we simply drove, tasted wine, and made love. It was all sweeter than the nectar of whatever gods there be. Knowlton and I were rhapsodic. Neither of us dreaded the three-days leave's coming to an end because we knew that that was simply the beginning of a lifetime of the same, and of the rest of eternity in a thimble of time for us, and of mutual experiences we could not even imagine or prescribe. Little could we know at that time that there would be one experience we would frantically want to *pro*scribe were it in our power."

"Did you have a premonition, a particular dread?"

"No. Each of us was thoroughly immersed in the other and completely captivated by the present."

"Was that a good thing? A blessing in retrospect, or do you have regrets about not looking ahead?"

"In retrospect, it was a blessing. Nothing regarding the future—not even an apprehension nor a premonition, had it gripped us—could have caused us to savor those initial months of marriage more fully. We made love every night, engaged in intellectual intercourse every day followed by social intercourse every weekend. By virtue of his graduation from Annapolis, Knowlton arrived in San Diego as an officer and, within a short period of time, achieved the rank of lieutenant commander. Numerous were the occasions we dressed to the nines to attend naval formal dances, dining with other officers and wives. It was a charmed life we lived for more than a year. But by early summer of 1942—the attack on Pearl Harbor having drawn the United States into the war—a great dark cloud settled over the San Diego naval base, and the curtain was raised on the soon-to-be written tragedy played on the Pacific theater stage. Knowlton was assigned as one of the six lieutenant commanders to the *USS Juneau*."

A remnant of that dark cloud from nearly half a century before fell upon Stephanie Statler in that instant.

"Do you know about the *USS Juneau*, Mr. McCutcheon?"

"To be honest, Mrs. Statler, I don't. By reason of a Scottish heritage, I suppose, I apparently neglected American History studies."

"There were five brothers—the Sullivan brothers—who decided to serve in the U.S. Navy, and they insisted on serving on the very same ship. Ostensibly, the Navy was opposed to their request, but, finally, they succeeded in convincing the upper naval echelon to assign them to the *USS Juneau*, an antiaircraft cruiser. They said that they would fight as one and, if need be, die as one. They did. Fought as one . . . and died as one. To be sure, Mr. McCutcheon, nearly an entire crew of seven hundred seamen died as one."

"Where in the Pacific?" McCutcheon inquired reverently.

"Iron Bottom Sound off Guadalcanal. It was during the Battle of Friday the Thirteenth, 1942. The previous day, on November 12, the *Juneau* was part of a thirteen-ship fleet that dropped anchor off Guadalcanal near the airfield, which had been captured by the Allied Forces in early August. The fleet's mission was to guard the transports that were delivering troops and supplies to the island. That afternoon they fought off an aerial banzai charge, destroying every Japanese plane except one. Then that same night they encountered Japanese warships and submarines. In that skirmish the *Juneau* was hit by a torpedo from a Japanese destroyer, which put a hole in the left side of the ship. Soon after, another enemy battleship was shelling the deck. But the *Juneau* miraculously survived those attacks. It was the next day, in the Battle of Friday the Thirteenth, when the *Juneau* met its ultimate fate. Only six ships of the thirteen-ship fleet emerged from the previous battles. Now they were making their way to Espíritu Santo, the nearest U.S. naval base. Only two out of the six had come through the previous night's engagement virtually unscathed. The other four were severely crippled. One of the two destroyers that were relatively undamaged was sent ahead to radio headquarters, leaving a vulnerable remnant of five. It wasn't long before a Japanese submarine seized the opportunity to zero in on the vestige vessels. It launched two torpedoes, aiming at the *USS San Francisco*, but missing. The *USS Helena* swerved to the right just in time to avoid the intended impact. But one of these missiles that missed the mark with these two ships found its target in the *Juneau's* side. Reports indicated that the *Juneau* blew up at 11:01 a.m. on Friday the Thirteenth and, in a matter of seconds, it sank."

"And your husband was on that ship," McCutcheon said haltingly with a vague disbelief.

"Yes, along with six hundred ninety-two other seamen."

"Were there any survivors?"

Stephanie Statler looked down at her crooked fingers holding the faded letter. She remained silent, motionless. Without looking up, she said, "ten."

"Ten," McCutcheon repeated incredulously.

"Ten . . . ultimately. Ten . . . more than a week after the *Juneau* went down." She raised her eyes to McCutcheon. "But that wasn't the whole of the matter, Mr. McCutcheon. While hundreds of sailors went down with the ship, more than one hundred forty men, who one way or another made it into the water, were left to die, abandoned by the other four ships . . . in shark-infested waters. According to the ten survivors, most of the men bobbing about in the oil-slick waves were devoured by sharks."

A pained expression seized Stephanie's countenance as if she were reliving another nightmare, the same nightmare that visited her recurrently. No words of comfort occurred to McCutcheon. Speechless, verbally constipated, he sat frozen in his chair.

"Ah, Mr. McCutcheon, I said I can't bear to recollect the worst of it, and here I am talking about just that . . . the worst of it. This is the first time I can recall talking about the worst of it."

"Can you say more, Mrs. Statler, or would you rather not?"

"The *more* of it, the rest of it, is the worst of it," she answered in a whisper. "The burning question, sir, the question that assaults me repeatedly, incessantly, is whether Knowlton went down with the ship or whether he was attacked by sharks, systematically mutilated, limbs torn from his body, his heart ripped out of his chest by razor-sharp teeth. That beautiful body I had tenderly caressed—the stately soul mate with whom I had soared into inexpressible ecstasy—violently debased by the ravaging of dastardly sharks! The very image decimates me over and over again. Can you believe it, Mr. McCutcheon? The blessing I ask for is knowing that Knowlton had the better death, the good death—that Knowlton went down with the *Juneau*. My God! What a pathetic request: to know that a watery grave was the more merciful death, the preferred death over that of a shark's tooth!"

"That could surely be only a modicum of comfort," McCutcheon offered quietly.

The assisted living staff nurse appeared at the door, apologized for the interruption, and engaged in the routine 3:00 p.m. check of vital signs before leaving for the day. Upon her exit, McCutcheon pointed to the letter in Mrs. Statler's hand.

"I see you receive correspondence," he said.

"Not much these days," she replied benignly. "This is a letter from Knowlton, years ago, before that fateful mission to Guadalcanal. There is very little I have left by which to remember him: this letter, a photograph of us at an officers' dance, and this—his Navy cross."

"May I see the photograph, Mrs. Statler?"

Stephanie reached into her nightstand and pulled out a small box. She passed him the photograph from its contents and smiled with a warmth that apparently radiated from a memory of long ago. There in McCutcheon's hand was a portrait of matchless beauty and irretrievable youth, of spontaneous joy and immeasurable optimism.

"After Knowlton had received intelligence that the *Juneau* would be leaving dock in August, he insisted that I return to Albany until after his tour of duty, which I did in

May 1942. Before he deployed for the Pacific, he wrote to me nearly every day. I have them all, but this letter was particularly special."

"In what way?" McCutcheon inquired tenderly.

"He informed me that, were anything horrible to happen, he would always be present with me, and we could communicate through the ether, which, he said, is always eternal. The *eternal ether* is the exact phrase he uses in this letter. This was the only letter of his abundant correspondence that ever alluded to a possibility of his never returning. This letter has never been out of my sight, Mr. McCutcheon. I hold it, and I talk with Knowlton, and Knowlton talks with me; all the time I clutch his Navy cross. When it comes to making important decisions, I ask Knowlton, and he helps me decide."

"Then he is always present, Mrs. Statler," McCutcheon said. It was a statement of affirmation, not a question to confirm her allegation. "In other words, you actually *feel* his presence."

"Yes, I do," she said with a sad smile. She held up the cross she had mentioned earlier. "I cherish not only his presence and this letter . . . but also his Navy cross, which he enclosed." She handed McCutcheon the cross, which he studied with a deep sense of awe before he returned both the photograph and the cross to the box she held. After a lengthy silence, she laid the box back into the nightstand drawer.

"You may be surprised to know, Mr. McCutcheon, that I remarried."

"I suspected as much . . . as indicated by a different last name from Knowlton's," McCutcheon rejoined with a soft smile. "Was that a choice that Knowlton helped you make?"

"Yes. Most certainly! We spoke about it at great length . . . through the ether."

"Was it a wise decision? A good marriage?"

"I believe so. It was a number of years after the war. After earning my PhD, I had returned to Sarah Lawrence College to teach Classics. At an educator's conference held at the college, I met Mr. Statler, a secondary school superintendent in the tri-city area. After nearly a year of dinner engagements and attending cultural events together, he proposed to me. I still missed Knowlton desperately, and Mr. Statler knew it. I told him I could never love anyone the way I loved Knowlton. He told me that he understood, that he would honor those feelings, but, by the same token, he would value a life-long companionship: a marriage of convenience, of living together liveliness, of dinner engagements and cultural events mutually-enjoyed. In my conversations with Knowlton, Knowlton agreed. So I agreed, and Mr. Statler and I were married at Madison Avenue Presbyterian Church long before you arrived as pastor. He kept his word. He was good to me. I was good to him. Our marriage was principally characterized by a rare, ongoing intellectual exchange I could never have found with anyone else I have ever known . . . not even Knowlton Williams."

With this, she looked to her lap, where Knowlton's letter lay in its eternal ether.

Raising her face to the small sunlit window, she said, "Mr. Statler died five years ago last month, Mr. McCutcheon, and it's still Knowlton I long for . . . or, to be precise, *ache* for."

"Yes, I can see that it's Knowlton whose presence surrounds you," said McCutcheon reflectively as he stared at the letter on Stephanie's lap. Another sacred silence ensued.

"Mr. McCutcheon?"

"Yes."

"Earlier I mentioned *providence.* I took the joy Knowlton and I experienced in San Diego as a sign of divine providence. As horrific images of Knowlton in shark-infested waters continue to haunt me, I wonder about divine providence. Where was the providence of God at all evident in Iron Bottom Sound? Where, Mr. McCutcheon . . . where?"

McCutcheon's eyes—shamelessly, uncontrollably welling up—were riveted on Stephanie's face. Again the curse of words sticking in his throat tormented him. There must be comforting words . . . if he could only find them. There must be some explanation . . . if he could only think of one. He looked away.

"Undoubtedly you remember, Mr. McCutcheon, Virgil's words: *deep in her breast lives the silent wound.* I haven't yet determined whether the silent wound that lives deep in my breast lives on wounding me because Knowlton is dead, perhaps devoured by sharks, or because God did not intervene. And I ask you, Mr. McCutcheon: is God useful? It makes me wonder, Mr. McCutcheon, is God of any earthly use at all?"

McCutcheon remained silent, as silent as the silent wound that lived deep in Stephanie Statler's breast. He wondered whether there exists a faith so profound that no anguish—no matter how enormous or crushing—could ever nullify that faith in the believer.

Unlike other occasions, there was nothing awkward about the silence. McCutcheon knew that no words could possibly cauterize Stephanie's silent wound . . . but only the Word, hanging listlessly on a cross. As the image of that beautiful Christ fractured on that heinous cross came into McCutcheon's focus, Stephanie Statler's question rang in his ears: *is God of any earthly use at all?*

† † †

A month later, McCutcheon—on his monthly rounds of members in care facilities—entered Stephanie Statler's room with his home communion set, prepared to celebrate Holy Eucharist with Knowlton William's only love. It occurred to McCutcheon that not only is the Presence of the Living Christ in the bread and wine but also the presence of Knowlton Williams would be in that room as well. McCutcheon started at its sterile appearance. The bed was stripped, all personal items gone, and a housekeeping staff member was washing all surfaces.

"Excuse me," McCutcheon said, "isn't this Stephanie Statler's room? Has she been moved to another?"

"You'll need to check with the nurse at the nurses' station," replied the housekeeper.

McCutcheon approached the head nurse. "Excuse me. Do you have a new room number for Stephanie Statler, please? I'm Stirling McCutcheon, her pastor."

"Mr. McCutcheon, I'm sorry to say that Stephanie died last week," rejoined the nurse on duty.

"Why wasn't I contacted?" asked McCutcheon incredulously.

"Our chaplain took care of the arrangements and officiated at the funeral here at the home. We had no idea that you would want to be involved or that she had a church affiliation."

"How could you not know!" thought McCutcheon as his ire rose rapidly. Despite his indignation, he maintained his composure. "When was the funeral?" he asked coldly.

"The day before yesterday; Saturday morning."

"Did she by any chance leave a letter from her husband Knowlton, dated in the forties?"

"No, sir, but she did leave a note indicating that if you came by she would like you to have this box." The nurse opened the top drawer of the desk and handed McCutcheon the box Stephanie had shown him previously. He recognized it.

"Thank you," he said wryly and walked away a short distance, sat in a lounge chair, and opened the box. There, isolated and alone—without picture or letter—lay Knowlton Williams's Navy cross. All these years it had been a constant reminder to Stephanie Statler that *deep in her breast lived the silent wound.*

"Her breast is no longer bleeding," thought McCutcheon. "Perhaps Stephanie Statler now resides with Knowlton Williams face-to-face in that eternal ether," he whispered, "where neither sharks bite nor breasts can be wounded."

26

As Dying Man to Dying Men

McCutcheon opened the box of crosses on his desk in the manse study and, as was his custom every Sunday morning, lifted out his Sunday Greek cross with imprinted affirmation: *ICH BIN BEI EUCH ALLE TAGGE.* He smiled, slipped it into his suit coat pocket, and said in an attitude of sacred prayer, "I am with you always." Today, October 2, marked his sixth World Communion Sunday at Madison Avenue Presbyterian Church. Before making his way across the road to the church, he sat at his desk, picked up his manuscript and reviewed his sermon for the day: *No Need for Ghosts*, based on Jesus's parable of Lazarus and the rich man, Luke 16:19–31. In this sermon, McCutcheon contended that the Lazarus we see in this parable is the same Lazarus we see throughout our world today . . . or, rather, the Lazarus we *don't* see, that is, the person among people our self-interest causes to be invisible. The sermon concluded: *this is the table of our Lord Jesus Christ. No one is invisible here; no one grovels for crumbs beneath this table; no one is a beggar at this feast; people will come from east and west, from north and south to sit as sisters and brothers at this table . . . with Christ in our midst.*

McCutcheon tucked the manuscript into his briefcase and made his way to the church. He missed Daphne most on high Sundays such as this one, in which the Kirkin' o' the Tartans occurred, when a vast variety of Scottish plaids were displayed in kilts and flags, all presented in a magnificent processional behind a Scottish bagpiper. In his second year at Madison Avenue Church, McCutcheon introduced the Kirkin' o' the Tartans, which had now become a tradition celebrated on World Communion Sunday, the first Sunday in October, and on the Sunday closest to St. Andrew's Day, November 30. It became immediately clear to McCutcheon that Freda Chamberlain wasn't the least enamored of Kirkin' o' the Tartans—actually, she literally detested the idea—but in light of her initial pledge of *active allegiance* to McCutcheon, there was little she could say against the tradition. Besides that, virtually all the members of the congregation had embraced the custom with unbounded enthusiasm.

Perhaps out of deference to Freda Chamberlain's feelings or to the firmly established traditions of Madison Avenue Church requiring the Sunday cross and academic hood, McCutcheon didn't wear his kilt or other Scottish attire for Kirkin' o' the Tartans, but he did add to his clerical vestments a clergy stole woven with the Mc-Cutcheon plaid of brilliant blues, rich greens, and thin red and gold lines. Who could be critical of such a miniscule nuance on these two occasions in which he celebrated his Jacobitical heritage?

With Scottish pride swelling in his breast at the familiar sounds of the bagpipes, McCutcheon took his place at the end of the processional and followed the impressive array of tartans, the chancel choir, and elders to the front of the sanctuary, where he entered the chancel and commenced the service of worship. What surprised him—though he took little notice of it—was his tripping on the second step into the chancel; but since he had gracefully caught himself, he attributed his misstep to his preoccupation with the splendor of the tartans and immediately dismissed it. Within the same first half-hour of the service, however, there occurred yet another anomaly, which could have given him cause for concern had he not ignored it as a sign. When he mounted the steps to the pulpit, he looked at the ornate wooden pulpit desk for the words he read to himself each time prior to preaching: *We would see Jesus* and *Preach as never sure to preach again; preach as dying man to dying men.* But the words were blurred. He knew them by heart, but he couldn't make them out. Three times he lost his place in the sermon manuscript, and sentences came in and out of focus. But who could tell except he, himself, since he knew his sermon well enough to carry on without raising unease in the congregation. The people's ensuing alarm, however, could not be dismissed when McCutcheon presided at the communion table and found difficulty in tearing the loaf of bread. *Take, eat. This is my body given for you*; and it was a noticeable effort for him to break the bread. *In a like manner also, Jesus took the cup and gave it to his disciples to drink, saying, 'This is the new covenant in my blood, which is poured out for you and the forgiveness of sin.* McCutcheon poured the wine from the tankard into the chalice, but the chalice slipped out of his hand and landed on the white cloth of the communion table, drenching it with the blood of Christ. Elders, who were serving communion to the people, came to his assistance, lifted the trays from the table instead of receiving them from McCutcheon, and distributed the cups of wine.

The remainder of the service concluded without further incident, but rather than waiting to greet the people, McCutcheon made his way to the manse and sat quietly in the study. He ached for Daphne, but she was in the midst of intense rehearsing for Mendelssohn's *A Midsummer Night's Dream*. Numerous people dropped by the manse to express concern, but he simply excused the falling chalice as an unfortunate slip of the hand, suggesting that he hadn't wiped his hands thoroughly enough after the ceremonial washing prior to handling the bread and chalice. Apparently everyone accepted this explanation as plausible except for Helga Wenzell, who insisted on coming into his study and sitting with him.

"What's happening, Stirling?" she asked pointedly. "I think it's more than excess water after ceremonial hand washing."

McCutcheon sat silently for a long time, his hands folded beneath his chin, his eyes trained on the box of crosses. Helga waited patiently, determined to learn the truth.

"I don't know, Helga," he answered, bewildered. "I was fine this morning when I left for church . . . filled with anticipation . . . sorry that Daphne couldn't be here with us. I tripped on the second stair of the chancel but thought nothing of it. Then the words on the pulpit desk were blurred, and my eyes wouldn't focus consistently on my manuscript. But I got through all of that. Then, quite apparently, by the time I arrived at the communion table, I had lost strength in my hands, so much so that I couldn't tear the communion loaf or firmly hold the chalice. And you saw the result, Helga. Everybody saw the result. Every last person witnessed firsthand the desecration of the Lord's Table . . . I don't know, Helga! I don't know what's going on."

"We should call Daphne," said Helga reflectively, concerned about the potential magnitude of the matter.

"No, Helga! We can't. She is right in the middle of a hectic rehearsal schedule, and it's such a demanding role. I can't do that to her. I won't, Helga, and you have to accept that."

"I'm not leaving you alone, then, Stirling, and you have to accept that."

McCutcheon nodded agreement, leaned back in the easy chair, and closed his eyes.

"You must see a doctor right away, Stirling. Dr. Tillman. How fortunate to have our own neurologist here in the congregation. He was there today. Let me call him."

"I shall feel foolish if it's nothing, Helga."

"No. You will feel grateful if it's nothing. Do you have your directory here or at the church office?"

McCutcheon stood unsteadily, reached into his desk drawer, and handed Helga the church directory. She looked at the listing for Dr. Tillman and dialed the telephone.

"Helga, I'll meet you and Rev. McCutcheon at the Albany Medical Center emergency room in an hour. Tell the staff there you are expected to meet me."

Helga drove. McCutcheon rode quietly, mystified by this sudden onset of baffling symptoms. Dr. Tillman was waiting for them when they arrived.

"I wondered this morning what happened at the table, Stirling," he said kindly. "Something seemed dreadfully amiss during the sermon. I thought I detected a slight slurring of your words. Then of course, the event at the table seemed to verify my suspicions."

"I was fine until the service began, Martin," McCutcheon rejoined. "Then a slip on the chancel step and words wouldn't come into focus at the pulpit and, finally, weakness in my hands at the table."

"Well, let's find out what the problem seems to be," Tillman said with a compassionate smile. "It would be well to get to the bottom of this."

After conducting a thorough physical exam, he ordered a brain MRI and remained at the hospital to read the report.

By midafternoon, Dr. Tillman had read the results and entered McCutcheon's room.

"Stirling, you said that everything was fine until the service began. Have you noticed any of these symptoms before today? Have you noticed anything unusual in your physical health previously?"

"Such as what, Martin?"

"Such as, problems with balance, bouts of nausea, more frequent headaches, excessive fatigue, difficulty in concentration, numbness . . . any of these symptoms?"

"Headaches, for sure, Martin. Frequent and intense. Loss of equilibrium at times."

"Have you fallen recently?

"No. Just issues with balance."

"Concentration?"

"That's okay. No problem there."

Tillman looked down at his folder, then up at McCutcheon. "Stirling, I'm sorry to say that the MRI shows you have a high grade astrocytoma, also known as a glioblastoma multiforme. As well as I can tell, it's malignant and inoperable. And, unfortunately, it's one of the fastest growing brain tumors we can identify."

"The headaches are on the top left side of my head."

"Yes, of course. That's where you will continually feel the pressure and the pain; and it will undoubtedly increase as the days go on . . . I'm sorry, Stirling."

McCutcheon sat frozen, as if his entire body as well as his head were in a vice, until he finally spoke, "Thanks for seeing me so soon, Martin, and getting at the source!"

"My colleagues and I will follow up with you tomorrow and suggest a treatment plan."

"What will the decline look like? Is there a pattern to the rate and characteristics of the deterioration?" McCutcheon asked with a calculating look into Tillman's eyes.

"Stirling, you'll be able to function much as you have been for weeks, but then you'll notice a rapid decline as all your symptoms intensify, particularly headaches, balance, nausea, and fatigue."

McCutcheon nodded, shook Tillman's hand, dressed, and met Helga in the waiting room. During the car ride to the manse, he could think of no reason to disguise the truth, so he told her exactly what Dr. Tillman had related in his diagnosis. Helga turned down her street, stopped at her house, and, within minutes, returned to the car with an overnight valise.

When they arrived at the manse, Helga asked Stirling what he felt like eating.

"Something light, Helga, please. There's thawed tilapia in the refrigerator . . . enough for both of us if you wish."

"All right," she smiled and turned to take an evening residence in the kitchen.

"Helga," said McCutcheon. She looked back sadly. "Thank you, my dear Lady!"

He sat down at his desk. There was a lump in his throat, and he swallowed numerous times to get rid of it, but it stayed. His eye caught the flashing light on his desk telephone. A message: *Stirling, this is Bill Schumann. I need to see you as soon as convenient for you. Would tomorrow, late morning, work for you? I would need you to come here to the house, if possible.*

McCutcheon picked up the directory Helga had left on the desk, found Bill Schumann's telephone number, and dialed.

"Hello, Bill. This is Stirling."

"Thank you for calling back, my friend! You got my message?"

"Yes, and I can see you at your place at eleven."

"Good. Thank you, Stirling. Babbs will be here also, and we'll look forward to seeing you."

"'Til tomorrow, then."

"Goodbye, my friend."

McCutcheon broke the silence at dinner. "My apologies, Helga, for dropping August's silver chalice during communion this morning!"

Helga leaned her head back a little and laughed good-naturedly. "Stirling, that, my dear, is the very least of anybody's worries today. If I believed that a new bargain with God would restore you to perfect health again, I would give up the entire sterling silver communion set—given in memory of my loving August Wenzell—to make that bargain in good faith with the Almighty!"

"Well, to quote you, Helga, *I know that God does not bargain.*"

"Yes," said Helga with a twinkle in her eyes, "but I think he did, which means that now I might think he does."

"On another matter," said McCutcheon seriously. "I think I'll be needing help during the next few months. I'm wondering if you would be willing to move into the manse with Daphne and me for a while . . . and be a member of our family for the time being? The guest bedroom is quite large, well appointed, comfortable, and could be suitable for your stay . . . if you are willing. The telephone calls to your house could be forwarded to the second line here at the manse, and there's a telephone with that line in the guest bedroom. There would be privacy for you. You would have keys to the manse, a parking space for your car in the garage, and you can come and go as you wish. But, if you say *yes*, you will need to allow me to pay you a stipend for living here and assisting us in getting on while I carry around this uninvited interloper in my brain. What do you say, Helga?"

"I don't need the money, Stirling. I'll be happy to live here for the time being and do whatever I can to make the way easier for you and Daphne. If Daphne, for some reason, however, doesn't feel comfortable with this arrangement, I'll certainly understand."

"Of course, I'll discuss it with her when we talk about everything that has gone down today, but I feel certain she will be grateful and agree fully with your being here."

"All right, Stirling, but I insist that you tell me if she disagrees with your decision . . . even in the slightest. The scenario of two women with responsibilities in the same house is usually not a pretty one. It's often a formula for incalculable disaster. I wouldn't want that for the three of us."

"I understand," laughed McCutcheon knowingly. "I've seen that dynamic playing itself out to the detriment of various households, but I'm certain it will not be a problem for us . . . Helga," McCutcheon continued after a solemn pause, "my diagnosis and future treatments need to be a family matter. Would you be willing to keep this information confidential until I announce it to the board and the congregation, which could be some time in the distant future?"

"Of course."

"I'll continue my pastoral duties as long as possible, but I don't want any reluctance by my people to call on me due to this condition."

Helga looked sadly at the lighted candles on the table and tacitly agreed.

"And as I intimated before," said McCutcheon with resolve, "the stipend is an imperative, Helga, and we cannot proceed without your agreeing to it."

Helga smiled, nodded her head. "Whatever we need to do to help you manage is the first consideration in all of this, as I see it, Herr Pastor."

They put down their forks, stood together, and embraced as warmly as do a mother and son.

Late that evening, McCutcheon called Daphne. In light of her current plan to be back home in the manse on Wednesday, McCutcheon played down the occurrences of the day, joking that his being so much older than she was at last catching up with him and that he was obviously losing his grip . . . literally . . . at least on communion chalices. He intimated that there was so much to talk about; he would meet her train and take her to dinner. "I'm in the mood for candlelight, red wine, long gazes into your eyes, and a whole lot of Daphne Astor McCutcheon, all to myself," he said, as he mentally laid the groundwork for dispensing a symptomatic auguring.

As daylight infused the manse, it found Helga already up and in the kitchen. An aroma of a dark roast coffee permeated the room, and ingredients were laid out and ready to be prepared for breakfast. She had explored the pantry, the cupboards, the appliances, and had become deftly acquainted with the food supply. A grocery list was growing by the minute on the granite coffee bar, and a trip to the Grand Union lay in her immediate future.

"Good morning, good morning, my dear Helga!" said McCutcheon in a jovial voice. "What an unparalleled delight to find someone in the kitchen when I descend the stairs . . . rather unusual these past couple of years! I hope you slept well in strange surroundings."

"On and off," she admitted. "It will take a night or two to become accustomed to a different room, but, as you claimed, it is comfortable, large, well-appointed, so I shall sleep like a child in just a matter of a couple of nights. Coffee, Stirling?"

"Yes, thank you! How well you know me, Frau Wenzell!"

McCutcheon sat at the breakfast room table, sipping hot coffee and examining his Day-Timer. Within minutes, Helga served their breakfast of eggs, toast and grapefruit. As they ate, he related his schedule for the day, including his eleven o'clock home visit (without mentioning Bill Schumann's name) followed by a luncheon at the University Club on Washington Avenue. He would be making hospital calls in the afternoon and expected to be home by five thirty. If she wished to prepare dinner, they could eat at six, and he would leave at seven fifteen for the Session meeting."

"Of course, I'd love to make dinner. And what if Dr. Tillman calls?"

"Tell him I'll return his call in the morning."

"Not your top priority, Stirling?" Helga asked with a mild tone of reprimand.

"Today's schedule is full, Helga. Tomorrow will have to do. Thanks for breakfast, dear Lady!" he said as he stood to leave. "I'll be on my way to the church momentarily. But here," McCutcheon said as he thrust his hand into his suit coat pocket, "here's a set of keys to the house, including a key to the garage on the ring. Please have your calls forwarded here, to the second line number, which is there by the phone stand. Also $250 for groceries as you need it, and an envelope with your first stipendiary install-ment." He laid everything on the breakfast table in an orderly fashion.

Helga protested the latter, suggesting that they wait until he had talked with Daphne, but McCutcheon insisted, smiled broadly, embraced her and left.

For a second time, McCutcheon reviewed his schedule from his Day-Timer when he arrived at the church office and sat with Caryn Corrigan. They were accustomed to discussing the calendar a week at a time and, during Advent and Lent, a month at a time. This morning, however, McCutcheon demonstrated a reluctance to talk about days subsequent to today. He felt a sharp underlying uncertainty, a razor-edge blade that could cut away a stone foundation beneath his feet in any given minute, and he would fall into a timeless pit, into a non-future, devoid as well of past and present.

"What happened yesterday, Stirling?" Caryn asked with her characteristic concern.

"I'm not sure, Caryn," aiming at a fine line between obscurity and transparency, averse to being disingenuous but unwilling to adopt a premature honesty. "The chalice simply slipped. At first I thought my hands were still moist from the ceremonial wash-ing before handling the bread and the chalice, but I can't be sure. What I am absolutely sure of is that the white communion cloth is indelibly marked, like the Shroud of Turin soaked in Jesus's blood. I can admit to you, Caryn, without equivocation, that it was the most humiliating day of my life . . . ever."

"I'm sorry, Stirling," Caryn rejoined compassionately. "The Chancel Guild insists it can come clean; but, if not, there are funds in the guild's coffers to replace it. Not to worry! Can I be helpful in any way this morning?"

"I have the Session agenda ready for you to copy for this evening's meeting. Ordinarily you don't attend those meetings, but I wonder if you could be available to take notes for me . . . not, of course, in place of the Session Clerk, but, rather, the notes I would ordinarily take for myself. It would help."

"Of course, Stirling, I can be free to do that," she said, surprised at this first-time request.

"Thanks!"

Caryn Corrigan had no idea and no suspicion what was going on with Stirling McCutcheon, but she was aware that an ominous shadow was eclipsing the sun in her usually radiant disposition, something like a huge Rorschach inkblot, the configuration of which could not be comprehended, only dreaded.

At ten forty-five McCutcheon left for Schumanns' house, arriving two minutes before eleven. Babbs opened the door, embraced him for an unusually long moment, and led him into the living room. Bill was lying on the long sofa and did not get up to greet him. A pole with an intravenous bag stood behind the sofa, a feed line to his arm. McCutcheon went to him, clutched his free hand and asked with a playful tone, "What's this? Our Bill Schumann flat on his back?"

Schumann laughed sardonically. "Something you seldom see, Stirling!" He then became suddenly serious.

McCutcheon turned to the loveseat and sat where he had sat numerous times, on numerous pastoral visits, on numerous occasions, for numerous discussions, both intense and playful. Babbs assumed her usual place in the matching chair.

"What's happening, Bill?" asked McCutcheon somewhat gravely.

"You remember . . . Babbs and I told you we would celebrate our thirty-fifth anniversary in Bermuda, where we had spent our honeymoon?"

"Yes, I remember."

"Six weeks at the Hamilton Princess Hotel and Beach Club—August 1 through September 15. A great place to be, not too shabby, and we loved every minute of it until the third week. Half-way through our planned stay there, I started to feel sick . . . deathly sick, vomiting, abdominal pain that was so excruciating I couldn't lie down to sleep, or sit up to eat, or stand up to get relief. It was constant, like I've never known before."

"It was absolutely unbearable, Stirling," offered Babbs emphatically, affected yet again by Bill's relating the details. "The pain was unbearable for him, and it was unbearable for me to see him going through such agony. Nobody could help us. I certainly couldn't help him . . . that horrible helpless feeling that leaves you empty and desperate!"

"What did you do, then?" asked McCutcheon, looking to each in turn.

"Babbs took the reins and chartered a flight to the States," Bill answered with an affectionate glance at Babbs. "We landed in Charleston, and I was admitted to the Medical University of South Carolina. That was on August 23, and the next day the doctors had a diagnosis."

"What was it?"

"Pancreatic cancer."

All three remained silent, each hearing the death knells in the silence, tolling, tolling, tolling. Again that helpless feeling that left all of them empty and desperate.

"What did they do for you, Bill?" asked McCutcheon with a soft resonance, *soft* because he was overcome by compassion, and *resonant* because he needed to sound confident.

"Chemotherapy and then radiation, and then nothing. By the end of September they told us, *There's nothing more we can do. We think you have a month or two at the most, Mr. Schumann.* So Babbs chartered another plane and brought us home." Another affectionate glance.

"I'm desperately sorry! This seems too unreal to assimilate," said McCutcheon dolefully. "We have been intimate friends for so long . . . as long as I have been your pastor."

Schumann smiled. "Yes, and you've been more than a pastor . . . you've been a pastor and friend."

"I have loved the two of you ever since that first evening Heather and I had dinner with you here . . . with the DuBoises and the Harlansworths . . . that evening you asked about our identity, and we discussed genome editing. That was the most stellar, erudite evening I think Heather and I have ever had here in Albany. Genome editing and its ethical implications."

"Do you recall," asked Schumann, "that one of the scientists said genome editing of DNA is both wonderful and scary because it's so easy to employ, and that they can't put the genie back in the bottle. It's already here, and I'd add, for good or for ill."

"Could editing your DNA create a healthy pancreas, Bill?" asked McCutcheon, acknowledging first his own naiveté.

"No, the genie is out of the bottle, but she's not granting me three wishes. The CRISPR scientists aren't that far along yet, Stirling. I'm boxed in by an inscrutable inevitability. It's a dead end."

Silence—a silence that resembled that vast silence beyond the grave—claimed center stage.

At last McCutcheon inquired, "How are you managing the pain now?"

Pointing to the pole behind the sofa, Schumann said, "With a morphine drip."

McCutcheon nodded his head. "I see."

Schumann lay quietly for a few minutes, his eyes closed. He turned his face toward McCutcheon, opened his eyes, and said, "There's something I want you to do for me . . . if you can, Stirling; and if you can't, that's all right too."

"What is it? I will if I can."

"I'm asking if you could sit at the end of this sofa, with a pillow on your lap, and let me put my head on that pillow . . . because I'm uneasy about dying—perhaps to say the least. I want you to talk to me about eternal life for as long as you can stay, and as long as you are willing to talk about it. Would you?"

McCutcheon thought carefully and long. The pulpit desk with the carved inscriptions flashed before his eyes: *We would see Jesus* and *Preach as never sure to preach again; preach as dying man to dying men.* He thought, how fiercely ironic is God's timing, bringing a man with an inoperable, fast-growing brain tumor into the home of a man dying with pancreatic cancer: one dying man to another dying man: *preach as never sure to preach again.*

"Sure," he said.

McCutcheon rose from the loveseat, and Babbs immediately after. She approached the sofa, lifted Schumann's upper torso slightly, enough for McCutcheon to sit on the sofa, enough for Babbs to place the pillow on McCutcheon's lap, and enough for Schumann to feel relief as she laid his head back upon the pillow . . . upon McCutcheon's lap.

"I'm on the threshold of death, Stirling. What's it going to be like . . . to die, perhaps to know nothing after this lifetime of seeking to know everything? Tell me, Stirling . . . tell me."

McCutcheon found himself in a unique encounter, one that was like none other he had ever known, not with a dying father or dying mother or dying child, whom naturally it would have been familial to hold and stroke their hair or wipe their brows. But never before had he held the head of a dying parishioner, a dying friend, on his lap. Now his hand lay on Schumann's forehead while his other hand cupped the back of his head and the hair he had not lost with chemotherapy. He gazed at the Maltese cross on a silver chain around Schumann's neck; and as the vision of a wounded soldier's holding a dying fellow soldier in his arms eased the initial awkwardness of the moment, McCutcheon relaxed into Schumann's request.

"Babbs," he said, "may I use your Bible? I didn't think to bring mine."

She went to the bookcase and lifted the Bible from the shelf.

As McCutcheon turned the pages to John 20, he initiated his reading with the words from Hebrews: we are reminded that *here we have no lasting city, but we seek the city that is to come.* "Bill, the passage I'm about to read is from the Gospel of Saint John, chapter 20, and it's about Mary Magdalene, who, after Jesus's crucifixion and burial, wants to see Jesus.

But Mary stood weeping outside the tomb, and as she wept, she stooped to look into the tomb; and she saw two angels in white, sitting where the body of Jesus had lain, one at the head and one at the feet. They said to her, "Woman, why are you weeping?" She said to them, "Because they have taken away my Lord, and I do not know where they have laid him." Saying this, she turned round and saw Jesus standing, but she did not know

that it was Jesus. Jesus said to her, "Woman, why are you weeping? Whom do you seek?"
Supposing him to be the gardener, she said to him, "Sir, if you have carried him away,
tell me where you have laid him, and I will take him away." Jesus said to her, "Mary." She
turned and said to him in Hebrew, "Rabboni!" (which means Teacher). Jesus said to her,
"Do not hold me, for I have not yet ascended to the Father; but go to my brethren and say
to them, I am ascending to my Father and your Father, to my God and your God." Mary
Magdalene went and said to the disciples, "I have seen the Lord"; and she told them that
he had said these things to her.

"As I see it, Bill, Mary Magdalene's agony is intense, a fathomless well of blood and gall, of biting and bitter memories that assault her palsied equilibrium. *Mary stood weeping outside the tomb.* Jesus, the presumed gardener, approached her and asked direct questions: 'Woman, why are you weeping? Whom do you seek?' Mary was weeping because the human heart is fragile, and because human life is all too brief. Besides that, she was seeking the true Essence of her life and love. She had told the angels who asked the same question of her, 'Because they have taken away my Lord, and I do not know where they have laid him.' She is sweeping up the ruins of her life, now shattered into a myriad of sharp and brittle shards of tinkling glass. 'Woman, why do you weep? Whom do you seek?' Gazing into the tomb, which holds the macabre mirrored image of her emptiness, Mary rejoins, 'They have taken away my Lord, and I do not know where they have laid him.'

"Bill, at some given moment in life, everybody is taken away, and our taking away is perhaps more imminent than others, ostensibly more imminent than Babbs's or Daphne's or your children's or mine. It's commonplace to speak of death as the unknown, but that is precisely what we face, and that is specifically what we all fear: that unknown realm to which everyone ultimately transcends but from which no one ever comes back. During the night sweats, when you and I are awash with that fear, peace of mind is elusive. But this is the truth you and I have to hold onto these days: if there is anything we can glean from Mary's encounter with her Risen Lord, it's the realization that the human spirit in Christ is indomitable, stronger than death. And the key?

"Bill, the key to our peace in dying, the key to a coveted resolution regarding our own death, is the recognition of Christ as risen from the grave, alive for eternity, and victorious over death. I'm speaking here of the very heart of the scandalous gospel: that is, that Christ, the Son of God—crucified, dead and buried—has been raised from the dead, comes back to life, which sets forth enormous—even preposterous—implications for each one of us and for those whom we love." McCutcheon turned to First Corinthians. "The Apostle Paul emphatically states it in a profoundly convincing apologetic in his first letter to the Corinthians: *but if there is no resurrection of the dead, then Christ has not been raised; if Christ has not been raised, then our preaching is in vain and your faith is in vain . . . but, in fact, Christ has been raised from the dead, the first fruits of those who have fallen asleep. For as by a man came death, by a man has come also the resurrection of the dead. For as in Adam, all die, so also in Christ shall all be made alive.* There's no equivocation for Paul, who's speaking here of resurrection for all—*since in Christ shall all be made alive*—here he is affirming the reality of eternal life for every single person.

"Some people—even people you and I are acquainted with—insist that this simply is not true, that categorically it makes no sense at all, no sense logically or as an outcome of empirical analyses or the scientific method; but, for you and Babbs, and for me, Bill, who are people of faith as well as reason, the resurrection of Christ and our future resurrection to eternal life are facts of faith. . . . *in fact, Christ has been raised from the dead.* In the Risen Christ, our shattered hearts are not only swept up but also restored. The human spirit in Christ is indomitable, stronger than death. *For he*—Christ—*must reign*, says Paul, *until he has put all his enemies under his feet. The last enemy to be destroyed is death.*

"The burning question for you and me at this crossroad in our lives, Bill, is this: can we believe it? Undoubtedly, that's one of the main reasons people come to Madison Avenue Presbyterian Church—to determine what's reliable in our belief system. Some are inquiring: I have heard there is a loving God who created this universe and who presides over it. Can I believe it? Others are making a similar inquiry: I have heard there is a God who knows when even the tiniest sparrow falls from the sky, and that I matter. Can I believe it? Yet another: I have heard that because God so loved the world he gave his only Son, that whoever believes in him might not perish, but have eternal life. Can I believe it? And another: I have heard that God can transform my life. Can I believe it? Still another: I have heard that God forgives me and blots out my shame and guilt? Can I believe it? Another: I have heard that I can let go of the past that plagues me and live in a present that delights me. Can I believe it? Another: I have heard that I can live in the beautiful layers of human and divine experience, rather than on the litter of old griefs and open wounds. Can I believe it? Bill, you can be certain that everyone inquires in one way or another: I have heard that Jesus Christ was raised from the dead and that because he lives, we too—and those whom we love—shall live. Can I believe it? We all ask the question; and as people of faith, you and Babbs and I say, *yes, we can believe it!* Because he lives, we too shall live . . . eternally.

"Bill, there's a hymn that sustains me every day of my life, composed in the seventeenth century to the words of Ernst Homburg. The first stanza is this:

> *Christ, the life of all the living, Christ, the death of death, our foe,*
> *Christ, yourself for me once giving, To the darkest depths of woe:*
> *Through your suff'ring, death, and merit, Life eternal I inherit.*
> *Thousand, thousand thanks are due, Dearest Jesus, unto you."*

McCutcheon paused, looked at Bill whose eyes were closed, laughed quietly and asked, "Are you still with me, Bill? I'm accustomed to people falling asleep when I go on and on like this from the pulpit."

"No," said Bill, "I'm imagining the scene at the tomb. I'm with you . . . all the way, Stirling."

McCutcheon continued, "There are two vignettes I think of that put it all into perspective for me. The first is summed up by Antonio, who makes the observation to Sebastian in Shakespeare's *The Tempest*: *What's past is prologue*, he says. As Christians we attach a theological significance to this simple observation. Everything that occurs in our past—our work, our relationships, our sweet or sour personal encounters, our accomplishments, our failures, our faith and obedience, our dreams, visions, hopes, whether realized or unfulfilled, our pain or pleasure, our agony and ecstasy, the best of times, the worst of times, our total life, our untimely death—everything that comprises our past is prologue to our eternal life, given as a gift to us by our crucified and Risen Lord.

"The second vignette occurred when I was attending a conference in Rochester, New York. The guest speaker referred to James Denny, the great Scottish preacher and theologian, who, later in his ministry, stood before the General Assembly of the Church of Scotland and said that if he had his time to do again, he'd go the length and breadth of Scotland and stand in every Presbyterian pulpit; he would hold up a Roman crucifix and say to the people: God loves you like that! God loves you like that! He holds nothing back. He gives himself totally to you.

"Bill, I am certain that you and I are friends. I am certain that we love our wives and they love us. I am certain that you are an extraordinary scientist and inventor. I am certain that the people of Madison Avenue Presbyterian Church are faithful disciples of Jesus Christ; and—were you to ask me, and you have—there is nothing more certain than the fact that God is giving himself totally to you in this very minute and offering you the gift of eternal life. The cross of Christ proves it . . . through his suffering, death, and merit, life eternal you inherit.

"I know it's difficult to accept, my friend, but because God is giving himself totally to you, the wound in your body is the sign of the ultimate blessing of the God who encounters us. The wounds of the crucified Christ are the means by which he identifies with us. Our wounds correlate to his."

Schumann raised his free hand to Stirling's face, brushed the knuckles of his clenched fist gently along his cheek, and said, "God bless you, dear pastor and beloved friend!"

McCutcheon took that hand in his, nodded to Babbs, who approached the sofa and joined hands; they prayed, and held one another, and wept, expecting any minute to see two angels in white.

As Babbs walked McCutcheon to the door, she made it clear that Bill would want the members of the church to know about his illness, since there were innumerable friends whom he would like to see before his last days. McCutcheon agreed to inform the congregation without employing intimate details.

The University Club business luncheon, the subsequent hospital calls, dinner with Helga, the Session meeting with elders—Caryn's sitting beside him while taking notes—and back to the manse at 10:30 p.m.: in every moment of each of these events, McCutcheon suffered a preoccupation with an intrusive image of Bill Schumann's lying in a casket—an ornate, elegant casket that inherently implied a tragic irony. Neither the abundance of wealth nor the ingenuity of genome editing could change the direction of his fateful pathway.

At the Session meeting, Caryn and the elders were deeply grieved at the news. At dinner, before the meeting, Helga was both incredulous and saddened. McCutcheon asked Helga if she had ever heard the story of James Denny and the Roman crucifix. She hadn't, so he told her. "God loves you like that," McCutcheon concluded. "He holds nothing back. He gives himself totally to you."

They finished the meal in silence.

At 3:15 a.m. McCutcheon's bedroom phone rang. It was Babbs Schumann's voice. "Stirling, Christ has risen . . . so has Bill."

27

The Question Revisited

McCUTCHEON PACED IMPATIENTLY BACK and forth on the Amtrak platform at Albany-Rensselaer Station. The Ethan Allen Express was due at five forty-five, but the station clock had struck six o'clock ten minutes earlier. His head throbbed. His throat tightened. His chest pounded. His eyesight blurred. In the past two days, he seemed to identify with Prometheus chained to a rock while an eagle ate his liver. In his own case, however, he deemed the eagle was eating his brain, standing above him with its talons piercing his skull and its beak repeatedly pecking at the left top of his head. *Chained to a rock* served as a fitting imagery for McCutcheon's inexorable predicament, a fate that he could neither alter nor redirect nor postpone. Neither could he rail against it without coming off as abjectly apostate.

As McCutcheon paced, he couldn't determine whether his restlessness grew out of his ongoing, unavoidable peering over the jagged edge into a bottomless abyss; or Bill Schumann's death and pending funeral, at which he would need to *preach as never sure to preach again;* or his desperate need to hold Daphne so tightly that their bodies would literally meld into a single transcendent entity, a mystique that could be described only as an eternal union. The antithetical thought of leaving her behind, while going on ahead of her, was not so much frightening as it was lonely, solitary. "Ah," he thought, "if she would only hold me in her lethal scissors and never let go, I could let go contentedly."

The whistle blew; the train pulled into the station and came to a deafening stop . . . *deafening,* that is, to McCutcheon. Daphne stepped down onto the pavement and danced into McCutcheon's arms. She was dressed in autumnal colors, rust and yellow and red, all of which enhanced her natural beauty, her fair skin and long, flowing hair. Her Ballerina cross hung from the silver chain around her neck. Neither was willing to relinquish the embrace, so they remained engaged for literally minutes. No words were required for each to know they were wrapped in an invisible web of immutability, that is, that nothing can change the imminent outcome while, ironically, that imminent outcome will change everything.

At the University Club, the valet attendant parked their car as they made their way to the main dining room, where Maurice led them to the secluded table McCutcheon had previously requested. Formally dressed in tuxedo and black tie with savoir-faire suitable to his elegance, Maurice lit the candles and seated Mrs. McCutcheon. They agreed upon a bottle of Carnivor Cabernet Sauvignon and toasted their love before ordering two entrée specials: Cilantro Lime Salmon and Trout Almandine.

"Stirling, Mother and Dad called yesterday afternoon to tell me that Bill Schumann died," said Daphne with a puzzled look.

"Yes, he did. Babbs called me at three fifteen yesterday morning."

"I realize you're reluctant to interrupt my rehearsal mindset with sad news, but I need to know these things, especially if you are being affected in any way by it. Please, Darling! You could have mentioned it when we spoke last night."

"No, Daphne. I told you Monday that we have a lot to discuss this evening." His pancreatic cancer was one of the topics. "Meanwhile, I refuse to weigh you down with the events of church life and negatively affect your concentration."

Daphne leaned partway across the table, stretched out her hand and took his, firmly. "Listen to me, my darling!" she said quietly but emphatically. "You have to trust me. I can carry anything you tell me and, at the same time, maintain my concentration. I know how close you were with Bill Schumann, and how sad it must be for you. Don't shut me out, Stirling."

"It isn't shutting you out, Daphne! It's protecting you. It's honoring our mutual understanding that our love and passion will not diminish your first love and passion, nor mine. I need to remain true to our agreement. It has worked so far with great success, and I have no desire to insert added stress into your craft, your profession, your creativity."

"I understand, Darling."

"To tell you the truth, Daphne, I have to admit that there are times I miss you terribly, when I actually ache for you. I'm not expecting our original understanding to change. It's simply a fact that I miss you desperately at certain times. Just saying it. No expectations."

Daphne tightened her grip on McCutcheon's hand, looked down at their touching, and said, "Me too . . . same for me. I look out at the audience and long to see your face. I fall exhausted into bed after the performance and reach for you when you're only a vision lying there. I want to wake up beside you and greet you with our morning kiss of blessing. Then coffee, lox, cream cheese, and bagels at the breakfast table with a long view of Central Park. Sometimes your absence is enough to make me cry, Stirling, when I can't bear it."

"Someday we'll have to bear it," said McCutcheon wistfully.

"Yes, I know, just as Babbs has to now," she said, searching McCutcheon's sadness. "When is Bill's funeral?"

"Friday morning."

"I'll still be here, Stirling. The final week of rehearsals begins Sunday afternoon. "Are you still planning on the opening night next Friday? It would be lovely if you could come as you usually do."

McCutcheon hesitated, smiled wryly after another sip of wine, nodded his head in agreement, and said, "Yes. I wouldn't miss it: your enormous leaps, stunning pirouettes, and magnificent *pas de deux* as Titània with Oberon. Shakespeare's genius and Mendelssohn's brilliance merging into *A Midsummer Night's Dream*! What could make for a better evening than that, my darling prima ballerina wife!"

Dinner arrived, the sure signal for small talk among small bites, stories, vignettes, shared information, information exchanges, conversations she had had with her parents, long-distance communications he had had with his parents and sister, notes and cards to and from his children, news in the parish, news in the ballet company . . . all the stuff that makes for verbal discourse between two lovers, between this married couple . . . over a candlelight dinner on a Wednesday evening at the University Club . . . not at home.

Daphne looked around the ornate dining room, remembering that this was one of her favorite places to eat with Stirling. "I love being here with you, Stirling, although I could have prepared dinner for us this evening at home. We could have had candlelight and wine there, as well."

"Actually I wanted us to be alone, Daphne . . . I mean *alone* in a secluded nook here."

"But wouldn't we be alone there?" she asked curiously.

"Not quite. Helga Wenzell is staying with us for a while."

"Oh, dear, dear Helga!" she responded warmly. "I have known and loved Helga a much longer time than you have, my dear Stirling . . . ever since I was a little girl." She stopped, frowned, and asked, "Is there something wrong with Helga? Is she sick?"

"No, no, she isn't," answered McCutcheon slowly. "It's simply that we shall need some help during the next few months, and I have asked her to become a part of the family for a while, to move in and occupy the guest bedroom. She'll do some cooking, cleaning, washing, and so forth. Only if you agree, however, she said. I told her I thought you would be fine with the arrangement."

Daphne looked bewildered. "Stirling, I'm delighted. You know I love dear Helga Wenzell. But why? What's going on, my darling?"

McCutcheon drank his wine, reached across the table and took both of Daphne's hands in his, looked down at his plate and then back to her eyes. "Daphne, my dropping the communion chalice during service on Sunday was not because I'm older than you or my hands were still wet after ceremonial washing." He paused, then said, "It was because I have a fast growing brain tumor that is both malignant and inoperable. I have asked Helga to stay with me at the manse to help wherever needed. She has agreed, but only if you want her there."

"Of course I want her there!" Daphne's face took on an ashen hue, her eyes wide with disbelief. "And I'll be there, too," she continued. "I'll take a leave of absence from the ballet company . . . as long as needed."

"No!" rejoined McCutcheon forcefully. "No, no, no! We have had an agreement, and we are going to honor that! There is nothing—short of your own death—that would induce me to allow you to give up ballet, even for a week. I am absolutely intransigent on this matter!"

Daphne's eyes welled up, and, as she pushed her hands forward and gripped his forearms, she began to weep quietly, lowering her head and sobbing silently. McCutcheon motioned to Maurice and requested their chit, their coats, and their car. He stood, lifted Daphne by her hand, and in due course, they were on their way to the manse.

Helga's bedroom door was closed; the old grandfather's clock struck ten bells, and within minutes after the mechanical grandfather's greeting, the two were firmly ensconced in their intimate solace beneath the covers of their warm, familiar bed. Only the Ballerina cross adorned Daphne's figure. So tightly were they entwined that McCutcheon deemed this would be as close as they would ever get to that single transcendent entity he thought of earlier. Daphne placed her tearful face in his neck.

Since his lips were close to her exposed ear, McCutcheon whispered, "The Heidelberg Catechism, Daphne, begins with a question: *What is your only comfort in life and in death?*"

"Yes," said Daphne, "I know the answer. The answer is: *That I, with body and soul, in life and death, am not my own but belong to my faithful Savior Jesus Christ.*"

"That's the answer I know as well," said McCutcheon with a long kiss on her cheek, the one not buried in his neck. "There's another parallel question for mere mortals such as I, Darling, and it's this: *What is your only other comfort in life and in death? And my answer is: That I belong, body and soul, in life and in death, not only to my faithful Savior Jesus Christ, but also to my beloved Daphne Astor McCutcheon with whom I am in eternal union . . . together, in union with Christ.*"

McCutcheon switched off the light beside the bed and returned to their *pas de deux*; both kissed passionately and fell into a deep sleep of fused melancholy.

By virtue of her profession, Daphne had cultivated the pattern of late nights and late mornings. By the time she descended the stairs from their bedroom, McCutcheon had left for the church office and Helga was at work in the kitchen. There were no words exchanged. The two women reached out, embraced, and clung to each other as they wept. When they finally separated, Helga poured coffee for the two of them, and they sat at the breakfast room table.

"Thank you for being here, dear, dear Helga!" said Daphne with an affection as genuine as Helga had ever felt before. "How could we possibly manage without you?"

"I need to be here, Daphne," Helga rejoined, "not only for you and Stirling, but for myself as well. Otherwise I would have felt so utterly helpless and of no use whatsoever."

"I told Stirling that I intend to take a leave of absence from ballet, but he refused to hear of it. In truth, Helga, there is nothing more essential to me than Stirling . . . not even ballet. But we had made an agreement to love each other without giving up our love for ballet or the church; so now he's holding me captive to that agreement."

"No, Daphne, he is right. I know when the time comes for you to be here, you will be here, just as he will need you then . . . and only you will do. But now he will continue to be the fine pastor he is, subscribe to all his duties anew in the face of this disease, and the day he can no longer perform his pastoral functions—but not a minute before—he will inform the church of his inevitable decline. Until then, he will go on traveling to New York City to watch you perform. Believe me, Daphne, it would kill him sooner if you relinquished your role and were not on stage to dance the great masters' ballets."

"Will you stay with us, Helga . . . and with him when I'm not here?" Daphne asked, knowing the underlying intent of her question was to officially register her full, honest desire for Helga to become a member of the family during these seemingly impossible days.

"But of course. You must let me know if I step over the line, or if the two of you need to be alone in the house on any occasion. As you know, I have a house of my own to which I can retire whenever you need me to do so."

"No, that won't be necessary, except those times when you need to be away from the demands of the manse."

The two women worked in the kitchen together, prepared breakfast, and ate silently side-by-side. When they had finished, they poured more coffee, and Helga related all the details of Sunday's symptoms and worship episodes followed by their visit to Dr. Tillman at the medical center emergency room, including the immediate testing and resulting diagnosis. Martin Tillman had followed up with Stirling on Monday; Stirling had been to the doctor's office Tuesday afternoon after he had spent the morning with Babbs Schumann; at that visit, he had categorically declined the treatment plan presented by Dr. Tillman's oncology team. "If ultimately there can be no positive results from an aggressive program of radiation and chemotherapy," Stirling had concluded, "I'd rather spend the remaining weeks or months I have left with an element of dignity. I'd truly detest incessant leaning over the commode, retching again and again." Dr. Tillman had acquiesced to Stirling's decision and promised to do what he could when he recognized the onset of McCutcheon's rapid decline.

"Is Stirling absolutely determined to keep all of this under wraps until he becomes virtually debilitated?" Daphne asked earnestly.

"Yes, absolutely, although, I should say, with two exceptions. Caryn Corrigan will have to be informed. As you know, she is extremely tight-lipped. And Marcel DuBois.

Stirling told me he intends to compensate wherever he needs to in order to keep all appearances as normal as possible. He plans to meet with Marcel DuBois early next week. He'll take him into his confidence and request that, as an elder, he co-preside at the communion table with him on communion Sundays. He'll ask Marcel to share the liturgy and handle the communion chalice and wine in particular. Those two would be the only exceptions . . . at least for the time being."

"All right, then. I'll not tell my parents," said Daphne with a sad smile, "at least for the time being."

"Anything for the wash, Daphne?" asked Helga as she rose from the table.

"No. No, thank you just the same. Nothing yet. But you needn't wait on me, dear Helga."

With this, the two women separated into their lugubrious solitudes.

Once again, proclaimed McCutcheon, *we are reminded that here we have no lasting city, but we seek the city that is to come*: the City of God.

Yet again, this particular Friday morning provided the occasion for the community of the faithful to haplessly acknowledge another death, the death of their beloved departed, William Blythe Schumann, and summon up hope to bear witness to the Resurrection of the Lord Jesus Christ. Yet again. There had been so many deaths and funerals in the parish during the past year that McCutcheon wondered—sardonically at that—if Chamberlain's reference to Nietzsche's description of *churches as sepulchers* had merit. But of course not! He knew better. This particular death, however, seemed a little more than McCutcheon's scarred psyche could accommodate objectively. There wasn't a single constituent of his congregation who had died that he didn't love as a dear parishioner—an integral member of the body of Christ. But Bill Schumann was a confidante and friend like none other . . . actually Schumann and DuBois together.

The sanctuary was full to overflowing with church members, dignitaries from the community, members of the Think Tank on Genome Editing from Tufts University, and medical staff from the Medical University of South Carolina. McCutcheon *preached as never sure to preach again*, affirming emphatically the reality of eternal life about which Bill was ultimately so certain. Babbs had informed Stirling that Bill requested open communion for the congregation, so DuBois assisted, handling the chalice and tankard of communion wine.

It must have been by sheer will of purpose or a steely determination that McCutcheon flawlessly *preached as a dying man to dying men*. His eyes couldn't bring into focus those words on the pulpit desk, but it mattered little since they were emblazoned on his heart, seared into his psyche. As his euphonic encomium in praise of Bill Schumann captured their imaginations, the people in the sanctuary seemed shackled to a singular silence, and an impalpable charisma encircled each.

A seemingly endless serpentine caravan followed the hearse to its destination. McCutcheon stood at the head of the casket, soon to be lowered into that shallow abyss. *Forasmuch as it has required almighty God to receive out of the world the life of our beloved departed, William Blythe Schumann, we therefore commend him to God and commit his body to the earth, remembering that if the tabernacle of our earthly house be destroyed, we have a building of God, not made with hands but eternal in the heavens.* McCutcheon's head throbbed. There were oscillating images assaulting that growing pebble ensconced in his left brain, images of Bill's body lying in that descending casket giving way to images of Stirling in Bill's place.

In the great hall at the University Club, without conspicuously hovering, Daphne attended to Stirling with the grace of a ministering angel. She detected the pillaging strain in his countenance and noted the numerous times he inconspicuously put his hand to his head as he spoke warmly with each person who approached him. Suggesting that he sit at the table with her parents and Helga, she brought him coffee and hors d'oeuvres from the buffet.

When all was quiet, Babbs Schumann stood and greeted everyone, thanking them for coming to the funeral and welcoming them to the luncheon in Bill's honor. McCutcheon returned thanks again for Bill's life among them and for the meal prepared in praise of his generous and kind character. Prior to dessert, many who knew Bill well gave touching, even humorous, reminiscences of significant incidents in their relationships with him. When taken as a grand and pleasant pastiche, the remembrances served as an eclectic central theme of Bill's life story: a ravenous hunger for truth pursued with intellectual curiosity.

The great hall was now nearly empty. Only Babbs, Daphne, and Stirling remained while servers cleared the tables. The empty hall—with much to put in order—seemed an apt metaphor for the cavernous emptiness Babbs was already feeling . . . or, more accurately, had been feeling since 3:15 a.m. Tuesday morning. Ironically, her frequent, muffled weeping echoed in a vast, resounding hollowness that only she could hear. And, so much to put in order. They sat together over final cups of coffee.

"It was a beautiful service, Stirling," Babbs said when she had looked up from her coffee.

"He was a beautiful man . . . he *is* a beautiful man," said McCutcheon, adjusting his statement.

"Daphne, I'm pleased you could be here," said Babbs warmly. "Seeing you and Stirling together brings me such joy . . . as it does so many people in our church."

"You and Bill presented an impeccable model, Babbs . . . a high standard for other married couples to emulate," rejoined Daphne. "Stirling and I have been inspired by the obvious love and mutual respect the two of you have for each other."

"Thank you," Babbs said as she nodded affirmatively and looked down at the table. "When do you have to return to New York?"

"Tomorrow. The last week of rehearsals for *A Midsummer Night's Dream* begins Sunday afternoon. I actually told Stirling I wanted to stay . . . because I've missed him so much," she said with a sideward glance at McCutcheon, "but he insisted I leave . . . and what do you think of that, Babbs," she quipped with a little laugh, "a husband who wants me out of the house?"

Babbs smiled knowingly. "I think it's a husband who is extraordinarily proud of his wife and honors her brilliant profession with an unmistakable avidity."

"It's true. Just like you and Bill, isn't it?" Daphne observed affectionately.

"Yes, I believe so." Babbs lifted her handbag from her lap to the table and opened it. She pulled out something wrapped loosely in tissue paper, removed the paper and held up a silver cross. "This is Bill's Maltese cross. I want the two of you to have it." She set it on the table. "For years Bill studied the meaning of this particular cross, which, according to him, is associated with the Order of John from the sixteenth century and worn by the Knights of Malta. Why all that fascinated him, I'm not at all sure, but he was definitely enamored of the meanings attached to these eight points here . . . two on each arm of the cross. As you see on this little card he kept with it, *the eight points symbolize eight aspirations of the knight: truth, faith, repentance, humility, justice, mercy, sincerity, and endurance.* Everyone who knows Bill is aware that each of these qualities was an integrated part of his character."

"Then wouldn't you want to keep it, Babbs?" asked McCutcheon gently, undoubtedly awkward about accepting such a treasure valued by one of his dearest friends.

"Stirling, weeks, months or years from now, I will not need a symbol to remind me who my husband was. Those integrated aspects of his character were infused into our mutual essence. A concrete symbol would only detract from vivid memories and accentuate his absence. In other words, a physical symbol would remind me of his physical disappearance. I can assure you, Stirling, his Maltese cross is not the nepenthes I need for the road ahead."

"Babbs, the day I held his head in my lap," said McCutcheon reflectively, "I saw this Maltese cross and chain around his neck. It would be an honor for Daphne and me to preserve both the cross itself and the recollection of his eight aspirations. Thank you."

The three rose from the table, embraced affectionately in turn, and left the great hall and its great emptiness.

Daphne and Stirling went home, placed Bill's Maltese cross in the box of crosses, ascended the stairs, and made gentle love in the afternoon, characterized by a note of foreshadowed, rationed scarcity. That evening they took Helga out for an exquisite, gourmet dinner at Yono's Restaurant on Chapel Street, where virtually everything among them was laid on the table. From that time on, there was never a doubt, not even the slightest doubt, as to how the future would unfold and with what unwavering determination it would be managed by each of them. *Truth, faith, repentance, humility, justice, mercy, sincerity, endurance.* Each point would make its contribution to the arduous course ahead.

† † †

The following Tuesday noon Maurice seated DuBois and McCutcheon at a table on the periphery of the main dining room. The University Club, more than any time in the past six years, had recently taken on the semblance of a meeting annex to the church. Confidential conversations, when completed, had been wadded up in these linen tablecloths and sent undetected to the club's commercial laundry service.

They ordered from the menu, shared their thoughts about Bill Schumann's death, funeral, and luncheon, and expressed mutual concerns about Babbs's challenging adjustment. McCutcheon dropped an apparently innocent question into the middle of their small talk. "When's your next international field trip with the students, Marcel?"

"Not until spring semester . . . actually during Lent again," replied DuBois casually. "Why?"

"Just curious," said McCutcheon.

The waiter brought the meals, McCutcheon returned thanks, at which time he took the opportunity to close his eyes with a fierce pressure to alleviate the shooting pain in his head. It helped.

"Fourteen students have already signed up. We have room for twenty-five altogether."

"What's your destination this time?"

"Greece, with most of our stay in Athens. Six weeks of the great philosophers can't be all bad, McCutcheon."

"No," laughed Stirling, "it can't be bad at all."

"Want to go with us . . . you and Daphne?" DuBois asked enticingly, fully suspecting he knew the answer. But the answer that came wasn't the answer he thought he knew.

"No, thanks, Marcel, I won't be here."

"No, no, Stirling! What do you mean, 'you won't be here'? Where are you going? You aren't resigning are you?"

"No, not my position at the church, anyway," answered McCutcheon. "Actually, confidentially, Marcel, I need your help."

"Sure, anything. What can I do.?"

McCutcheon explained it all, from the mishaps at the Kirkin' o' the Tartans World Communion service to the present moment, including Dr. Tillman's diagnosis, Daphne's offer to give up ballet, Helga's moving into the manse, and Caryn Corrigan's being the only other person who knows . . . "and now you, my friend." DuBois sat and stared. He pushed his plate toward the center of the table, wiped his mouth with his napkin and laid it on the tablecloth.

"What can I do, Stirling?"

"I need you to assist me at the communion table on communion Sundays . . . handle the cup and the tankard. I think I'll be able to manage the bread. As I am able to do less and less, I wonder if you might do more and more, such as more of the liturgy, the readings. If we had an associate pastor on staff, he or she would be able to do all of the assisting; but you know as well as anyone, we haven't and we don't. I'll refrain from telling the elders and the congregation as long as I possibly can."

"Why, Stirling? Why would you deprive them of caring for you when you need them?"

"My calling is to care for them, not them for me."

DuBois emphatically disagreed but conceded to McCutcheon's wishes.

"Marcel, on a related subject, you know that for decades I have been wrestling with the impossible question about a loving God who allows unimaginable suffering in his beautiful world. Why? How does he allow it? Why does he allow it?"

"I know. We have discussed it numerous times with no adequate answer."

"I don't think there's an adequate answer, Marcel. Certainly if there is, I'm not about to discover it in this life. The closest I can come is that the Crucified Christ is the Crucified God, and the cross—the crucifixion of Christ—is an inimitable act in which God encounters those who also carry a cross up their individual paths to their unique versions of Golgotha. So having gone through this himself, Christ is going to carry me through all of this, while I'm asking *why*. And while I'm asking *why*, I'm in a direct face-to-face encounter with him.

"But mark this, Marcel: I am not asking *why* for myself, but for all of my people whose beauty has been fractured during the vicissitudes of their lives. Why? And to that *why*, I do not have an answer, since I cannot say to any of them—even on their behalf—as you carry your cross, the Christ is encountering you, and that encounter is more precious than gold; it is the pearl of great price."

DuBois nodded his head, understanding everything McCutcheon was saying and what he was not saying, that is, what he was saying in the unarticulated agony of the *why*.

"Marcel, you know I have been a man haunted by this conundrum for years. I doubt that I shall be inclined to a deathbed confession, so what I'm about to say is as close to one as I shall ever make. And it's this. I have revisited the question of *theodicy*. I've set it aside, and the new question for me is: *was it worth it?*"

"Was what worth it?"

"I was determined to know nothing but Christ crucified. I was riveted to my call to the people of Madison Avenue Presbyterian Church. In refusing to return to Scotland, I lost Heather and my children. Was it worth it? I missed watching them grow up, of being an integral part of their lives, of sitting with my arms around them, of providing fatherly guidance and family interactions, the Sunday afternoon equestrian rides, the safe and comfortable living at Farquharson Heights, the joy of being near my parents and sister, as well as Heather's parents. I can't have any of that back, Marcel! Was it worth it? If I had returned to the luxury I knew in Scotland and turned my back on my people here, would I have been saying that God is expendable?"

"Is that what you would have been saying?"

"Yes, I think so."

"So was it worth it?"

"I don't know, Marcel. What I know is that an ocean separates us. I am an out-of-reach father, inaccessible and, therefore, the worst kind of father."

"Give yourself some slack, Stirling. I've seen you with your children—when they were here with you for three years. You were close to them . . . accessible."

"Daphne."

"What about Daphne?"

"She makes it all worth it, Marcel. There's nothing theological about this marriage to Daphne, but it certainly felt sacred."

Maurice brought the chit, McCutcheon signed, stood and embraced DuBois. "It's to be a short road, Marcel, but a narrow one with lots of jagged rocks. Thanks for walking it with me!"

Opening night of *A Midsummer Night's Dream* came off as nothing short of spectacular, even as the opening night of *The Nutcracker* did in early December. Both as Titânia in the former and the Sugar Plum Fairy in the latter, it was vintage Daphne Astor, brilliant as usual. Whatever shadow she carried in her heart, or whatever preoccupation sought to cloud her mind, there was no evidence that it affected her concentration. *The body remembers,* she had told McCutcheon once. Apparently that remained true.

On both occasions, they observed their treasured routine: Friday morning train from Albany, lunch in their apartment at Two Lincoln Square, love in the afternoon, the performance, after-theater dinner at the Plaza, breakfast with the usual view, and McCutcheon's ride back to Albany aboard the Ethan Allen Express. These days, whenever she could manage it, Daphne made more frequent trips to the manse, each time having to assure McCutcheon that she wasn't giving short shrift to rehearsals.

The decent began the third week in January. The pain in his head was nearly constant, at times unbearable; his vision was so blurred that he had to memorize his sermons; he turned more and more to DuBois for assistance in the worship services; he asked DuBois to process beside him and up the chancel steps each Sunday to help steady his balance; acute nausea had become a pressing issue. The previous month, he succeeded getting through the rigors of three Christmas Eve services, including holy communion at midnight, as well as one service on Christmas morning. By mid-January, however, the suspicions in the congregation had launched, and serious concerns were rising. Daphne had broken the news in detail to her parents on January 25th, and on the following morning McCutcheon had called for a meeting of the Session to be held immediately after the worship service.

Attempts at retarding the inevitable, swift decent into that shallow abyss—to say nothing of stopping it—were as fruitless as stopping a one-person bobsled, mid-course down the Lake Placid Olympic bobsled run. What Dr. Martin Tillman could do, however, was to dispense the blessings of Morpheus directly, before the bobsled shoved off.

28

The Low Road

DELIRIUM HAD SET IN the previous day. Hallucinations attacked McCutcheon's cerebral cortex like so many rhythmic breakers assaulting a rocky shore—relentless, merciless, unstoppable. Grotesque figures—whose faces were distorted, unrecognizable—rose up from their chairs, or beds, or desks, and wagged boney fingers at him. Some were dressed like royalty, some like beggars, some scantily clothed, most were naked with their secrets no longer hidden, their needs no longer disguised. Where had he been when he was needed! Why didn't he have the answers to their pain! Why had he been mute when a word of sensible solace would have served as a balm for open wounds! An explanation! *In Christ's holy name, give me an explanation!* All that was required was an explanation to put horrific, meaningless tragedy into a creative perspective.

Where is it, Mr. McCutcheon, man of God! Say something! Say something sensible that would lend at least a modicum of meaning to this world's madness. Tell me why! God loves me, you say! Such a naive fool! Is that all you can muster! Clichés come trippingly off your tongue! You certainly know how to screw up people's lives! You screw up people's lives with what you say, and you screw up people's lives with what you don't say! All the lamentation begging for meaning—the pleas of parishioners and complaints of colleagues—came surging in those breakers against the rocks, scourging him with irresolution.

McCutcheon twisted in his bed, his fists clenched, his knees drawn up to his chest, his breath halting, irregular, held, then expelled. The top left side of his head throbbed with these incriminating inner voices.

"The wound . . . the wound . . . the wound is the sign of the . . . blessing," moaned McCutcheon with dry lips and a thick tongue.

I don't want to die, Mr. McCutcheon. Jeremiah said to choose life. I chose life, and I am given death. I had no choice. But choose I will. I choose to spend my virginity, not bewail it. Mr. McCutcheon, if you don't come right now, I'll kill myself. Let me pour you a glass of whiskey. My lover bites me, draws blood; she has returned my letters. Burn them after I die. If she'll be dead by the time I arrive, there's no sense in my going to see her. Stirling, I found her in the garage with the car running. Dead. Mr. McCutcheon, how absurd is that . . . to want the better death for him, to go down with the ship rather than bleed at the shark's tooth! The wound is the sign of the blessing. There is no room for a divorced pastor in the pulpit of this church, Stirling. If gold rusts, what will iron do? No, we do not baptize the dead. But it would comfort us, and when he is buried, it will be too late. Besides, Stirling, how would it ultimately destroy your theology? How would it besmirch your integrity?

Daphne entered softly, swiftly through the study door, seated herself bedside the bed, and touched McCutcheon's shoulder. McCutcheon awoke with a start. "Sh-h-h, Stirling, my darling." He straightened his legs and rolled onto his back. She placed a steaming compress on his forehead. His eyes focused, and he recognized his study, where the hospital bed had been set up in the very room he loved so well, surrounded by his books and wall hangings . . . and there, the box of crosses on his desk. He closed his eyes again and leaned into his pain.

Daphne spoke slowly with a comforting tone. "I'm here. Helga's here. There's nothing to fret about. So many of our people have come by to wish you well. You are being wrapped perpetually in prayer by our congregation, held close in the warmth of one large human embrace. Marcel DuBois was here, saw you were sleeping and refused to disturb you. He observed that God is using your people to enfold you in his arms. I think he's right, Stirling."

McCutcheon opened his eyes and smiled at Daphne, nodded his head slightly, then turned to Helga on the other side of his bed. "What do you think, Helga? Is God doing that?"

"Oh yes, Stirling, he surely is! *He's giving himself totally to you. He's holding nothing back.*" They smiled knowingly.

"Are you sure, Helga . . . are you sure?"

"Nothing is more certain, Stirling! Nothing!" Helga assured him with a quiet, emphatic affirmation.

McCutcheon nodded small nods in agreement, smiled, closed his eyes, reached for Daphne's hand, and grasped it tightly.

"Stirling," Daphne said as she leaned closer and raised his hand to her lips, "Freda Chamberlain is here and insists on seeing you. Could you manage it?"

He opened his eyes, looked at Daphne with an inquisitive frown. "Why?"

"She needs to talk with you . . . said it's very important. Do it if you can, Darling, please; but if you can't, we understand."

"All right," McCutcheon conceded.

Daphne removed the compress from his forehead, left the room and momentarily returned with Freda, who sat beside the bed. Helga and Daphne turned to leave, but Freda motioned them to remain.

"No, please stay," she said with genuine sincerity, perhaps with uncertainty as to how McCutcheon would respond to her. "There is nothing for me to hide, nothing that anyone should not know." Then turning to McCutcheon, she asked, "Stirling, may I take your hand?" He reached for hers, and their joined hands rested on the side of the bed as Freda leaned forward.

"Stirling, I have come to apologize with the most sincere remorse I can ever remember feeling." McCutcheon raised his eyes to hers to be attentive to what she was saying, to reach for a clear understanding of the words she was speaking, to hold on with all his remaining cognitive force to words that so easily jumble in his mind these days. "I told you that the pulpit in this church is no place for a divorced preacher, but I was wrong. For every Sunday since that time you have laid before us the magnificent, concrete reality of the God of forgiveness and grace. Perhaps you did the same before your divorce from Heather, but, if you did, it never came home to me until you had your own cross to bear. When I told you how lonely my life with Sinclair was while he was forever sequestered in his study, night after night, it never occurred to me that you could fully understand until Heather left and demanded a divorce, and you too were alone—in the most abject sense of the term. On that Sunday of your and Daphne's engagement reception, I posed the rhetorical question, *if gold rusts, what will iron do?* But look at this time you and Daphne have been married. It's obvious to me and to everyone else how deeply your love for each other pulsates at the heart of your marriage, which, I admit freely now, is the gold, not the iron, and it will never rust. Stirling, please accept my heart-felt apologies . . . and my admiration for you and Daphne . . . and, if you will, accept my love as well." With this comment, she stood, bent over the bed, and gave McCutcheon a kiss on his cheek.

"Thank you, Freda," McCutcheon said weakly, warmly, still holding her hand. "Do you recall the first time we met, you gave me the cross I wear on Sundays?"

Freda sat again. She smiled graciously and said, "Oh yes, Stirling, I remember it so well."

"*Ich bin bei euch alle tage,*" he recited. "I believe it is true for me, Freda. I also believe he is by you every day. By virtue of that, we are by each other always. Thank you!"

Even as Daphne had done, Freda raised his hand to her lips and kissed it; she stood, embraced Daphne and Helga, and left the room.

McCutcheon fell into a deep sleep . . . a troubled sleep, the relentless breakers resuming their ruthless assault on the white sands of his memory. *Where's McCutcheon? The service begins in five minutes. Hey, McCutcheon, what are you doing in the broom closet?* Howls of laughter from fellow clergy. *Ha! He's praying in the closet before he preaches! Come on, time to preach it, brother!* Then the pain, the excruciating pain woke him. A little more morphine and back to sleep. *Could you not watch with me one hour? Sleep and take your rest. See! My betrayer is at hand.*

Daphne touched his shoulder tenderly.

"Stirling, Heather and the children are here," Daphne said. "I asked Helga to call them in Edinburgh, and now they've come."

McCutcheon smiled and attempted to sit up but couldn't. Daphne raised the head of the bed and arranged his pillows in a comfortable configuration; then she brought in Heather and the three children.

Heather approached the bed and greeted him. "Hello, Stirling, it's been a long time . . . ages, it seems." She embraced him as well as she could in his sitting position.

"Hello, Heather. Yes, a long, long time." He kissed her cheek affectionately. "Our children are fine, young adults, I see." McCutcheon studied each of them as a rush of remorse and conflicting pride rose in his throat. Angus stood much taller than he had remembered him. But, of course, he would. He could see that Angus still possessed that weight of responsibility McCutcheon had seen in the airport before their return to Scotland. Annabella's quiet self-confidence was still self-evident, and Fiona's radiating joy convinced McCutcheon that Heather's decision to take them back to Scotland was the wise choice for all of them. If he could admit it to himself, he'd have to acknowledge that none of the children was truly happy here, though each suffered it more tacitly than Heather did. In turns, they embraced their father with warmth and, it seemed to him, with longing. In turn, Stirling told each of them how much he loved them and how much he had missed all of them.

Angus made his way to the foot of the bed and remained there, holding his father's right ankle through the bedding. It seemed strange to McCutcheon, who could not discern its significance until he remembered Angus's summer course with Professor McLaughlin and the class discussion on *Prometheus Bound*. Stirling smiled knowingly at Angus, who smiled broadly in return and nodded affirmatively, affectionately. The girls, on the other hand, stood on either side of the bed and laid their heads on his shoulders, their hair against his cheeks, holding his hands resting on his upper thighs.

Addressing all three of them, McCutcheon said with difficulty, "I think I was a good father, but out of reach and, therefore, a bad father."

"No, Father, don't be woeful. You *are* a good father," said Angus, gripping his ankle firmly. The girls kissed him lovingly on either cheek respectively, holding the kisses for a full minute.

After a long interval of affection between Stirling and his children, Heather moved closer and suggested that the three children wait in the living room while she spoke with their father. When they had left, she sat beside McCutcheon and waited patiently for him to speak.

"They are wonderful children, Heather. You have done a magnificent job raising them to full height, so to speak. Thank you."

"Stirling, you didn't have the seven more years you wanted here. I'm sorry it turned out the way it did; but you know I couldn't stay."

"I know."

"And I know you couldn't leave your people."

"Yes."

"But I would be less than honest if I didn't admit that I've missed the years we could have had together at Farquharson Heights. Mom and Dad send their unchanging love to you. They also miss the years they could have enjoyed your presence, the lively conversations, the sense of security my father felt when you and your ardent faith surrounded him. Occasionally, after the divorce, at the dinner table, when my parents and I were alone, Dad would say, 'I would have given anything for him to stay.' The last day he said it was the day I knew he had accepted the finality of our parting. It was indeed a sad day, Stirling, in every respect as sad as the day they learned my brother had gone down in his plane . . . into the sea. To them, our divorce was the loss of a second son."

"Yes," responded McCutcheon, "I know. It's sad, to be sure. I look back . . . but can't find my way back . . . to make it different. And now, I wouldn't choose to make it different if I could, Heather. Daphne unintentionally danced her way into my life after you left, and now my soul would be splintered without her. I'm sure you understand."

"Yes, strangely enough, Stirling, I do. Even as my soul would be splintered without Scotland, and our children in Scotland."

"Heather . . . do you remember . . ." McCutcheon continued with effort. "Heather, do you remember when we used to sing *Loch Lomond* together? Just you and I . . . singing *Loch Lomond* . . . do you remember, Heather?"

"Yes, I do, Stirling . . . yes . . . I do."

"Would you sing it to me . . . like in the days gone by?"

Heather sang softly, actually with feeling in her breast and water in her eyes and a catch in her voice and every word laced with a gossamer layer of sadness.

> *By yon bonnie banks and by yon bonnie brae,*
> *Where the sun shines bright on Loch Lomond,*
> *Where me and my true love were ever want to gae,*
> *On the bonnie, bonnie banks of Lock Lomond.*

McCutcheon joined his weak voice with hers:

> *Oh! ye'll tak the high road and I'll tak the low road,*
> *And I'll be in Scotland afore ye;*
> *But me and my true love will never meet again*
> *On the bonnie, bonnie banks of Loch Lomond.*
>
> *The wee birdies sing and the wild flowers spring,*
> *And in sunshine the waters are sleeping,*
> *But the broken heart it kens nae second Spring again,*
> *Tho' the waeful may cease frae their greeting.*

Oh! ye'll tak the high road and I'll tak the low road,

And I'll be in Scotland afore ye;

But me and my true love will never meet again

On the bonnie, bonnie banks of Loch Lomond.

Heather gently placed her face in Stirling's neck and wept silently . . . for all that might have been.

When she emerged from the study, Daphne and Heather embraced affectionately, each fully aware that the other had played a profound part in Stirling McCutcheon's life.

"The children and I will stop by tomorrow before we leave for the airport," Heather said. "What time would be best for Stirling?"

"I think around nine, if that gives you enough time to make your flight."

"Yes, that would be fine," said Heather.

Daphne put her hand on Heather's forearm to stop her from leaving. "Heather, I heard you singing to Stirling . . . *Loch Lomond,* I believe. I have never known the origin of that beautiful ballad. Could you tell me?"

"Yes. It's based on an ancient Celtic myth, which claims that the soul of a Scot who dies outside the homeland will find its way back home by the spiritual road—that is, the low road. Supposedly during the 1745 uprising of the Scots against the English, one captured Scotsman was condemned to death while his fellow Scotsman was set free. The condemned Jacobite, before he was hanged at Carlisle, said to his compatriot, *Oh! ye'll tak the high road and I'll tak the low road, And I'll be in Scotland afore ye.* The high road is the road of the living; the low road the spiritual way of the dead back to Scotland."

"So beautiful, Heather! Thank you!" exclaimed Daphne softly. She turned to the children and said, "I know your father loved your being here . . . and I know he loves you deeply! Thank you for coming all this way to see him!"

The three embraced Daphne and exited by the front door with their mother. The entire scene that afternoon had possessed an element of the surreal, as if all the players had come to this ineffable moment on this particular stage surprised to find themselves in a familiar but foreign state, or perhaps as in a midsummer night's dream. The roads taken and those not taken have a mysterious way of crisscrossing countless times so that the ultimate configuration resembles the work of a weaver's shuttle plaiting with brilliant hues a tapestry depicting the tree of life.

Twilight encircled the manse, an ominous prologue to dense nightfall. All the dear friends and parishioners who had stopped by as well-wishers had left for the day. McCutcheon's pain levels fluctuated between mild and intense, intense and mild. The small doses of morphine brought a measure of relief but, at the same time, increased his hallucinations.

His state could be described as unusually quiescent when he awoke with a start to see Honeysuckle sitting by his bed, simply staring at him. As McCutcheon's eyes came into sharper focus, he saw Glynnis Vandeusen standing near the study door, speaking with Daphne. As usual, Honeysuckle's large, protruding nose was running profusely, and he held his huge, dirty, white handkerchief to wipe it.

"Honeysuckle," whispered McCutcheon with extraordinary effort. "Welcome, Honeysuckle. I'm rejoiced to see you."

Honeysuckle grunted, reached for McCutcheon's hand and took it in his. In that very moment, Honeysuckle's face took on the countenance of Christ. It was just as Glynnis had described her encounter with him under the bus . . . and McCutcheon was at perfect peace. With his free hand, Honeysuckle lifted the Shepherd's cross over his head and placed it around McCutcheon's neck, and said, "Well done, thou good and faithful servant!"

Glynnis moved to the other side of the bed, bent down and spoke softly to Stirling, "Often, often, often goes the Christ in the stranger's guise."

Had it not been for the tangible Shepherd's cross around his neck, McCutcheon—looking around the room later with no sign of Glynnis or Honeysuckle—might well have attributed all of that to hallucinations.

The clock struck eleven. Daphne told Helga that she should go to bed and get some sleep. "I'll stay with him, Helga. Thank you."

Helga rose from her chair, kissed Stirling on the cheek, embraced Daphne, and wished her *goodnight*. Daphne undressed, pulled a sleeveless, short, white cotton nightgown over her head, put on her blue robe, dimmed the light, and moved to the easy chair near McCutcheon's desk.

Shortly after midnight, McCutcheon awoke and looked at Daphne dozing in the wingback chair.

"Daphne!" he called at the only volume his voice would permit. "Daphne!"

She came to his side. "Yes, my darling?"

"Come lie with me, please . . . hold me. Wrap your scissor legs around me."

Daphne removed her robe, removed her ballerina cross from her neck, removed McCutcheon's Shepherd's cross from his chest, went to the box of crosses on the desk and laid them wistfully side-by-side among the others. Flickering shadows cast by the streetlight outside the study window danced frivolously upon the bed quilt. Daphne pulled back the covers and slid into bed beside him, thinking all the while how those dancing shadows were reminiscent of their splendid *pas de deux*. She pointed the toes of her right foot so that it resembled a weaver's shuttle, pushed her leg beneath the small of his back, laid her other leg across his abdomen, and enfolded him in her body.

"Daphne," whispered Stirling mysteriously, "I see Honeysuckle's face against an azure sky."

"M-m-m . . . yes," she said reassuringly. Ever so gently, she placed her hand upon the left side of his head, looked at him intently, and said, "my darling Stirling, I do believe your wound is the sign of your blessing. How dearly I love you, my Cavalier!"

"And I you . . . I love you . . . my beloved Sugar Plum Fairy . . . with my best love and adoration."

Intertwined in each other, they fell into a deep sleep of contentment and synchronized breathing . . . until early morning.

Daphne awoke in what she recognized as the final position of their *pas de deux* . . . and wept. She placed the palm of her hand against his sallow cheek, kissed his cold lips, and laid her head again upon his chest, where it remained for an indeterminate time, rehearsing beatific memories of the last two years.

At nine o'clock, Helga knocked on the study door and opened it for Heather, who stood silently in the doorway. Daphne rose from McCutcheon's bed, approached her, and embraced her.

"Stirling took the low road, Heather. He'll be in Scotland afore ye."

Acknowledgments

It would be audacious on my part, if not arrogant, to think of *A Box of Crosses* as a likeness to a Rembrandt. Yet, when I consider the overall contrasting effects of this novel on my own temperament, there is one undeniable characteristic of the book that resembles Rembrandt's works, namely, the pervasive use of the artistic technique termed *chiaroscuro*: the contrast of light and shadow, the contrast of what is bright with what is dark, the contrast of what is clear with what is obscure. The shadow, the dark, the obscure serve as foils to the light, the bright, the clear and, in part, account for both the profound essence and the irresistible magnetism in Rembrandt's paintings. *A Box of Crosses* is a work of religious fiction that is characterized in large part by its chiaroscuro. The shadow of the cross falls across nearly every page; that shadow seeks to serve ultimately as a foil to the light.

A deep debt of gratitude belongs to Wipf and Stock Publishers and specifically to their Resource Publications imprint, to Matthew Wimer and the editorial staff. The novel manuscript could never have approached the status of impeccable accuracy without the diligent scrutiny of Karen Comstock, my extraordinary proof-reader, who generously spent innumerable hours with a keen eye for errors in the initial draft. At two different stages of the manuscript development, my competent copyeditor Ralph Yearick meticulously examined each sentence and offered recommendations not only for editorial improvements but also for structural enhancements and content refinement. Hearty thanks to Frank Logano and David Harmon, both of whom read the first version of the manuscript and gave me invaluable feedback.

Photographs of the nineteen crosses were taken by Michael Good of Photographic Trends. Don Kimble of The Company Jewelers fashioned the sterling silver St. Andrew's Cross with the Drummond Scottish clan crest badge. Heather Hicks of Olive Tree Designs, LLC created the Butterfly Cross and the Ballerina Cross specifically for this project. To all three of these highly-skilled artists I extend my sincere appreciation.

Numerous clerical colleagues have deserved my extensive appreciation over the years that encompassed the formation of this work of fiction. Paul Cameron gave me the Greek Cross with the German inscription as a gift at my January 16, 1994 service of installation as Associate Pastor of Shadyside Presbyterian Church. F. Morgan

Roberts—with whom I served at Shadyside Church—has remained a close friend since that date of installation; he eagerly read the manuscript and led me to Wipf and Stock Publishers. Grafton Eliason, who returned from Peru with the gift of a Mayan Cross, has shared countless, vital insights while reviewing each chapter as it was developed. William Roemer offered a singular enthusiasm that was the essential stuff of an indispensable encouragement. Charles Partee was the incarnation of Hephaestus (Greek god of fire and craft) at lunch with me every other week, goading me on with *fire* to use my *craft* more readily, to "finish the novel before you die," and to draw a creative entity out of an unformed chaos.

Two other colleagues played roles of incalculable influence in my early years of ministry—an influence without which I should have been impoverished professionally and ill-equipped to create *A Box of Crosses*. Donn Vickers, my senior associate at Gates Presbyterian Church, modelled everything egalitarian in ministry—a ministry devoid of autocratic or hierarchical ecclesiastical relations. His leadership style served as the essential fabric of Stirling McCutcheon's professional demeanour. Dwight Ferguson, while serving as Senior Pastor of Bethany Presbyterian Church in Rochester, threw me a lifeline mid-career while I was at sea in a near-perfect storm. Thank you!

I owe a note of deep, deepest thanks to William Hamilton, who introduced me to Nietzsche's madman with his lantern, searching for God—declaring that he had come too soon—as he appears in chapter 2 titled *A Nietzschean Manifesto*; to Benjamin Wah Chin for his immeasurable contribution to chapter 11 titled *World-weariness*; and to James Ashbrook for his nuanced insight regarding Jacob's wrestling with the angel in Genesis 32, alluded to in chapter 21 titled *Pas de Deux*.

In the summer of 2015, I enrolled and participated in the Kenyon Review Novel Workshop at Kenyon College. There I became keenly aware that there are countless ways for an unschooled craft to go adrift and come to ruin. While there is no sure-fire certainty for the success of a work of fiction, to have sat with writing teachers who have effectively published and to engage with fellow participants who are passionate about their writing craft, challenges one to plumb the depths of creativity and rise to the heights of originality, regardless of an ambiguous outcome. For an opportunity such as this, I am grateful to David H. Lynn, the David F. Banks Editor of the *Kenyon Review*; to the workshop leaders: Nancy Zafris, Nick White, Ellen Weeren, and Greg Michalson; and to the workshop participants: Waqar Ahmed, Lori Huth, Minnie Jeong, Tara Lindis, Rachel Lippolis, Tonja Reynolds, and Alison Strack.

It seems a truism that the journey of faith is a personal journey initiated by each person to believe or not believe, to accept the gift of faith or to reject it. There are hosts of people who have enriched my journey of faith/personal journey and to whom I am infinitely grateful, including a myriad of members of the numerous churches I served in New York and Pennsylvania; my kindly parents who loved me with an invincible love, who taught me to believe, and whose passion for writing was contagious; my family of origin, comprised by six older sisters and brothers, whose love and support resembled a kaleidoscopic portrayal of beauty throughout my life; Nancy Jane, who made the journey with me in the early years and shared the inestimable gifts of children/spouses and grandchildren, each of whom is a cause for rhapsodic joy; Nancy Ann, who made the journey with me during the middle years and introduced me to the Pennsylvania Ballet with lovely evenings of ineffable beauty in choreographed motion; and Elizabeth Slayton, who makes the journey with me these later years, who expanded the family circle to include more precious people to love, who has been the most intimate advocate of my writing, and to whom I owe an eternal expression of gratitude.

What is your only comfort in life and in death? There's a parallel question for mere mortals such as I: *What is your* other *comfort in life and in death?* My answer: *That I belong, body and soul, in life and in death, not only to my faithful Savior Jesus Christ, but also to my beloved Elizabeth Slayton Wilson with whom I am in eternal union . . . together, in union with Christ.*

www.ingramcontent.com/pod-product-compliance
Lightning Source LLC
Chambersburg PA
CBHW081144020726
47504CB00009B/1990